TREACHERY AND TRUTHS

Erin P.T. Canning

H.C. BROWN LLC

To all the dreamers out there who were told they talk too much.

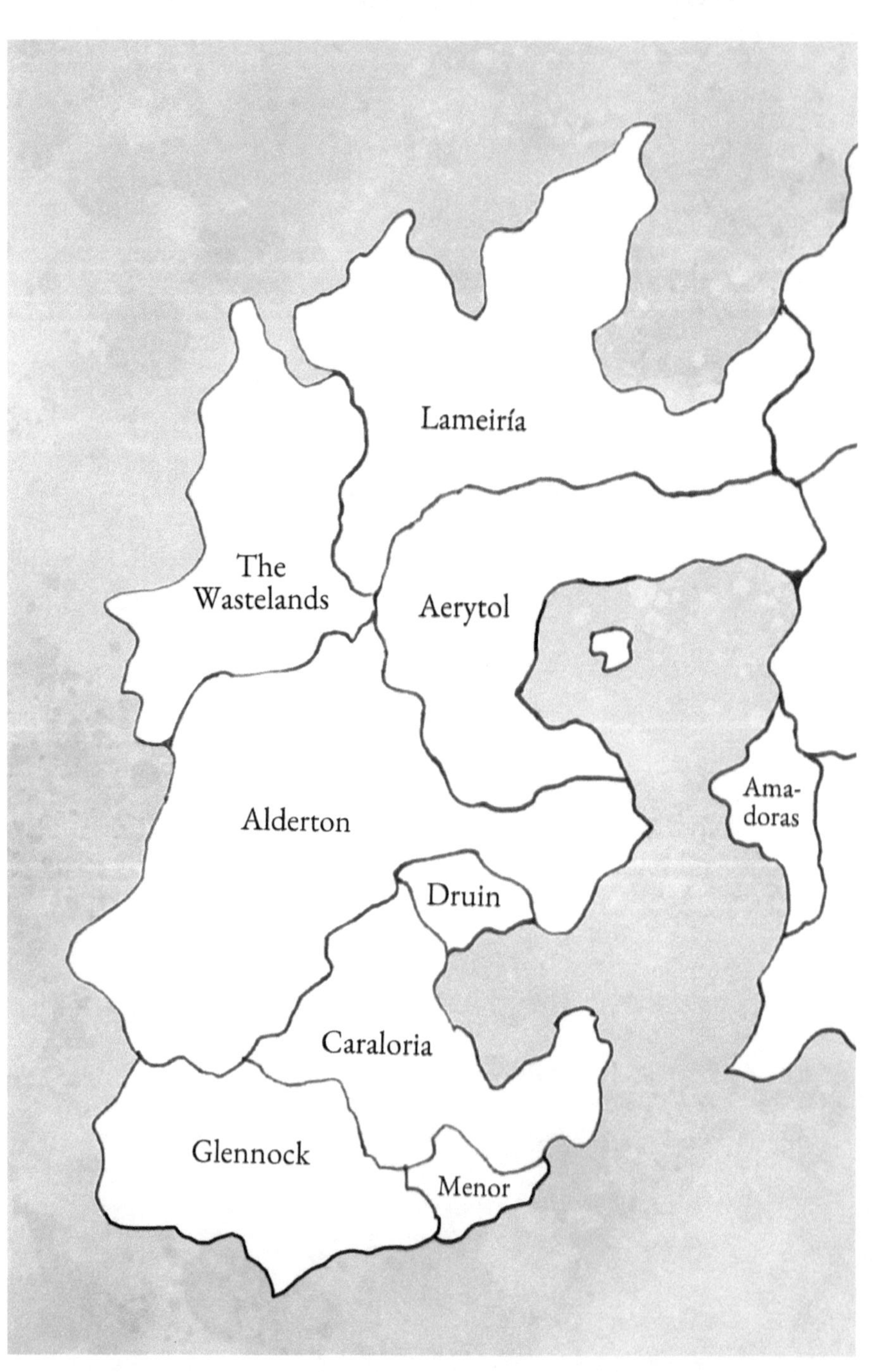

Lameiría
The
Wastelands
Aerytol
Ama-
doras
Alderton
Druin
Caraloria
Glennock
Menor

CONTENTS

Chapter One

A Permit

Adaline tightens her grip around Ëólas's waist as billions of stars gleam above them. Heavy sea waves break against jagged chunks of broken rocks at the bottom of the cliff. The white foam disperses quickly only for another to smash against the cliff again.

Ëólas, with eyes three times wider than normal, guides Adaline away from the edge and toward the squat buildings rubbing shoulders. She slips her hand into his as they walk along the outside of the city, neither of them daring to break the silence. Adaline tries to time her breaths with the breakers, hoping to slow her pulse and keep her mind as sharp and steady as Ëólas appears. From the moment they traveled to this new location, he began craning his neck, assessing their surroundings, and scanning the buildings ahead as much as the patterns of the stars.

Where the hell are we now? And why does this keep happening to me?

Ëólas halts, and Adaline nearly bumps into his back. He turns toward her, lowers his lips to her ear, and whispers, "I cannot tell if we're in human or elven territory." In the shadows, his golden eyes glow brighter, like the halo of candlelight.

Adaline's eyes widen. *If we're outside of the Neutral Territory, then one of us is in serious danger. Oh god, how can I keep him safe?* Adaline squeezes his hand.

"We'll proceed with caution," he says, squeezing her hand too. "There's an opening in the outer wall up ahead. I want to get closer and explore. Stay close to me."

They take ten more steps before Ëólas freezes. He tilts his ear toward the archway, but whatever he's listening for, Adaline can't hear above the roaring sea. He nods once, leads her a few steps backward, and whispers into her ear again, his lips brushing against her lobe. She shivers as she strains to hear him.

"We're in elven territory, though I'm uncertain where. Take off your snood, and make sure your hair covers your ears." Ëólas pulls back to give Adaline space, but he doesn't move away.

With his eyes locked on her, she reaches up and pulls out the pins Kayla, her lady's maid, secured just this morning. She tugs the hairband away, but a few unseen pins hold fast, and she winces as her hair plucks her scalp. Ëólas reaches past her shoulders and gently removes the remaining pins, not snapping a hair on her head. Her curls fall around her shoulders and down her back. Without hesitation, Ëólas slips his fingers through her hair, combing the strands so her curls can breathe and stretch now that they're free.

As he assesses her, he crosses his arms over his chest, tucking her sword beneath his elbow, the sword he'd given her to keep herself safe, the sword she'd thrown onto the ground after her last training session. He saw her then too, all the doubt that had taken hold, that she fought her way through. Once again, his eyes sweep over her body to examine her from head to toe. He takes in every detail, every curve, every imperfection that screams human, not elf. Unable to hide from him against the moonlight, Adaline blushes and worries her bottom lip. His gaze flicks to her mouth, and the silence between them drags on.

I'm going to get us both caught, aren't I?

She shifts her weight to her other foot and clears her throat, hoping to end his prolonged stare. Surprise flashes across his face as he returns from his ruminations, or maybe that was just the spark from someone lighting a candle in the room far above them. Ëólas exhales loudly through his nose, and his eyes darken as he loops Adaline's sword around his belt. His eyes flick to her dagger. He doesn't move though, letting her choose whether to give that one up too. The blade's not visible under her skirts, but God forbid she falls down or something else happens and an elf catches her armed. *Damn it.* She relinquishes her last weapon, which he also fastens to his belt.

Again, he brings his lips to her ear, his cheek brushing against her own. "Let's hope for a calm night and no wind. If anyone asks, you're my wife."

Adaline leans forward and places her hands on his chest to keep herself steady. *Can we really pull that off? Is it even possible?* She forces herself to whisper, "And if they notice?"

His chest tightens. "Then you're my prisoner."

When he stands tall again, his concerns cast a shadow over his face, and the reality of this world sinks inside Adaline's chest, weighing her down and crushing the hope that the Neutral Territory engendered.

She drops her hands and looks down. *Because most elves and humans fear each other. But this is Ëólas. Who taught me how to use a sword. Who carried me out of the palace ruins. Who knew where to find me when I was abducted.*

The wind roars as she murmurs, "I'd rather be your wife," and carries her words over the cliff, dropping them into the ocean below.

Wait, what did I just say? Her eyes snap to his, and her cheeks catch fire. "Oh, I didn't mean—"

"Me too." The corners of his mouth twitch upward.

Adaline swallows her heart as he leans down and whispers, "Our only exit is through the city. I need you to trust me. I will get you out of there. I promise."

The weight of his words hangs around her neck. As he gives her a moment to process the severity of their predicament, she peers into his eyes, which look like dark melted gold in the moonlight. He's always known the reality of his world. After all, he's the one who told her that humans who set foot in Lameiría face life imprisonment. Her experience in the Neutral Territory, that humans and elves can form relationships, that is, friendships, is not the norm.

Their two peoples have lived apart for five hundred years. It stands to reason most of them would prefer to keep the borders between the kingdoms closed. The very idea of the Neutral Territory, of humans and elves living side by side, might offend many of them, which would explain the recent attacks on Ëólas and Magnus's efforts—all of which is why Adaline and Ëólas are here in the first place. Whatever deity or power or magic whisked them to this seaside cliff in the blink of an eye must have heard their mutual declaration to seek answers.

And we're not going to achieve that just standing here. Besides, Ëólas must have massive skills as the commander general of Lameiría's defenses.

Adaline nods her head with a single, decisive nod. "Let's go."

Ëólas smiles, and the corners of his eyes crinkle. "I also need your help though. Your accent is too exotic. I need you not to speak. At all."

I'm exotic? Adaline smirks and adopts Nan's British accent. "How about I speak like this? Would that be more suitable?"

Ëólas jerks backward. "Um. How?"

"Your accent isn't that different from my grandmother's. I used to speak this way too, when I was little, before we moved to another…kingdom."

Ëólas chuckles. "Well, isn't that convenient."

Hell, yes. "So, you think I'll pass?" Adaline grabs the folds of her skirt and curtsies, keeping her movements light and fluid like the ballerina she used to be.

He looks her over once more and gulps. "Most assuredly."

Great. Let's pray for no wind. Adaline fluffs her hair around her ears once more.

Side by side, she and Ëólas pass under the arch leading into the city and walk down the long, narrow alley. Up ahead, the din of city life grows louder until it suppresses the sounds of the sea. When they step onto the street, ladies and noble elves stroll past them, not paying Ëólas or Adaline any heed. Their satin gowns and long trumpet sleeves flow like water around their limbs. Many of them wear shades of coral and turquoise. Thankfully, Ëólas's navy tunic and Adaline's lavender cloak and sapphire-blue gown blend in.

Resting his hand on the small of her back, Ëólas guides her down the street. She latches onto the warmth radiating through her spine to keep her feet moving forward. Halfway through the city, they turn a corner and enter a market with a rainbow of canopies covering the length of the street. Streetlamps hang from the canopies' poles and cast a soft orange glow upon the market.

The first person to pass in front of Adaline makes her gasp out loud.

The man pauses, bows his head, and asks, "Is there anything you need, my lady?"

Unable to form coherent words, Adaline shakes her head, and the man continues on his way. Even though she cannot yet move the rest of her body,

Adaline slowly turns her head toward Ëólas, who stares down at her with his mouth agape. While they both examine the market, humans stroll up and down the street, wearing clothes similar to the elves and creating a river of silks and satins. Many humans work beside elves at the same shop, as if they share a joint business.

Holy shit! Not even the Neutral Territory is this integrated.

As humans and elves approach the merchants, they speak to each other with ease. Shoppers carry goods with smiles on their faces and a lightness to their steps. No one appears tense or cautious. Both peoples move about with the ease and confidence of long-term residents who feel safe in their own, secure homes.

So, the Neutral Territory isn't the only city to create a haven for elves and humans alike? Is this why we've been sent here, to see that the world is more open-minded than Ëólas or Magnus thought? Watching the humans and elves come and go together helps all of Adaline's concerns to dissolve one by one.

"Did you know?" she asks, remembering at the last moment to mimic Nan's accent.

"No. I've not heard of another city like ours."

A single nudge from Ëólas's hand on her back encourages her legs to begin moving forward again. She can't stop smiling as they make their way through the crowded street, even as the moon rises higher in the sky. The canopies keep the wind at bay, and their hanging lights twinkle as if the stars surround them. Several children run past, three elves and one human, their laughter lingering behind them. A woman hands a wrapped package to an elf who nods his head in thanks. A lady elf examines a collection of bags as a man behind the stall works the leather into a new design, chatting with her all the while and incorporating her requests into his current project.

Ëólas approaches the same stall slowly, never taking his hand far away from Adaline, and selects from a display rack an army-green knapsack with leather shoulder straps. After he shows her the bag, particularly its roomy interior, he slips it onto his back, waves goodbye to the shop owner, and leaves. With her brows furrowed, Adaline points to the pouch tied to his belt and stops herself from asking outright why he's not paying the man. Ëólas only smiles, takes her hand, and tugs her to continue walking with him.

They repeat the same process with Ëólas using the five-finger discount. He picks up, in front of everyone, two leather canteens shaped like shells, two small metal bowls and spoons, and a large canvas blanket like the canopies overhead—all items they'll need during their trek back to the Neutral Territory. No one stares at him. No one stops him. No one yells, *Stop, thief!*

Elves don't use money?

They pass a shoemaker polishing a pair of riding boots, and Adaline spies a stall displaying bolts of fabric. On top rests a bundle of rope. *Never go camping or hiking without rope*, her father always said.

"May we use this?" Adaline asks the tailor.

The elf nods and passes the bundle to Adaline, who drops it into the knapsack Ëólas holds open. *Whoa. If only people were giving away horses too.*

As they continue shopping, she also collects a bag of almonds, two wheels of cheese, and a dense loaf of barley bread. When she reaches for another loaf, Ëólas shakes his head, giving Adaline the impression that either she's overstepping boundaries or they have enough. Still, none of the shopkeepers stop her from taking what they need.

Mercia mentioned the Neutral Territory would have to do something about its two economic systems. I must be right that elves don't use money. Jósep made me that bench. Delós gave me that mandolin. They never asked for anything in return. Huh.

The memory of Jósep's bench and his forever unfinished statue pings her heart again. After passing her goods to Ëólas, she places her hand on her chest and tries to rub away the ache another loss has left inside her.

Stepping off the main path, Ëólas kneels down to arrange their new belongings neatly inside the knapsack, but one bowl rolls off the blanket and into the street like a runaway tire. Adaline dashes forward, dodges three people, and stoops down to grab it. Her hair falls like a curtain beside her cheeks. When she pops back up, an elf, a foot taller than Ëólas and with bright gray eyes, halts abruptly so he doesn't knock into her.

"Terribly sorry," Adaline says, bowing her head.

Rather than walking around her, the elf places his thumb under her chin and lifts her face. His eyes bore into hers as he slightly tilts her chin to study the shape of her jaw and her long neck. Her chest caves inward as his gaze travels downward. He doesn't regard the shape of her body with lust, thank goodness, but his cold, unyielding assessment makes her heart beat faster and her legs tremble. Determined not to risk her and Ëólas's efforts to find answers, she forces herself not to flinch, not to scowl, not to smack his hand away. Within a few seconds, Ëólas is beside her, having abandoned their sack, and she can once again breathe.

"Fei na méla morelno?" the gray-eyed elf asks Ëólas but doesn't look away from Adaline. He doesn't release her chin either.

Ëólas nods. "Ei."

The elf narrows his eyes. "You're a pretty little thing. Quite lovely, indeed. Are you a good ward? Do you listen to your mentor?"

Mentor? Does he know I'm Magnus's ward? No, he must mean Ëólas.

Adaline tries to nod, but the elf tilts her face higher as he examines her body again.

Stop, stop, stop. How do I make this stop?

Finally, the elf lets Adaline go and turns to Ëólas. "She looks healthy too. Does she have a permit yet?"

Pausing a fraction of a second to calculate his answer, Ëólas forces a shallow smile onto his face. "Not yet."

"Shame." The elf steps aside and points to two young men behind him. They appear to be in their twenties with wide jawlines, lean torsos, and long hair down their backs that makes them suited for modeling. "I have two male wards at the moment myself. Both have earned their permits. Your ward would do nicely. Her waist is rather slender, but her hips are plenty wide. When she has obtained her permit, come find me at my compound. She can choose which of mine she'd like to mate with."

Bile rises up Adaline's throat, and her brain slows down as each word hits her harder. *Earned. Permits. Mate. With them.*

She stares at the ground, waiting for the street to open up and swallow the elf whole. If only that kind of magic were real.

Ëólas's calm expression never falters. He steps in front of Adaline, forcing her to move backward, to distance herself from them, to give her a shield to hide behind so she doesn't have to endure the men staring at her like starved animals.

Folding his arms casually behind his back, Ëólas clenches his hands into fists as he speaks with the polished, neutral tone of a seasoned politician. "That's extremely generous of you. Thank you, my lord."

I hate politicians.

Ëólas bows his head, and Adaline does the same. When they look up, the elf and his wards' backsides disappear into the crowd. Ëólas drops his arms to his side and exhales. Together, he and Adaline stand side by side for a while longer, neither ready to look at the other.

His pinky brushes against hers, an outreach of kindness before he says in a cool, steel voice, loud enough for all to hear, "Come along."

After he retrieves their packed sack, they make their way further into the city even though every hair on her head and every bone in her body tell her to get the hell out of this place as quickly as possible. But they need to learn more about what's going on.

She places her cool hands on her stomach to ease her discomfort. *We're on the right track.*

Further into the city and beyond the market, a ray of moonlight lights the path in front of them. Adaline fixes her hair and covers her ears again, and Ëólas returns his hand to her back. She leans closer to him, to his warmth, to his tangible reassurance that they'll get through this, that they'll make it home.

Home. Is that my condo or the castle?

Magnus and everyone else must be eating dinner now. Are they worried yet? Have my guards reported us missing?

Am I going to keep disappearing on people, leaving them to worry about what's happened to me and if I'm safe?

And now Ëólas has been caught up in this too.

Even though part of her keeps wishing that whatever brought them here would send them back, Adaline steels herself to keep listening for clues and observing how these people live, just like she did when she first arrived in the Neutral Territory. Observe first. Granted, this time she has no desire to participate in this society.

They pass by two elven ladies sitting in front of a wide, shallow fountain. One lady rests her head on the other's shoulder and wipes away her eyes. "It's so exhausting. You raise one ward perfectly, but they're dead the next day. We have to start all over again and pick a new hopeful to sponsor."

"I know. They age too quickly," says the other lady. She scrunches her nose as if she suddenly smelled something moldy. "And they get so wrinkly."

Adaline drifts away from Ëólas. His hand slips off her back. They keep pace together, but every step makes her heart grow heavier.

Several streets later, they enter a town square. Small, sporadic groups of people engage in conversation, laugh together over some inaudible joke, or dance around the mandolin player. Other people sit on colorful blankets that designate picnic areas while floor pillows encircle dishes laid out family style. The music and overall lively, joyful attitude radiating from the people remind her of the elven tavern she visited her first night after arriving in this world. If only Merith, Fólas, and Delós were here with them now.

Safety in numbers.

Beyond a few rows of picnic blankets, a post with a rectangular piece of wood across the top stands in the center of the town square. Adaline squints. The horizontal block of wood features three holes, a large one in the center and a smaller one on either side. She squints a bit more to peer through the scattered candlelight that hovers like fireflies. The holes contain a head and two hands.

Adaline covers her mouth with her hand. *Someone's in the pillory.*

Long before her father and Nan died, they spent a summer in England, not to visit Nan's hometown but to enjoy touring off-beat paths and the countryside. When they stopped in Cheshire, they strolled past the pillory where Daniel Defoe had been imprisoned for three days. Adaline snapped a picture. Afterward, they ate at a café up the street that served the most delectable homemade scones with clotted cream and jam.

She'd forgotten about Cheshire's relic until today.

No one in the elven square comments about the man forced to bend at the waist and stay on his feet so that he doesn't suffocate himself. In fact, most people here keep their backs to him, until an elven lady walks over and stands next to Adaline.

"A shame, isn't it?" The lady neither takes her eyes off the man nor hides the sadness in her voice. Turning her back on the festivities, she drifts away.

Some of them are empathetic? Or she's disappointed in that man's actions?

Ëólas scans the crowd. When he concentrates on a particular gathering, Adaline follows his line of sight. In the center of a group, sitting around a buffet of dishes, the gray-eyed elf from earlier laughs with friends as though he is merely enjoying his summer vacation.

Stuffing his hands in his pockets, Ëólas still doesn't look Adaline in the eyes. "I should go socialize with him."

She releases a long, silent breath. *I know we're on the same page. Lameiría can't be like this. No way.*

Reminding herself they're here to investigate, she steadies her hand and points toward a group of humans nearby, all of whom appear to be in their teens or early twenties. A few girls giggle and wave hello to her.

"If it's alright with you," Adaline says, in case anyone's listening, "I'd like to meet some friends."

Ëólas swallows so hard that even the corner of her eye catches his Adam's apple bobbing up and down. Finally, he knits his brows together and faces her. His voice remains cool, but his gaze wavers. "Stay within my sight at all times."

He's ordering me around? No, he's just acting. We both are.

"I want to make sure you feel safe, given that you're new here," he adds, emphasizing the words *feel safe.*

Adaline nods and presses a smile onto her face. He gazes at her a while longer, waiting for her resolve to waver. When it doesn't, he walks toward his people.

Well, not his people. Ëólas couldn't possibly be friends with people like them. He just couldn't.

As Ëólas approaches the others, his chuckle mingles with theirs.

So much for being his wife.

Pushing her shoulders back, Adaline stands taller, giving her stomach more room so her bile doesn't rise up again. She walks up to the nearest group of humans and clasps her hands behind her back, pressing the pressure point between her thumb and index finger to reduce the heaviness compounding in her skull.

She can do this. She can observe and mimic and blend in. She's just working onsite today, exploring another culture, and not judging them.

Inhaling deeply, Adaline strolls over to them. She doesn't interrupt the girls discussing the skills they want to learn next. One hopes to work in a perfume shop. Another wants to design dresses. A third has already begun her apprenticeship, learning how to fold crabmeat into fish cakes that make everyone practically drool. When the clouds release the moonlight, the bags under their eyes become more visible, along with their slouched shoulders and slowing gestures.

A boy yawns, stretching his arms overhead. "I'm so tired."

A deep voice vibrates directly behind Adaline, his breath brushing her shoulder. "Enjoy tonight's celebration, little one. Our mentors have worked hard for this."

The hairs on the back of her neck rise to attention. Stepping aside, Adaline makes room for the man while also giving herself space and immediately recognizes his chiseled face.

Despite the others in their group, Mr. Chiseled looks only at her, his eyes exploring her just as he did when his mentor said Adaline could choose to *mate* with him. "You must be new to the city, the way you take everything in with those bright green eyes of yours."

Adaline gulps. *Don't look away. Keep him talking. You can do this.* "Oh, yes." *Great answer, Adaline. That'll surely encourage conversation.*

"I'm certain you'll love living here. Life in the city is so much easier."

Easier than what? "Indeed." *How can I ask questions without sounding like I don't know what I'm talking about?*

"I hope you weren't too embarrassed earlier, about the lieutenant's recommendation. But I do hope you'll consider his offer."

Adaline tries to ignore the girls nearby giving her the stink eye. "I, I, I'm so overwhelmed with everything."

"I understand." His smile slowly transitions into a cocky grin. "But after you've had some time to adjust, I hope I'll see more of you. I have enough credits to apply for a marriage and birthing permit, and the lieutenant will grant me and my bride a home of our own within his compound. We'll have space for the two of us. Just something to keep in mind. No pressure, of course." He winks at her.

Adaline nods. *Marriage permit. Birthing permit. They're controlling population growth.* "Being the lieutenant's ward, you must have your choice among all the ladies here."

Mr. Chiseled discards the banter. "The lieutenant doesn't approve of most."

"I'm sorry." She almost touches his arm but pulls her hand back, not wanting to give him the wrong idea.

"Don't be." Bringing his knees to attention, Mr. Chiseled looks at the man in the pillory as if he were a cockroach that deserved to be squished. "The elves know best, of course. I'm honored my mentor wants the best for me."

Can we say brain washing?

When he looks at Adaline again, his eyes linger on her breasts, and he licks his lips. Adaline can't stop herself from grimacing.

Annnnnnnnnd I'm done. Get me out of here. Angling herself away from Mr. Chiseled, she searches for Ëólas, praying for a rescue. The moment his eyes lock with hers and he recognizes Mr. Chiseled, Ëólas motions for her to come.

"My mentor's summoned me. If you'll excuse me." Adaline bows slightly and leaves the man behind, forcing herself not to run. As she approaches, Ëólas's laugh booms louder, but his voice doesn't contain the ease she's come to know.

"Ah, and this young ward is Menna," the lieutenant says as Adaline approaches.

Okay, so I'm Menna now. Does Ëólas have a fake name too? She curtsies and sits beside Ëólas, mirroring the ladies across from her by tucking her skirts beneath her legs and sitting with them off to the side.

Again, the lieutenant gazes at Adaline. "A beauty, isn't she? Perfect evidence of the success of our lord's program."

Adaline flinches and quickly pretends to re-adjust her skirts. *Program? Oh god. They're not just controlling population growth. They're, they're breeding humans, aren't they?* The aroma of baked fish clogs her airways and punches her stomach.

While the conversation continues around them, Ëólas points to a pile of empty plates and ignores Adaline shaking her head. "You haven't eaten much today. It's important you take care of yourself."

Translation: Eat. We have a long trek ahead of us.

Without rolling her eyes, Adaline leans forward and makes herself a plate from the assortment of fish that's cooked, filleted, and marinated in every way imaginable. Even though she needs to fill her belly now, admitting her *mentor* is right makes her stomach sour more. Still, she pushes a chunk of baked fish into her mouth.

"What a good girl," says a lady next to the lieutenant.

Adaline gnashes the fish, swallows the lump, and bites her tongue. *I'm a pacifist. I'm a pacifist. I'm a pacifist.*

While she eats, Ëólas steers the conversation, laughing when necessary, poking for openings, teasing out weaknesses, until the lieutenant and his friends boast about the city, about its success, about its clever arrangement and where everything's located, including the main gates. Ëólas feeds them compliments and shares his admiration for the city and its progress over the last several hundred years.

With the lieutenant relaxed and in good spirits, Ëólas stares his puppet in the eyes and assumes that neutral, stoic expression he used when Adaline first arrived, when she couldn't read him yet. "This is quite the celebration tonight. Although, the city feels somewhat empty."

"I know." The lieutenant, discarding his plate of fish bones on the ground in front of him, leans back on his palms and grins as he gazes up at the night sky. "But

I have every faith our soldiers will be back within a month. As long as the terrain cooperates, Lord Āranol and the Morgai will need less than a day to eradicate the Neutral Territory."

Oh god!

Every muscle in Adaline's body stiffens as if rigor mortis has already set in. Only her heart pounding in her chest reassures her she's still alive. Plus, the lieutenant's prediction isn't set in stone. Being here, at this moment and in this hell, means they have a chance to stop this, to warn their friends, to save their city. She can't lose hope. Not now. Not when she needs it more than ever.

Āranol. Morgai. I have to remember those names. But why do I feel like I've heard them before?

Āranol. Adaline repeats his name in her mind, trying to remember where she might have heard that before, but the memory remains buried in the back of her mind. She rips off a chunk of meat and stuffs it in her mouth.

We need to leave. Now.

Ëólas sits perfectly still, preserving his stone-like indifference, but his chest stops moving as if he's not breathing anymore. "I'm impressed our lord does not fear starting a war with Lameiría."

The lieutenant chuckles. "Impressive, indeed, considering the fault will lie with Alderton. When we're done, that kingdom's demise will be inevitable. Serves them right, daring to create something as abhorrent as that territory. Lord Morgán knew truth."

Morgán?

The lieutenant lifts his goblet into the air. "And soon the rest of the world will too."

The other elves do the same. Likewise, Ëólas doesn't miss a beat. The lieutenant narrows his eyes at Adaline while he waits for her to toast her mentors. Reaching forward, she grabs a bottle of wine and fills her cup without spilling a drop.

When she lifts her goblet, the lieutenant toasts, "To a bright future, when we bring the most hopeful under our guidance and exterminate the rest."

Instead of grabbing her sword from Ëólas and impaling the lieutenant, Adaline lifts her glass high into the air, cheers with the rest of them, and drinks every last drop of the wine. Then she smiles at the lieutenant, all the while remembering her first dinner in the Neutral Territory when Seira had cornered Adaline into confessing, *Okay, I don't show spiders mercy. But only when they invade my territory! When I'm on their turf, I leave them alone.*

At the time, Adaline wanted to hide under the table to avoid the glee on Seira's face, the glow of anticipation in her eyes, and the delight in her voice when she announced, *Exactly.*

Now, Adaline understands. She's not a pacifist after all.

Chapter Two

THE RULE OF THREE

After another hour of conversation, Ëólas excuses himself from the lieutenant's company, and Adaline follows behind. They head farther away from the town center, away from the sounds of jubilation. Neither of them speaks. Before they reach the main gates, Adaline fixes her hair and conceals her ears once more. Then they stride past the guards and cross under the iron arch with their heads held high, each of them lost in their thoughts as they drift away from each other but forge ahead.

Beyond the warmth of the canopies, the vegetable gardens fronting every house, and the wide wells full to the brim with fresh water, the land beyond the city wall offers only shades of gray, from the rocky terrain under their feet to the miniature mountains in the distance.

Life is easier in the city, Mr. Chiseled had said.

Well, he certainly told the truth.

Adaline doesn't slow her pace until Hell City by the sea shrinks to the size of a dime. Still, she presses onward, trying to get as far away as quickly as possible. Distance is what matters most to her right now, not her soft mattress back home, not the steaming hot breakfast Kayla would bring in the morning, not even the questions piling up about Ëólas's plan. After everything they both saw, she can't bring herself to speak to him, not yet. Part of her fears his response, that maybe he's seen or heard about something similar before.

Ëólas tugs on the shoulder straps of the knapsack, repositioning the bag across his shoulders, and looks nowhere but ahead. His long strides propel him forward as if he's walking on playground foam rather than the unyielding, solid stone pounding the bottom of their feet. His cloak flaps madly against his calves.

He must be worried about his friends. Our friends.

When only a speck of the city remains, Adaline's head droops forward. She opens her heavy eyelids every so often to make certain she's still going straight and that she won't trip over any rubble or boulders. Every jagged stone jabs the bottom of her flat slippers and bruises her feet. Her blue skirts may hide the truth, but every time her foot falls sideways, rocks scrape her ankles.

Please, don't let me twist my ankle.

God forbid she's stuck here and dragged back to that city. She bites the inside of her cheek to ignore the burning sensation overtaking her feet, to stop her thoughts from drifting back to the humans left behind. The look in those elves' eyes—they didn't see her as a person. To them, she was a pet. Maybe even a prize.

Sometimes, her ex-boyfriend, Derek, looked at her the same way, especially when he gushed about her achievements to his friends. He would hug his arm around her waist, pull her close, and beam a spotlight onto her while he recited all of her recent projects and findings. Adaline tried nudging him to stop, but that just made him want to show her off even more. "Adaline, sweetheart, you have to stop hiding," he'd say.

Well, fuck. He sounded a lot like Seira. At least she can't send me a we-need-to-talk text message.

Adaline's foot dips sideways, and a rock lacerates the inside of her ankle. Warm liquid trickles downward, into her shoe, and begins to pool under her arch. "Fuck."

Ëólas halts and opens his mouth, but he doesn't say anything as Adaline squats and sits down. While her muscles sigh with relief, she hikes her skirts over her knees, making Ëólas immediately turn away, and bends her foot so she can closer examine the ripped flesh. "Damn it."

The last thing we need now is an infection.

Adaline pulls out her dad's Swiss army knife, stabs her chemise undergarment, and tears off a long strip. If only she had her field kit to disinfect the open wound.

Keeping his distance, Ëólas glances over his shoulder. "You alright?"

"The rock cut me."

Setting aside her makeshift bandage, she hunches over and uses the bottom of her skirts to dab at the wound, cleaning away the excess blood. She leans sideways and feels the ground with her hand to search for the bandage. Not finding it, she looks up, and her head nearly collides with Ëólas, who's squatting in front of her. He leans over her ankle and presses his lips into a thin line. Before she can protest, he takes her ankle in his hand, sits down, and repositions her foot across his lap. He slips off her shoe and, using her underskirt, brushes away bits of gravel. With the bandage he stole from her, he wraps her ankle.

Adaline leans back on her hands and grumbles. "I know how to dress a wound."

"I don't doubt that."

He concentrates on his work, making certain the bandage overlaps itself at perfectly even intervals and pulling tightly while not causing her to wince. As he lifts her heel, her skirts slide toward her knees, revealing the scars along her calves from when the guard who abducted her used his sword to pin her dress to the ground. Ëólas's eyes and mouth twist toward each other, but his hands continue their steady work. She leans forward and, in a quick motion, tosses her hem over her legs.

When he finishes tucking the end of the bandage underneath itself, he slides her shoe onto her foot, stands up, and offers Adaline his hand. His palm, hovering in front of her, never wavers. She presses her hand into his, and he pulls her up.

Face to face, he finally looks her in the eyes as the sky behind him shifts from black to red and orange. "I managed to get some information from the lieutenant. Āranol has a three-day head start, but we have the advantage. His army comprises less than a thousand soldiers. If we can reach the Neutral Territory sooner, Magnus and I can assemble a legion. Āranol and the Morgai will never reach our city."

"How do we get ahead of them?"

"They can move only as fast as their horses can endure. They also have wagons with them, and that alone will tire their horses more quickly. There's only two of us, which means we can move faster. Which means you don't have to push yourself so hard."

She rolls her eyes, gives him her back, and crosses her arms over her chest. *Like he's not pushing himself too.*

"Adaline." He waits for her to turn. When she glares at him, he tries again. "In order for us to achieve our goal, we must rely on each other. Ãranol..."

His gaze falls to the ground, and his brow wrinkles as if he too has to keep fighting back the memories of what they saw tonight. His stoicism falters for only a moment, a second really, but the flash of disgust across his face tells Adaline he's equally upset about the city by the sea.

Her hands fall to her sides. "Okay."

Letting the knapsack slip off his shoulders, Ëólas rests their supplies on the ground, rummages inside, and pulls out the canvas blanket. "Good. Now that we understand each other, I need you to be honest with me. Let me know when you need rest, when you need water and food, and above all else when you are unwell." With one flap of his arms, he unfolds the material and lays it on the ground. As he pats the blanket, his eyes focus on her again. "Will you help me? Please."

A gust of wind pushes Adaline's long curls across her face. She looks away, shielding her eyes with her forearm. She wants to keep going. She wants to make certain she never sees that city again. She wants to prove she's not weaker than Ëólas, that she won't slow them down.

Damn it. "I'm tired."

"Thank you. Get some rest." He folds the blanket in thirds to give her some cushion, but the width is meant for only one.

As Adaline lays down, each of her limbs collapse and melt into the rocky terrain beneath her. She tugs the cloak Seira made across her body, and the silky material turns into a luxurious blanket fit for a queen. "You're not tired?"

"I'll let you know when I am. I promise." He sits beside her but keeps his distance while his face turns to stone.

He's formulating. I bet he won't move for hours while he's thinking things through. Adaline chuckles to herself. She used to hate that about him.

"Éólas," she mumbles while her eyelids flutter shut, "where are we? How far until…"

"We'll discuss that after you've had some rest. I'm afraid you won't get much now, but we'll rest longer mid-day."

Her voice fades to a whisper. "Mmm. Because we don't have shelter."

"Exactly."

With the sun peeking over the horizon, Adaline rolls over, letting her hair cover her eyes from the rising sun, and everything about the past day fades into nothingness. In her dreams, torches peek awake and surround her. As they slowly close in, her father hoists her into his arms and runs. She buries her face in the crook of his neck, inhaling the scent of wet wool.

When her father skids to a stop and puts her down, the lieutenant looms over them. "Lovely," he hisses. "A perfect specimen."

The elf's shadow grows longer, stretching like a river beneath her father and sucking him downward. She reaches for him, but before her fingers can touch her father's, the lieutenant blurs and shifts into her abductor. Once again, he grabs her wrist, yanks her backward, and drags her behind him while her father claws at the rocky terrain, unable to get a hold of an anchor. She twists and turns and tries to wrench her hand free.

Her captor squeezes her wrist. "Too late, cockroach."

When Adaline looks up, the shadow swallows her father and his screams. Her abductor releases his prey, allowing her to collapse in a heap on a hard, barren surface. Nothing but darkness surrounds her. She tugs her knees to her chest and sobs silently. Not even sound survives here. Each time she gasps for air, a coarse blanket scrapes her cheek. Alone, she cannot recall what hope feels like. Even the word fades from her memory.

A warm hand brushes against her forehead. Adaline envisions tucking that hand under her cheek and going back to sleep, but she blinks her eyes open. The blanket pressing against her cheek is damp. Pushing her hands against the ground, she sits up and rubs her eyes with the back of her hands. "How long was I out?"

"Only a few hours. I'm sorry." Ëólas passes her a leather canteen.

She takes a few gulps and puts the cork back in place. "Where are we?"

"The Wastelands."

Adaline closes her eyes and tries to conjure an image of the map Magnus had laid upon his desk. Lameiría, Ëólas's home, is to the north. Alderton, Magnus's kingdom, is to the south. And the Wastelands are... "That's west of the Neutral Territory."

"Yes."

"Well, the name is spot on."

With the sun still low in the morning sky, Adaline can more clearly see rocks, rocks, and more rocks around them. The mountains in the distance offer the only variance to the landscape. At least the terrain is flat.

Ëólas uses Adaline's dagger to cut a few slices of cheese and the loaf. While she eats the dry bread and buttery cheddar, he cleans the blade, sheaths it, and passes the weapon back to her. After her last bite, she ties the dagger around her calf again, glad to once more feel the familiar leather straps around her skin. Standing up, she dusts off her hands and folds up the blanket, which Ëólas stuffs into their knapsack. He hoists the bag onto his shoulders, and, once again, they set off.

"We can take turns carrying that," Adaline says.

"I'll let you know when I need the help. Thank you."

Even though his voice contains no hint of sarcasm, she doubts he'll ever take her up on that offer.

Okay, let's see what I do know. We have to cover a lot of ground each day to get ahead of that army. Thankfully, I've got pretty good stamina due to years of dance classes and living in a city. We have food and water, but we didn't take much, which means we must be close to Aerytol's border, and Aerytol, thank goodness, isn't a wasteland. If only we could teleport back home too. Now would be a nice time for Seira to follow through and—

Adaline hits her forehead with the heel of her hand. "Oh, shit."

"What?" Ëólas glances at her sideways but never slows his pace.

"I sort of got into a fight with Seira yesterday morning." Adaline hunches her shoulders and waits for Ëólas to chastise her. She did, after all, promise Ëólas she wouldn't upset Seira.

He exhales slowly and keeps his eyes straight ahead. "About what?"

"Well, she kinda pissed me off. She said I was less myself and that I needed to make a decision but wouldn't specify what kind of decision and basically said if I didn't do something, the Neutral Territory would be in greater danger, and you know how much she loves to be vague."

Ëólas releases a puff of air out of his nose that almost sounds like a laugh. "Indeed."

"She just kept staring at me and putting this pressure on me, so I sort of, kind of, yelled at her and said that maybe she could do something for once."

Now, Ëólas pauses, turns his head, and looks directly at Adaline. "And?"

"She yelled at me, which honestly was a nice change of pace from her usual dream-like aloofness, and said she would do something. And that it wouldn't be subtle."

"And?" Ëólas closes his eyes and waits for the final blow.

"Well, look around? How else do you think we got here?"

Throwing back his head, Ëólas looks up at the lone cloud drifting above them. "I don't know, Adaline. But traveling like that is no small feat. I can't comprehend the amount of magic required to achieve that, let alone how the elf would survive afterward."

"Oh."

"I truly don't know how we came to be here or who granted us this upper hand, but I do know that the rest is up to us, and we're not going to squander this gift. So let's keep going."

Adaline nods, and they continue beating their feet against the unforgiving wasteland. As the hours pass, the scenery never changes. The mountains never appear taller. Not even a tumbleweed rolls in front of them. The silence, the lack of life, eats away at Adaline's faith. Despite the thousands of questions that pop into her head, she can't bring herself to interrupt Ëólas's own ruminations. Plus, the fact that he hasn't commented on what they saw back there makes her begin to wonder if those elves' actions didn't surprise him.

What's Lameiría like? What do his people think about humans, the ones who didn't join Ëólas in the Neutral Territory?

When the sun reaches its zenith, eradicating all shadows, Adaline's mind quiets down while the rumbling in her stomach for lunch grows louder. The sun focuses all its attention on the two of them, as if its sole purpose is to melt them into a puddle of ooze that will just evaporate in this barren land. What's worse, the sweat tricking down her back and the miles they've walked mean she's burning far more calories than they have food to replace. Adaline's upper body sags.

This isn't good. I trust him, but something about this plan isn't adding up.

As if reading her mind, Ëólas sidesteps in front of Adaline and spins around, turning off her autopilot. "Now seems like a good time to rest."

Adaline nods but doesn't sit down. "Ëólas, how many days do you think we'll be out here?"

He scowls at the horizon, in the direction of Hell City. "Anywhere from ten to fifteen days."

Adaline gasps and stumbles backward. Her heart starts pounding, and her mouth dries up. "But, but there's no food for us to forage for out here. I haven't seen a single bird in the sky, let alone mountain goats or lizards or anything edible." *He's got to have a plan. What the fuck is it?*

"The river that flows through the Neutral Territory, and around our castle, eventually splits in two and creates the Wastelands' borders. The closer we get to one of those rivers, the terrain will shift from rock to moors. We should easily find food in five, maybe seven, days."

Adaline hugs her stomach, concentrates on slowing her breath, and speaks only when she's certain her voice won't sound ten times higher than usual. "And until then? What about water? The same?"

"If we don't have rain, yes."

When Adaline doesn't move or speak, he tilts his head at an angle and hesitantly takes a step closer to her. Her knees quiver, and her feet feel as if she's standing on a bed of hot coals. Ëólas, on the other hand, stands tall with the confidence of a general, his shoulders back and face relaxed.

"Adaline? Are you ready to break now, before the worst of the day's heat peaks? You haven't rested enough as it is."

"We can't afford to," she whispers, trying to keep at bay the panic rising in her voice.

Without waiting for Ëólas to respond, she pushes forward, walking past him and urging herself to take wider strides. The shoulder she injured during her abduction throbs, and the old twinge returns. She cradles her left arm against her stomach, holding it in place to limit its movement.

Ëólas grabs her other elbow to stop her. "Adaline, you're clearly exhausted. I need you to rest."

"We'll die out here without water." She spins around and yanks her elbow free, ready to fight him tooth and nail and scream at him for his shortsightedness, but his eyebrows tilted downward and big eyes reduce her anger to a simmer. She exhales a single, loud huff of breath. "Ëólas, how long can you go without food and water?"

He shrugs and kicks the ground with his heel. "A while."

"I don't have time for vague answers, Ëólas. Answer the damn question." When he flinches at her curse, she instead begs. "Please, help me understand."

He rubs his hand over his face. "The typical amount, Adaline. The rule of three. Three hours without air. Three weeks without water. Three months without food."

First, she scoffs. A tiny, single bubble of a laugh escapes her. Then she drops her sore arm and clamps down on her lower lip. "I'm sorry to be the bearer of bad news here, but that's not how it works for humans. We can't survive beyond three minutes without air. Food is three weeks. And water, three days."

Ëólas's mouth falls open. His eyes dart around the horizon, void of animals, of water, of shelter. When his gaze falls on her, he snaps his mouth shut, stitches his brow together as he formulates, and hardens his voice with determination. "We need to double our pace."

"That's not possible, not for humans. I can't burn twice as many calories with nothing to give me energy. It's not possible." Adaline closes her eyes. Images of Ãranol's city fill her mind. The stalls handing out free food. The wells bursting with fresh water. How could she explain returning without her *mentor*? Would they feed her if she had to spend days in the pillory? "Go on without me. I'll head back, and when you defeat Ãranol's army, you'll come get me and—"

Ëólas grabs both her arms and looks her dead in the eyes. "I will never, ever leave you in that sordid place. Do you hear me? Never."

"I'm just one person, Ëólas. In the grand scheme of things, I don't matter." Even though she sounds brave, dread and uncertainty spread throughout her body and threaten to erode her resolve. She needs him to leave quickly, before her cowardice wins. "The most important thing now is warning our friends. I won't be the reason they die too."

"I said we have enough time."

"I'll slow you down."

Adaline tilts her head up to the heavens. *Please, whatever, whoever, brought us here, send us home. Or at the very least, send him back.* She waits for the rocks to vanish, for the training room to return. But the wind howls past her, the sun beams down harder, and all she feels inside is the hollow void of hopelessness.

"Adaline, look at me." He cups her cheeks and tilts her head until his eyes lock with hers. "We're in this together, okay? We're both getting home safely. I give you my word."

She should argue with him, maybe even push him away. She could try threatening him with her dagger or saying something cruel that would turn him against her. But she just got those big, golden eyes to see her as more than an impossibility, as more than a problem, as he once called her. The thought of having him revert to hating her crushes her from the inside out.

I'm so selfish, to care what he thinks of me.

Only when Adaline nods does Ëólas release her arms. After she devours half the bread and half a cheese wheel, she wills herself to stand up again, ignoring the sting in her eyes that begs her to close them for a while. Even the rocks look inviting to sleep on.

Before she can take a single step, Ëólas moves beside her, loops his arm under hers and across her back, and pulls her close. As the side of her body presses against his, her arm hooks around his neck, her elbow hitting the knapsack. She inhales sharply, tries to lean away, but the scent of lavender and that hint of pine confuse her senses.

She hugs his neck tighter, her fingers curling around his shoulder. "What are you—"

"We have a better chance of doubling our pace this way."

Praying she doesn't smell sweaty, she allows him to take the lead. He nudges her forward with his arm supporting her back. Whenever sharp rocks jab her soles and her knees start to buckle, he hoists her up around the waist, taking half the pressure off her feet. Her legs move in sync with his. Sometimes, she even feels weightless.

"I'm sorry," she mumbles. "I hate not being able to carry my own weight." *Literally, in this case.*

"You need not apologize. If anything, I'm the one who owes you an apology. The way those elves... I loathe to even call them that. I have never—"

"You're not them." She says that with as much certainty as if she were confirming that the sky is blue. She can't have him doubting himself. He's carrying enough already. "You're a good person, Ëólas. There's no one else I trust more than you. I'm glad I got stuck here with you."

He stumbles over a rock.

Even from beside him, Adaline can make out his eyes darkening as he loses himself in his thoughts. Still, he resets his grip around her waist and resumes his brisk pace. His quick, light steps prove he had been moving slower up until now to keep pace with her, but together they're able to trek faster—not as quickly as he could move on his own, but the journey is easier now. Every time his arm tightens around her waist, Adaline relaxes against him more and more. He never falters. Never grunts from her weight. Never complains. He just keeps going.

They both do.

Chapter Three

Another History Lesson

*H*e's really something else. What makes him so different from Āranol's people?

With every other step, she side-eyes him. "Have you heard of them before, Morgán and Āranol? Why do they hate humans so much?"

Ëólas's chest heaves up and down, but he doesn't respond, not for a long while. When he finally answers her questions, he speaks slowly, cautiously. "Āranol, no. Morgán, yes. All elves know of him."

Again, a long silence stretches between them. *Do all elves take this long to think?* "Who is he, this Morgán?"

"You've heard of Aerytol's last queen?"

"Yes. A bit."

"Morgán was captain of the queen's guard, her guard."

"Oh. Does this..." She doesn't want to say it. She doesn't need more evidence why elves and humans should remain apart. "Does this have to do with the time when humans betrayed the elves? Why the old palace is in ruins?"

Ëólas exhales a single, sad laugh. "As observant as ever."

Another long pause drags on, so Adaline pokes his arm. She narrows her eyes and stares him down, making certain he knows she won't let this go. "I need you to trust me too. What happened, Ëólas?"

Being this close, he can't retreat behind his placid expression. The grief that overshadows him makes Adaline regret her question, but he focuses on the horizon and doesn't hold back. "I do not mean to shut you out. We simply do not speak often about the Great Betrayal because the loss is indescribable. But I'll try." He inhales deeply, filling his lungs, expanding his chest, and bracing himself for an uncomfortable conversation that he'd rather avoid. Letting go of his reservations, he speaks openly. "Those elves are refugees."

"What?"

"It's probably best if I start at the beginning." He runs his hand through his dirty-blond hair. With their roles reversed, he becomes the storyteller and she the listener. "When the world was still new, fae descended from the Immortal Realms. At the Source's request, they nurtured this land. Their breath gave birth to the wind. Their hair became the grass. They gave us a spark of their soul so we'd have fire, and their spit filled the oceans."

"Okay, most of that was beautiful. The last image was a little gross though." Ëólas arches an eyebrow and pinches her waist.

"Ouch. Okay, sorry. I didn't mean to be disrespectful."

"Do the children interrupt your stories?"

"All the time!"

He chuckles. "I'll keep that in mind. Some say their tears of joy filled the ocean."

"I like that version better."

"Noted." He hoists her closer to him and jumps over a gap in the rocky terrain. "Anyway, when the fae completed their mission, they entrusted the world to us, the elves, and departed. From among us, we chose a leader, a lady named Aeríoléna, who had received the blessings of the fae. We trusted her guidance above all else and eventually declared Aeríoléna and her husband, Tólen, our queen and king."

"Whoa."

"Over time, we watched the apes evolve. They grew smarter and mimicked us, eventually walking on two legs, and—"

"For the record, we learned to walk on two feet without you all in my world, so you can't really say they were...mimicking...you. I'll shut up now. Just saying it was inevitable. But okay. Go on."

Ëólas massages his temple. "Are you going to keep questioning the story of my people?"

"Yes. But don't take it personally. It's my job."

"At least you're honest."

"I try."

With a loud exhale and a smirk, Ëólas continues. "The point is that we've called Aeríoléna's family beloved since the beginning of time. As we spread further across the land, she and her family settled where now stands Aerytol, named after Aeríoléna and Tólen."

The nostalgia in his voice laces around Adaline's heart, tugging her to mourn with him. "They must have been magnificent."

"Indeed. For several millennia, the humans revered the Aerytolíans too and looked to the elves for guidance, but mankind grew impatient and insisted on doing things their way. About thirteen hundred years ago, they started declaring portions of land for themselves and electing their own kings, which forced the elves to do the same before we had no free lands left."

"Typical."

"Mmm. Even though we elected additional leaders to guide us in the different regions, we still viewed the Aerytolíans as our high queen and king. Soon, the humans began warring with each other, and the division between our two peoples grew greater."

The adoration on his face cracks and crumbles. "The last queen of Aerytol tried to reunite our peoples. She welcomed humans into her homeland, and their numbers grew until humans outnumbered elves four to one. The humans began to fear the queen would rescind her invitation, denying them her grace and the bounty her land offered. Some humans feared worse, that she planned to enslave them and reduce their numbers."

"Oh no."

Ëólas nods. "Four hundred sixty-two years ago, they stormed the palace and killed the royal family." As his chest caves inward, his eyes turn misty. Each word he utters makes him grimace further until his face is as gray as their surroundings. "They initiated a war that devastated all of Aerytol. The humans who betrayed their queen fled to the Wastelands, and Morgán pursued them with the aid of his guards, the Morgai. After a few hundred years, we never heard from him. We suspected he and his people settled somewhere new but wanted to be left alone. So we did. We wanted to give them peace."

So, the Morgai are Morgán's followers. And they're still fighting the same war that happened hundreds of years ago. No wonder they hate us so much. How are we ever going to convince people like that lieutenant that not all humans are bad, that what Morgán's done isn't okay?

Adaline stops walking and lets go of Ëólas. She wipes her eyes, smearing her tears across her cheeks, and stares at the tips of his boots. He inches closer. Her chin quivers, and her shoulders shake.

"We're going to stop them, Adaline."

When he slides his arms around her and rubs her back, she falls against him, rests her cheek on his chest, and hiccups. She curses herself for not making him feel better. He's the one hurting, but something about this story gnaws at her until her bones feel raw. "I'm so sorry, Ëólas."

He presses his chin against her forehead. "You don't have anything to apologize for, Adaline. It took me a long while, but I realized that the humans of today aren't responsible for the past. We can't keep punishing them. We can't keep hating them. And you? You have done nothing but foster peace."

The longer she holds him, the more her chest compresses. She tries to swallow, but her mouth has turned to cotton. As Ëólas steps back, his hands slide down her arms. His gaze trails from her eyes to her lips, and warmth creeps up her neck. She licks her bottom lip, and Ëólas stiffens.

Broken bits of skin make her lip feel like sandpaper.

He lets go of her and unties a canteen from his bag. "Drink this."

After she guzzles the rest of the first canteen, they continue onward with Ëólas helping her to move faster. She wants to ask him more questions, but she's not sure if she can stomach more answers. She's still trying to comprehend how Morgán's pursuit turned into brainwashing and breeding humans, not to mention how Hell City went unchecked for hundreds of years.

No one heard from Morgán after a few hundred years. A few hundred.

"Ëólas, how old are you?"

"Older than you."

Fucking vague answers. "I figured that. The question is how much."

He shrugs. When Adaline's eyes finish boring a hole into the side of his face, he smirks. "What's it matter? We're both here now."

"If it doesn't matter, why won't you tell me?"

"Because." Ëólas sighs and massages circles into his temple. It would seem elves suffer headaches too. "Because the more humans see how different we are from them, the more they view us as a threat."

Adaline winces. That's why she intentionally made mistakes in her ballet classes, because she was tired of prima donna Nicole turning the class against her. Most of the students had been studying ballet since they were three, whereas Adaline had become the teacher's pet within her first year when she was eight. "I get it. But not being yourself also makes it really hard to find people, to find friends, who truly love you for who you are."

The moment she utters the word love, her cheeks flush, and she looks away. "I'm not trying to guilt you. I just hope someday you find someone you trust enough so you can be yourself around them."

"You're fearless, you know that?"

Adaline laughs and looks away from him again. "I wish."

An hour later, grass pops up in patches. The ground feels softer, but Adaline leans on Ëólas more. Yesterday, she trained for hours, before magic launched them into this new adventure, and she's had maybe three hours of sleep. She needs her adrenaline to kick in. Now. Instead, she drags her feet forward, only for her toe to catch on a sharp rock, and falls. With Ëólas holding onto her, she swings in front of him. Her free hand clutches his belt buckle, which she uses like an anchor as she tries to stand upright.

Once she's on her feet, he gently clasps her hand and pulls her fingers away from his trousers. "I think you've reached your limit."

"Sorry."

"Don't be." He lets go of her and slides the knapsack off his back. "We can cover a few more miles while you rest. Put this on." He hands her their bag, which she stares at in confusion until he turns his back to her, squats down, and waits for her to climb on.

"You can't be serious. Ëólas, I need you in top shape. You can't carry me."

"Stop arguing and trust me. Do you want to starve to death and let our friends die? Of course not, so let's go."

What the hell. Elf superpowers?

Too tired to fight him, Adaline pulls the rope out of their pack. "Fine, but use this to better distribute my weight. I don't care how strong you think you are; you'll kill your arms carrying me piggyback style for more than a few minutes."

He glances over his shoulder and arches an eyebrow. "Have experience with this?"

"Oh, stuff it."

Adaline tosses the pack onto her shoulders. Sadly, their meager supplies weigh almost nothing. She wraps her arms around his neck and lays her body against his. Luckily, her skirts are wide enough that she can spread her legs and drape them around his sides. She positions the rope beneath her bottom, crosses it in front of his chest and around her back. When she passes the rope back to him, he knots it in front. He stands up in one swift motion, hoisting her up with him, folds his arms behind his back, and grips his wrists, creating a bench for her to sit on. She doesn't dwell on the fact that his hands are under her round bottom.

Trying to find a more comfortable position, she pushes down on his shoulders, just a bit, to move her torso higher, but her bottom grinds against his back. With her heart pounding in her ears, she tries to squeeze her legs shut, but that's not possible with his lean, solid body beneath her. As her cheeks burn, she hugs his neck too tightly.

"Relax," he chokes. "I've got you."

No kidding. She loosens her grip. "Sorry."

He chuckles once and starts walking, his steps as quick and agile as before. *Show off.*

The more she watches the same rocks pass beneath her, her muscles collapse. She rests her cheek on his shoulder and against his dirty-blond hair, grateful to have something soft amidst this harsh environment. Her eyes follow the curve of his jawline, up and down and up again, before her eyelids grow too heavy. As the horizon fades from view, she whispers, "Thank you," and surrenders to her dreams.

By the time Adaline opens her eyes, the sun has nearly finished its journey across the second half of the sky. Instead of only shades of jagged gray, the ground sports larger patches of grass and the occasional twisted, skeletal remains of a bush.

She lifts her head. "I can walk now."

Ëólas unties the rope and sets her down.

She stretches her arms high above her head, then rests her hands on her butt and arches her back. "Whew. I feel a lot better, thanks." When her stomach rumbles, she covers her belly with her hands.

With a frown, Ëólas hands her the bag of almonds but holds onto the other half of the cheddar. They walk as she munches.

"Don't you need rest?" She pops a single almond into her mouth, chewing slowly and sucking on each crumb.

"Not for a few more days." He keeps side-eyeing her, and the frown he wears won't lessen. He cuts a single slice of cheese and passes it to her.

She nibbles the corner. "You okay? I was too heavy, wasn't I? We should stop and—"

"Do you always have nightmares?"

Her hand freezes in front of her mouth, and the rectangular slice droops in half. "Oh. They come and go. They've just been a bit more intense lately."

He waits for her to finish the morsel in her hand and passes her another. Again, she takes her time, savoring the cheese melting on her tongue and delaying the moment she has to swallow.

Ten. I'll allow myself ten almonds. And six, no, five slices of cheese. That can get me to dinner.

The longer he stares at her, she decides they both need a distraction. "I used to have nightmares a lot after we moved to the States, um, to a new country. My dad would sit next to me and read until I fell asleep, or he'd share random facts he learned from his studies. Sometimes, we'd be awake for hours, just him and me, in our own little universe." Adaline laughs to herself, even though the memories threaten to drown her too. "He used to puncture holes in cardboard, turn on the flash—um, torch, and cast constellations on my ceiling. He'd tell me stories about them too."

"He sounds like a kind man."

"He was. Very."

"I'm sorry for your loss." The heaviness of his words snuffs out a corner of Adaline's pain. "How did he—never mind."

"It's okay. He was on his way home from work. It was raining, and his, um, wagon drove off a bridge." When she closes her eyes, she can hear the Potomac roaring in her nightmares. "It took us two months to find his car in the river."

"I'm sorry."

"You have nothing to apologize for," she says, repeating his words from earlier.

"What sort of stories did he tell you? Like the one about the girl who falls down a rabbit hole and enters another world?" When Adaline nods, he hands her slice number three. "You promised you'd tell me that one."

"A deal's a deal."

They continue walking forever. Just landscape after landscape with no option for a montage or fast-forward button. After she tells him *Alice in Wonderland,* he tells her a story about the elf who turned into a tree and the lady who sang the moon to sleep. Adaline records his every word in her mind, and his voice keeps her fears at bay. The more he opens up to her, the more she admits to herself she's glad they have this time together, outside of the training grounds and without someone trying to kill her.

All too soon, the sun sets, and the moon rises. They sit down facing each other on a grass patch big enough for two. Without warning or asking, he pulls her foot onto his lap.

Adaline tips backward onto her palms. "What are you—Aah! Don't do that!"

He takes off her shoe and holds her dusty, smelly foot in his hand. She tries to yank her leg away, but he holds firm to her ankle.

"Calm down, Adaline. I want to see how your wound is doing."

She thanks the moon for staying behind her so he can't see her face turning beet red. Biting her lip, she whimpers when he unwraps the bandage. She can smell her foot from where she sits. *Stop. Stop. Please, stop. I'm going to stink him to death.*

He tilts her foot sideways and examines her ankle as if he were a surgeon. "I don't think you need this bandage anymore."

He presses his hand into the ball of her foot, and her upper body arches backward as she gasps.

"If only you had those curious boots from your world," he says.

Her laugh surprises her. *I can't believe he remembers my Timberlands.*

His fingers rub circles on top of her foot while he digs his thumb into her arch, making her wriggle and try to pull away again but to no avail. "The night will be cold. We need to walk then to remain warm, so you should rest now."

"Ugh." *I hate when he's right.*

With him continuing to massage the kinks out of her foot, she lays down. Every ache dissolves under his attention, his fingers kneading her flesh until her skin is soft and compliant. Her eyelids flutter shut, and her leg grows warmer with each compression despite the temperature dropping. His hands skate down the length of her calf, easing those muscles as he pushes and pulls, making her skin tingle. Her breath turns shallow. Her inner thigh pulses, and she squeezes her legs together. Not stopping, his fingers brush over her skin. His thumb rubs circles around her inner ankle bone. Round and round he goes over that nub until she whimpers. Although faint, the sound of her moaning makes her eyes pop open.

She rips her foot away from him. "That's enough."

"The other."

She's never heard him so demanding, and her heart rate speeds up. Not sure what to do, she contemplates rolling over to attempt sleep or stealing the rest of the cheddar from him.

But he extends a hand and waits for her to comply. "My apologies. I got lost in my own thoughts. I'll keep the second one shorter."

His patience outlasts Adaline's irritation. She entrusts her foot to him again, and her cheeks grow redder as she lays back in the grass and prays she doesn't moan again.

What the hell is wrong with me?

She wakes up to Ëólas leaning over her, brushing her hair off her cheek.

"Adaline, we need to walk now." His hand is the only warm object nearby. She pushes herself up, and they continue onward as the moon shines above them.

Once again, Ëólas is right. The night got cold fast. How didn't she notice that the first night? Because she was running on adrenaline to get away from hell?

Adaline grabs her stomach. The cramping worsens with every step, but miraculously her feet no longer hurt. She's swapped one pain for another.

How on earth will I keep going? I peed only twice today. Not the best sign.

When her stomach roars, Adaline hunches over as if that will stop her muscles from clenching. She has one wheel of cheese, three quarters of the almonds, and one canteen of water left. If they double their pace, they can find food in two days. Maybe. This is doable, so long as Ëólas's back doesn't give out.

Not that I have any idea how much he can endure and if I'm endangering him.

"How about another history lesson?" Ëólas asks, drawing Adaline's attention away from her stomach.

Are all history lessons as depressing as the last one?

She tries to imagine the fear those humans must have felt, a fear strong enough for them to choose destroying their own home. But nothing Ëólas said indicated they had proof of the queen's ill intent. "You really think humans are that stupid?"

Both of Ëólas's eyebrows rise up. "I only meant to—"

"No, no. Not about your question. About Aerytol. I just don't get it. Okay, we can be impetuous and greedy and blindly follow the wrong asshole who feeds us the lies we want to hear, but—oh, okay. I guess I can see it."

Ëólas wrinkles his eyebrows into a zigzag of amused disbelief. "Are you always so critical of your own kind?"

"Sometimes. Especially when we make choices that hurt ourselves. Still, someone had to stoke the fire, you know, for them to take such a big risk and destroy a whole kingdom. I don't understand."

"You wouldn't."

She closes her eyes and stumbles in the dark for a while. He must have meant to pay her a compliment. She knows he no longer sees her as a threat to his species, but she can't let go of the other meaning behind his words, the one he didn't intend but believes. "But other humans would."

Ëólas's puff of breath forms wisps that float around them before vanishing for good. "Yes. But I have never... Lameiría has never... That doesn't make Morgán right." Ëólas clenches his jaw and grinds his teeth. "I cannot stomach calling them elves. Their actions go against our very nature."

"What do you mean?" Broken chunks of rubble roll beneath her shoes, threatening to send her flying onto her backside. She teeters sideways and spreads her arm outward to rebalance.

At the same time, Ëólas grabs her elbow to stabilize her. "We encourage and nurture life, not control and subdue it. Their methods are appalling, and I will personally see to it that we tear that city down brick by brick."

Adaline stops abruptly. "You really mean it?"

Looking her in the eyes, Ëólas vows, "Absolutely," and his grim expression transitions into a ruthless smile, showing Adaline he already has a plan. "By attacking the Neutral Territory, Āranol has initiated war with not only Alderton but also Lameiría, which means I have every right to defend my people. When Magnus and I defeat him and the Morgai, I'll have evidence to present to all the elven kingdoms. Because of Ãranol's crimes, the elves will grant me permission to invade the Wastelands and claim this territory our responsibility. So, I give you my word, Magnus and I will make certain those who contributed to the atrocities here will pay for their crimes."

Hope takes root inside her again. The seedling is small right now, but it's enough to tell her why she's going to survive the Wastelands. "Somehow, someway, I'm going to help."

Ëólas searches her eyes for a moment. A cloud drifts in front of the moon, dimming its light and casting a long shadow over his face. He nods his head, but the darkness conceals his expression.

CHAPTER FOUR

THE PEARL

Adaline wakes up with a grumble, her cheek smushed against Ëólas's shoulder, and her arms draped down the front of his chest. She lifts her head, her eyelashes brushing his cheek, and looks ahead, waiting for her nightmares to materialize in front of them. But she and Ëólas are alone. He unties the knot at his navel and sets her down. Tilting her chin up with his thumb, he locks eyes with her until she blinks away the haze clouding her vision. She yawns once, rubs her eyes, and starts walking. Neither speaks. All that matters is covering more ground, and thanks to Ëólas's insane stamina, she can do her share for a while now. She has to.

The wind picks up, blowing her curls across her face and whipping her cloak sideways. She glances at the gray sky that mirrors the gray landscape. Their merger erases the faint graphite line that's supposed to separate the two. The clouds blocking the sun deny her the opportunity of guessing the time of day.

How long did he carry me this time? "Ëólas, you need to rest."

"Tomorrow."

Over the next several hours, he says the same thing each time she tries to coax him to pause. He doesn't glance at her as much now. He keeps his gaze focused on the horizon, telling her he won't rest until he's found her water and food.

No matter what, she'll forever regard him as a guardian angel. Well, a guardian elf. Her personal savior. With so much endless expanse around them, he's the one tangible thing she can hold on to.

The wind settles down, and Adaline's curls fall limp around her face. The clouds increase in thickness as they grow heavier, darker, taunting her with the idea of rain. With her mouth chalky, she tries not to think about vending machines with rows upon rows of bottled water and only a sheet of glass keeping them at arm's length.

The inside of her stomach feels hollow now, numb even, allowing her to close her eyes, relax her abdomen, and forget for a moment the last day that had her hunched over, clutching her stomach, and ready to claw Ëólas's eyes out every time he glanced her way with concern. Maybe that's why he doesn't look at her now. He's afraid she might pounce.

When she pockets her hand, her mobile phone bumps her palm like a dog trying to get her attention. In her contacts lists, she's saved the numbers to her favorite restaurants that are only a Metro stop away. Pad Thai. Butter chicken and garlic naan. Crispy beef with white rice and pork egg rolls.

I'm going to lose my fucking mind out here.

As if she already has, she chuckles loudly. The sudden, musical sound that doesn't match this scene makes Ëólas jump.

Is he afraid I'll eat him? "Sorry. I just miss public transportation."

Slowly, Ëólas unwrinkles his brow and smooths away his scowl. "A carriage would be a luxury right now."

"I was thinking more about planes, so we'd be home already."

Without ceasing to walk, Ëólas turns around in a full circle to examine the miles of rocky terrain surrounding them. "I believe we have more than enough plains for now."

Her laugh sounds like wind chimes, tin-like, empty on the inside, and carried off with the wind. Still, the momentary levity makes her steps lighter. "No, a plane, spelt differently, is how we fly."

Ëólas gives her a sideways look while his eyebrow slants upward, as if he's waiting for more information or the final line of a joke.

"I'm not teasing. Don't tell Magnus, but we created long, cylindrical, mechanical objects with wings that fly us around the planet. I don't really get how they work, but they have wheels on the bottom and use fuel to take off. Inside the planes, we have cushioned seats and windows so we can watch the land shrink below us until we're higher than the clouds." She floats her hand in the air like a child pretending to fly a toy.

"You cannot be serious."

"I don't lie. Ever." When he cocks an eyebrow at her, she smirks and adds, "There's no point. I'm terrible at it."

Ëólas chuckles and passes her the remaining cheese, which Adaline slices into paper-thin shavings. His laughter dies in his throat when she fails to hide her hands shaking. The next time she uses her dagger to slice the cheese, she focuses all of her attention, all of her strength, all of her energy on keeping her hands steady. The moment the cheese curls away from the wedge, Ëólas releases a faint exhale, and his frown lessens.

While she eats, she imagines Nan's kitchen counter covered with hundreds of mini tarts filled with homemade apricot or fig preserves and topped with three flaky pastry stars fanned out to create a decorative topping.

Stop thinking about food!

Ëólas answers her prayers. Pulling her attention away from her thoughts, he tilts his head up to the clouds, lifts his arms, and spreads them out, just a smidge, as if he's ready for takeoff. "I can't imagine what the world must look like from so high up."

"It looks peaceful. There aren't any lines drawing borders. It's just one landmass and a patchwork of green, brown, and blue."

His eyes glaze over as he disappears inside his own head. Whatever troubles him pulls the corners of his mouth downward. Before Adaline can ask him one more time to consider resting, he clears his throat and tosses aside his worries. At least for now. "What do you miss most from your world?"

She blurts out her first, random answer. "Indoor plumbing."

Arching an eyebrow, he waits for her to explain, which results in Adaline providing a full speech about city water, treatment plants, and underground pipes, along with descriptions of tap water, showers, baths, and, above all else, toilets.

With her hand, she mimes pushing down an imaginary lever. "When you flush the toilet, the water goes wa-oosh and gets sucked down a pipe, taking all the waste out of the house. Oh, and when you go to the sink, there are two more handles that let you choose hot or cold water to wash your hands or get a glass of water. All you do is turn the handles, and water pours out of the faucet and disappears down another drain in the basin."

Finally, with most of day two behind them, Ëólas stops walking. "Wait."

"What?"

"This indoor plumbing, it handles all water in your home?"

Adaline beams. But when his face turns a shade of yellowish green, she scrunches her brow. "Are you okay?"

Pushing his fist against his mouth, he swallows hard as if trying to stop himself from throwing up. "That's horrid."

"No way. Hot or cold water the instant you want it? It's amazing!"

"Alright, let me see if I understood you correctly. Water sucks the waste out of your home." When Adaline nods, he gags but continues. "Only for that water to return to you, so that you may *drink* it?"

"Oh my god! Nooooooo. Eww." Adaline dry heaves while Ëólas exhales with relief. "Different water. Different pipes. Different destination. Never do the two cross paths."

His eyes follow her hands as she gestures how the pipes run past each other. As she flaps her arms and waves them about frantically, he chuckles so deeply that his whole chest vibrates, and the clasp for his cloak jingles at the base of his neck. Within the darkness folding around them, his joy dances across the land. Surely trees should start growing from that sound alone.

"Indoor plumbing," he repeats. "That seems convenient. And being able to fly? You must think us simple."

"No. Not at all." Adaline shakes her head while the last slice of cheese disintegrates on her tongue. She keeps talking, keeps thinking about anything other than food. If she dwells on her inability to twitch her nose to conjure a meal, her legs will give out beneath her. "My world has made massive progress in terms of technology and whatnot, but we've made lots of mistakes along the way. Your world feels almost brand new. You have the opportunity for elves and humans to work together and balance each other out, which means you might be able to avoid the pitfalls humans alone fell into. Maybe you can bypass the tragedies my world has suffered through. Who knows what you will achieve with both peoples working together."

"Are you usually so optimistic?"

Am I really optimistic, even now? "Sometimes. My grandmother, Nan, she didn't have such an easy life. She had to raise my dad all by herself, and when she was in her sixties, she had to raise me too. She's the one who taught me to look for the possibilities rather than lose myself in the gloom."

We can't let the gloom swallow us forever. Huh, I guess I am still optimistic. Thank you, Nan.

Ëólas peeks at her from the corner of his eye. "I understand now."

"Understand what?"

"Why our citizens enjoyed your stories so much. They introduced new possibilities. And they all ended with hope."

How many of my stories did he listen to? "Not all of them."

"Mmm. The one about the mermaid was tragic."

Adaline nods. "Unrequited love is tragic." She crosses her arms over her chest to brace herself, to hold herself together, to protect herself from the gloom that lies ahead.

"I don't understand how the prince—never mind." Ëólas kicks a rock that rolls twenty feet ahead of them.

"What?"

"Nothing."

With his eyes fixated on the horizon, Ëólas suddenly halts, squints, and sprints ahead. Once he reaches the outline of a bush, he kneels down and sticks his hands between the brittle branches. He's careful enough not to snap a single one. When Adaline stops beside him, he stands up and places in her hand ten berries, ten fragile gems that roll around her palm. A few are tiny and shriveled, but the plump ones almost burst at the seams. Their bulbous forms start to blur.

"Thank you," she whispers, cupping all ten to her chest.

Ëólas's grin rejuvenates his entire face. "Eat. I'll find more."

She savors every one, each a pearl that bursts with hope inside her mouth. She offers Ëólas half, but he waves his hand in refusal. When two remain, she pockets one and reaches for Ëólas's hand. His head jerks back at the sudden touch, but his hand quickly warms in hers. Carefully, she places the last berry in the center of his palm and folds his fingers over it, creating a dome shield.

When he opens his mouth to protest, she says, "All of us need hope."

His breath hitches. He nods once and presses his fist against his heart. As he bows his head, his shoulders seem lighter. Slants of sunlight break through the clouds, encouraging Adaline to start walking with more gusto. Of course Ëólas keeps up, but to her left, she watches him ponder the berry in his palm. He contemplates it for a long while, then places the gift in his mouth and follows the daylight ahead of them.

When nightfall shades their gray surroundings and the clouds switch off the moonlight, Adaline squints into the void ahead. A raised, jagged piece of rock catches the tip of her shoe. She tumbles forward a few steps and whispers a string of profanity that makes Ëólas cringe and shrink away.

"You don't like cursing, do you?" Finding solid ground again, she flings her curls behind her shoulder, away from her face.

He tosses his head from side to side while he debates his answer. "It's just not something elves do."

"Huh. My father cussed like a sailor. He loved using colorful language to punctuate his points."

"Do all sailors cuss where you come from?"

"Ha! Yes. It's a thing."

The fourth time Adaline trips, Ëólas halts in his tracks. "Alright, you need a respite."

"I'm not getting on your back." She drops her hands to her side and stands taller, overstretching her abs that fight to contract and make her hunch over.

"Adaline, we need to—"

"*You* need to—"

"Just get on."

"I'm not sleeping on you again!"

They both break eye contact and stare at the ground. A slight pink blush creeps up and warms Adaline's neck while Ëólas shifts his jaw from side to side.

"Fine." He drops the bag from his shoulders, which lands with a quiet thud.

Still not looking at her, he spreads the blanket out and gestures for her to lay down. She collapses into a fetal position and turns away from him so he can't see her grabbing her waist and grimacing. If she could claw the earth for water, she would. Her stomach contracts, seizes, and screams deep inside her. Her joints lock into place, and every muscle in her body burns. Venturing from sword practice to enemy territory to walking for two days straight with limited food and rest has introduced a new realm of torture. She's slept maybe eleven hours in three days. But her brain can't handle math right now. As her thoughts switch off, her lips part and release a loud sigh, and she sinks into oblivion.

Her dreams don't offer rest though. She's plagued with images of Cindy and Dax banging on the door to her condo and the elven lieutenant chasing her through downtown D.C. When her father finds her, he takes her hand and leads her into a forest so they can hide. "Find that abomination," yells a man's voice. The torches close in around her, their heat singeing her back. Her father pulls her into a bear hug just as fire engulfs them.

With a scream, Adaline jumps off her blanket and searches the endless horizon of midnight. No lieutenant. No soldiers. No fire. Exhaling, she closes her eyes and places her hand on her heart to suppress the thumping.

We don't have time for stupid, pointless nightmares.

A second later, before she can finish steeling herself, Ëólas rests his hand on the small of her back. That small source of warmth, pulsing through her body, fortifies her. Despite their world turning upside down, his lavender and pine scent hasn't faded. She takes a few more breaths, syncing her heartbeat with his. Then she gets up and puts the blanket away.

Again, he doesn't ask for details, and she doesn't offer any.

They start walking again. Aside from more patches of dirt and the occasional decayed bush, the terrain feels smoother and gradually slopes downward. Eventually, the ground turns spongy, reducing the impact on Adaline's knees.

"Moss?" she asks.

Ëólas squats to study the squishy, green flowerless plant. She expects him to announce this is what they had been hoping for because grass and moss must mean they'll soon spot animals. And animals mean food.

Adaline licks her lips. *Thank goodness Ëólas grabbed that frying pan back in Hell City.*

But when Ëólas stands up, he doesn't jump for joy. He doesn't announce they're close to food. He doesn't even glance her way.

She grabs his hand to make him remember she's standing in front of him. "Is everything okay?"

He blinks a few times and presses his mouth into a thin line. "Fine. Let's keep going."

Without waiting for her, he continues onward, and she follows, pretending everything's peachy, because they have enough to deal with already. And they sure could use a break right about now.

At least the moss is much softer.

As she rolls her feet from toes to heel, they bounce with lightness. *Huh.* Actually, now that she thinks about it, her legs no longer burn. Neither her ankles nor her feet have suffered cramping or aching since she woke up. Just like yesterday. After Ëólas had massaged them.

Staring at his back, she opens her mouth and closes it again. *How am I ever going to repay him?*

Time moves faster only when they're talking, so Adaline forces herself to break the silence and ask him about his favorite childhood memories. That he openly shares pieces of himself, windows into his world, encourages her to keep going. She can vividly picture him learning to ride horses, climbing the highest tree in

Lameiría, and learning how to cook in the middle of a forest with no one to help him.

When he asks her the same, she tells him about the hours she spent in her father's library. She listened to all of his stories about the colonists fighting for their independence from the king overseas, how merchants and farmers and everyday people fought for the right to govern themselves, to reshape their lives and build a better world. A master storyteller, her father would leap around the living room, duck behind sofas, and stab cushions as he brought those stories to life. He made her fall in love with history, even when Nan told them to shop for new cushions.

In between their reminiscing, they easily fall back into a silent rhythm. While Ëólas plans, she pulls her hair over her shoulder, giving her neck a chance to cool down, and braids her curls that now, thanks to Seira's spell, fall past her waist. *I hope she hasn't turned me into Rapunzel.* When she finishes, she drops the braid and watches her work slowly unravel.

Will the Neutral Territory come apart once everyone knows about the approaching war? What about now, with Ëólas missing? No, I can't think like that. Our city is too important. It's a symbol of hope for all of us.

She can't believe anyone in the Neutral Territory would give up. Its citizens have worked too hard to turn that portion of Aerytol into a thriving city. *Granted, they should give the city a proper name. Like New Hope. Meh, overused.*

Sticking out her tongue, Adaline grabs her braid and begins toiling away again, keeping her hands and mind occupied. *Besides, the city's name should be half Elvish and half English, er, Common Tongue. Leira means hope. New Leira? Oh, I love that.*

Giving the city a proper name makes it feel closer, not hundreds of miles away on the opposite side of a river. A river that they have to find a way to cross. With no boat. No wood. And no oars. Damn it.

It's okay. Magic brought us here for a reason. Our story can't end like this. We will make it back to New Leira. I know it in my bones.

Ëólas leans forward until his profile catches Adaline's attention. "It's been a while since you've smiled like that. What's so amusing?"

"Nothing."

He arches an eyebrow.

Adaline purses her lips to the side. "I just renamed the Neutral Territory. Were you and Magnus ever going to give the city a proper name?"

"Yes, once we knew the city was viable. That's on next year's agenda. Dare I ask what you renamed my city?"

"It's not *your* city. I renamed it New Leira."

After Ëólas scoffs, he pauses, silently moves his lips to test the name, and rocks his head from side to side. "Not bad. I'll submit New Leira to the council for consideration."

Adaline swings her arms as she walks faster, envisioning that moment when New Leira will pop up in the distance, when the castle's turrets will rise above the horizon, when Seira and Magnus will run out to greet them—and chastise them for going missing in the first place. She can picture so clearly the Venetian-esque bridges, the vines climbing the sides of buildings that make alleyways feel like gardens, and the stalls and conversations lining Front and Market Street.

Suddenly, Ëólas grabs Adaline's elbow, causing her to stop and fall back a few steps. Standing as tall as a statue, he cranes his neck and squints into the darkness ahead. His face falls.

Adaline peers into the distance but sees nothing noticeable along the horizon. "What's wrong?"

"There's a bog several miles ahead."

"A bog?" Adaline throws her hands onto her hips. "You can't be serious. How can there be a bog ahead?"

"We've been walking downhill for a while now. The rain must collect there."

"Fan-fucking-tastic." When Ëólas lowers his eyebrows, Adaline bites her upper lip. "Sorry."

"No, it's okay. Your sentiment is quite accurate."

That's not reassuring. "Can we go around?"

Ëólas looks left, right, then left again. "I can't see how far the bog stretches. We may waste more time trying to find a way around."

"So we go through?"

He glances at her shoes. "You'll lose those slippers the moment we enter the bog. We still have a few miles, but—"

"Wait, how do you know there's a bog *several miles* ahead?"

He ducks his head and massages his neck. "Oh, well. You know."

"You can see it? From here?"

Ëólas shrugs. "We have good eyesight."

"Fascinating. What other super senses do you have?" Lifting her eyebrows, she tilts her nose toward her armpit, sniffs, and backs up several steps. "Oh no."

"You don't smell as horribly as you fear."

"That doesn't make me feel better."

With a shrug, he goes back to glaring in the direction of the bog. "If we go around, we could spend days—"

"We'll go through."

"Your shoes."

Okay, what resources do we have on us? A useless frying pan. Adaline stifles a sob. *Cheese cloth. Rope.* "The rope. I can use it like the ribbons on ballet shoes."

"Ballet?"

"The details don't matter. Just pass me the rope, please." Pushing her cloak aside, she sits down, pulls up her skirts, and shows him what she means as she crisscrosses the thin but durable material around her foot and her ankle. One side of the rope falls in a pile of loops at her side. "We need to cut it."

Which means no more sleeping on Ëólas's back. Careful what you wish for, Adaline.

They lock eyes, each weighing the pros and cons. Adaline pulls out her Swiss army knife, folds the rope over the edge of the blade, and waits for a sign that Ëólas agrees with her. He steps back, hangs his head, and runs his hands through his hair. Again, he scans the horizon. Finally, he looks at her, juts out his chin, and nods. Adaline pulls the blade upward, and the long side of the rope falls away.

"Let me do the knot." He stoops down in front of her and reaches for both ends of the makeshift ribbons.

"I know how to tie a knot."

"Yes, but..."

She cocks an eyebrow at him and holds fast to the rope. "But?"

When he rests his hands on top of hers, a warm shudder travels up her arms and down her back. Her chest tightens. Still, she doesn't let go. She can't release her hope that he'll open up to her even more. That he'll let her in.

Taking a deep breath, he exhales his resistance through his nose. "My knots won't come undone if I enchant them."

"Enchant them. You know how to cast spells?" Her eyes widen as she leans forward.

Tilting his head toward her, he whispers, "Not quite. But..." As his gaze falls to the ground, he relinquishes his hold on her.

The way his demeanor shifts from warm to cold reminds her of their conversation on the balcony, after their waltz together, the way he didn't let her fall, only to push her away. Sure, they've come a long way since then. Hell, they hardly ever fight now. But his words from that day still hold truth.

She quotes him, "But magic is for elves, not humans."

He shrinks away. "I'm sorry. That's the law of my people, of my queen. I can't—"

The guilt weighing him down pains her too. "It's okay. Maybe someday, when things change, we won't have these barriers anymore."

"I hope so."

The way that he looks at her, like she just gave him a glimpse of the world he's been working toward, makes her heart stop. She passes him the rope and plugs her ears with her fingers. In muffled silence, she watches his long, slender fingers manipulate and secure the rope quickly. When he lowers his mouth to her ankle, his lips move ever so slightly. The warmth of his breath travels up her inner thigh until the rope glows brighter. A second later, the light diminishes, and he repeats the process once more, making her legs quiver. Finished, he slaps his hands on his thighs and stands up. Offering her his hand, he pulls her onto her feet.

They face forward and march ahead, ready for the bog.

Chapter Five

THE TOAD

Carrying her skirts and cloak around her bottom, Adaline grits her teeth and steps into the pool of murky water. The liquid soaks into the bottom of her shoes, under the arches of her feet, and between her toes. As the bog hugs her ankles and creeps toward the stitches along her inner calves, she prays the green, fuzzy water won't infect her wounds that had been healing so nicely thanks to Loríen's crystals and herbs. At least she's not barefoot. Her slippers prevent buried rocks from shredding her feet.

She takes another step, then another, shuddering each time. Further into the bog, the mud sucks her down. Moving the bunched-up, bottom layers of her clothing into the crook of her arm, she grips Ëólas's forearm with her other hand and tugs her foot free. Together, they squelch their way through the stagnant, murky water sloshing around Adaline's bare calves and Ëólas's leather boots. He doesn't seem as worried about the border of his cloak turning muddy.

I can't believe we're going through all of this because some stupid-ass humans betrayed and murdered the queen of Aerytol. And not just any queen but an elven one who wanted to bring elves and humans together.

Adaline side-eyes Ëólas as he scrunches his nose at the moldy salad smell surrounding them.

"Ëólas, there must be more to the story, about what happened to Aerytol. Don't get me wrong; I'm not justifying what happened to the queen. But it doesn't make sense. If she wanted elves and humans to come together, why did the humans think she changed her mind? What does Magnus say?"

Careful not to splatter more mud on Adaline's thigh, Ëólas takes quick yet light steps. "Magnus knows less than his forefathers. Whereas my parents remember the war as if it occurred yesterday," Ëólas reduces his voice to a quiet, reverent whisper as if he entered a church, "the humans think of Aerytol as nothing more than ancient history. To be fair though, my mother doesn't remember much of the war. She was only forty-four when Aerytol fell."

"Wait, wait, wait. Forty-four years old? She was forty-four years old...four hundred and sixty-two years ago? Your mom is five hundred and—" Adaline yanks her foot out of a sinkhole and shakes off the excess mud, as if that makes a difference.

"Five hundred and six. Yes."

"I know how to count, thank you." She elbows him while her heart pounds faster. *He, he openly confessed facts about elves.* "Ëólas, be careful."

"I'm not talking about magic," he whispers in her ear.

When he stumbles, his smile tickles her lobe. She smushes her lips together and focuses on her next step, on only what she has control over.

Ëólas keeps talking as if they were taking a leisurely Sunday stroll. "When I first met Rioran, he insisted that we become friends. But I saw only his naivety. That humans could so easily forget the war infuriated me. But as Rioran kept trying to cross the divide, and then Magnus, I realized neither of them were their ancestors. I ruminated for a while—"

"You? Ruminate? No way," she says, her voice dripping with sarcasm.

"Surprising, I know." Wrapping his arm around her middle, Ëólas lifts Adaline up, pulling both of her feet free from the mud that seems to like her more. "Anyway, while I was ruminating, the wind told me it was time for change."

"The wind?"

Setting her down again, Ëólas nods and relinquishes her waist. "I knew the wind was right. If elves didn't wish the divide to widen further over the next five hundred years, I needed to meet the humans midway. Like Rioran, Magnus is forward thinking, creative, headstrong, and hopeful. And, as someone pointed out earlier, we all need hope."

Adaline looks away to hide the blush she can feel overtaking her cheeks, her chest inflating at the evidence that he listens to her, that he's always listened to her. Nibbling her lip, she dares to ask, "So, how old are you?" From the corner of her eye, she peeks at him, searching for a scowl or any other sign of agitation.

The corner of his mouth pulls upward. "How old do you think?"

He didn't shut me down! "I have no idea."

"Guess."

"More than one hundred?" She chews the inside of her cheek and waits.

He nods.

Wow. Despite the bog belching a foul stench in front of them, she can't stop the grin spreading across her face. "More than two hundred?"

He releases a long exhale but debates only a few seconds before responding, "Not yet. One hundred eighty-five."

He must be extremely talented to be the commander general, but she's not ready to push her luck and broach a new topic. *I'll ask about that another day.* "One hundred eighty-five," she repeats with awe, followed by a low, long whistle. "Dang. You're old."

They both laugh.

"I'm really not. The average elf lives between eight hundred and a thousand years."

Concrete information. That he just volunteered. To me. With her eyes alight, her hands itch to get a hold of her field guide so she can write down this conversation, to preserve it, to safeguard this milestone. Having her book would also mean they escaped this damned swamp.

But without warning, an image of him hundreds of years from now, unaltered and standing among strangers, flashes in her mind, and the corners of her mouth droop. Her entire face mourns a future she'll never see. *I'm nothing more than a fleeting moment in his life, a single leaf among an orchard.*

"Thank you," she whispers, "for telling me." But she can't erase the frown that's overtaken her.

Ëólas sighs. "Humans don't usually do well with our differences. That's why we don't share such information readily."

She closes her eyes. Her steps slow, but she doesn't stop treading one foot in front of the other. "I'm not jealous, if that's what you mean. This world will benefit from having someone like you in it for so long. I just... It must be hard for you, becoming close to humans, only for us to disappear from your life so quickly."

Ëólas's cheeks deflate as his skin turns ashen. "It is. I pray Magnus's heir is like him. If he'll produce one, that is."

"Huh."

So, Ëólas doesn't know about the girl Magnus met when his father banished him to Meadowbrook. Is that because he's still embarrassed about his past behavior? That doesn't seem right. He humbly told Adaline how rotten he'd been as a child, so much so that his father made Magnus live like a commoner for years under Thoren's semi-protection. That means Magnus must be protecting either himself or Nora, maybe both. They did, after all, meet when they were teenagers. If twenty years have passed, she must have moved on, and Magnus's council wouldn't have approved of such an unorthodox union.

Bullshit like that is why I hate politics. No one would think a nobody like her would be good enough for him. Burying his feelings must be easier than facing an impossible future. Fucking pointless love. All it does is torture people.

Stomping onto a thick, elevated patch of moss, Adaline curses the false ground that sinks and floods beneath her weight. She also kicks a tuff of grass with her heel, gouging out a piece of soggy earth.

"You're worried about Magnus?" Ëólas asks, rupturing her thoughts. "Thoren worries as well, but he has his own preferences for Alderton's next queen."

Adaline whips around and shoves her finger in his face. "Don't you start with me too." *Not him. I can't have him pushing Magnus on me too.* Her heart cracks. A piece chips off and crumples into dust. "I am not in love with him, and I will not marry him." She glares at Ëólas until he nods his understanding. Only when he raises his hands like white flags does she back off and lower her finger.

Ëólas releases a quiet breath, and his upper body relaxes. "Just so we're clear, I would never encourage you to do something you don't want to."

Adaline sizes him up, and with a *damn-right* nod, she continues marching onward. "Don't you think humans deserve the chance to find *the one*?"

"Yes. I've just not known many willing to wait." He shifts the pack on his back, re-dispersing the weight.

Does he mean wait as in remaining celibate? No way. If Ëólas has been around for nearly two hundred years, surely, he's... Her chest curls inward. *Never mind. That's none of my business.* "How long does it take to find the one?" *Three, four hundred years? He must have a while to go.*

"I have no idea. My mother found my father centuries ago. She hadn't even celebrated her first one hundred years." Talking about his parents' youth makes Ëólas appear younger too, until something pulls his thoughts down a darker path, and his voice drops. "Traveling beyond our own borders was safer back then."

"So the war has also made it harder for elves to find their soul mates?"

He nods. "Some of my friends made the journey elsewhere after they reached three hundred. A few didn't survive the journey. Elf hunting, I hear, is quite the sport."

Hunting? A particularly deep well of mud makes Adaline teeter off balance. Flapping her free arm wildly, she re-centers herself and avoids falling on her face. She stares at Ëólas wide-eyed. *How could anyone hunt him? He's so... I mean, he's just... No. No one's allowed to hurt him. Ever.*

As he steps on a hidden tree limb, the opposite end rises out of the bog. The twisted, decayed branches reach for him, but he bends backward at the waist to avoid the claw from impaling him. Grabbing Adaline's arm, he clings to her as she pulls him closer to safety. "Well, the Wastelands must have had trees at one point."

"Apparently." She closes her eyes for half a second, and her exhaustion uses that opportunity to flood her again. But the bog doesn't offer opportunities to rest, let alone sit down. *I'm ready to go home now.*

Ëólas brushes his hand along her back and stays close, carrying half her weight again as he pulls her against him, and they continue. Her head drifts toward his chest, but she pushes her eyes open.

Is it a bad sign to have adjusted to the discomfort of practically no food? No water. She glances at the pool around her feet. *Maybe...*

"Adaline," Ëólas whispers. His lips close to her ear pull her attention away from the whirlpool their footsteps create. "Do you see that?"

She follows his line of sight but sees nothing out of the ordinary. "No."

"Up ahead. About a mile. To your right." He raises his hand in front of her face and points, directing her eyes.

As she squints, the shadows separate, and in between them a dark, solid square appears with maybe a triangle on top. "A house?"

"It wasn't there earlier."

"As in it just appeared? Out of nowhere?"

"Exactly."

"Huh. Friend or foe?"

"No idea."

Without other options, they continue forward, watching the horizon for any other house-like buildings in the middle of a bog. Seeing none, they approach the cabin. When they near the front door, the lanterns sitting on the three steps ignite all at once. Leading to a small deck, their flames flicker within their glass confines, casting a dancing orange glow on the bog.

"Ah, more guests," croaks a voice from within. When the door swings open, a withered old man crosses the threshold. Warts cover his face, and his mouth spreads into a grin so wide that he resembles a toad. He plops his hands on his hips and spreads his webbed fingers. "Well now, aren't you two a most surprising couple."

Adaline glances at Ëólas, whose mouth hangs open. His golden eyes slowly dim, and his shoulders sag as if he's on the cusp of falling asleep.

"We are, aren't we," Adaline says, drawing Mr. Toad's attention toward her. "Have you by any chance seen others come this way? Many of them?"

"Oh, yes. Yes, I did." He licks his lips and stomps his foot once. The length of his porch lights up with hundreds of glass jars, each containing a single bluish-white flame. The one closest to him, he picks up and cradles like an infant. As the light swirls inside the jar, an outline of a face appears, along with transparent hands pressed against the jar. The face cries out, but its plea remains trapped behind the glass. The ghost's eyes and mouth dissolve into the rest of the light, like paint in water.

"I'm so lonely here, you see. I was happy to have so many visitors." Mr. Toad curls his bulbous lips into a snarl. "But the last lot weren't very polite."

Stay calm. Stay calm. Stay calm. "I'm so sorry to hear that."

Mr. Toad flashes another wide grin, which Adaline returns despite every hair rising on the back of her neck.

She slips her arm behind Ëólas's back, beneath his cloak, and grabs onto his tunic. "I hope they didn't give you trouble."

Mr. Toad flops down the steps, one at a time, his bare, webbed toes curling around the edge of the boards. On the last step, he stands at half Ëólas's height. Algae covers his thinning hair and coats the hair on his chin. He cocks his head to the side, not that he has much of a neck, and scans Adaline and Ëólas from head to toe. "You're trespassing."

"Oh, I'm so sorry. We didn't know."

"Not my fault." He steps into the water. An empty glass jar floats by and bonks into his ankle. Mr. Toad stares at Ëólas, who still hasn't moved.

"You're right," Adaline says, the pitch of her voice higher than normal. She begins speaking faster too. "And we're terribly sorry. Might I offer you something, as a thank you for your kindness?"

"Oh, yes," says Mr. Toad. His thick tongue extends from his mouth and licks his squat nose.

In the recesses of Ëólas's irises, a pale bluish-white light flickers and grows longer like a thread Mr. Toad could eventually latch onto and pull out of Ëólas's body.

"How about something you've never seen before? Something quite rare?" Dropping her skirts, Adaline shoves her hand into her pocket and pulls out the wooden flower Denós gave her and her father's Swiss army knife. When Mr. Toad's eyes snap to the knife, Adaline cringes and bites her bottom lip, but Ëólas still isn't moving or talking. Worse, the tip of that pale-blue light pokes out of his irises.

No, no, no. Not him.

She breathes slowly through her nostrils so her eyes won't blur further as she faces Mr. Toad, now at her outstretched hand. "Might any of these grant us safe passage through your land?"

He glances from the treasure on Adaline's palm to the empty jar bobbing up and down around his legs. While rubbing his belly, he eyes Ëólas. "For him too?"

Adaline nods fervently. "Absolutely."

Mr. Toad sighs once and croaks loudly. In one swift motion, he snatches both items from Adaline's palm, and the jar sinks under water. "Best you get going. And since you were so polite," he clicks his tongue, and submerged lights illuminate their path forward, "follow this, and you'll leave my bog within the day. Don't stop though, deary. Or I'll collect another fee."

He waves goodbye with her father's knife.

Turning away, she digs her fingers into Ëólas's upper arm and pushes up against his side so that he begins sidestepping toward their path. His movements are mechanical, but at least she doesn't have to drag him. After twenty steps, his eyes return to normal. She doesn't look behind them, not until they're about half a mile past the cabin. When the last porch light turns off, the cabin blends into the shadows, its shape no longer discernable. Ëólas blinks a few times, jerks backward, and looks about them wildly.

Adaline tugs him forward. "Don't stop. He told us to not stop walking."

"What, what was that?" Ëólas presses his palm against his forehead as if he has a migraine.

"I don't know. But my father," she stops to choke back a sob, "he told me a Slavic myth once about a wetland creature that resembles a frog and keeps people's souls in porcelain cups. It's called a, um, a vodyanoy."

"I've never heard of such a creature. Where did he go? How did we get past?"

Adaline shrugs but grips his shirt more tightly. "I gave him stuff."

"What stuff?"

"It doesn't matter. What does is that we're both safe, and we have pool lights guiding us out of here, so let's not waste this opportunity. We just, we can't stop, okay?"

Ëólas nods. He opens his mouth to say something more but changes his mind. Instead, he places his hand on his side, on top of hers, and doesn't let go, not for several hours.

CHAPTER SIX

TWO SPELLS

When Adaline's pace slows to a crawl and her eyes droop, she hugs Ëólas's arm and rests her head on his bicep.

"We're almost there, Adaline."

She tilts her head up and looks at his golden eyes that once again have their natural, warm glow. "Really? You see dry land?"

"I do. Just a little more. We can do this."

"Mmm. We can." She glances back, the first time she's done so since losing another piece of her father, of the life she's left behind. The shadows neither move nor illuminate nor take shapes. Adaline sighs and loosens her grip, just a tad. "So, what were you saying about your friends? Did they find their soul mates?"

Did our conversation about souls conjure that thing?

He studies her face for a few moments, and his eyes dim with concern. Letting go of her hand, he tightens his grip around her waist and, without stopping, stoops down to pick her up.

"No!" She swats his hand and pushes herself to walk faster. "We have to leave this swamp."

"I won't stop."

"But I would!" The image of all those blue flames trapped in jars pops back into her head. An ice-cold chill numbs her joints and limbs. "Please, just tell me about your friends."

"Alright." He pulls her close again, dispelling her chills. "Yes, some did find the one destined for them. Most stayed in their new home with their spouses. Two returned, one wed and the other alone."

"I can't imagine having to wait so long. It sounds awful."

"I don't think about it much, save when curious humans inquire."

"I'm sorry!"

"I jest. I do not mind," he says, easing her heart.

"If you're not always thinking about it, do you all have crushes?" *Wait, what? This isn't what I should be distracting myself with. Pick another topic, Adaline. Elven architecture?*

Ëólas simultaneously arches one eyebrow while pushing the other down. "What should I be crushing?"

A laugh bursts free from Adaline. "Oh, my. A crush is when you see someone who's attractive and you think, hey, maybe they could be the one, and you go on dates and, um, do stuff and see if it can become something." A dust of pink colors her cheeks. *Architecture.*

"What is a date?" When she doesn't answer, he pokes her side and repeats his question.

"I heard you. It's usually dinner at a restaurant, to start. And if the guy's really trying to impress you, it'll be something fancy. Not a coffee date. Um, a hot beverage. If your first date is a coffee date, he's not serious."

"Sounds complicated."

"It is."

"Have you had many a coffee date?"

She almost stops walking but settles for smacking his chest. "You think I'm worth only a coffee date!" *I mean, he made it pretty clear the first day we met that elves don't fancy humans, but seriously?*

His eyelids jump open, and his voice takes on an unnatural high pitch. "I mean restaurants. Many restaurant dates. Too many, surely."

She whacks his chest again. "Now you think I'll date the whole town?"

"I have no idea how to get myself out of this situation. Please, help."

Adaline chuckles but gets a stitch in her side. Tilting slightly sideways, but not enough to draw Ëólas's attention, she pushes her fist into her side and forces her eyelids to stay open. "For the record, yes. I've had my fair share of restaurant dates. Though sometimes it's a movie—the theater. Though it's really not what you do or where you go but who you spend the time with. So, okay, a coffee date with the right person can be the best."

"Huh. And then what? Proposals?"

"Oh my god! You're skipping way ahead."

"I don't understand human courting!"

"Ugh. Sometimes it takes a while to know you've found the one, to admit that to yourself, let alone to them." *Not that elves would understand that.*

However, Ëólas nods his head as if he does understand. Before Adaline can ask him about that reaction, he asks, "How long does that usually take?"

"Oh, I don't know. Depends on the baggage?" When Ëólas curiously glances over his shoulder at the knapsack he's carrying, Adaline sighs. "Sometimes people are together for years before they decide to get married. Take Cindy and Dax, my best friends. They were together in high school but went their separate ways when they went off to college. They wanted different things back then."

Adaline's shoulders slump down. She's not being entirely truthful. "Actually, Dax's family wanted him to marry someone from back home, from their home country. Dax and Cindy weren't ready to fight that battle. So, they dated other people for a while, but after three years, they found each other again."

"And they fought for each other this time?"

Adaline closes her eyes and conjures Cindy calling and squealing with delight. "The night I came here, Dax had planned to propose to Cindy. He showed me the ring after he bought it." *I hope she's asked her cousin to be her maid of honor, that she's not waiting for me.*

"Ring?"

"Um, yeah. A man gives a woman a ring when he proposes. It's a symbol of never-ending love because a ring has no beginning and no end. Granted, it's also really pretty with a diamond in the middle." She contemplates telling him the full story behind wedding bands and why the ancient Egyptians chose the ring finger, but giving a history lecture right now requires too much brainpower.

"Ah, I see. So, you spend years waiting to discover if you love each other enough for the man to give the woman a ring?"

"Sort of?"

"But why would you waste the precious time you have together? I do not mean to insult you!" He bites his tongue and winces at the same time. "Our courting and marriage customs are so different from humans that I don't understand."

"Different how?"

Ëólas opens his mouth but promptly closes it again. As Adaline stares him down, his cheeks turn a darker shade in the moonlight. "We, um, well, we don't—never mind."

"Dude! Spill it."

"Dude?"

"Ëólas! Come on. I told you about ours."

"You'll think poorly of us."

"Never."

When he still doesn't answer, Adaline doesn't press him further. She returns to leaning against his side and entertains herself with images of kicking his ass during their next training session. Her pace gradually slows again, but the fact that they're inching upward and that the bog no longer rises above her calves gives her one more boost of energy. She can't worry right now about what they'll do once they exit the bog. She snuggles closer to him, and her eyes droop closed, even as she drags herself forward. Endless sleep doesn't sound so bad right now.

After ruminating for almost half an hour, maybe longer, Ëólas exhales loudly. "I've watched humans." His voice jolts Adaline awake. "I've seen how they sneak off together and how afterwards both must deny the encounter; otherwise, the woman's deemed ruined. They view physical pleasure as, well, shameful."

Adaline nods her head emphatically. "It's ridiculous, right? That's what you're getting at? Not to mention the double standard. I mean, where do they think guys are sewing those seeds? But nooooooo, women shouldn't get to enjoy themselves."

With one eyebrow raised, Ëólas stares at Adaline as if he's seeing her for the first time. "Are you unique among your kind?"

"Ha! No. Well, yes and no. Most people back home don't wait until marriage before jumping in bed with someone." She stops talking while fire slowly creeps up her neck and burns into her cheeks. "Not that I jump in bed with people regularly. Or at all. I mean, not—"

"No, of course not," he says, dragging his words out with a smirk.

"Shut. Up."

"It's alright. We don't jump into bed with just anyone either. We choose our lovers thoughtfully."

Hearing the word *lover* leave Ëólas's lips makes Adaline's heart pound so quickly that she might have a heart attack and die right here in the bog. When the hell did this conversation take this turn? Too much personal information. She doesn't need images popping up in her head, images of him, doing things, in bed, with other people, too gorgeous for this world or any other. No, no, no. She doesn't need those types of thoughts pushing through her boundaries and making her hands turn sweaty. *Oh my god! When the hell does this bog end!*

"For someone so forthcoming, your cheeks have turned crimson." He dares to poke her cheek too.

Swatting his finger away, she glares at him. "We, we just, we don't use that word, *lover*. We say boyfriend or girlfriend."

"Sounds rather juvenile."

"Huh. Yeah, it does." She shrugs. Now that she thinks about it, she's never used that word herself. She's always managed to avoid describing someone as her boyfriend.

"You've had one then, a boyfriend?" He looks ahead, but his irises dart her way.

Derek flashes in her mind. After being together for six months, she royally messed that up. "I did. But my last relationship ended the day before I came here." Ended in a big, flaming pile of shit, the day after Derek asked Dax to help him shop for rings.

Whatever. The past doesn't matter—says the person who preserves the past. But the last person she wants to have this conversation with is Ëólas. Besides, someone like him probably already found the one. She's probably graceful and quiet and dignified and most certainly doesn't curse. *Not that I care. He deserves someone amazing. Someone out of this world. I mean someone in this world. From this world.*

"Taking a lover doesn't last long for us either," he says.

Her head whips up faster than she intended. To soften her reaction, she pretends to stretch and massage her neck muscles. "Why's that?"

"Without the emotional connection, the physical pleasure fades after some time."

"How much time?"

"Twenty, thirty years."

Huh. In thirty years, I'll be fifty-eight. Elves would consider me decrepit by then. Just like that elven lady cried in the city from hell, that we get so wrinkly. "So, you enjoy a bunch of lovers until you find the one?"

"Well, I imagine not many more than you have restaurant dates."

Adaline laughs, and her heart feels lighter. "You said your marriage customs are different. How so?"

He glances at Adaline, his eyebrows narrowing while he debates whether to continue this conversation. "We say our vows, which are actually a spell." He swallows hard, and his thoughts disappear into the distance as he searches the horizon, searches for his soul mate. Returning Adaline's stare, he whispers, "The one is our other half, so we give them half our soul. Literally." He quickly looks away, embarrassed or maybe afraid of what she'll say.

"That's beautiful."

"Really?" He glances at her again.

"Yes." She tilts her eyes up to the heavens that she imagines exist beyond the night sky. To be so connected with someone. To never be alone again. To trust someone so thoroughly. Back home, her world is bursting at the seams with billions of people. The idea of sifting through all of that makes her heart break more. "I hope you find that." She can't look at him, not right now. "What's the spell?"

"Well, I can't very well say it aloud," he says.

"Oh, right." Adaline laughs awkwardly, but she needs to know these words, needs to record them, needs evidence that something so magical and powerful actually exists.

"But I can write them."

"Oh. Where?"

Ëólas stops walking. With a gasp, Adaline jerks forward, out of his embrace, and grabs his arm, pulling with all her might. "Walk! You have to—"

"Adaline, stop." He grabs both her arms and gestures with his eyes for her to look down.

On both sides of them, she finds nothing but solid rock and one patch of dry, not moist, dirt. The bog is behind them. Far behind them. Already reduced to a memory. Or a nightmare. She doesn't move. Her entire body has locked into place while the last of her adrenaline drains out of her shoes, along with the remainder of the murky, green water. She drops her skirts, which swish around her legs and her damp undergarments. She could collapse now, but if she does, how will she ever get up again?

"Here, to satisfy your curiosity." He sets down his pack and, with his fingers, etches into the ground the vows.

In her mind, she reads the spell, translating the phonetic Common Tongue spelling into English. As she hears the words inside her head, the sounds of the wind, of Ëólas shifting on his feet to peer up at her, of her own breath become muffled and fade away.

> *My love, my one,*
> *all that I am,*
> *all that I was,*
> *all that I'll ever be,*
> *I give to you*
> *for all of time.*

She stares at each word until her eyes burn, until she hears Ëólas clear his throat, until she can move her body again. She rubs her eyes, resetting her focus, and pretends like she's analyzing nothing more than a poem. "It doesn't rhyme."

"Why should it rhyme?" Although he sounds incredulous, his voice betrays an undertone of humor.

"I don't know. I guess I kinda thought spells would rhyme."

"Well, the words themselves don't matter as much. They simply help us to—" He stops abruptly and scowls, not at Adaline but into the distance where his people reside.

"It's okay." With her foot, she brushes the words away, erasing the evidence. Besides, she's already committed them to memory. The moment she read them, they etched themselves into her soul.

"Thank you." He opens the knapsack and pulls out the blanket. "Let's rest here for a bit. I can undo those knots and see about tying our rope back together again. I'm sure we can make it still work."

While she waits, she sticks her hands in her pockets, and the emptiness of one opens a cavity inside her chest, until her fingers brush a small object tucked into the corner. She jiggles her dress, and the berry she saved rolls into her palm. She clutches the pearl, taking heed not to crush it, and releases her sorrow. If anything, her father helped her out one last time.

Thank you, Poppa.

When Adaline sits down, Ëólas disappears into his own thoughts, hopefully not trying to remember what happened with Mr. Toad or berating himself for breaking his people's laws by sharing information about magic with a human.

Not to mention the fact that a human has caused him so much grief lately. "I'm sorry," she whispers.

"What for?"

"That you're here with me." With a long sigh, she looks up at the faint moonlight fighting to break through the clouds. "I don't understand why this keeps happening to me, teleporting across worlds or locations, and this time I dragged you with me."

"I'm relieved I'm here."

When Adaline looks at him curiously, he nudges her side with his elbow and shakes lose her stupefied expression. "You said you wanted answers, and we got them. Some of them at least. And if I hadn't been here, I shudder to think... Right now, this is where I'm needed most. I firmly believe that, Adaline."

Where I'm needed most. Is that back home, or New Leira? "Still, it sure would be nice if we could just poof home again."

Ëólas bends his legs and rests his forearm on his kneecaps. "Indeed. Though, perhaps we have more to learn."

Out here? With almost no resources? We better find whatever that is soon. Her stomach growls, and she hugs her legs to her chest to crush the hollow space inside. "When we get back and stop Ãranol, you and Magnus should throw another party so all of New Leira can celebrate together."

At the mention of New Leira, Ëólas arches an eyebrow, and a mischievous thought makes his golden eyes almost glow. "Agreed, but you'll have to teach us another dance."

"Ha! Deal." Closing her eyes, she tries to conjure the warm lights, the soft music, the room swirling past her as she and Ëólas dance circles around the room. "Fox trot. I love a good fox trot." She leans her head against his shoulder. Once again, the world is silent around them with endless miles of nothing, of no one, except the enemies marching ahead of them. Adaline's stomach growls so loudly that it tears through her body. A whole day without food or water. Not that the other two days counted much in terms of hydration.

"Ëólas," she whispers, "I'm scared."

With his chin, he nuzzles the crown of her head. "Me too." As she closes her eyes and sighs, he says, "But you owe me a fox trot, so we can't give up now."

She nods, rubbing her cheek against the silks of his sleeve.

"May I lift your skirts?"

She freezes, her cheek still pressed against his shoulder, but when her initial panic passes, she smiles wickedly. "Do as you please, *Lord* Ëólas."

His entire body turns rigid, every sculpted muscle beneath those silky coverings. "Look at you, so eager to please these days."

Touché.

Shifting into a squat beside her, he pushes her muddy dress up to her knees, unwraps her sticky legs and feet, and re-coils the slimy rope. After he replaces her skirts, he sets to work knotting together the frayed ends, his fingers nimbly manipulating the rope saturated with muck into sturdy knots.

Ever the gentleman, er, gentle-elf. Granted, that's super easy when there's zero attraction. I wonder if he's so restrained with his lov—Nope. Not going there.

"Alright. Let's give this a try, shall we?" He pops up and leans forward, waiting for Adaline to climb onto his back.

"Ëólas, you can't keep going like this. It's been three days, I think, and you haven't slept once."

Standing up straight, he looks down at her and rests his hands on his hips, the rope dangling at his side. "That's not entirely true."

"Huh?"

"First, if necessary, we can go four days without sleep, so you needn't worry about that. And while you slept, I meditated, which allowed me to enter a state of half consciousness, which means I can keep going for a while."

Adaline purses her lips to the side and crosses her arms over her chest. "And strength. Where the hell are you finding the stamina to keep carrying me this long?"

Ëólas drops his hands and looks away, pushing his lips against each other until the top lip pushes into his nose. "Just for once, can you not ask these questions?"

She jumps up, well, more like hobbles quickly onto her hands and knees and pushes herself up to stand with a loud groan. Hobbling over to him, she jabs his chest with her finger. "What don't you want me to know?"

"It's fine. I'm fine."

"No, no. *Fine* is a bad word that conceals a lot. What's going on?"

Resting his hand over hers, he pulls her finger away from his body and flattens her palm against his chest, beneath his heart. "I'm borrowing strength."

"What does that mean?"

"It's a spell Seira taught me. She said I'd need it someday." His thumb brushes against her palm, against the soft flesh.

No distractions. "And?"

"And it allows me to borrow strength from tomorrow."

Pulling away, she covers her mouth and takes a few steps backward. *What if he drains himself completely? What if he runs out of strength and the enemy finds us? What if he gets hurt because of me?* She buries her face in her hands. "This isn't okay. You can't. I won't. If you. Oh god!"

"Adaline, I've thought this through. Trust me." Gently, he peels her hands away from her cheeks and peers into her eyes. "I've calculated the time, the potential paths we'll take, and when I'll rest myself once you're okay. I know this—"

"You can't *know*. What are the consequences, Ëólas? Borrowing means you need to give something back. What happens then?"

"When we've returned to the Neutral—to New Leira, I'll sleep. While Magnus and Merith handle matters. And while you recover properly."

"Sleep for how long?"

"As of right now? An entire day. I can stand to sleep a few more. Once we bypass the enemy, time is on our side, and we can resume a more natural pace until we reach New Leira, meaning I won't need to borrow anymore."

"I'll never forgive myself if anything awful happens to you."

Folding her hands into his chest, he bumps his forehead against hers. "Likewise."

They both allow a moment of stillness. Fingers intertwining. Slow breaths mingling. She'll always believe in him. They'll get home. They'll win the day. They'll stop this war. They'll prove what elves and humans can accomplish together. And they'll celebrate. Even though home feels so far away, like another lifetime, she clings to that image of friends surrounding them, a buffet of food, a warm hand holding hers during a time of levity. She just needs to keep moving and stay with him. For now. Once she knows they're safe, she can leave them be and return to her own world. But that thought hurts more than the cramps tearing up her stomach.

Removing his fingers from hers, he slides his hands up her arms, skates under her cloak, and squeezes her shoulders with a small massage. "Let's keep going,

Adaline. Just a little more. We must be at least halfway to the moors by now. We can do this."

She nods, her forehead still pressed against his. "Okay."

She doesn't move. She's not ready to leave this moment behind, so she waits for him to make the first move, to force her to face reality and all the obstacles that lie ahead. Sure enough, Ëólas straightens his torso and stands tall, removing his brow from hers and severing the connection. Her shoulders slump, and her willpower falters, but only a tad. She'll recover. She has to. Because when she goes home, she'll be on her own. Again.

Instead of releasing her arms, he snaps his head to the left and scans the horizon. She follows his line of sight, praying they don't see Mr. Toad, but sees and hears nothing, neither distinct shapes nor crickets. The Wastelands, per usual, are unnaturally quiet.

The longer they stand still staring into nothingness, a chill creeps up Adaline's back. When she shivers, Ëólas glides his hands down the length of her arms and up again. The heat he generates envelops her, dissipating her worries. As her body temperature rises, her cheeks flush, and her heartbeat suppresses all thoughts. He takes one more step, closing the distance between them, and tilts his head downward. As his lips inch toward her, she stops breathing altogether and closes her eyes. She raises her hands, resting them on his upper chest, which hums under her touch and gives her confidence. Sensing his face moving closer, she leans into the warmth and rises onto her toes. His breath brushes her cheek, and instinctively she lifts her chin. His voice tickles her ear, and she shudders as he whispers, "We're being watched."

CHAPTER SEVEN

THE CAVES

Adaline's eyes snap open. Staring at Ëólas, she waits for him to confirm if Mr. Toad has returned and to signal a plan. But he stands still and resumes rubbing her arms. His calm washes over her, telling her subconsciously that they're not in immediate danger. Again, she squints into the horizon, waiting for something mythical to show itself. The fact that Ëólas hasn't reacted drastically gives her some hope.

When he's done thinking, he looks at Adaline with a mixture of sympathy and pleading. "I'm sorry. We should not rest this night, but I don't want them to see me carrying you. You've done wonderfully today, more than you should have, but can you manage a bit more?"

Releasing a long, shaky breath, she could drift off to sleep, right here, in his arms. Instead, she nods.

As they continue their trek across the Wastelands, Adaline refocuses all of her energy on not constantly scanning the horizon and searching for silhouettes, maybe even torches. How many hours roll by, she cannot keep track. Time seems to both slow down and feel endless at the same time. That Ëólas hasn't suggested they stop must mean that whatever's out there is still watching them. He doesn't know the human body isn't made for this. She cannot fathom how she's managed thus far. Is her desire to survive that great? Or is something else keeping her going? Neither matter. Not anymore. She's reached the end now. She knows it. She can feel it. One of these next steps will be her last. Even if she wakes up hours from now, without water and food to nourish her, that's it.

Maybe, before I pass out, I should tell him, tell myself...

Adaline stumbles. Before she hits the ground, Éólas's arms are around her waist. He doesn't let go of her again. At his side, he keeps her with him. Yesterday's shroud of clouds gives way to daybreak as the sun peeks above the horizon.

"You were close to your father?" Éólas asks.

Dad. Poppa. Can he see her now? Can his spirit travel between worlds? What about Nan's? She cried for them both for months. Every day without them felt empty, shallow, fake. When she lay in bed at night, she used to wish she could see them again, that she could go back in time to when she had them both.

"Adaline?"

"Mmm?" Her throat crackles like peanut brittle.

"Your father? Were you close?"

"Mmm. Not just with me. Cindy's dad left when she was fifteen. Our families, we spent most holidays together."

"What holidays do you celebrate?"

"Éólas, I, I don't want to talk anymore." *Please, don't make me keep...*

The ground disappears beneath her, and she feels weightless, as if she's floating downward into a void of oblivion. Éólas's shoulder turns into a pillow, and a sigh escapes her parted lips. Her arms and legs hang lifeless as gravity stretches them and extracts the tension from her muscles. Having forgotten where she is or what she is doing, she inhales the scent of autumn that clings to his hair, the lavender that eases her aching, that evokes relief. The world drifts away.

In her dreams, she's still moving, still traveling, or at least her body bobs up and down in time with a walking gait. Her body isn't her own anymore. At least there are no torches, no enemies, no pain in this vast nothingness. Or so she thought. Through the night-like barrier of consciousness, Éólas's voice fades, resurges, and echoes around her. Is he calling to her? He doesn't sound like himself. He sounds scared. And he's not alone. Other voices, bodiless and unfamiliar, filter in and out of this dreamless dream.

"Please, the lady needs water."

Who? What lady? Should I be dreaming about a lady?

"Release her, and we'll..."

Release whom? From what?

Her pillow disappears. A cold, jagged surface presses against her back. She tries to roll over but can't lift her limbs, and she misses her new pillow. She's not safe without it, not whole.

"...cannot trust..."

"...a trap..."

"...mean no harm..."

"...bind him..."

Bind whom? Why does this dream have no images?

She fights through the veil of sleep to open her eyes, but her body's floating again. When her body collapses onto a softer surface, one that yields with the curve of her spine and the shape of her bottom, she loses the battle to resurface. Not for a long while.

When Adaline yawns and opens her eyes, a flickering light a few feet away greets her. She rubs her eyes to clear away the fog clouding her vision and stares at the light again, trying to discern if that speck belongs to a firefly or ghost. Shifting her weight, she rolls onto her side, her arm falling off her chest like a dead weight. A light blanket scratches her cheek. As she pushes herself up, her hands crush the stacked blankets beneath her that act as her bed. Once she's fully sitting up, she brushes her hair away from her face while her eyes refocus and discern the lantern emitting the light.

Thank God the flame is yellow.

Aside from the pile of blankets and the lantern, the dome-shaped room contains little else. No windows. No wardrobe. No door. Just a round, open archway. The room is hardly bigger than a walk-in closet, and a bucket releasing a putrid smell sits the furthest away.

An elderly woman enters the room. "Oh, thank goodness you're awake."

Her hair pulled back in a high gray bun reveals her small, round ears. A mole decorates the corner of her mouth, and she smells like freshly turned soil. Sitting down next to Adaline, the woman rests another candle on the stone floor, beside Adaline's cloak that's been neatly folded. In her other hand, the woman carries a bowl of soup. Hot soup. With who knows what in it. But Adaline can't take her eyes off the broth.

The woman pulls out of her pocket a wooden spoon and passes both it and the bowl to Adaline. "Drink slowly."

Adaline doesn't wait to shovel the unexpected offering into her mouth. The broth hints at flavor with small chunks of meat and some specks of herbs. It's horribly bland and the most delicious meal she's ever had. Not caring about manners, she slurps the soup and tilts her head back until the last drop rolls down her throat. Her relief's gone too soon, until the woman brings her another bowl. When Adaline finishes tipping the last drop into her mouth again, she looks pleadingly for more.

The old woman's shoulders droop. "I'm sorry, dear. That's all I have."

"Thank you. Thank you so much."

"Here, I have this for you though."

Crossing the room, the woman picks up the handle of a different bucket near the entryway and drags the seemingly heavy wooden pail to the bed. Taking Adaline's bowl, the woman dips it into the bucket and fills the shallow bowl to the rim with water. Cupping the gift with both hands, Adaline blinks at the offering, at how much there is right now and in her hands. She doesn't care where the hell this woman came from. She's an angel.

"You poor dear. Drink some of that, and why don't you rest more? You're safe down here."

Each drop of water rolling down her throat is liquid ambrosia. "Down here?"

The woman nods. "Yes, underground. There's a whole network of caves, and we use them to—"

"Where is he?" Her panic makes her swivel sideways and look about the room. She wills Ëólas to appear in the corner, to be resting soundly, safely, at the foot of her bed, but the cave's emptiness hammers at her heart. How long has she been there? Did he leave her with this woman? Pushing the blanket off her legs, Adaline staggers to her feet and drops the bowl, the water spattering across the cave floor. "Where's Ëólas?"

"The elf?" The old woman hobbles over and rests her wrinkled hands on Adaline's shoulders. "Don't you worry about him, dear. You're safe from him now."

"What do you mean? He saved me." *No, no, no, no, no. He can't be. He can't have.* "Where is he?" Adaline shouts, ripping herself free from the woman's grasp.

The old woman staggers back and clutches her hands together in prayer, as if to ward off the devil in disguise. "He's being kept further down. They must be close to deciding his fate by now."

His fate? Oh god!

Her knees almost give out, but she can't give up now. Adaline lunges forward. "Take me to him. Please!" When the old woman stares at Adaline with a stupefied expression on her face, Adaline clutches the woman's hands and pours every ounce of prayer into her words. "Please, I owe him my life. He's not like those other elves. He's good and kind. He looked out for me time and again, and he never gave up on me. Please, help me." She locks eyes with the old woman, not allowing her to look away as Adaline's bright green eyes darken with every horrible thought of what could be happening to him.

"Oh, alright." Taking up the candle, the old woman leads Adaline out of her room and down a long tunnel that finally splits in two.

Even though Granny doesn't move quickly, Adaline maintains her sanity by repeating over and over again that they didn't come this far only for her to lose him now. She refuses to accept a world in which he doesn't exist.

Further into the cavern, Adaline can't see much except for the soft, wide glow of another light up ahead. When the sound of deep voices fills her ears, the old woman stops, not willing to take one more step, and points ahead.

Adaline squeezes Granny's hand. "Thank you." She peers into the entrance of a large chamber, not that different from the one she entered nearly a month ago with her colleagues, only this one's illuminated with several torches. Adaline's heart pounds, and her breaths turn shallow as she counts a group of eight people standing in a circle. Most of them are young men, aside from the one woman with shoulder-length dark hair and a man old enough to be Adaline's grandfather.

"But he brought the lady to us," says the skinny man. "I don't get it."

"That's what makes this more suspicious," says the woman.

The much older man with a thick gray beard scratches the length of his side as if he has a rash beneath his tattered shirt. "He didn't fight us when we dragged him in here." Flapping his tunic away from his body, Gramps cusses, and flakes of dead skin scatter to the ground. "He surrendered. That has to mean something."

"Yes, that it must be a trap." When the broad-shouldered man growls, everyone stops talking and turns to him. He holds their attention with the confidence and command of a police chief. No, like a mafia boss.

Only Gramps dares to break the silence. "Well, what does he say?"

"You think the elf will speak the truth?" says Mr. Mafia.

"We should ask the lady," says Gramps.

Trying to find a sign of Ëólas, Adaline inches forward and scans around the mob and the chamber. When Mr. Mafia takes half a step forward with his behemoth leg, Ëólas's knapsack appears. She clutches her hands into fists and shoves them into her pockets, only to remember she doesn't have her father's knife anymore. She can still surprise them with her dagger though, if need be.

But are they my enemy? The old woman did help me, twice. And if they know the elves from Hell City, of course they'd be leery of Ëólas. Maybe this is just one big misunderstanding.

"Calvden," Granny says, appearing beside Adaline, "the lady's here."

Mr. Mafia, or rather, Calvden, turns his torso to look Adaline over. As he walks toward her, the rest of the group parts, each of them studying her and drawing their own conclusions about the noble woman wearing a fine muslin and silk dress with a muddy hem and patches of bog splatter, not to mention her dingy hair, dirt-lined nails, and most likely a smudged face. But she doesn't acknowledge any of them. She stares only at the center of the dispersed group where, pushed up against the back wall, Ëólas sits on the ground, his hands bound to his feet. A blindfold covers his eyes, and they shoved into his mouth a dirty rag secured with a rope around his head.

Not waiting for introductions, Adaline runs past Calvden and the group, her sudden movement and direction causing them to step back in confusion. She doesn't breathe until she's kneeling in front of Ëólas and pulls down his blind fold. The moment his eyes lock with hers, he exhales, and the relief that washes over him crushes Adaline's chest, that he has a false sense of hope that she can somehow help him escape these people who judged him so quickly and who could very well be those elf hunters he mentioned earlier. She can't let him down.

She reaches for the rope to pull that soiled cloth out of his mouth, but a meaty hand grabs her wrist. She winces at the touch, and Ëólas shouts a guttural protest that the cloth muffles. Before she can pull the gag out, the man holding her yanks her backward. With her other arm still extended, she grasps for Ëólas's arm, but he quickly falls out of her reach.

"What do you think you're doing!" Calvden hisses.

"Let him go!" Adaline twists her wrist free.

"Are you insane?"

"You're free of him," says the woman. "He can't punish you for not obeying him anymore."

"I don't obey anyone!" Adaline jumps to her feet, pulls her shoulders back, and glares at Calvden and the rest of them in turn while taking a few steps to place herself between them and Ëólas. "And I don't obey him. He's my..." *Trainer? Ally? Friend?* None of those feel right, but she doesn't have time to search through a thesaurus.

"I don't like it," says Skinny Man. "It's only a matter of time before the others come looking for him."

Calvden's face turns red, and the veins along his temple pulse. He grabs the back of his shaggy, long black hair and glowers in Ëólas's direction. His hatred becomes so palpable, so visceral, that even the torches shrink back. "Let's kill the thing and be done with it."

Thing!

Calvden reaches behind the knapsack and retrieves Adaline's sword, tossing the scabbard away. As he stalks toward her, he squeezes the hilt so tightly that his knuckles stand like mountains. He raises the tip of the blade so it's level with

Ëólas's head, the reticent general who pushed her away for weeks only to make that very weapon for her, that he trusted her with, so she could protect herself.

The day he walked into the training room and handed her that sword, she admired the craftsmanship that went into forging it, the vines that twist around the hand guard, the diamond in the center, the etchings in the pommel of people celebrating in a garden.

It's a weapon, he had said, *that we use to protect what's dear to us.*

She never forgot his words. *My sword isn't meant for murder.*

Leaning forward and placing one foot behind her the way Fólas taught her, Adaline grounds her feet and stares Calvden down. Both her trainers showed her how to dodge, how to defend herself, how to avoid being pinned down. But none of that seems applicable in this situation, and neither of them mentioned how to protect someone else. Dodging would give Calvden access to Ëólas, and staying in place means she'll need a damn strong defense to keep this giant at bay. She doesn't care what happens to her next, how heavy her arms and legs still feel. All she needs is to get this brute to listen or keep him distracted enough to catch him off guard with her dagger. And, if need be, she could wound him enough so he backs off and hopefully not kill him. She got lucky once. Maybe in this fantastic world, she can get lucky again.

Ignoring Ëólas's protesting grunts behind her, Adaline raises her hands and folds her fingers into fists. Although Calvden takes slow, deliberate steps meant to intimidate her, Adaline doesn't flinch. She grinds her teeth and watches his footsteps. The moment his weight shifts, Adaline leans sideways to avoid his hand reaching for her. She steps forward, spins into his embrace, and elbows him in the chest with every ounce of strength she has left. Calvden, who most likely expected a weak little poppet, wheezes as his shoulders curl inward. He clutches his chest and staggers backward, but only one step. When he looks at Adaline, he no longer sees her as a weak victim but a deranged traitor.

"We're not your enemy, Calvden. If you'd wait just a moment, I can explain what Ëólas and I are doing here. Where we came from. And why—"

Calvden lunges forward. Once again, Adaline sees the intention beforehand and dodges, but she also refuses to take a single step away from Ëólas. The moment she bobs up again, Calvden grabs her behind the neck and pulls her against him, using his other arm to lock her in place with a bear hug. The flat side of her blade presses against her back. Ëólas's louder, muffled cries, combined with Calvden breathing on her face, make her skin crawl and vision blur.

How can I get away from him? What do I do? How do I save us both? "We're not—"

"Anyone who would defend an elf is my enemy." He spits on the ground beside them and throws her to the side, flicking her away like a fly. "I'll deal with you later."

Chapter Eight

A PROMISE

As Adaline falls backward, she lands against Gramp's legs, which save her head from hitting the cave floor. Placing his hands under her armpits, he helps her scramble to her feet. When Adaline looks up again, Calvden towers in front of Ëólas, still bound and defenseless. He locks those golden eyes on the human ready to kill without knowing anything about his prisoner, without just cause. The expression on Ëólas's face flashes from anger to defiance. Calvden widens his stance and tightens the muscles along his back. His entire frame grows larger as he looms over Ëólas.

Adaline inhales sharply, and the torches' flames freeze mid-flicker as if they too are holding their breath. A bead of sweat sticks to the side of Calvden's brow. Half the people behind him look away. The others wear half-formed grins, while Adaline, pushing off her back foot, reaches one arm toward Ëólas. As he stares not at the blade but the man behind it, the light in Ëólas's eyes dim, not from fear but from what Adaline senses to be regret, maybe even shame. She pulls his strength inside of her, steeling herself so that she won't spend the rest of her life reliving and regretting this moment.

As Calvden raises the blade at an angle, Ëólas closes his eyes, denying the world that earnest golden light that has the ability to draw people to him, to ease their fears, and to make them believe in the impossible. Launching herself between them, Adaline lands in front of Ëólas and pushes herself up against him, shielding his torso and neck and staring into the face of death, or at least the face of its deliverer.

A single exhale is all that's needed to lift the veil between this moment and the afterlife. She considers closing her eyes, but Ëólas—rocking his body and nudging her with his head to get her out of the way, to save her—reinforces her resolve. She won't leave him now. She won't back down and hide either.

With a sneer and a shake of his head, Calvden slides one foot backward. The muscles driving the sword tighten. He inhales and—

Last chance.

"You're just as bad as them!" Adaline's words reverberate off the chamber's walls, bashing Calvden's ears and forcing him to listen. When he cringes, she clings to that ray of hope. "You're just like those elves in that city of hell by the sea."

He stares at her in disbelief, either because he's not used to people talking back to him or because her words stung. Whichever the case, he lowers his sword. Adaline drops her shoulders from her ears, exhales, and curves her back between Ëólas's arms. But her reprieve doesn't last long. Calvden stabs the blade into the cave floor, and the clang ringing throughout the cave vibrates inside her ears, making her shrink backward. She seals off one ear against Ëólas's cheek. Using the sword like a cane, Calvden leans on the hilt, kneels down on one knee, and pushes his face into hers, leaving less than an inch between them.

When he speaks, the vitriol of his words drips down Adaline's back, making her shudder. "I am nothing like the monsters from Feídra né Morna. All they do is twist, torture, or enslave us."

Matching the intensity of his gaze and tone, Adaline tips her head forward, making him back up half an inch. "You're ready to murder an innocent person, who can't even defend himself, just because of *what* he is. How is that different from those who keep hunting and killing you?"

"He's one of them!"

"No, he's not! He's kind and noble and brave and the only reason I'm still alive."

"Elves are none of those things," he hisses.

"Then all men are irrational, cowardly beasts with no faith and no ability to show mercy."

"His kind murdered my grandfather, enslaved my mother, and—"

"And that gives you the right to kill every elf you meet? All that does is continue to justify in their minds why they keep hunting every human they find." Adaline shifts her feet under her bottom, forcing Calvden to rock back onto his heels and stand. Slowly, Adaline rises too, keeping eye contact with Calvden and physical contact with Ëólas as she backs her heels up against his wrists still bound to his ankles. "When does it stop? If you want to be better than those elves, prove yourself to be a person of morals and hear me out!"

"Let the lady speak," says Gramps, touching Calvden's shoulder.

When Calvden grunts at the old man but doesn't object, Adaline doesn't waste time. She lifts her chin and elongates her spine, making herself taller the way her ballet teacher taught her, the way her grandmother modeled, the way Magnus exemplifies when addressing his people, the way Lady Marzella does when commanding those around her.

Pretend you're a noblewoman, Adaline. You can do this.

With all eyes on her, she can't show any signs of weakness, neither in her convictions nor in how she holds herself. "I am Lady Adaline of Alderton and ward to King Magnus."

Calvden relaxes his wrinkled brow a smidge and eyes her from top to bottom once again. "Alderton? They fought against Lameiría in the war."

They what? I knew they didn't get along in the past, but they fought each other? Process that later, Adaline. "Yes. And yet my traveling companion is Lord Ëólas, commander general of Lameiría. King Magnus and I have been working with him and Lameiría to create the Neutral Territory in what was once Aerytol."

"The neutral what?" asks Gramps.

"The Neutral Territory, where elves and humans live side by side, as equals."

"You're mad," the woman says, followed by a loud scoff.

"No, I am furious." Gritting her teeth, Adaline looks at each of them in turn as she speaks, keeping her words crisp and her rage simmering beneath the surface. "Individuals from this land attacked the Neutral Territory and threatened our people, elves and humans alike. Lord Ëólas and I wanted answers, so we took it upon ourselves to come here and learn who has been threatening the peace we've been working so hard to secure."

Not having lost their attention yet, Adaline continues but laces her words with fire. "Those elves who have done you wrong are planning to destroy our alliance. They have an army that's headed toward our friends, and instead of helping us get ahead of them, you're putting even more people in grave danger. I will not allow the hell that is the Wastelands to spread into Aerytol." When she turns to Calvden, she lifts her chin higher and says in a commanding voice, "With or without your help, we have a mission to fulfill, and I will not have anyone undermining our efforts. Return to me my sword at once and let us go. Now."

No one speaks while they try to understand everything Adaline said. She contemplates taking her sword from him, but she doesn't want to break the trance he's under. Instead, she gives Calvden one last defiant look and turns her back to him. Keeping her posture strong and confident, she kneels in front of Ëólas. When his golden eyes peer into hers, the intensity of his gaze and the pride emanating from him knock her off kilter.

He, he must know it's all an act.

Focusing on his gag, she casts her eyes downward and wills her hands not to shake. She squeezes her fingers under the rope crushing his cheeks and rolls it downward. When it falls to his neck and dangles over his cloak's clasp, she yanks out the filthy gag, chucking it behind her. Hiking up her skirts, she pulls out her dagger, her last line of defense. From the corner of her eye, she catches Ëólas use the tip of his tongue to push a remaining piece of lint out of his mouth.

He leans closer to her ear. "It would seem I am indebted to you, though I don't think this is the first time."

"Well, you're still a few more saves ahead of me."

"I'd rather neither of us need saving."

"Good point. How about we just avoid capture and starvation from here on out?"

"I like that plan." He sounds content, amused even, but something about him seems off. His normally flawless, creamy white complexion looks slightly gray, and a bead of sweat trickles down his temple.

I've never seen him sweat, not even during training practice on a horrifically humid day.

Pushing her concerns aside, she saws at the bindings around and between his wrists while taking heed not to wound him. Before she cuts halfway through the thick rope, Ëólas's head and eyebrows snap up as he shouts, "Adaline!"

Swiveling around, she raises her dagger, only for Calvden to grab her forearm and yank her upward. Her sore shoulder pops out of the socket, not entirely, but enough to make her tendons twinge, and the resulting pain sears through her spine. As her scream rebounds around the chamber, Calvden twists the dagger out of her grasp and lets her go.

"Be gentle with her!" Ëólas says, twisting his wrists to loosen the rope. "She's not slept or eaten properly in days."

"I don't trust you. Either of you." While Adaline grabs her arm and blinks to clear away the tears, Calvden passes the dagger and sword to the woman. With Adaline defenseless, he pushes her between two other men who grab her arms and hold her steady without any consideration for her shoulder.

"I'm the one you don't trust." Using that regal voice, Ëólas addresses Calvden as if he were an equal, as if Ëólas were offering a deal to another obstinate council member. "Let Lady Adaline leave, and I will stay. Just help her to cross the river into Alderton."

"Ëólas!" *No, no, no.* The thought of leaving him behind fills her with an emptiness worse than when her father died. *I, I can't do this on my own. I need him.*

"I give you my word, Calvden. I won't fight you, but she must warn the others, or your fate will become Alderton's too." Ëólas lowers his head, surrendering himself once again. "Warning King Magnus is what matters most."

If that were true, he wouldn't have stopped me from returning to Hell City. And he wouldn't have brought me here, to his enemies, for help. He should have left me on day one.

Calvden considers Ëólas's words for half a second. "That's the biggest load of shit I've heard yet."

The two men clutching her arms let go as Calvden grabs her throat and pins her against the chamber wall. She claws the back of his hand and tries to kick his shins, but he nudges his leg between hers.

"Get off her!" Ëólas uses his teeth to rip at the rope until the man holding Adaline's sword points it at Ëólas's throat and mouths, *No.*

Snarling in her face, Calvden squeezes harder. "The rivers are well-guarded, and the elves won't let us leave. Which means there's no way you could have crossed the border in the first place. You are a liar."

Without weapons or the ability to run, she's lost the fight. The façade is over. She's nothing more than a girl out of place and out of time. She stops pulling at his fingers and looks Calvden in the eyes. For the first time, she sees him, not the behemoth shadow of another threat, but the human being standing between her and his people. A flawed person with leathery, sallow skin from lack of sunlight, a thin scar that runs from his temple to his jaw, and deep brown eyes that have seen more injustice than Adaline can imagine.

She lifts her hand and touches his forehead, brushing his shaggy black hair off his brow. Her gentle touch confuses him enough that he lessens his grip just enough that she can speak freely. "I'm sorry you've suffered for so long. I'm sorry for what your family has endured."

She remembers the faces of all those humans left in the city, those who never had the chance to discover themselves and those who have to silence their voices every day. "It's not fair. It's not right. No one should condemn an entire population because of the crimes of a few. You've fought for your freedom your whole life. You guard these people every day. You're a protector, Calvden. And now you have the chance to do even more good. You can prevent thousands of others from suffering a fate similar to yours. You get to choose whether you want to continue this endless violence, or if you want to help us end it. The people in that army, they are evil. What kind of person do you want to be?"

His fingers loosen around her neck until she can barely feel them, and his snarl fades. As he releases the tension in his shoulders, he drops his hand away from her throat. He withdraws his leg from between hers and stands back, but he doesn't seem to have the words to express his thoughts.

Skinny Man walks up to them. "Let them go, Calvden."

He shakes his head once, not from disgust or fury, but from a lack of hope, something he's probably been without for a long, long time. "A woman and an elf are going to make a difference?"

"Two kingdoms fighting as one, yes." Although she speaks softly, her voice conveys zero doubt. "And when we stop this army, we're going to level that city by the sea to the ground and free the people trapped there." In her peripheral vision, she sees Ëólas nod his agreement.

"You're going to destroy Feídra né Morna?" Calvden chuckles. "I have believed in nothing but revenge for the last forty-five years." He could stop there, could run her through with her dagger. But he doesn't. Maybe it's desperation. Maybe it's exhaustion, but he gives in to the people he's protected, the people urging him not to throw away this chance. Backing up, he shakes his head, not believing his own words. "Don't disappoint me."

Without hesitation, she says, "I give you my word."

When Calvden nods, she extends her hand to the man holding her weapons and eyes him until he relinquishes both. With the set returned, she walks over to Ëólas, rests the sword beside him, and uses the dagger to finish cutting his bonds. The rope falls to the ground, a dirty clump of knots that can no longer divide them.

This time, she meets Ëólas's gaze, which contains an admiration she doesn't shy away from. As a moment becomes a lifetime, she settles into herself. Not the orphan who stumbled in the dark the last nine months. Not the emotionally numb woman who made the wrong choices. Not the king's ward who dressed up like a noblewoman. And not the traumatized girl who let her nightmares eat away at her confidence. No, in this space, she's just Adaline. And for the first time since she arrived in this world, that feels like enough, even to Ëólas.

After they both stand up, Ëólas massages his wrists. Even though they bear no visible marks, he winces, just once, but that small display of discomfort sets Adaline's nerves on edge again. She touches his arm and parts her lips to ask him what's wrong, what's hurting him, and how she can help, but he doesn't give her a chance to inquire, shaking his head *not now* and turning to face his captors.

"Thank you, all of you," Ëólas says.

Calvden grinds his jaw, turns his back to Ëólas and Adaline, and goes to the other side of the chamber, putting as much distance between him and them as possible without actually leaving his people. Gramps and Skinny Man take over with giving directions, asking the old woman and a few others to bring more food and water. Sitting beside each other, Ëólas and Adaline fill their water bladders and thank the group profusely for the little food they have to share. Granny returns Adaline her cloak, but most of the other people keep their distance from Ëólas, whom Adaline refuses to let out of her sight.

Ëólas doesn't seem to mind though, focusing instead on their next course of action. "Take this opportunity to close your eyes, Adaline, before we set out again."

With her adrenaline gone, she's too tired to argue, but she doesn't accept Granny's offer to use her bedding again. Instead, Adaline rests her head on Ëólas's shoulder and closes her eyes. Her breathing slows, and her head droops, but she's too wired to fall asleep here. The oddly numbing, pulsing sensation in her shoulder keeps her awake too.

Gramps's voice announces his approach. With Ëólas's consent, Gramps sits down in front of them. "There are some of us free folk left. We have other groups, other leaders. We've survived because we've learned to hide down in these caves. Getting water is the hardest. We're able to collect rainwater, but we have to be careful not to anger the cave dwellers, and I don't mean the rats." He whispers, "Don't tell the lady what was in her soup."

"I won't, thank you," Ëólas says, a hint of humor in his voice.

I'm so hungry that I'd eat ten bowls of rat soup.

Gramps clicks his tongue. "Never did I think I'd see the day when an elf thanked us."

"I hope to continue to prove many firsts to you. Why don't you come with us to the Neutral Territory, or New Leira, as Adaline calls it."

"I can't." Gramps sighs. "With the army away, we must make use of our time wisely."

Oh my god. They can't be planning to attack that city, Feídra né Morna, by themselves?

Ëólas sighs but keeps his upper body still so Adaline's head doesn't slip off his shoulder. "They will see you coming from afar. You'll need a diversion. If the situation seems dire, get out. I'll return with Alderton's and my own forces within two months."

Someone far off scoffs, but another person says they saw the army less than a day ago.

"Did you see how many there were?" Ëólas asks, wanting specific numbers.

"Sorry. I can't count that high."

Gramps and Ëólas talk more about food and resources, about how he found the caves when he was a child, and about the family he lost a decade ago because of illness. "We all waste away in the Wastelands. Why ever would King Magnus allow his ward to venture here?"

Ëólas laughs softly. "She did not ask for his permission."

"She's too lovely to be out here," Gramps whispers. "Too kind a soul."

A long pause passes, long enough for Adaline to worry if Ëólas agreed, but he says, "She's strong too."

A smile returns to her face, and knowing he's safe, she drifts off to sleep, ready to face the next challenge that comes their way. Ready, because she knows now that she and Ëólas can overcome any obstacle together.

CHAPTER NINE

THE HUNT

Muffled voices lure Adaline's consciousness away from a dreamless nap. When someone shakes her shoulder, her good one, thank goodness, she lifts her floppy hand and taps a slender nose to shoo the person away. "It's too early."

"Adaline." The urgency in Ëólas's hushed whisper tugs her eyes open. "Ãranol's soldiers have entered the caves. You need to—"

"The Morgai!" Pushing herself off the ground, Adaline jumps to her feet and scoops up his cloak, which he must have folded and tucked under her head for a pillow. When she hands it back to him, the navy-blue material unfurls and ripples like a waterfall as he spins the cloak around his shoulder. Securing the silver clasp at his neck, he lets his perfectly-in-control façade slip. His skin looks less glossy, maybe even paler, despite the flickering orange glow from the torches. The corners of his mouth droop, and his eyelids appear slightly puffy. But an instant later, he looks into Adaline's eyes and projects that can-do confidence, making her doubt what she saw. Still, she can't shake the unease that something's off with him.

Is that spell wearing off? His strength can't crash now.

Placing his hand on Adaline's back, Ëólas escorts her over to Calvden and his men, all of whom look ready not only to decapitate more elves but also to piss their trousers.

Calvden glares at Ëólas but lets him and Adaline enter the circle. "I don't suppose you have any ideas?"

"I do," Ëólas says. "All of you take an opposite route and escape. I'll buy you time."

Gramps looks at Adaline. "The lady should come with us."

"Agreed." Ëólas, glancing at the sword tied to Adaline's belt, extends his hand.

"What? No." She clasps the hilt and narrows her eyes. "I'm not leaving you. Not now. Not ever."

They both freeze until Adaline feels her cheeks turn red, and Ëólas clears his throat. His expression remains cold, unyielding, while she scowls and grits her teeth.

Him and that damn blank expression. It's not like I said anything unusual. Even he said we're a team. While we're in the Wastelands. Once everything's settled, I'll resume trying to find a way home. Obviously.

Her scowl melts into a frown, and her resolve weakens. Home feels more like the fantasy these days, which is crazy. Who wouldn't be eager to get the hell out of here and leave behind Mr. Toad, killer elves, and noblewomen trying to marry her off?

It doesn't matter. None of that matters right now. "Ëólas, I can—"

"Please, don't argue. Not now. When they see me, I can delay, misdirect, or fight them. But I can't do any of that if I'm worried about you the entire time. Go with Calvden, and I'll find you. I need you to trust me." A second bead of sweat clings at his hairline, threatening to fall into his eye, but he doesn't break eye contact as he wills her to comply.

Despite the logic behind his thinking, separating now doesn't seem like a wise idea either. Not if he's feeling unwell. Plus, he's never fought his own people before. How's he going to manage that? But if she stays with him, she will only be in his way. With one sword between the two of them, the blade belongs in his skilled hands, not hers.

His gaze intensifies as more seconds tick by. The other humans huddling near the exit fidget uneasily and glance behind Ëólas, waiting for the apocalypse to arrive at their doorstep. The safer option for them would be to abandon Adaline and Ëólas to their fate, which Adaline's fine with, except she'll place Ëólas at a disadvantage.

Cussing under her breath, she gives him the sword, ramming the sheath into his hands. "Fine. But we're resuming my training immediately after this."

"Agreed." As he ties the sheath to his belt, he somehow appears taller, unbreakable even, like the warrior she's glimpsed during training but never actually met.

Even though she's not sure what changed between one breath and the next, the determination on his face helps her own stomach to settle and her hands to stop shaking. A look passes between Calvden and Ëólas, that they're both trusting the other because they don't have any other choice. With a final nod, Calvden grabs Adaline's wrist and pulls her behind him. She doesn't look forward until Ëólas vanishes from her sight.

Please, if anyone's listening, keep him safe.

Running behind the others, she picks up her blue skirts and keeps her eyes focused on Calvden's back. They turn once, and the light from within the chamber no longer reaches them. The tunnel swallows them whole. The torch leading the way reveals horizontal layers of rock that mark the decades with various shades of gray. They run for what feels like forever while Adaline tells herself over and over again to trust Ëólas, that he knows what he's doing, that he won't get himself killed and leave her here to die, or worse. If the enemy does catch up with them, will the Morgai slaughter them all? Or would they too think she's pretty enough for breeding?

A gurgle of bile stings the back of her throat.

Maybe twenty minutes later, the tunnel leads to another corridor with six archways of shadow. She follows the others through the third from the right. No one slows down, even though Adaline doesn't hear anything behind her. They make several more turns as if they're ants burrowing deeper underground. The only sounds come from their breaths, their feet scurrying along, and the torch crackling.

He must be done with them by now, but how is he ever going to find me down here?

The smooth cave walls offer no direction, no distinction. But a recess carved into the bottom right displays a pile of stacked stones. Adaline counts four as she runs past. She scans the cave wall until she spies another niche holding only three rocks. By the time she counts down to one, the group turns right into another tunnel, this one with gems counting downward like mile markers. If only she had noticed these sooner, she could have mapped out how to find Ëólas.

After more time passes, maybe fifteen minutes, the group slows down, but they all take long strides to hurry along. Maybe now she can risk asking where they're going. She doesn't get the chance. Despite the lack of airflow down here, a familiar, disembodied, female voice whispers in her ear, "Adaline."

Oh shit. That's not good. "We have company," Adaline whisper-shouts.

Calvden's people skid to a stop, and Adaline halts before she collides into his shoulders. She spins around, hiking up her skirts to find her dagger, and the dry layer of mud coating her hem cracks. As her fingertips brush the hilt, four sets of eyes pierce the darkness: two blue, one green, and one gold. Each pair glows with a supernatural ring of light around the iris. The first three emerge with their swords drawn. The tall, lean silhouettes she's come to associate with safety now make the cave feel smaller and her chance of escape impossible.

Adaline looks to the golden orbs in the back and holds her breath, waiting for Ëólas to emerge and reveal that they have surrounded the three soldiers. But the fourth elf isn't him. The owner of these pale-gold eyes also has flawless skin and handsome features, but his white hair and sharp nose accentuate the severity of his disgust that tells her he'll choose option one: slaughter them all.

Panic festers under her skin, making her bones wriggle, but her muscles lock. *Where's Ëólas? What have they done with him?*

Calvden, Mr. Skinny, and another man push past her, knocking her into the wall and not waiting for the elves to speak first, let alone attack. Calvden pulls a small bottle out of his pocket, pops the cork off with this thumb, and dumps the contents into his mouth. As Gramps yanks Adaline's arm and warns her to look away, Calvden raises a torch and spits out a clear liquid. Squeezing her eyes shut, Adaline shrinks against the wall but not before catching sight of the torch's flame bursting forward into a wall of fire. The inferno of heat radiates against her back, as if she's jumped into a volcano and her cloak caught fire. She pulls her hair around front, shielding her cheek. The strands turn dry and brittle. The heat penetrating the layers of her clothing feels like someone's ironing her alive, but before the temperature becomes unbearable, the light diminishes, along with the heat. Plunged into a darker cave, she searches for the elves, wiping the sweat away from her brow and making herself as small as possible. Black spots float along the sides of her vision.

Pressing the heels of her palms to her eyes, Adaline blinks away the darkness. "What? How?"

Grunting and cussing, Calvden has sidled up to another elf. Their shoulders rub against each other as Calvden tries to wrestle a sword free. Mr. Skinny and the man tackle the remaining elves, who keep staggering backward and brandishing their swords as if they're fighting ghosts they cannot see.

Gramps, holding another torch, grabs Adaline's hand. "They've got this."

The woman up ahead waves at Adaline to follow, to hurry, to escape while the guys distract the elves, but how can Adaline leave the others to fight alone? Her dagger vibrates against her calf.

I should go help them, shouldn't I?

As she yanks her wrist away from Gramps, the elf with the white hair greets them, his face void of empathy. The humans are little more than the rats skittering in the shadows. Even though he locks his yellow eyes on her, he rams his sword through Gramps's abdomen and doesn't bother to acknowledge the old man hitching forward and clutching the elf's shoulder. The tip of the blade strikes the cave wall with a ping behind Gramps. Thrusting his arm backward, the elf wrenches his sword free, and Gramps crumples into the ground, a pile of bones and tatters that the elf uses to wipe his blade clean.

Beyond the white-haired elf, the other woman has vanished. The scuffles and grunts behind Adaline block her only other exit. She curls her fingers, ready to claw out his eyes the moment he moves, but the elf only tilts his head sideways and looks her up and down, the same way the lieutenant did back in Hell City. That single comparison makes Adaline snarl and lunge at him. Instantly, the elf dodges sideways, grabs a fistful of her hair, and drags her toward his friends, forcing her to bend at the waist. As she screams and twists and pulls, he tightens his grip, and her hair lifts her scalp away from her skull.

Rather than crying, Adaline lets go and digs under her skirts, fumbling with each step until she pulls out her dagger. She runs forward, dragging his arm in front of him and blocking him from taking another step. As he stumbles into her, she shoves the tip of her blade into his thigh. At least, she thought she was aiming for his thigh. With her head pushed downward and her hair falling over her face, she can't see where she got him until he screams and falls backward, releasing her as he clutches his groin. Blood spurts between his fingers.

Fólas's lessons about what would happen if she ever stabbed the femoral artery come rushing to the front of her mind. If she doesn't apply pressure to the wound, he'll bleed out in minutes. His pale-yellow irises fade like a dying sun. Adaline vomits in her mouth.

I don't want this. I didn't mean to.

She glances down at her cloak, gathering the fabric in her hands, one of which holds the dagger now dripping blood onto her dress. She could use her cloak to stop the bleeding, but more elves run toward them.

Taking a step back from the white-haired elf, she mumbles, "I'm so sorry," and runs, leaving him writhing and crying for help.

She turns down a different tunnel, this time without a source of light. Keeping the dagger close to her chest, she presses her palm against the wall and follows the curve. Sediment rubs her fingertips raw, but she doesn't get far. A halo of light chases after her. She looks ahead into the abyss, wills her heart rate to slow down enough so she can hear beyond the blood pounding her temples, and counts the shadows heading her way. One. Only one.

I can take one more. If it means living or dying, I can. Or maybe it's...

"Lady Adaline!" Mr. Skinny sprints toward her. He rounds the curve, the light revealing his lanky frame. His eyes, forced open with adrenaline, still sink into his skull from exhaustion. "Don't go that way. You'll—"

Another shadow catches up to Mr. Skinny, two black blobs merging into one. Wrapping a hand around his forehead, the elf pulls Mr. Skinny back, exposing his long neck. As the torch hits the ground, the light kisses his throat and illuminates the red line from which blood seeps down his torso. Gasping for a breath he'll never get, Mr. Skinny falls to the ground and doesn't move.

She can't help. She can't help anyone. How is she supposed to help herself?

The elf stalks toward her. His blue eyes flick to the dagger she clutches, and he raises his sword.

Would the elves offer any of them mercy? If she got down on her knees, dropped the dagger, and begged, would he let her live?

With her back pressed against the wall, Adaline inches away from the elf, her cloak sliding along the stone. Her hands shake. The dagger quivers against her chest. *Ëólas, what do I do? Please, come back. Please. I can't. I don't know how.*

She lowers the dagger to her navel, but the elf pauses and gestures with the tip of his sword for her to fall onto her knees. Guilt and bile mix together, locking her legs in place. A voice in the back of her head screams at her that she's being stupid, that she's taking too long, that this elf won't wait much longer. And yet she can hear Ëólas admonishing her in her mind, repeating what he told her just before they came to the Wastelands: *If anyone dares to hurt you again, I won't forgive you if you let them win.*

He was right. She has to fight back. *They killed a defenseless old man. I can't possibly think he'll let me live.* And if she surrenders now, what will happen to their friends? To the Neutral Territory?

Grabbing the dagger like a hammer, she lifts the blade in front of her face. Even with the light flickering behind him, she sees him roll his luminescent blue eyes at her. Still, he rushes toward her, sword raised, not willing to drag this moment out any more than need be.

With a half effort, he slashes at her sideways. Adaline, catching the shift in his footing and the bend of his waist, moves one leg behind her for better support and blocks the blow with her narrow blade that never buckles, never breaks. The sword catches on her hilt. With a sneer, the elf pushes against her blade and shoves her into the cave wall. Her arms burn as she pushes back, stopping the edge of the elf's sword from fileting her chest. He releases the tension between them just enough to grab her hand and twist it backward, forcing her to drop the dagger, and presses the edge of his blade along the clasp of her cloak as if he plans to use the length of her silver chain as a guide.

He moves his hand one millimeter. "Learn your place, Vermin!"

Her skin sears, and tears spill down her cheeks. *Not like this. Not here. Not alone.* "Please," she cries.

The elf releases a half laugh, but she wasn't speaking to him. She prays to the voice that's been warning her all along, the angel watching her back or the fae that summoned her here or to the belly of the cave that's consumed them. "Please," she repeats.

A crack echoes in the cave, and both her and the elf's eyes widen. The warning stills his hand, and they both look up at the uneven chunks of rock that form the ceiling.

Is that why Mr. Skinny said don't come this way, that the tunnel isn't finished? Isn't stable?

The ground rumbles, subtly at first. Sediment and dirt fall from the ceiling. The elf tips backward and staggers sideways. When he hits the opposite wall, Adaline tries to run, but the shaking makes her legs buckle, and they both fall to the ground. She scrambles onto her knees and crawls away, but the elf releases his sword to lunge forward and drag her beneath him. As he straddles her, he picks up her head and slams it against the floor. Black spots block out his features and merge with the darkness surrounding them. Unable to see, she feels the ground with her hand, searching for something, anything. Her fingers find the recess carved into the cave wall, along with a sharp flint of rock that she grabs. The elf reaches for his sword, but Adaline's faster, jamming the flint into his ear.

The elf bellows and rears upward, but before Adaline can wriggle away, he clasps her throat. She digs her fingers under his, trying to peel them away one at a time, while he squeezes and pulls a knife out of his boot. This time, he spins the handle around so that he grips it like an ice pick, ready to ram it through her throat.

Adaline stares at the tip, at the fine point upon which her life balances, a miniscule end that can rob her of everything she has yet to do. As the elf inhales and pulls his arm back, she sees within the tip Nan planting another row of tulips in a garden bursting with color, her father guiding her hands at the drum kit to help her tap out a beat, Cindy dancing out of the dressing room and modeling her dress for her engagement dinner, and Ëólas lifting his arms as he laughs at the wonder of airplanes.

"Ëólas," she whispers. *Is he dead too? Will he find me dead, bleeding out on this floor?*

How can her chest contain so much pain, so much pressure, that only keeps building, keeps condensing, keeps suffocating her as every possible future collides together in one spot at the hollow of her neck so that someone can shatter her entirety with a single breath?

"No," she hisses through clenched teeth. She glares at him, at his icy blue eyes that see her as nothing more than a nuisance, and screams, releasing a carnal torrent of refusal that he dismisses as he lowers his blade. She lets go of the hand choking her and catches his other wrist, stopping the blade from piercing her skin. Sweat beads on her forehead. He lets go of her neck and uses both hands, trying to drive the blade into her throat. The tip scratches the hollow of her neck.

When the metal cuts into her flesh, the cave shakes again. A rock the size of her fist falls from the ceiling. The chunk drops effortlessly, as if it had been holding on by a thread, and smashes the back of the elf's head. He groans but doesn't yield. Shaking his head, he pushes down harder, the metal tearing her skin apart millimeter by millimeter, until the ceiling cracks. A narrow beam of light penetrates the tunnel, and the elf glances upward with relief. Sunken cheeks and pasty skin mar his otherwise perfectly symmetrical face. As he inhales the hint of fresh air, his face becomes less splotchy.

He turns back to Adaline and leers over her with renewed vigor. Letting up on the dagger, he grabs her wrist and pins one above her head. The cave shudders again. A large chunk of rock the size of a basketball plummets onto his back, followed by another. The elf yelps and rolls off her, but not to his freedom. The cave ceiling cracks again, the breakage so loud that Adaline shrinks back from the cave's thunder, and a boulder larger than a trashcan drops onto his legs, shattering his calves.

Adaline presses her hands against her ears to shut out his screams as he attempts to push the boulder away. She retrieves her dagger and starts down the tunnel, eager to leave behind his pleas. But then she hears her question to Calvden: *What kind of person do you want to be?*

Pausing at the edge of darkness, she looks back at the elf, defenseless now and pleading for help. Her shoulders fall, and her chest grows heavier. But her feet take her back. She stands beside the elf, whimpering from a pain she never wants to feel herself, and pushes her shoulder against the boulder. It teeters a smidge, and the elf screams again as he leans back on his hands. She shoves her back against the boulder and pushes with her thighs, her cries mingling with his as her muscles burn. The boulder teeters again, but her feet slip, and the boulder falls back into place.

The elf's leg bones crunch. "Stop. Stop!"

She does. They both look at each other, his blue eyes now raw and pulsing like a heartbeat slowing down, counting down. She stands up and rests her palms on the boulder to try again.

"You have to leave." His hoarse voice is barely above a whisper. "One of my own is coming. Run away while you can."

Adaline steps back and glances at the torch, its flame failing. "What about my friend? He's an elf with long dark-blond hair and gold eyes."

"Your friend?" The blue-eyed elf swallows hard and knits his brow together, trying to comprehend her words.

"Yes, is he okay? Did you see him?"

"You have to go. Leave now!"

This time, Adaline doesn't look back. She runs for what feels like forever until she's taken too many turns and has lost her way in complete darkness.

Chapter Ten

THE BLUE LIGHTS

S hivering under her cloak, Adaline clasps her hands together and brings them to her mouth where she blows hot air onto her palms. The heat tingles her skin for only an instant. She hunches her shoulders close to her ears, rubs her arms, and pulls her cloak shut. She can't stand the sight of torches, thanks to her nightmares, but she'd give almost anything to see one now. She's tried going back the way she came, but too many turns have trapped her.

How am I ever going to find my way out of these tunnels? Think, Adaline, think.

She turns off her emotions—or, at least, ignores the tendrils of panic curling around her heart—and focuses on what she does know.

I don't have a whistle, but I can whistle fairly loudly. The sound might travel far, but it would also bounce off the cave walls, confusing anyone looking for me. And that anyone could be friend or foe.

Taking a deep breath, Adaline slowly counts to ten and presses the meaty pad between her thumb and pointer finger. The tension in her temples dissipates, even though the back of her head still throbs.

I could have a concussion, so I need to stay awake. I could wait here until Ëólas finds me.

A sudden sob clogs her throat, and panic crushes her heart. She takes a shaky breath and concentrates on her breathing again.

It's not pitch black, meaning light must be filtering down here from somewhere. That means there's also a way to get to the surface. What do I have on me?

She reaches into her pockets and pulls out her phone. Bending down, she unsheathes her dagger. *I can mark the wall on the left side to know where I've been.* Powering on her mobile, still at eighty-five percent battery, she turns on the flashlight and scratches the wall with her dagger, making an X mark.

Ëólas will find me. He's so damn honorable and persistent that he won't be able to leave me here.

Steeling herself, she marches ahead. When she reaches a fork in the tunnel, she closes her eyes, quiets her breath, and listens. The sound of water dripping directs her to the right. Marking the cave as she goes, she walks faster as the sound of rushing water grows louder. At the next turn, she enters a chamber that beaches up against an underground river. The cave stifles the roar of the current flowing past. Adaline shines her flashlight over the river that looks to be at least forty feet wide, but her light can't penetrate the darkness on the other side.

Maybe this waterway connects to one of the two rivers that border Aerytol?

She meanders forward and sinks to the ground at the river's edge. With her phone at sixty percent power now, she taps the flashlight off and powers down her mobile, stashing it back in her pocket. Closing her eyes to shut out the darkness, she brings her knees to her chin and clasps her hands around her calves.

This river could be our ticket out of here. But what can we float on? And how will I find Ëólas? And what if he's hurt?

Time ticks by. Turning her face, she presses her cheek against her knees and listens. She hasn't heard anything from the cave tunnels, so either she's so far gone that no one can find her, or no one's left. Then again, she has no idea what other creatures might exist in this world or what Gramps meant by cave dwellers.

I hope he didn't mean goblins. Or krakens.

She lifts her head, squints, and stares at the faint pencil line of what she thinks is still the tunnel entrance. Nan always said if she's ever lost, she should look to her own feet for answers. But her father taught her to stay put until someone finds her. Who does she listen to now?

As the loneliness starts creeping up inside her, she hides her face in her knees, which smell like moldy linen. The emptiness of the cave reminds her of home, of her empty condo and abandoned childhood house.

After Nan passed, Derek filled the void for a while, his presence a respite from the storm that threatened to overtake Adaline. He'd pop into her office with a fresh chai latte and flash his sweet, boyish grin. If he sensed she was down, he would hang up the phone and show up at her condo twenty minutes later. They'd curl up on the sofa, his arm hugging her shoulders, and they'd watch a movie, pushing back the emptiness with laughter. At night, he'd curl up behind her, draping his arm over her abdomen, but the moment he fell asleep, she'd escape his grasp and lie awake, staring up at the blank ceiling, waiting for morning and work to silence her thoughts, silence her memories, silence her growing concern that she'll never find someone who knows her inside and out.

Too much quiet made the truth inescapable, palpable even. Like every time she returned home after her father died. She'd find Nan waiting in her garden, facing the lake that borders the backyard. With her eyes shut and her silver hair blowing in the wind, Nan seemed ready to float away. In those moments, Adaline knew the end was coming. She couldn't pretend Nan wasn't slowing down. They'd sit on the porch swing, arm in arm, both at a loss for words. Nan continued to project strength, and she never faltered to offer Adaline perfectly timed advice. But something in Nan broke when dad died. Her light dimmed with each passing day, and she got older a lot faster. She never seemed sick. Just worn out.

The day after Adaline got the green light to start her excavation, she drove home to tell Nan, to see the pride gleaming on her face, but she wasn't outside in her garden. The worst possible reason flashed through Adaline's mind, but she dismissed it. She let herself into the house through the kitchen. The air, which always hung heavy with the scent of sugar and baked bread, smelled instead like Pine Sol. That artificial lemon-fresh scent and the silence that had already settled throughout the house told Adaline the truth.

Slowly, she walked up the curved stairs to Nan's side of the house, Adaline's hand pulling on the banister to tug herself along, and down the corridor that elongated with each step. She didn't bother to knock on the door. She pushed it open and sat on the edge of the bed, her weight jostling Nan's silver hair. She lay with one hand on her chest and the other on the empty pillow beside her, the one that should have belonged to Adaline's grandfather. She rested her hand on top of Nan's and held on just a little longer.

In the cave, Adaline opens her eyes, but there's no waking from this nightmare. No Ëólas to massage her back. No Seira to hold her hand. No father to sing her to sleep.

The memory of her father throwing his arms into the air and belting out "Let It Be" at four in the morning pulls her cheeks up into a smile. Maybe he defaulted to that song because he was trying to tell her something. Maybe she needs to let it be, needs to stop running from the pain. She's suppressed it for months now, which led her to make the wrong choices with the wrong person. And since then, she's been running from one trauma to another. She can't wash away the blood of innocence lost. Not yet anyway.

Staring in the direction of the tunnel, Adaline channels her father and sings the first few words to a song she's known most of her life. When she gives voice to the troubled times she's found herself in, that she now finds herself in, her voice cracks and breaks. She pushes through the sob and half whispers, half sings about those words of wisdom that her father and Nan always gave her. Maybe even her own wisdom that got Calvden to reconsider killing every elf he sees. If he's still alive. When she sings about the light that can pierce her own hour of darkness, she knows deep in her gut, without any trace of doubt, that Ëólas will find her, and they'll leave this cave together.

Adaline lifts her head and listens to the steady rhythm of the water pulsing beside her. Her voice stops trembling, and warmth envelops her from the inside out. Singing louder, she holds onto the hope of living in a world where both sides lay down their weapons and choose to agree, to listen, to find an answer together.

From the corner of her eye, a flicker of light draws her attention back to the tunnel entrance, hoping to find Ëólas holding a torch. Instead, a soft blue glow hovers about four feet in front of her. With a sharp inhale of breath, she stops singing, and the light goes out.

Adaline tilts her head and waits, but she can't find any trace of the blue orb. So, keeping her eyes on the spot where she last saw the light, Adaline continues singing, praying that the people of this world might still have the chance to see the truth that Adaline discovered in New Leira, that the people of Alderton and Lameiría are mending the history of their broken hearts by agreeing to live together.

As she gives in to the song, the blue light flickers on again, almost like a firefly but brighter. She sings louder, allowing her voice, her hope, her acceptance of fate to fill the entire chamber. The cave comes alive with blue starlight that descends from the ceiling and walls to dance around her. Each miniature star illuminates the cave as if Adaline were floating in space.

I love this world. There's far more good than bad here. I won't forget that again.

One of the cave dwellers hovers nearer and lands on top of Adaline's knee. As the blue light dims a bit, the creature's silhouette becomes clearer, revealing not a firefly but a little person, a fairy or a sprite or a bluecap. Whatever he is, the little person measures no bigger than Adaline's thumb, a real-life Thumbelina, or rather, Thumbelino, with skin as blue as the ocean. Iridescent wings like a hummingbird's flutter behind his back, and a gold crown rests upon his head. The king crosses his arm over his tunic and bows at the waist, and Adaline lowers her eyes and nods her head in return.

When she looks up again, a tear slides down her cheek, and the tiny king watches the drop fall onto her chest. His eyes grow wider as he frowns, and Adaline marvels how someone so small can display such concern.

"They're happy tears." She wipes away the rest and smiles broadly. He's too precious for her to feel anything but joy right now.

The king beams, but his eyes become glossy as if he's overcome with relief too, although Adaline can't fathom what's affected him so greatly. Regardless, he seems sincere.

I wonder if he can help me.

"I'm sorry if my singing woke you. I, I lost my friend, an elf named Ëólas. I don't suppose you've seen him?" She gnaws her bottom lip and lowers her voice as if speaking aloud what she fears most might bring it to fruition. "I'm worried about him."

The king flutters his wings, drawing himself into the air, and hovers above Adaline's knee. He lifts his arm, which is as thin as the stem of a leaf, and points to the side. Adaline follows the direction of his gesture and looks at the tunnel. In the center of the opening, Ëólas stands as still as a statue. One hand rests on the hilt of Adaline's sword, hanging from his belt. The other dangles limply at his side. The blue orbs floating between them cast a warm glow on his face, illuminating his mouth hanging agape.

Adaline clamps down on her bottom lip as she jumps to her feet and runs to him, throwing her arms around his torso and pressing her cheek into the silky threads of the tunic covering his chest. When she hears his heartbeat throbbing beside her ear and his arms encircle her, all of her worries drain out of her body and into the river. Yes, this world contains horrible moments, memories that will haunt her the rest of her life and fuel her nightmares. But it contains so much promise too. "I knew you'd find me."

He rubs her back, his fingers tangling in her hair. "The singing helped."

Can we stay here, like this, for just a bit longer? Must we start running again so soon? Adaline frowns. *Of course we do. Who knows how much time we've lost now, after we'd nearly caught up to Āranol and the Morgai.*

Adaline leans back and checks Ëólas's torso and arms for signs of injury. His ripped sleeve hangs loosely from his bicep, but there's no sign of blood. She glances up to search his face, and her happiness falters. His flawless skin has turned pasty. His cheeks have sunken inward, and his eyes are glowing brighter than normal. "Ëólas, what's happening to—"

He tilts her head back and glares at her neck. "Who did this to you? What happened?"

"What do you—"

"Your neck, Adaline. You're bruised and bleeding." His eyes lower to her chest, and his irises zoom in. "You're covered in blood."

Adaline takes half a step back, not enough to leave his arms but enough so that she can examine herself. "Oh." She flinches at the flashing memory of Gramps falling to the ground. "It's not mine. They, the elves, they killed the old man. He wasn't even fighting. He was helping me, trying to get me to escape with him, but I, I hesitated." Tears fall onto her chest, clear splashes that dilute the rusty red. "It's my fault he's dead."

"No, Adaline. Do not hold yourself accountable for the sins of others." He checks her throat again, rubbing his thumb over the hollow of her neck. He keeps his touch gentle, but the trail of his thumb makes her shudder. "At least the wound doesn't appear deep."

"Like I said, I'm okay. Physically speaking." She dips her head to hide her tears, but they stream down her cheeks of their own accord. She can walk out of this cave, but many more people are going to die before this war ends. "I just don't understand how anyone can be so cruel. How do you kill someone like that, without mercy, without any sense of empathy?"

He lets her go, taking back the comfort of his warmth. She stares at the spot where he had been, when he hadn't hesitated to embrace her too. He takes another step back. When she peeks up at him, his hardened expression makes her shut her mouth.

I didn't mean you.

She has no idea what he must be going through right now, after fighting, maybe killing, his own people. Elves don't war with elves, that's what he'd said when they first met. She doesn't even know how to help him feel better. Not that it's her place, being on the other side, the side that the elves already blame for all this strife.

He glances at the splatter of blood that's soaked into her sapphire bodice. "Is the one who did that dead?"

The hardness of his voice makes her chest curl inward. She stares at him for a long moment, not sure what answer he's looking for, hoping for, or fearing most. "When, when we were fighting, a boulder fell from the ceiling and crushed his legs."

Ëólas's lips fall open, but he doesn't speak.

"I tried to help him. Really, I did. But it was too heavy for me to move. I'm sorry." She pulls her cloak shut, hiding the blood.

Closing the distance between them, he tilts her chin up, pushes her cloak aside, and eyes her wound. As he scans her body for more visible signs of injury, Adaline hopes he doesn't notice her heart racing. "Why would you try to help him? You're lucky—" His words falter while he ponders something unpleasant, something that makes him wince. But he shakes the thought away. "Are you hurt anywhere else?"

Under his intense gaze, she stares at the ground and searches for a way to change the topic, to end his scrutiny, to stop her brain from trying to unravel what about this reunion and conversation feels off-key. She takes a deep breath but accidentally smells herself. Gagging on her body odor, she scurries away, closer to the water's edge and near a large cluster of floating blue people. The king lands on her shoulder. Maybe his nostrils are too small for obnoxious fumes.

"I made some friends," she says with an awkward laugh.

Releasing whatever unpleasant thoughts plagued him moments ago, Ëólas follows her, his movements less graceful than usual. "So I see." He bows to the bluecaps' king. "Hello, Your Majesty."

The king nods at Ëólas but doesn't leave Adaline's shoulder. Glowing brighter, he rests his fists on his hips and eyes Ëólas with a frown.

Does the little king begrudge Ëólas fighting elves too?

Ëólas doesn't seem bothered though and keeps his voice gentle. "Thank you, Your Majesty, for keeping the lady company until I could find her. Might we benefit from your kindness again? Is there anything we might use to float down this river? The queen and king of Lameiría would be eternally grateful."

The king floats in front of Ëólas and crosses his arms over his chest as if he's waiting for something.

Adaline reaches into her pocket. "We don't have much to offer in exchange, but I do have this berry." Holding her hand out flat, she offers the king the last juicy morsel she saved from the first bunch Ëólas had found for her.

The king lands on her palm. With his hand pinching his chin, he walks around the berry, inspecting all sides. He stops in front of Adaline's nose and smiles with such kindness and gentility that Adaline wishes she could come back and visit him often. The king gestures toward a bunch of other blue orbs that follow his orders and disappear in a wisp of light upriver, their glow fading beyond the bend. Turning back to the berry, the king picks up and admires the fruit as if he were inspecting the rarest diamond.

Adaline looks to Ëólas for any indication if her offering worked, but his expression has turned sour again, and he seems to have disappeared inside his head. When he closes his eyes for a few heartbeats, the underside of his eyes sag.

We need to get out of this cave. I hope the others got out too.

"Ëólas, did you happen to see Calvden? Did he—"

"He's fine."

Adaline exhales. She opens her mouth to ask more but changes her mind. *Later. I can ask him later. If he's willing to tell me what happened to him.*

A few moments later, the bluecaps return, only they aren't flying. Instead, lined up like a string of fairy lights, they outline a raft made of reeds and push a pole, or maybe a lever, in the back that slows the platform. More bluecaps push the edge of the raft against the shore, preventing it from continuing downriver. As Adaline blinks in awe, the blue orbs jump about, dancing a jig. Puffing his chest outward, the king beams, hovers above Adaline's palm, and gestures toward her new transportation while two other bluecaps fly off with the berry.

She gathers her skirts, ignoring the cracking crust of dirt, and curtsies. "Oh, thank you. Thank you so much, Your Majesty."

The king bows. When he flies over to Ëólas, he wags his tiny finger back and forth.

"You have my word," Ëólas says. "And thank you immensely for your generous gift."

Wait, what? How does Ëólas know what the king is saying?

Ëólas steps onto the raft, and the rest of the bluecaps flutter away, leaving behind a dark square the size of a family sedan. Adaline gulps and hides her clammy palms behind her back. She didn't think this through, didn't consider what rafting would entail, didn't realize that she'd be forcing herself to ride a beast similar to the one that swallowed her father.

Taking hold of the long pole in the back, Ëólas offers Adaline his free hand. When she gnaws her bottom lip, he misinterprets her concern. "It's safe, I promise. His Majesty would never allow you on his barge otherwise." His shoulders droop from the weight of his outstretched arm. The blue lights make his cheeks look hollow, and he blinks slowly as if in a haze.

Unable to see him like this anymore, Adaline places her hand in his and teeters onto the raft. Once she sits down, he pushes the raft away from shore. She waves vigorously to the king and his people, and her heart sours as the river quickly carries them away, leaving the magic behind.

Chapter Eleven

THE GIFT

When she can no longer see the cave dwellers' starlight, Adaline digs her nails into the reeds. Whenever she's nervous, words fill her mind. Sometimes facts. Sometimes stories. Now, she wills her mind to shut the hell up, to suppress Shakespeare's words, to block out images of bones turned to coral and eyeballs bloated like pearls. This isn't the Potomac River, and she's come too far to drown now.

I bet he thought the same thing, on the cusp of discovery, only for his car to fly off that bridge.

Nope, those aren't the right words to stop this line of thinking. Adaline fumbles her fingers over the reeds, searching for anything to hold on to. "Why does someone who can fly have a raft?"

"I imagine flying all the time is exhausting. Besides, faeries love parties. This, I believe, is the king's festival barge." Ëólas pulls a side lever that locks the pole in place and sits down, crossing his legs and resting his hands on his knees.

Random beams of sunlight slide through pockets in the cave ceiling, creating uneven intervals of light and darkness so thick that Adaline can't see her hands. The fact that Ëólas has zero concern about them crashing into the sides of the cave gives her hope that this trip will be much easier than anything they've faced thus far. And, truth be told, not every moment was awful.

Some moments were almost perfect.

Adaline glances at Ëólas and absentmindedly rubs her hand over her chest to loosen her muscles. The soreness from all that walking and lack of sleep has left her limbs stiff, and her chest has felt tighter and tighter each day that passes. She glances at Ëólas, at his droopy posture, and nibbles her bottom lip. She's not the only one struggling.

Despite their most recent escape, she can't help but ask questions. "Why didn't you mention there are fairies in this world before?"

"It's not my place. They choose whom they reveal themselves to."

Huh. And they chose me? Because I was singing? Yeah, that sounds like fairy logic. Adaline smiles to herself, careful to make sure Ëólas doesn't see and think she's unaffected by his illness. Which seems to be getting worse. Which he's not fessing up to.

"What's wrong?" When he doesn't answer, Adaline scooches her bottom closer to him until their knees touch. The heaviness of her fears reduces her voice to a whisper. "Please, tell me what's wrong. How can I help?" Hesitantly, she wraps her fingers around his hands.

He opens his eyes but needs a moment for his pupils to focus on her. "Elves, we're a part of nature. We need the flora and fauna as much as they need us. The caves," he pauses and takes a deep breath, "being cut off from nature makes us sick."

"I won't tell anyone."

The corners of his mouth twitch upward. "I know."

Adaline squeezes his hands.

"Can you distract me?" Shutting his eyes again, he curls his fingers under hers. "I can feel us getting closer to land, and my nausea is dissipating. But I'd rather think about something else."

"Um." Adaline wracks her brain for something that might possibly entertain him. She stares at their linked hands, and her mind numbs.

"What was that song, about the light that shines upon you?" Ëólas asks.

"Oh, 'Let It Be.'"

"Mmm. It's a nice song."

"My father and I used to sing a lot of Beatles songs together. That's one of the best, but my favorite is 'Imagine.'"

"May I hear it?"

"Oh, uh, yeah."

She's sung that song a million times in the shower, while cooking dinner, and walking from her office to class. Not once did she reconsider belting out the lyrics. But here, in front of Ëólas, her voice hardly reaches above a whisper. Still, the cave's acoustics boost her range, not permitting her to hide. As she sings about a world with no countries and no borders, a soft smile takes over his face, and his hands hold hers more tightly. He exhales and seems to release the weight he's been carrying around since they met back up again, so she sings louder. She cuts loose her fears and lets the water carry her along, and the tension leaves both of them. He looks younger, lighter, wistful even. By the time she's done, the cave echoes the last line about people someday being able to live as one, and sadness touches Ëólas's face again.

"I can see why you love that so," he says.

Adaline lowers her head, not sure how to respond. But focusing on the song helps her to lighten the mood, to not dwell on whether Áranol and his Morgai will crush Ëólas's dreams. "My father bought me my first guitar, uh, mandolin, when I was nine. He was tired of me stealing his. That's the first song I learned to play."

"Birthdays. Birthdays are fun." He still doesn't open his eyes.

"When's yours?"

"Oh, we don't celebrate every year. That'd become quite boring soon enough. We initially celebrate every five years until we reach maturity, between thirty and fifty years. Depends on the elf. Then we celebrate every decade. After we reach five hundred, we pretty much celebrate every century. But collectively, we have a grand summer festival every year."

Adaline nods to herself. "So, the big two hundred's coming up for you. Know what you want already? You have fifteen years to plan."

With a chuckle, Ëólas opens his eyes and inhales deeply. His voice is thick with longing. "I hope to travel the world. Safely. We're not meant to be locked into single territories. We're supposed to be able to roam the earth. Otherwise, well, life can get a bit boring. We're natural explorers; traveling calls to us."

Just like me.

"How about you? When's your next birthday?"

"Oh, it's a few months away. Well, a couple now, I suppose."

"And what do you want?"

His thumb moves ever so slightly across the back of her hand, creating an electrical pulse that races over her skin, across her palms, up her arms, and into her chest, overtaking her. Once again, her palms turn clammy. His golden eyes draw her in, tugging her further away from all the buts and what ifs. She parts her lips and starts to speak, only to seal her mouth shut and trap the words inside her throat, words that would embarrass her, words that would repulse him, words that would destroy the friendship they've built.

She gulps and tugs a hand free just as the cave swallows them again. When the light returns, Ëólas releases her other hand.

"You're looking less pale. Maybe some food would do you good. Where's the—oh no!" Adaline glances around the raft and sees nothing but themselves.

"I didn't have time to backtrack. We'll be okay though. We're getting closer to greenery."

So that's what's making him feel better. Thank goodness he'll be okay. "We really do owe His Majesty." Adaline waits for the next beam of light to ask, "What did the king say, when we were leaving, when you gave him your word?"

"He told me to make certain you remained safe."

"Really?" Adaline tilts her head sideways. "That was sweet of him. A berry's that valuable?"

Turning his hands over, Ëólas stares at his empty palms. "He didn't value the berry itself. He valued what it symbolized."

Thrust into darkness again, Adaline stares at the spot where his hands might be. When a few, thin rays of sunlight return, they both glance around at the raft, the cave walls, and the river until they settle into a comfortable silence and while away the hours, grateful for a chance to rest not only their limbs but also their minds. Adaline, for once, allows her mind to remain empty while she lets her shoulder rest. In her mind, she imagines herself in front of the drum kit, playing through the beats and singing the lyrics of various songs so she won't forget them.

As the beams of sunlight fade into the night, she decides to restart their conversation and prays she's about to make him laugh, not horribly offend him. "You know, we have stories about elves where I come from."

"Dare I ask?" He arches a brow, but his cheeks have a pink sheen to them, like he's coming alive again, becoming himself.

"Well, some think elves are only knee high, live in perpetual winter, and help deliver presents to good little girls and boys all over the world one day a year."

He looks at her like she's lost her mind, like any moment she might turn into a sprite and reveal the extent of her tomfoolery. "You jest."

Adaline fidgets with the side of her cloak, trying to hide the extent of her amusement. "Sorry. But what's worse? That, or elves who live in trees and bake us cookies all day long?"

Sliding his hands behind him, Ëólas leans backward and scoffs. "So, in all of these ridiculous scenarios, we basically tend to the needs of humans?"

Adaline purses her lips into an O-shape and squishes it to the side. "More like fulfill dreams."

"I'm not opposed to fulfilling dreams, but of cookies and presents?"

"Yeah." Adaline can't help but chuckle.

Thankfully, Ëólas does too. "I'm not sure why I'm setting myself up like this, but what else can you tell me about your world?"

"What do you want to know?"

"Your mother. You don't mention her."

"It's hard to miss something I don't remember."

"You said that before. But I wonder, forgive me, if she might have anything to do with your nightmares?" He waits patiently, but when she doesn't respond, he tries again. "What are they about?"

They're picking up speed now with the river sloped more downward, and the water has become choppier. The currents will most likely be worse once they exit the cave, especially if it spits them out further from Aerytol and closer to the ocean.

Adaline folds her hands in her lap and plays with the hem of her skirt, flicking off dirt scabs that molded to the fabric. Her dress is more dingy than blue. "My, my mother died in a fire. I don't remember much, but I tend to dream about fire. A lot. Right now, it's torches and people chasing me. Sometimes it's…" *the guard who took me or the lieutenant. Elves.* "I don't know. It doesn't matter."

But speaking about her dreams aloud reignites her memories. The longer she stares at the shadows across her lap, the quicker the world fades from view. The flames flicker in her eyes. A woman screams, and—

Adaline shrugs. "It's fine. It's hard to miss something I don't remember."

Ëólas looks at her longer than she likes, so she swings her legs sideways and dips her hand into the river, wishing she could dunk her whole body in it—for only a brief second and with a one-hundred-percent guarantee that she'd come out safely—so she could take an overdue bath. If the raft's magical, maybe she could get away with that. A bonus gift from the little king.

"Could you actually understand him, the king?" Adaline asks, not looking at Ëólas. Not yet.

"Of course. Elves and faeries have more in common than we do with humans." His curt tone catches her off guard.

"Oh." *Did she offend him about the Keebler Elves? No, his laugh was genuine then, so what upset him? Does, does he suspect whom I dream about?*

Adaline glances up at him, waiting for him to say something else, something that will make his words sting a little less, something that will bridge the gap that's suddenly reappeared, that snuck in between the light and dark patches, that first resurfaced when he came back from fighting his own people. But he doesn't say anything. He goes back to closing his eyes and remains oblivious to her, lost in his own world while he meditates or ruminates or continues whatever he's doing that has shut her out.

"Well, he was very sweet," she whispers, hoping her words reach him and nudge him out of this funk again. Anger, she can handle. Comfortable silence doesn't bother her either. But seeing him like this, indifferent, it's like someone's squeezing her windpipe. "They all were. Seeing bluecaps, or fairies, was like something out of a dream." Hugging her legs to her chest, she taps her chin on her knees. "This world is magical," she mumbles.

He cocks an eyebrow. "We've been on the run for almost six days now, and you're going on about faeries?"

"They may be ordinary to you, but they're everything I dreamed of as a child. I used to draw pictures of fairies and write my own stories too, especially about one named Lee-Lee. My grandmother loved reading about them."

"Of course you did." His tone is off. Edgier. The melody gone.

"I didn't mean to offend."

"I know. I didn't mean..." Not looking back at her, he exhales sharply. "You shouldn't get too attached, Adaline. You don't belong here."

What? Where the fuck did that come from? I know, I mean, I can only imagine what he went through in those caves, but is that how this is going to be from now on? As long as neither of us are in danger, then good riddance?

Adaline crushes the pressure point between her thumb and finger. The sharp, endless pain draws all of her attention to that single spot so she has zero chance to feel anything anywhere else. She bites her lip and wills herself not to scream at him.

He's not himself, fucking moron.

How could he not realize how much she's come to care about h—the people in this world? Obviously, they're becoming close friends. What an idiot. Both of them. If only she had something she could throw at him, wake him up from his own stupid, thoughtless words. But her hands are empty, and pulling her cloak out from under her bottom and rolling it into a ball would make her look childish. But she is a child to him. To all of them. She releases her hand and turns her head toward the river, resting her cheek on her knee. She's stuck on the river that had absorbed her emptiness moments ago, and now its cold waters are seeping through the reeds and numbing her.

Fuck him. How could he be so kind one moment and an asshole the next?

The hand that appears on her forearm draws her eyes upward. When she peers into his eyes, those damn golden orbs from which she cannot hide, she curses the tears that have made her eyes glossy.

His gaze softens, as do his words. "Please don't misunderstand me. I only meant that our world doesn't have the right to steal you away from your own."

Somehow, this hurts Adaline even more, but in a different way, a deeper way.

All she can do is nod once at him. He accepts that lone acknowledgement and sits back. As he grabs onto the pole and maneuvers the raft a few inches into the center of the river, which is now wider than an interstate highway, Adaline studies his face. The hard lines have evaporated, but he wears the faint mask of sorrow. Did he regret his earlier word choices, or might he actually be sad that she needs to go home?

Can't be the latter. He's always thought I don't belong here. He made it a point to tell me that from the beginning.

Standing up, Ëólas stares down the barrel of the cave. "We should emerge soon."

From what Adaline remembers of Magnus's map, only a tiny portion of the river that forms the Wastelands' border touches Aerytol. They have a greater chance of winding up in Lameiría. Or Alderton. "What happens if this river dumps us out in Alderton?"

He glances down at her and says calmly, "Then my life will be in your hands."

Shit. "And if we come out near Lameiría?"

"I will see to it that you're treated as a guest. Besides, I already informed my mother about your unique situation, and she's our best resource regarding magic."

Adaline's eyes spring open. *I'm going to meet Ëólas's mom, and I reek! Oh, God help me. But wait, what about the king and queen?*

A knot forms in the pit of Adaline's stomach. Which is worse? Meeting the royal family covered in dried muck and sweat, or meeting Ëólas's parents?

Definitely his parents. Please, let us end up in Alderton.

The moment she issues that prayer, an image of Ëólas bound in the cave with a sword at his throat flashes through her mind, and her heart stops.

I take it back. I can deal with Lameiría. A shady forest sounds like a great change of pace at this point.

Because if one of their lives must be in danger, she knows unequivocally he'll get her out safely. Even if he's a bit of an asshole afterward.

Chapter Twelve

THE RAPIDS

When they approach the threshold to the outside world, the cave unceremoniously spits them out into raging rapids that sweep them along like a piece of paper and propel them downstream as fast as a car. The raft toggles back and forth on all sides yet never spins them around or throws them off. Still, Adaline grips the edge, paying no heed to the reeds digging into her palms. Along the shore, a wall of slender ash gray trees greets them. Their trunks rise so high into the air that Adaline can barely crane her neck back enough to take in their lush boughs that brush the starlight.

Lameiría, here we come.

Fist over fist, Ëólas lifts the pole out of its holder. Like a magic trick, the length keeps going until Ëólas raises the pole over their heads. Both ends extend far over the sides of the raft. Swinging the pole sideways, he plunges it back into the river and pushes with all his might to rip the raft away from the rapids and thrust them toward the shoreline. His balance and strength astound her.

Within minutes, maybe seconds, Ëólas steers the raft into Lameiría's bank, wedging it with a thud along a narrow piece of land that juts into the river. Once they're stationary, he shoves the pole against the back of the raft, deep into the mud, using it as a break. The rushing water wobbles the pole.

"That should hold long enough for us to get off." Ëólas pushes his damp hair away from his brow and stares at Adaline still clinging to the side of the raft.

Water drips off her brow and the tips of her hair. "That was fun."

Ëólas chuckles. "Border patrol must have seen us by now. I'll disembark first so I may explain, but stay close to me. If the raft feels even slightly unstable, jump onto the shore immediately. Understand?"

"Got it."

While Adaline teeters and attempts to stand up, Ëólas strolls forward as if the ground beneath him were solid. He hops off the raft like a squirrel jumping from one limb to the next. To his back, Adaline sticks her tongue out. She takes one step and staggers when the reeds make her feet roll sideways. At the same time, four elves rush out of the woods, two with bows drawn and arrows aimed at Adaline.

Oh shit.

Instinctually, she raises both palms while she sways side to side. Before Ëólas can utter two words, an elf admonishes Ëólas. At least, his tone sounds like a reprimand; Adaline doesn't understand the words themselves. But her brain doesn't have time to process that fact. She's too busy staring at the pointy ends of the arrows, so she doesn't register another elf dodging around Ëólas until the patrol guard kicks the raft away from the bank. As Adaline falls forward onto her hands and face, the pole slips loose and disappears into the water, and the raft launches into the rapids.

Ëólas screams in horror, but he and his voice quickly shrink out of view, even as he races along the shoreline while the river hurls Adaline downstream, toward the ocean. Whatever he's yelling, she can't hear over the rushing water.

For the first few seconds, which feel like hours, Adaline can't move her body, and her thoughts grind to a halt. But she doesn't have time for fear. She doesn't have time to think about what might happen if she reaches the ocean. She doesn't have time to curse the elves who didn't give Ëólas two seconds to explain why she was there. With him. Did they even recognize their commander general?

What the fuck!

No, no. Now's not the time for that.

Adaline pushes herself onto her hands and knees while the raft tilts and wobbles and nearly flips upside down. Like before, the raft at least remains facing in the same direction as she speeds past the trees.

Logic brain. She needs her logic brain now.

If she jumps into the water, the layers of her clothing are too heavy; she won't be able to swim. She unclasps Seira's cloak. As the fabric falls beside her, she rises onto her knees and reaches behind her back for the laces securing her bodice, but the jostling raft causes her to yank only one side and form a knot. Forgetting her top, she reaches underneath her bodice and unbuttons her bottom skirts. Rolling over, she kicks off those layers, leaving her in her underwear and chemise, which is light enough for her to swim in. Before her skirts slide into the river, she pulls her mobile phone out of her pocket and shoves it into her bra. With her hands flat against her bodice, she searches the river for a spot where she can jump close enough to land.

What did her father teach her? Swim with the currents, not against them.

The sudden thought of her father dragged to the bottom of the Potomac River cuts off her air supply. All blood drains from her face, and her hands shake uncontrollably. Water splashes onto the raft, hitting her cheeks and stinging her eyes.

I can't do this. I'm going to drown. I need a miracle.

A miracle.

This world is full of miracles: Coming here in the first place. The tree root that tripped that guard. Ëólas hearing her plea. The cave ceiling falling onto that elf. Those bluecaps giving them this raft. This world is laced with magic, and, for some reason, someone has been watching over her.

Besides, she never feared water before her father's accident. She spent summers in Cindy's pool, floating for hours while listening to music, playing chicken with her siblings, and learning how to dive. At home, she spent evenings staring at the lake behind Nan's house or lounging on the dock and reading a long book. That lake defined her childhood.

Adaline slides to the edge of the raft and places her hand in the river. Closing her eyes, she focuses on the cool sensation as the water glides between her fingers, on the water's strength, on its ability to simultaneously bend and persist.

"Please, I need help. I have promises to keep. People to save. Please, help me get to shore."

Not two seconds later, an enormous wave scoops her up, tilting the raft so rapidly that Adaline screams. As her feet slide downward to the water and her nose hits the reeds, she jumps and grabs hold of the edge. Water sprays her face. Her hair adheres to her cheeks, and she can't see how to balance the raft again. Her fingers cling and stretch, but her grip loosens. When she's about to slide off and plunge into the river, the wave crashes against Lameiría's shore, sending Adaline and the raft sliding to a halt just before they collide with a tree trunk. The reeds, thumping over the forest floor, splinter apart like snapped toothpicks, and Adaline rolls into another tree, her back slamming against the trunk.

She lays there a moment, breathing heavily and staring at the broken raft littering Lameiría's shore. Her sodden chemise clings to her legs, and her hair has collected leaves, mud, and splinters. But she's alive. She's on land. And she's alone. She wiggles her toes first, then pushes herself up to a sitting position. Nothing feels broken. Slowly, she gets onto her feet, bends forward, and pulls at her chemise, releasing the suction to her legs.

Well, I did wish for a bath.

Flinging her hair out of her face, she lifts her head and turns back to the river. "Thank you," she whispers, and another wave sprays upward like a high five. "Dang. Maybe I'm in Narnia."

"You're trespassing in Lameiría," says an icy voice behind her.

Adaline spins around and searches the woods. Night conceals its depth, along with whomever spoke. "I'm sorry." Water dripping down her arms causes her to shiver. "I was traveling with—"

From within the folds of shadow, two elves emerge, one with his sword drawn. The other pulls out an arrow and slides it into the notch of his bow. As Adaline steps backward, her heels sink into the mud, and a third elf appears behind her.

"You have a choice," says the swordsman. "Leave our shore, or face life imprisonment."

She glances at the raft shattered among the trees. "You're serious? You expect me to just jump back into that river?"

"Not our concern," says the archer.

"Look at me? I'm hardly a threat. I'm not even armed. Well, mostly." *Damn it. What was I thinking? Maybe it's better they see that I'm truthful.*

"What do you mean? Show your weapon. Now!"

Pinching her chemise, Adaline draws up the hem, keeping her eyes on the elf with the bow and arrow and making certain that arm muscle of his doesn't twitch.

The first elf lowers his sword, tears at the straps around her calf, and yanks off her sheath. "Why do you have an elven dagger?" He holds the weapon in front of her face. His hard eyes have little room for scenarios he considers impossible.

"It, it was a gift." *This might not go over well.* "From Ëólas. We were traveling together, and—"

The elf behind her knocks her feet out from under her, causing Adaline to fall forward and her face and body to collide with the mud. He steps on her back and hisses, "Don't get up."

The three of them debate with each other, speaking so quietly and uttering words Adaline can't comprehend. Unable to keep lifting her head, she rests her cheek on the ground. The sandy mud squelches in her ear.

Maybe if they take forever to contemplate this situation, Ëólas will arrive and yell at the douchebag standing on her lower back. Unfortunately, they don't seem to ruminate nearly as long as their commander general. The elf does remove his foot but yanks her arm, pulling her up to standing, and shoves her into the woods.

"Wait, where are we going?" she asks, wiping mud off the side of her face. She glances back at the shore, praying she'll spy Ëólas sprinting toward her. But how far had the river taken her from him, and what if he thinks she's lost at sea now? "I need to find Ëól—"

"Lying will make your situation only worse," says the archer.

"But I came here with your commander gen—"

The swordsman spins around, grabs her throat, and shoves her back against a tree. "We receive word that our lord has been missing, and then you turn up on our shore with an elven dagger. You're lucky I don't throw you into the river myself. If we prove you've harmed our lord, I give you my word I'll slit your throat myself."

"I, I'd *never* hurt him."

The swordsman grits his teeth and pulls his shaking hand away from her throat. Based on what she's heard of Lameiría and their view of humans, he would have killed her already if he could do as he pleased. That she hasn't attacked or resisted are the only reasons she's still breathing. She doesn't dare speak again. The rage simmering beneath his eyes reminds her too much of Calvden's. They'd gagged Ëólas, not giving him a chance to speak for himself. She can't possibly hope the elves will give her more leniency.

Quietly, she follows them into the woods, with her cloak and half her dress gone. At least her phone is still wedged between her bra and skin. The swordsman takes the lead. The archer marches beside her, and the stomper takes up the rear. Soon, the leaves crunching under her feet and the crickets' songs are louder than the river's roar.

"Ëólas," she whispers. "Find me." A breeze caresses her cheek and whirls away, into the forest.

The archer glances at her sideways but doesn't say anything. Thankfully, they don't hike far. Once Adaline can no longer hear the river's murmurs, the shadows pull back and reveal the outline of an octagon gazebo, or at least a building with the same shape. As they get closer, the building and its roof grow in size until Adaline's certain it could accommodate at least a hundred people. Smoke rises from the two-tier cupola perched on top. The walls are made of the same ash gray trees surrounding it, and lights from inside peek through closed shutters.

As they approach the front, the double doors swing open. A tall elf with a pointy chin, sharp nose, and hair as black as the night sky descends the stairs and approaches Adaline's guards. Something about him tells Adaline he's old, even though he doesn't look it. His eyes and his demeanor match those of someone who's seen a lot. "Explain."

His willingness to use the Common Tongue surprises Adaline. She arches her eyebrows and peeks up at him, hoping he'll take pity on her sorry state. But he doesn't look at her, doesn't acknowledge her.

"The girl washed ashore, Lord Gerol." The swordsman gestures at Adaline with a nod of his head. Even with their superior in front of him, he still keeps his sword at the ready. With his other hand, he holds up her dagger. "She carried this upon her person and spoke Lord Ëólas's name. How she came to possess this dagger worries me more than anything."

"She said she came here with the commander," the archer adds, his tone hopeful.

The swordsman scowls. "She said no such thing."

"You cut her off."

"They are inherent liars. You can't trust a word of what they say."

"Enough." Lord Gerol waves his hand, and the swordsman steps aside, allowing his lord a better view of Adaline. He eyes her suspiciously, and his nose curls as if he smells a skunk. Without moving closer, he asks in a cool tone, "Where's our lord?"

"Upriver. We were unintentionally separated." *Unintentionally on our end, but I doubt you'll care to know the particulars.*

He ponders her words, mulls them over, and juts out his jaw. "Why were you with him?"

"That's a long, complicated story, but I'm King Magnus's ward, and Ëólas and I have been traveling together for five, six days now. I've lost count."

"Traveling together." He repeats her words as if he's testing them in his own mouth, tasting them for hints of falsehood. His eyes glance at the mud on her face, the stains of blood on her bodice, and her missing skirts. At least he doesn't eye her like a prize cow. "You speak of our lord so informally."

Adaline releases half of a tired laugh. "I tend to do that. He's my friend."

Lord Gerol's nostrils flair twice. Sucking in his cheeks, he turns to the archer. "Search upriver for our lord, and inform him what's transpired." As the archer races back the way they came, Lord Gerol turns to the swordsman. "Bring her inside."

"My lord, ought I not bind her?"

"I admire your desire to keep Lameiría safe, but I don't think her a threat. And *we* are not barbarians. *We* treat our prisoners well, regardless."

A prisoner. Adaline shudders.

With Lord Gerol leading the way, Adaline follows him and the swordsman into the building while Stomper guards her from behind, probably so he has the opportunity to kick her feet out from under her again. Inside, a large, open room welcomes them with a fireplace against the back wall. Doors flanked on either side depict forest scenes carved into the wood. A doe on one door and a stag on the other look across the fireplace, searching for their mate, and the bas-relief carvings appear as though they're emerging from the wood so they can cross the divide and unite. Thin tree trunks stretch upward, their branches curling into the door frames and providing play space for squirrels, birds, and other small animal carvings.

Lord Gerol knocks on the doe's door. "Lanía, we have company."

A lady emerges with white hair that reaches her knees and dim, gray eyes. She takes one look at Adaline, inhales sharply, and looks to Lord Gerol for reassurance. "Why?"

"I'm not sure yet, but the girl won't be here long."

Adaline opens her mouth and almost says *woman* to correct him. But when the swordsman steps aside to side-eye her better, all of Adaline's attention shifts to the long table in the center of the room with bowls of berries, apples, figs, nuts, olives, and mushrooms, as well as a large platter of various, glorious, cheeses. And a mound of sizzling strips of meat. The broken loaves of bread and stacks of plates look like a buffet for passing-through travelers or border patrol.

Adaline's stomach growls so loudly that Lord Gerol stops mid-sentence, and everyone stares at Adaline. She licks her lips and leans forward. Her eyebrows droop, and the sight of several pitchers full of water makes her teary-eyed. What she would give to drink just one pitcher.

"I think it's hungry," the swordsman grumbles.

Adaline glares at him, but not for long. Her eyes quickly drift back to the food.

Lord Gerol sighs. "Lanía, would you please make her a plate?"

Lanía nods once. When she's done selecting a few of each item, she passes the plate to Adaline, her hands shaking the entire time. Adaline wipes her fingers as best she can on her damp chemise and stuffs her mouth. The elves stand back and watch as if observing a wild animal. Right now, she doesn't care what they think.

Every flavor explodes in her mouth, making each ache fade away. Once again, the world is beautiful, and everything will be okay.

"She has no reservations about whether that food might be poisonous?" Stomper asks the other elves.

Adaline hesitates a fraction of a second, shrugs, and pops a sugary sweet date into her mouth. As she's eating her second helping, the elves look away from her and stare at the main door. Adaline wonders what they're searching or waiting for, but not enough to stop eating.

"Can that be?" Lord Gerol crosses the room to open the door.

Before he reaches the handle, the double doors fling open, and Ëólas runs inside.

"My lord!" Lord Gerol says, jumping backward.

All the elves bow their heads, but Ëólas looks past them. His eyes lock onto Adaline, sucking the stem of a mushroom into her mouth, and a smile of relief breaks through his haggard expression. She's never seen him out of breath before, and his rapid breathing makes her wonder if he never stopped running after her.

Setting the plate down on the table, she gives him a small wave while she finishes chewing. "Hungry?" She gestures to the buffet.

Lord Gerol points at Adaline. "My lord, the human—"

Ëólas launches across the room and pulls Adaline into a hug, wrapping his arms around her cold frame and tucking her muddy head under his chin. He holds her for a long moment while she inhales his scent and absorbs his warmth. After all they've seen thus far, she should have been more terrified of these people, his people, but she never doubted they'd be reunited.

"Did you hear me?" she whispers into his chest.

"Yes." He pulls back and kisses her forehead. Tilting his nose downward, he peers into her eyes. "I'm so sorry." His voice breaks, and his eyes turn glossy as he delicately cups her cheek. "How can I ever apologize for what happened? They were overzealous new recruits whom I hadn't met yet. But I can't forgive—"

"Just stop. I'm okay. See, all in one piece." She places her hand on top of his and nuzzles her cheek against his palm. "How about we convince your queen to reconsider how humans are greeted?"

Levity returns to his face, and their worst fears dissolve between them.

"You can propose that topic when you see her next. But first," Ëólas steps back and slides his hand down her arm until his fingers fold around hers, "you need to be tended to properly."

While he addresses his people, issuing orders Adaline doesn't quite register, she observes his clothing and notes that, even though he'd just been holding her, his own clothing has remained pristine throughout their entire journey, aside from the torn sleeve. Not a speck of dirt has touched him, and his hair looks as lush and silky soft as the day she met him. *Magic.* He also doesn't let go of her hand, as if he fears what might happen if he does.

"Lady Lanía, please see to it that Lady Adaline receives proper care. She's my honored guest and is to be treated like royalty."

Adaline baulks. "That's excessive."

"No, it's not," Ëólas says, leaving zero room for argument.

Lord Gerol takes a step forward. "Forgive the interruption, my lord, but the law dictates that we bring the girl before the queen now."

"The lady. And that is exactly where we're heading next. But first, my lady needs attending, and I will not hear otherwise. Bath, more food, a lot of water, and at least a few hours of sleep. We'll set off towards the capital at first light."

His lady? Adaline's heart thumps loudly in her ears.

CHAPTER THIRTEEN

THE FOREST

In the wee hours of the morning, the bed dips near Adaline's torso, and feather-light fingers brush her cheek. "Time to rise," Éólas calls, his voice thick like warm honey. He tucks locks that have fallen over her face behind her ear and strokes his thumb along her brow line.

"Nut-uh." Adaline stretches her arms overhead and hugs her pillow. An actual, fluffy pillow. With silk sheets. And a cozy mattress she could sleep a year on. She doesn't open her eyes.

"I know this journey hasn't been easy, but we can rest properly once we reach the capital." His voice is like a song, a coo, a jazz session meant to coax her onto her feet, but he has the opposite effect.

She buries her face in the pillow and falls into oblivion.

To call her back, his hand trails between her shoulder blades, beneath her curls spilling around her arms, and massages circles into the single-layer nightgown Lanía lent her. Adaline resists. Her desperate need for longer, uninterrupted sleep pulls her back into a half dream that causes her to sigh, or rather moan. Her soft flesh yields under his touch, and her heartbeat speeds awake as his palm travels down her spine. As he heads south, she scoots closer to the headboard, nudging his hand toward her rear. Her bottom would yield to him, let him do whatever he wants, but his hand is already traveling north. When he brushes her cheek again, she slides her hand over his. Their fingers intertwine, and she rolls over, dragging his hand with her and pulling his torso until he's leaning over her. The tips of his long, silky hair prickle her neck.

"Come on now. Or I'll have to take drastic measures." The rasp in his voice tickles Adaline's chin.

Her voice hasn't yet woken up. "Okay. Do your worst."

His breath heats her lips as he draws nearer. She tilts her head backward, just an inch but enough to raise her mouth. When nothing happens, she drifts asleep again, until Ëólas releases her hand and rips the sheets off her bed, flinging them over the edge and dousing her with a blast of cold air. As she gasps, he slides one hand under her back, another under her knees, and jerks her out of bed. Her eyes fly open as she clasps her hands around his neck, and he swings her away from the mattress. Still holding her waist, he drops her legs, and the cold wood bites her bare feet. She yelps and jumps onto his boots.

"Not fun." But she is fully awake now.

"I tried the gentle approach first."

Adaline scrunches her nose. "I liked that method better."

"But it didn't work. Come on now. Lanía has a dress for you. Will I see you outside in a few minutes, or will I need to come fetch you again?"

"Fetch me? No, thanks. I'm good. And how fast depends on how many layers this gown has."

With a chuckle, Ëólas exits the room, but his lively personality lingers like the fire crackling in the hearth. Within the few hours they've both been on Lameiría's soil, he's seemed more comfortable. Freer. Is that because he doesn't have to be on constant alert here, among his own people?

Adaline wills herself to stop dawdling. Getting dressed on her own proves easy enough, given the dress doesn't have many layers at all. Forget borrowed underwear, thank goodness. Lanía provided a simple chemise with thin straps as the only undergarment, but that first layer hugs her breasts close to her chest. The dress itself is a cream-white satin gown with inch-wide straps and a sheer, lace-embroidered muslin overlay. The delicate sleeves taper at the elbow, widening so greatly that the underside cascades to the ground. The hem reaches past her toes, but the rest of the bridal-like gown lays softly upon her skin, showing off every curve of her dancer's frame until just below her bottom where the layers drape freely. Even the low, square neckline hugs her breasts firmly, along with a ribbon beneath her chest that she ties behind her back, albeit a tad lopsided. To her relief, a pocket allows her to stash her phone. Overall, the dress makes Adaline spin around twice and roll her eyes that she could get caught up in her appearance when they're fighting to get ahead of Āranol's army.

Quickly, she combs her hair with her fingers and stares at her reflection long enough to note that the neutral dress enhances her dark curls, pink lips, and green eyes. She takes a page out of an Austen novel and pinches her cheeks to add a bit of color there too. Lifting her hem, she slips her feet into Lanía's shoes, which crush Adaline's toes.

In the main living space, she sits down at a small table already laid out with hot herbal tea; a fresh mushroom and cheese omelet; a bowl of berries; and two rolls of warm, fluffy, buttery bread. When her plate's empty, she steps outside the cabin Lord Gerol set them up in late last night. She had no clue when she first arrived how many more of those gazebo-like buildings surrounded the main one.

The guards, soldiers, or patrol, whatever they technically are, stare at her as she walks toward Ëólas, who's stroking a horse's mane while whispering in its ear. When Lord Gerol clears his throat, Ëólas looks up toward their cabin, and his eyes find her immediately. His good-morning smile freezes on his face, and his eyes widen. He blinks a few times and beams as she strolls over.

Adaline, carrying a bunch of her dress in her hands so not to trip, avoids looking at anyone else. Still, she fidgets with the layers. She must look ridiculous—a human dressed as an elf. Turning away from Ëólas's grin, she places her hand next to his and strokes the golden-brown horse too. "How do you have a horse in a forest?"

"We have roads," he says. "And the horses visit from Aerytol."

"Huh." Adaline side-eyes Ëólas, who watches her every move. "What?"

He rests a hand on her arm, drawing her attention away from the horse. "Lameiría suits you."

Her brain can't form words, so she turns back to the horse and lets her hair fall forward to hide her expression. She feels like she won a free cruise, only she keeps reading the fine print to find the part where she doesn't qualify.

Lord Gerol, however, distracts her from overthinking when he asks a second horse to stand next to the first, drawing both Ëólas and Adaline's attention. While Lord Gerol speaks, his eyes focus solely on his commander general, as if Adaline doesn't exist. "My lord, are you certain you won't allow me to assign you an escort? I have several volunteers ready, and—"

The bored look on Ëólas's face leads Lord Gerol to close his mouth. "I know my way around my own home, thank you."

Ëólas doesn't bother to comment on Lord Gerol's true concerns, but Adaline knows what they are. The elves in this clearing have been taking turns watching her, peeking up from their tasks and shuffling closer so that anyone might jump to Ëólas's defense at a moment's notice. Their constant alert reminds her every second that she isn't welcome, that she doesn't belong here, despite Ëólas's earlier compliment. She should appease them all by announcing that her goal is to leave Lameiría as quickly as possible, one way or another. After all, Ëólas said Lameiría has a sacred circle. She's closer to going home now than ever.

Adaline rubs her neck up and down as if to free her airways and tries to ignore the several eyes following her.

Turning his back on his people, Ëólas brushes Adaline's hair behind her shoulder so she faces him. "In about six to eight days, Āranol will reach Aerytol's border. Once they do, the Morgai will ditch the horses and speed up. In all, I estimate they'll reach the city within ten to twelve days."

Adaline nods her head slowly while she processes this information. "Once we reach the capital, how long will it take us to reach New Leira?"

"Elves only, with little rest? Four days."

Of course he's considered that option. "And with me?"

He pauses but answers truthfully. "Six."

"Shit, Ëólas. We don't have time to detour to the capital."

"We do. If we ride all day. Without stopping."

"How's that possible?"

"I sent messages last night so we'll have horses waiting for us along our route. But for us to go so quickly, I'm afraid that means the journey won't be pleasant."

Adaline nibbles her bottom lip while she thinks. *Six days to New Leira. Two or three days for Ëólas to finally sleep. And one day to get our ass to the capital. That's ten days. We're cutting it close.* "Tell me you sent word to Magnus too?"

"Of course. I dispatched his bird first. He and Merith are to start making preparations immediately. I just didn't specify the identity of our enemy. I thought that information would be best coming from you and me directly."

Together. So he doesn't mean to leave me behind. Even though I'm slowing him down. Again.

Adaline nods. "We'll do what we have to."

She gazes at the large, unsaddled beast that appears a few inches taller than a Clydesdale. The top of her head reaches the middle of its shoulder, and that one muscle is larger than Adaline's whole head. Despite being in this world for almost a month, she still hasn't learned how to ride a horse. A normal-sized horse. Now they need this beautiful giant's help, and once again Adaline's the dead weight, just like in the Wastelands when Ëólas had to carry her all those times. She'll never measure up to him. Never be good enough.

Whatever. If she has to ride this horse, so be it. Now's not the time for a pity party. "Am I riding this one?"

Ëólas chuckles. "When did you learn to ride?"

Shoving her fists onto her hips, she scowls at him and snaps, "I guess when I learned how to ride you."

The moment the words exit her mouth, she wishes time would stop. Actually, she'd rather rewind time and erase that entire exchange. But it's too late. Her words hang in the air for everyone to form their own visualizations. She can feel all the elves' eyes on her, the disgust on their faces, and the gag caught in their throats. Lord Gerol grimaces as if someone told him a foul joke that broke every rule of propriety he wrote himself.

She wills herself to ignore them all; their opinions of her don't matter. Usually, she would believe that, but knowing that these people, Ëólas's people, think poorly of her twists her gut and burrows under her skin like an infestation.

Her face turns crimson. "That, that didn't come out the, the way I meant." *Can I just mount this horse and get the hell out of here?*

When she peeks up at Ёólas, his eyebrows stretch upward, but not a speck of disgust mars his grin. "No, it most certainly didn't." Each word hints at a chuckle buried beneath it, which makes Adaline smile and shove his arm. Ёólas uses every muscle on his face to force his ballooned cheeks to deflate and his quaking jaw to stay shut so he doesn't release a howl of laughter. Both of them ignore another nearby elf who flinches that a human would dare touch his lord so informally.

Turning away from her, Ёólas places his hands on the first horse's back, pushes down while jumping up at the same time, and swings one leg across. His movements are fluid and effortless as if he just opened a car door and sat down.

"Come on, Adaline." Leaning down, he hooks his arm across her torso and hoists her onto the horse like carry-on luggage. With her side pressed against his chest, he reaches around her torso, grabs the horse's mane, and kicks his heels. "Make sure you don't kick him too, or he'll think we want to go faster."

Without any further goodbye, they leave behind Lord Gerol, and the extra horse gallops away to do as he pleases.

The ride isn't easy, especially when she's stuck sitting side saddle—without a saddle. Riding bareback and clinging to Ёólas's arm aren't the worst parts though; it's praying she doesn't slip off and get trampled to death while the horse bounces her rump in the air every other second. "Why bareback?"

"Saddles aren't necessary, aren't natural. We also communicate with horses better without one."

"Why use them in New—the Neutral Territory?"

"New Leira?" His smile helps her to relax or remember that he knows what he's doing. Maybe both. "We use them in the city because it's expected. As I said, we don't like drawing attention to how different we are."

"From humans." *From me.*

"Mmm. Now, riding lessons. Take hold of the mane." Ёólas lets go as Adaline twists sideways, pressing her back against him, and places her hands where his had been, her hands shaking the entire time. "Balance is paramount." He moves his hands to her hips and pushes on them, maneuvers her, so she rides in time with the horse. "You have excellent balance, so I have confidence in you, but let me know if you ever feel unsure."

"I, I don't like sitting sideways. Can I face forward?"

"Of course. I can ask for a pair of trousers at the next stop."

"No, that's okay. I can't stomach the idea of wearing someone else's trousers when I don't have my own undergarments on." *Oops. TMI? Nah.* "I've got this." Shaking off her embarrassment, she pulls her dress past her knees and lifts one calf, only to pause and clench her thighs together. "Um, is there anyone up ahead? Who might see me?"

"Huh?" Ëólas's cheeks turn rosy, probably from shock at her impropriety, as his eyes drift over her bare legs and upper thigh. He peels his eyes away from her to look ahead and scan the forest. When he focuses on a tree far ahead, he squints and mouths something. When he nods and sits up straighter, he says, "You're good."

"You're sure?"

"Mmm."

Adaline lets go of the mane long enough to swing one leg over the horse's head while Ëólas firmly holds her hips in place. Thankfully, the dress, tight around her bum, acts as undergarments, and her leg hair has always been so fine and sparse that she isn't embarrassed about exposing her legs, even if women most likely don't shave in this world. Now that she can face forward, she scoots her bottom again to find a more comfortable position. When her bottom cheeks graze Ëólas, his member perks up, poking her rear, and he quickly slides backward.

Oops.

She squeezes her thigh muscles to lock herself in place and not risk doing that again. Then she laughs at herself, at the absurdity of her reaction, at the assumption that he had responded to her touch. The first day they met, Ëólas made sure she knew that an elf would never be intimate with a human, and she's never forgotten the revulsion on his face when she brought up the topic. She's better off not thinking about today's non-incident again, even if she's stuck on a horse with him all day. With his chest pressed against her back. And her ass bouncing up and down. And his arms skating along her waist. And his face hovering over her shoulder. Yep, completely forgotten already. Easy peasy.

Thankfully, a few hours of her inner thighs and rump smacking against the horse drive away her concerns. Her lower spine throbs so loudly that her brain doesn't have room for self-doubt.

Breaking through her discomfort, Ëólas moves his lips closer to her ear. "Would you take the lead for a while?"

She gnashes her teeth but takes hold of the mane. She will do her part, damn it, until she collapses. As she directs the horse, Ëólas steadies her hips once again. He removes one hand only to massage her lower back, digging his knuckles into and along her spine, causing her breath to quicken, making her eyes roll back in her head. His touch, the pressure, forces her muscles to unlock, pop, and absorb the constant shock of impact. When he's done, he glides his arms around her torso, and she melts into him as if she's lying on that soft mattress again. While he directs the horse, he rests his chin on her shoulder, placing his lips near her ear, and tells her story about The Great Stag, the true king of Lameiría who permits the elves to inhabit his forest.

She can never stay mad at him.

Shifting between walking, trotting, and cantering, they make their way through the forest with trees growing so high that they look like the evening sky set on fire with shades of red. They encompass a whole world unto themselves. The air around these ancient trees feels thick with wisdom. The shade they provide keeps the forest cool, yet the boughs seem to move aside for the daylight, allowing slanted beams to warm the people below. Every now and again, Adaline spies a doe or fox, and the birds chat all day, as do Adaline and Ëólas.

They pass flowers with petals larger than Adaline's face and colors so vibrant she swears they were painted neon, and Ëólas humors her every ooh and aah, explaining which berries are eatable and which taste like the floor mats in the training grounds.

The tree trunks themselves grow thicker the closer they get to the capital, with trunks wider and taller than city skyscrapers. When they switch horses for lunch, they slow to a stroll so Adaline can eat without her food flying off her lap. They spend the rest of their journey conversing about the ordinary, everyday comings and goings that fill their life and hold little value to anyone else but fascinate each other.

The roar of cascading water pulls Adaline away from Ëólas's story about the first keepsake box he crafted with his father's help and the few opportunities he's had to indulge in his love of carpentry. With a kick of his heels, he spurs the horse into a gallop for a few miles, only for them to slow to a walk. Along the road, the rim of a crystal-clear lake reflects a halo of trees. Sunlight paints a gold road through the center that disappears beyond Adaline's line of sight. When the wind blows, the ripples blend the sky into brushstrokes of blue, pink, and violet.

Another long block of trees shuts the door to Adaline's view. But the sound of gushing water grows louder. She peers ahead, leaning forward and trusting Ëólas to hold her more securely, until they reach another gap within the trees. Several hundred feet away, a green mountain rises to meet the setting sun. From its summit, water plummets onto five tiers of staggered platform rocks, creating a Zen waterfall that would put Iguazu Falls to shame.

As Ëólas eases the horse to stop, Adaline fights the urge to jump off the horse and cannon ball dive into that lake. "I want to swim in that."

"Next time." The words roll off his tongue so easily, as if he invited his human friends over for lunch on a daily basis, as if they wouldn't be imprisoned for life, or as if he knows they will but at least he'll show them a good time. Adaline doesn't know whether his consideration should scare or comfort her.

Too many what ifs have plagued her this past month. She'd rather think only about now. Because that's all they really have, right now, before she must face the queen, before the war, before she goes home.

Carpe diem. "Oh, come on. Twenty minutes? The cold water would feel great on my muscles, and we'd be on our way in no time. I mean, people have to pay thousands of dollars where I come from to vacation in a spot like this." The fact that he doesn't respond right away leads her to believe she might have a chance here.

He opens his mouth, closes it, then opens it again. "I don't think that dress is meant for swimming."

"I'll take it off." She glances back at him and arches a challenging eyebrow. *Huh. That's funny. When it's just us, I don't feel embarrassed.*

Ëólas glances at the lake, and their pace slows to an amble. He tilts his head sideways, and a smirk slides into place, the gleam in his eye calling her bluff. "You jest."

"You know I'm a terrible liar. Oh, come on. Just a few moments of fun?" When he doesn't show any hint of disgust at the idea, she waggles her eyebrows and pulls one corner of her mouth up, making her mischievousness visible.

After one last look at the lake, Ëólas releases a slow breath that gives the commander general time to resurface, but a glimmer of his playful side lingers in his amused expression. "Let's reach the capital, and I'll consider other ways to entertain you during your stay here."

Adaline laughs aloud and faces forward, but her pulse races with the horse's canter. Leaning against him, she turns her cheek toward his and lightheartedly grumbles, "Fine. I get it. You're no fun."

"Oh, I'm fun. I assure you." He scoots closer to her, holding her tight while guiding their steed. "But now isn't the right time for us to engage in activities such as this. If you'll permit me though, I'll make it up to you. I promise." His lips brush the side of her cheek, and the flush around her neck spreads to her arms and chest.

Oh my god! Is he flirting? No, he's not. He can't be. Is he? No. Nope. No way. I'm reading too much into this.

Exhaling a puff of laughter, Adaline allows herself to rest against his sturdy frame, trusting that if he were uncomfortable, he wouldn't hesitate to correct her posture. Instead, he sits up straighter, and his chin nuzzles her temple while she sinks into him. With neither attempting small talk, the trees racing beside them count down the few hours remaining when she and Ëólas can be alone, when they have only each other to lean on, when they have a reason to spend every moment together. Soon enough, the sound of the waterfall fades into a memory, and they speed up into a gallop.

They ride in silence, a silence that feels as comfortable as a Friday night spent curled up on the sofa, tucked under a wool throw blanket, reading a good book, and sipping a hot cup of tea.

When did we become so familiar with each other?

She can't think of anything she might say that would offend him. Their teamwork has been effortless, even when Ëólas has to compensate for her shortcomings. They seem to drift together these days, always walking in step or holding onto an elbow, a back, or even a hand. And he's so damn reliable and considerate too, like making sure she ate a full lunch today while massaging her back so her muscles recover from this journey faster. Or the way he reads her, knowing when to ask questions and when to back off, to give her time to reveal pieces of herself at her own pace. He didn't even ask her about the raft, opting instead to give her time to feel safe in his home.

"Ëólas?"

"Mmm." He moves his lips close to her ear, his breath near her cheek.

"You didn't ask about the raft."

"Do you want to tell me? How you managed to reach the shore?"

She twists sideways to peer into his eyes, to make sure he won't think her crazy. "I, I asked for help, and a wave sort of pushed me that way."

He searches her eyes in return with an expression that seems thoughtful, careful, maybe even hesitant. "Has that happened before?"

She nods slowly. "A tree. The cave itself. And the wind."

His gaze intensifies as he stares not at but through her. She faces forward and waits, but whatever he's ruminating over, he doesn't share. Not yet. He needs time, or maybe his queen's permission. Whatever the reason, she trusts him. She just has to be patient a little longer. Wherever this journey has been leading them, they're much closer now, closer to discovering something that might change the course of this story. This feeling has been growing stronger, ever since they left that disgusting lieutenant and Feídra né Morna, but she still can't pinpoint the source. It's like her inner compass is spinning out of control, round and round in circles, as if something is interfering with her ability to find due north. Unless she's already standing on top of it.

By the time Adaline can't discern tree from shadow and she's convinced they're about to canter into a tree, they come to a stop and dismount. When her feet touch the ground, Ëólas lets go of her waist. A cool breeze rattles the leaves, and Adaline shivers so violently that her teeth chatter. Before the wind ceases, Ëólas drapes his navy-blue cloak around her shoulders, shutting out the cold air and leaving her with a layer of his warmth. As he fastens the clasp at her neck, he stares at her longer than necessary, his fingertips lingering on the clasp as if he's waiting to see if she'll tear the cloth off and toss his cloak in his face again. She pulls the garment tighter around her arms.

Accepting that signal, he wraps his hand around hers, says goodbye to their last horse, and leads her into the woods. "We enter the capital on foot. Are you ready?"

Adaline inhales deeply and pushes her shoulders back. "Yep. Let's do this."

They walk not even thirty feet before ten guards emerge from the shadows and surround them. Again, all drawn bows and swords point at Adaline.

Chapter Fourteen

A MEETING

Ëólas steps in front of Adaline and tucks her behind his arm. As the guards approach and seem to recognize Ëólas, all but one lower their weapons. The elf who opts to keep his sword at the ready nods at the others to halt, and they do. Despite their leader's height and confidence, his shoulders sag with a perpetual heaviness to them. The sharp angles of his diamond-shaped face make him too pretty to touch, and his sky-blue eyes contrast with his mahogany brown hair.

With little room for amusement in his gaze, he stares at Ëólas. "You disappear without a trace, only to reappear a week later back home, and with a human trailing behind you?"

Ëólas, crossing his arms over his chest, cocks his head to the side and says in a flat tone, "I believe my instructions were quite clear, Renor."

The elf glances from Adaline to Ëólas. "The queen is not amused."

"I am not aiming for amusement. I'm waiting for compliance."

Ëólas, be careful. I don't need you imprisoned with me.

Grinding his jaw, Renor shoves his sword back into the sheath but still won't look Adaline in the eyes. "We'll escort you the rest of the way, my lord." He steps back, as do the others who divide in half to allow Ëólas and Adaline to pass.

Ëólas offers his elbow, which Adaline accepts. That simple touch reestablishes their link, and Adaline remembers to stand tall, keep her head high, and pretend like she's fearless. They continue into the woods.

Several feet ahead and in the middle of nowhere, two maple-brown tree trunks stand like sentinels as they flank both sides of the entrance to a bridge or boardwalk that curves upward until its path disappears out of sight.

Ëólas pauses in front of the bridge and turns to Adaline, making certain he has her attention. "This is the entrance to Gladríen, my home and the heart of this forest." He doesn't hide his pride, and she doesn't blame him for it. If they didn't have to worry about the queen's reaction to Adaline's presence and their revelations in Feídra né Morna, Ëólas might almost be giddy with anticipation to show off his home.

Adaline pats his arm, picks up her hem again, and tugs him forward. His grin lights the path forward, which curves through the trees at such a gradual slope that their march toward judgement feels more like a pleasant evening stroll. As they ascend higher, orbs of golden light hang from higher limbs just out of reach. When they near one hanging lower, Adaline hurries in front of Ëólas and squints into the orb. A small flame flickers in the center of a tea light. That's it—a dangling tea light. But the flame glows brighter than a one-hundred-watt bulb, and its rays appear condensed or restrained to an invisible sphere that could fit in both of Adaline's palms.

"Enchantment?" she asks.

He nods, and they continue.

She waits for the smooth, golden-brown teak planks to tug at her hem dragging behind her, but the planks never do. She and the dress glide onward. With her free hand, she trails her palm over the thin yet sturdy wrought iron railing with its fine balustrade of branches curving in wide, elegant loops capped with gold leaves. Although light and dainty in appearance, the railing doesn't quiver once under her hand.

When they stroll past another massive tree trunk, thousands of lights twinkling up ahead draw Adaline's attention upward. Holding on tight to Ëólas's arm, she spins around every which way to take them all in, along with the homes, walkways, and stairs connecting the trees and buildings together. The city seemingly floats above them with buildings, streets, and people weaving around and through the trunks, branches, and boughs.

The multitude reminds Adaline of the view from her condo, after the sun has set and the lights of D.C. sprawl out before her window. "Huh. You're a city boy after all."

Ëólas's chuckle adds to the dream-like atmosphere. Its golden-brown structures, combined with the magenta, burnt orange, and gold leaves, trick her into accepting the city's warmth and safety. She could too easily forget why they're here and the laws forbidding humans from entering these woods, let alone this city.

Turning away from the glitter and gold, she focuses on the path ahead. "Ëólas, if, if I can't leave here—"

"That won't happen."

"But if it does—"

"It won't. I have a plan. I've had days to think of every scenario."

She can't argue with that. Is that what he had been doing every moment he was quiet, plotting New Leira's victory and Adaline's escape?

"Don't worry," he repeats, nudging her ribs with his elbow.

"Okay, okay. But what's the queen's name?"

"Right now? Your Majesty."

"Ah, okay. Got it." *At least if I don't know her name, I can't fuck that up and subconsciously address her by her first name.*

By the time they're halfway up, Adaline's breathing more heavily, and Ëólas lifts his hand to make their procession pause. She looks over the railing at the forest floor below, at the homes they passed that are now the size of postage stamps. At this level, the buildings encircle the trunks and curve upward with the walkway, while other buildings rest on limbs as wide as a highway. Wrought iron and gold filigree decorate the sides of homes, outline windows, and make each building appear inviting and cozy. Gladríen's too enchanting to remain scary.

Adaline keeps waiting for Ëólas to point out the direction of his parents' home, but he only whispers occasionally which shops have the best boots, linens, and books. The last one makes Adaline do a double take so she can record the shop's hanging sign above the door and its location next to the elf whittling miniature wooden spoons no larger than a pinky. Adaline furrows her brow but doesn't comment on that hobby.

When they wind their way past the city, the walkway opens up to a vast platform that could hold hundreds of people. On the opposite side of the open space, a cluster of a hundred or so similar buildings, spread over a few boughs and limbs, form what must be Gladríen's palace. The two main floors are surprisingly level with each other, including the cloistered walkways connecting buildings. Moss, vines, and foliage decorate the natural-wood exteriors, dressing the palace in several layers of autumn. The bell-shaped roofs, similar to bird cages, sometimes disappear under foliage or peek through the top of the trees, and several higher towers afford a view of the city. A lone building perched on the tallest limb peers over the entire forest.

Across the length of the platform, boughs of trees form a canopy ceiling, and the platform's railings eventually lead to the palace's towering double doors. When their group comes to a stop at the bottom of three tiers of steps, the doors swing open.

Ëólas moves his palm to the small of Adaline's back, reminding her that she's not alone, that they'll face this together. She takes one sidestep closer to him but lifts her eyes as the queen appears in the doorway. The moon high in the sky illuminates the palace courtyard, just like it did at the ruins when Adaline first arrived in this world a month ago.

With a quick glance at the group gathered before her, the queen descends the stairs, her movements slow and graceful like a principal dancer who's reached the peak of her career. The subtle sequence in her midnight-blue gown makes the form-fitting fabric draped over her body look like a waterfall under the moonlight. A matching sheer cape extends from her capped sleeves, adding an air of severity and elegance to her demeanor. Her long black hair shimmers down both sides of her slender, lean frame, and around her brow, she wears a delicate circlet of silver leaves. As she reaches the last tier, she locks her golden eyes on Ëólas.

Adaline glances from the queen to him. Aside from their similar eye color, they look nothing alike. Adaline exhales silently. *I guess gold eyes aren't rare among elves.*

When the queen speaks, she enunciates her first word with a strong, commanding voice. "*Where* have you been?"

Ëólas removes his hand from Adaline's back and takes a step forward. Left alone, she shivers from the snap of cold. She glances sideways, seeking clues as to whether she should bow or curtsy too. But no one seems to pay her any attention, so she focuses on standing perfectly still and remaining invisible for as long as possible. Which is ridiculous. Given most everyone here hates that she's in their forest.

One problem at a time, Adaline. Deep breath.

Crossing his arm over his chest, Ëólas drops onto one knee and bows his head low. "We were in the Wastelands, Your Majesty, where we discovered a plot to eradicate the Neutral Territory and turn Lameiría and Alderton against each other."

The queen tilts her chin upward. Both musical and fierce, her voice makes Adaline feel equally enthralled and cautious. "And this plot involves the army currently marching towards the Neutral Territory?"

Ëólas nods and rises, but he doesn't rejoin Adaline. Instead, he squares his shoulders and speaks clearly for everyone to hear, including the eavesdroppers from the towers and the other guards who have gathered near the courtyard. "Yes. Given the circumstances, I've instructed all of Lameiría's generals to head here immediately. I request a third of the army come with me and that we set off within three days."

The queen narrows her eyes. "You wish to pull our people into another war. To save your alliance."

Oh shit. Adaline itches to move closer to Ëólas. *Don't overreact, Adaline. He's got this.*

Ëólas doesn't move, and his voice never wavers. "Yes."

"And in the name of this alliance, you've taken it upon yourself to bring another human into Lameiría?"

Double shit. Adaline slows her breath to stop her chest from curling inward. Instead, she elongates her spine and pretends she's backstage, waiting on the side because her performance is next.

Widening his stance, Ëólas clasps his hands in front of himself and leans back. "To be fair, Your Majesty, I didn't actually bring the first two. Rioran snuck in of his own accord, and Magnus is much like his father."

"So he is." A hint of nostalgia tugs the queen's cheek into a half smile, but she releases the memory quickly and looks at Adaline from head to toe with an expression that reveals nothing about her inner thoughts. "None the less, you entered these woods of your own design?"

Adaline exhales slowly. "Yes, Your Majesty."

Ëólas turns back and extends his hand to Adaline. When she slides her palm onto his, he guides her to him and gives her hand a gentle squeeze. "Your Majesty, allow me to introduce you to Lady Adaline, ward of King Magnus, and the woman who saved my life, twice now."

So he does have some memory of Mr. Toad. "You're still in the lead."

"But who's counting."

The queen observes their banter before speaking to Adaline again. "You are aware of our laws, and yet you willingly ventured into my realm. Why?"

Honesty, kindness, and courage. "Because we had no other choice, Your Majesty. The river we took from the Wastelands brought us to your shore. But more than that, what matters most is making certain our friends have everything they need to stop this war from ever reaching the Neutral Territory. If I'm not allowed to leave Lameiría, I can live with that, so long as our friends back home are safe."

"Back home?" The queen sets the full force of her gaze on Adaline, leaving nowhere to hide. Even though the queen appears to be maybe thirty years old, the aura round her can strip everyone bare, knocking down internal barriers and exposing a person's innermost fears, and desires. "You've spent less than a month in the city and yet you call it home."

Adaline gulps but otherwise can't move. Running away isn't a possibility; she'd never be able to face Ëólas again, and the guards would stop her. More than that, she's certain that if she tried, the queen's stare would follow Adaline throughout the rest of this forest until the queen unlocked whatever information or truth she sought from within Adaline.

She may be formidable, but she's still a person. Exhaling her fears, Adaline returns Her Majesty's gaze.

The queen's expression softens a little. "According to our laws, I should have you imprisoned immediately."

Before Adaline can contemplate a reply, Ëólas interjects, pulling the queen's attention back to himself. "As I mentioned in my letters, the situation is rather complicated and extraordinary. But you need not worry about Lady Adaline. She's my personal guest. I take full responsibility for her presence here. If anyone needs to be imprisoned for breaking the law, that would be me. I'll head to my cell at once, Your Majesty, should you deem that necessary."

What? No! That won't help anyone.

As Adaline glares at him, ready to protest, a sly smile slides onto Ëólas's face. He knows the system. Hell, maybe he helped write a good portion of it as the commander general.

"But I do request first that we take this conversation inside where I can better inform you of all that's transpired," he says.

Again, a hint of amusement tugs the corner of the queen's mouth. "The generals are already on their way. When Merith failed to find you after your unexplained disappearance, your king began organizing our army in your stead."

"Ah. My sincerest apologies, Your Majesty. I would have sent word sooner, but I couldn't find a bird in the Wastelands." Ëólas pauses a moment and pushes his jowls outward. The gesture is hardly noticeable, but it's one Adaline's come to know well when he's recalculating his response. "Where is the king?"

"Now that you've returned, he should arrive tomorrow, I hope." The queen stands still for what feels like forever, scrutinizing Adaline's hand still resting in Ëólas's. "But let us continue this conversation inside." Turning away from their party, the queen walks toward the palace doors held open by guards.

As Ëólas takes a step forward, Renor grabs Adaline's arm and yanks her sideways. "You can wait with me."

Before Adaline can blink, Ëólas snatches Renor's wrist and underscores each growled word with an unspoken vow to end him if he doesn't follow orders. "Unhand her."

Looking at Ëólas as if he morphed into another person, Renor clamps his mouth shut. Reluctantly, he loosens his hold on Adaline's arm and looks to his queen for help. Her Majesty halts and glances back, her chiffon cape fluttering in the night breeze, and her eyes fall on Ëólas as he extracts Renor's hand from Adaline.

"Complicated and extraordinary, indeed," the queen repeats. "Renor, you heard your general. The lady is his guest. I have many questions for her myself; therefore, she will join me for tea as well."

Without another word, the queen climbs the stairs and heads inside the palace, leaving Adaline breathless and not sure if she should feel relieved or terrified that she has the chance to go deeper into the heart of Gladríen. Picking up her hem and taking Ëólas's arm, Adaline follows after the queen. She doesn't look back at Renor. She doesn't have to, because she can feel his hatred burrowing into her back.

Chapter Fifteen

NEW POSSIBILITIES

Inside the main building, the large reception room features benches along the walls and a grand staircase in the center. Adaline and Ëólas turn right and walk down a long corridor with several rooms on either side. As they pass a window, Adaline studies the night sky, which shows no sign of dawn. They pass several more rooms and make a bunch of turns, all of which confirm that she has no idea where they're going or how she could escape. Of course Ëólas knows the way, given he works here.

When they near a room with both doors wide open, Ëólas slows his pace, leans toward her, and whispers, "I apologize for the semantics. Duty must come first, but I guarantee my parents are quite forgiving and understanding."

Adaline exhales. *I hope meeting them will be a breeze after this tea-time interrogation.* "I look forward to meeting them after this."

They both pause outside the room. As Ëólas turns to Adaline, he knits his brows together, wrinkling his otherwise pristine forehead, and purses his lips into a question. He starts to speak but stops, then tries again. "You...you do know the queen is my mother, right?"

Everything Adaline thought she knew shatters into a million tiny pieces. She clutches her hands to her chest as if she could collect those pieces and preserve a few, but she only feels emptiness within her grasp. "What!"

"My mother. Lady Élara, the queen, she's my mother."

"N-no. I didn't kn—why would I know that?" Her voice rises ten octaves.

Ëólas lifts his brow as he thinks of the easiest way to explain this. "Well, my role as commander general, it automatically goes to the eldest child to help prepare us to lead and defend our people. It's common knowledge."

"No. No, it's not. Not for me."

"Ah." Ëólas presses his lips into a thin line and nods. "I see your confusion."

"But, but no one ever referred to you as a, a prince." *Even calling him that feels unnatural.*

Stuffing his hands in his pockets, Ëólas rocks back on his heels and scrunches his nose. "Oh, well, we don't really use that title much. Besides, my official role—in New Leira—is as commander general. I don't have much authority as the queen's son. But as the commander general, I'm in charge of our entire army. It's through that role that I was able to convince my queen and king to support my collaboration with Magnus."

That's why he controls half the Neutral Territory and acts like Magnus's equal. How stupid am I that I never even considered him to be more than a general? But he doesn't act like a prince. Not that I would know how a prince should act. But still. I just didn't... I couldn't... I wouldn't...

Her exhaustion must have caught up to her because she's not certain if she's experiencing hunger pains or if the horse ride has led to the cramp in her side. Either way, her muscles clamp down and twist her insides. She grabs her stomach and takes a few steps back from him. From Ëólas. Who is not just a gifted commander general. Not just some guy who's been thrown into her sphere and has taken up every moment of her life. No, he's a prince. A fucking prince. Who will someday be king.

She can see it clearly now, his entire future planned out, the crown he'll wear one day, the responsibility he'll never shirk. The queen he'll need by his side. His one. Someone meant to help him be what this world needs most. Someone equal to him. His entire life is bound to this forest in which Adaline's an unwanted guest. In the grand scheme of his long existence, she's still a speck of dust easily carried away on the wind.

"Hey." Grabbing onto her, Ëólas rubs her forearms up and down. Apparently, he thinks friction can wake her up. "Are you alright?"

"Yes. It's just been a long day." Her voice sounds hollow. Fake. It belongs to a liar.

"It has. I'm sorry. We'll keep this conversation short, and I'll make certain we have a guest room ready for you afterward. I'm sure the queen will understand."

"You mean your mother."

"Well, when we're dealing with official business, it's easier to think of her only as my queen."

Adaline nods. "I get it."

She glances at him, at the worry etched on his face as he holds her up. She rolls her shoulders, forcing him to let go of his hold over her. "So, *Prince* Ëólas, lead the way." She nibbles her lip as she turns toward the room where they left the queen waiting. *I'm always so disrespectful.* "I'm sorry I was so rude to you. I never treated you like royalty."

"Well, to be fair, you've never treated Magnus like a king, now have you?"

They both burst out laughing, rupturing Adaline's swelling concerns. She swats his arm, which he dodges, and he pops his elbow out to his side. As her arm slips through his, an image of them dancing the night Lori was born flashes in her mind. They were finally friends by then, or at least on their way to becoming friends. Even that night, he kept appearing and disappearing in front of her as the music swept them together only to pull them apart again.

Ëólas leads her inside a spacious room with honey-warm walls lit with lanterns. An oblong wrought iron coffee table divides two long sofas in the center of the room. Potted plants, both on the floor and on display tables, bring the outdoors inside and complement the sofa's green and gold brocade fabric. At the back of the room, double glass doors open onto a deck overlooking a private garden bathed in moonlight. Servants prepare tea and place biscuits on the coffee table before leaving.

Queen Élara angles herself on one sofa as Ëólas walks toward her.

"Do you disagree with my orders to the generals?" he asks.

He's not wasting time.

"They are under your command, and I trust you." She gestures at the sofa for him to sit while Adaline hangs back, near the exit.

"But."

"But they do not yet know this enemy you spoke of are elves. No elf has willingly taken the life of another elf. You cannot expect—"

"That's not accurate." He stands tall as ever, unafraid to face this mother, his queen. But his hand twitches beside the hilt of Adaline's sword, still tied to his belt.

Adaline walks forward and places her hand on his arm. "The caves."

He pats her hand, their connection, but faces his queen. "I had no other choice."

Rising from the sofa, Queen Élara walks around the table. As Adaline steps back, the queen cups both of Ëólas's cheeks and peers into his eyes that mirror hers. "My son, do you suffer greatly?"

"No. I stand by my decision."

She stares at him for a long moment, searching for evidence of his well-being. When she drops her hands, her expression shows only a mother's love and the pride she has for her child. "As I said, I trust you. But you will need to help our people understand."

"I know." Ëólas kisses her cheek.

A look passes between them, one Adaline can't guess the origin of, but she senses they're on the same page after all. Tilting her head, the queen sets her sharp eyes on Adaline. "Come here."

Fuck. Can't I just stay in the background? No. Okay, don't curse in front of the queen. And don't call her Élara.

Adaline walks up to the queen and stands next to Ëólas, mentally telling him not to budge from that spot. "Yes, Your Majesty?"

"You must be eager to return home after such a long time away. We have a sacred circle here, nearby. I can speak with the priestess to grant you access. Would you like to head there now?"

"Oh." She glances at Ëólas, who only looks ahead. How she'd love to smack that neutral look off his face. "I, um, I hadn't thought of that as an option. Humans aren't invited."

"True. But you're here now, and, apparently, I owe my son's life to you."

Oh. That's why Ëólas said that earlier. So, that's it? We've reached the end of the road?

After all this time, after all those near-death experiences, after their long trek cross-country, she might be able to step into that circle and, poof, go home. It can't be that easy, can it? To just go back through the rabbit hole. Without ever saying goodbye to Magnus or Seira or the others. Without knowing how this war will end. Without ever seeing—

Adaline looks down at her toes, her hands hidden beneath Ëólas's cloak. When she lifts her face, she doesn't care her eyes have turned glossy from lack of sleep. "I don't have an alibi yet, to explain to the police or my job where I've been. Um, and it's been such a long day; I can't even think straight. And Ëólas needs to rest first too and undo that damn spell." Adaline flinches. *Damn it. Never quite a lady.*

"What spell?" Élara looks at Ëólas as if she just caught her son stealing money from her purse.

Do queens have purses?

"It's just a small spell," he shrugs. "That I learned from Seira. To borrow strength. From future days."

"That's dangerous. Cancel that spell now."

"I'd much rather be in my own bed before doing so, and I need to make sure Adaline's situated first."

Élara glares at her son but sits down, her movements graceful even though she's bunched her face in disapproval. "Fine. Adaline," the queen gestures to the opposite sofa, where Adaline and Ëólas automatically sit down. "How exactly did you come into this world?"

After Adaline retells her first meeting with Ëólas, leaving out the part where he turned into an asshat when he realized she was human, she also recounts, with Ëólas's encouragement, the two attempts on her life. She doesn't mention the magical assistance though, and Ëólas doesn't give her away. "And if that's not enough, while Ëólas and I were talking about wanting to find answers, we went poof again into the Wastelands where we discovered who our enemies are, and we've spent the last week trying to escape."

Ëólas takes over from there, sharing all that's transpired in the Wastelands under Morgán's command and now Ãranol's, as he leads the Morgai. When he's done, he drapes his arm along the back of the sofa and crosses one leg over the other.

"I see." The queen pours herself a cup of tea, drops in an orange-colored sugar-like cube, and stirs her drink, never clanging the teaspoon against the sides of the cup. She takes a sip and rests the cup on the saucer still in her hand. "And Adaline's been at the center of all this?"

Adaline looks to Ëólas, not sure how to tread here.

Leaning forward, he braces his elbows on his knees and nods. "Yes. The first attack occurred the day Adaline arrived, but that must be a coincidence. As for the other attacks, well, she's brought our peoples together in more genuine ways than Magnus or I could have imagined."

Oh. Adaline sits back against the sofa, wishing the cushions would swallow her whole, or let her fall asleep on them. With the nausea in her stomach returning at full force, she grabs a biscuit and admires the crunch as she nibbles. *Oh, that's nice. It has a hint of something extra. Cinnamon. Lovely.*

"Adaline," Queen Élara waits for Adaline to swallow and set down the biscuit, "does your world know about the fae?"

After wiping her mouth with a linen napkin, she places her hands on her lap to hide the crumbs on her dress. She ignores Ëólas's brief smirk. "We consider fae to be a myth."

"Like elves?" Ëólas says, side-eyeing her.

They both press their lips inward to ward off a snicker.

The queen never removes her gaze from the two of them, as if she's taking notes on their familiarity. "The fae serve the Source of all life. After they've done all they can to help build a new world, they leave for the Immortal Realms. Yet every now and again, when the world is at a crossroads, the fae have been known to travel back to this world and help nudge everyone onto the right path. The fae are natural travelers."

"So, you're implying a fae brought me here. To help?" Adaline asks.

Élara nods.

If people suspect she's here to help, that could be why the guard abducted Adaline in the first place, because they don't want her to keep bringing humans and elves together. And if other people think the fae brought her here, that might also explain why her abductor guessed she's from another world. But both of those mean that maybe she shouldn't go home—and that she has twice as many possible enemies, humans and elves alike.

Going home would be safer. But—Adaline jumps up. "Can I have a moment of fresh air, please?"

Without waiting, Adaline walks through the double doors, places her hands on her hips, and tilts her face up to the moon. She never once considered the possibility that maybe she came here for a reason. Not once. The idea that one person could be so important seems impossible to her, even as her brain lists historical figures who turned the tide of whatever situation their people were facing. But history loves heroes. They don't name the everyday people who made those victories happen, and the last thing she wants is to become another Joan of Arc, not only in terms of becoming a leader but also being condemned.

Weaving around a bench and some plants, Adaline grips the railing and peers up at the canopy of leaves surrounding her. The orbs of candlelight, the stars peeking out from between the leaves, and the scent of the queen's fragrance garden stops her hands from shaking. "Breathtaking."

"I'm glad you think so." Ëólas stands beside her, resting his hands on top of the balustrade.

Once more, they're side by side on a balcony. He watches her as she studies the buildings behind and above them, the designs, the layout, the architecture. Spinning around, Adaline takes in the breadth of the palace, most of which tree limbs and leaves conceal from this angle. Again, the enchantment ebbs her fears. She'd much rather enjoy this world.

This is one hell of a treehouse.

Out of nowhere, Ëólas's reaction to her stories during their river cruise pops into Adaline's mind, and humor bubbles up inside her. She covers her mouth to hide her amusement, but it's no use. Her shoulders start shaking as her laughter grows louder.

"What?" he asks.

She locks her lips together, forcing herself to stop, but she can't deflate her cheeks. "You're an elf."

"Yes?"

"And you live in a tree." She bites the inside of her cheek, but not even that helps. She cracks another grin.

"Alright, fine. I do. But not for the sake of baking you cookies all day. Stop laughing." He wags his finger in her face, but his own cheeks expand. They both chuckle so loudly that anyone awake must hear them.

Adaline stops only when she gets a stitch in her side, and she grabs her waist to pinch away the twinge of pain. When she looks inside the tearoom, the queen gracefully retreats from the glass doors, and Élara's sweet smile confuses Adaline most of all.

"I think you have enough to ponder for the time being." Taking her hand, Ëólas guides her back inside. "Mother, I expect to be asleep for two, maybe three, days. Will you—"

"Of course. Adaline will be treated as an honored guest for the duration of her stay in Lameiría. You have my word, Ëólas. No harm will come to her."

Woo-hoo! No life imprisonment.

The queen turns to a servant who had silently entered the room and asks him to show Adaline to her room. When the servant steps out, the queen turns back to Adaline. "I imagine you'd prefer to spend most of the day recovering from your journey. How about the day after you join me and Aiden for dinner?"

"Aiden?"

"My father," Ëólas whispers.

"Oh. Yes. Thank you. That would be lovely. But to be completely honest, Your Majesty, if I am here to help in some capacity, I'd love to discuss the laws regarding humans who enter your woods." Adaline holds her breath as she waits for the queen's reaction.

Élara clasps her hands in front and watches Adaline for an uncomfortably long moment, so much so that Adaline tucks her arms behind her back and wipes her palms on her dress.

Finally, Élara acknowledges Adaline's boldness with a nod. "Very well."

After they bid the queen goodnight, they follow the servant to the guest room. In the hallway, several guards come and go, but none stand at attention like in New Leira.

Reaching her room, Ëólas opens the door but doesn't go inside. "Rest well, Adaline. Sleep away all of tomorrow if necessary. Whatever you need, someone here can fetch it for you, or you can shop at the market. But please, despite your natural inkling to explore, promise me you won't wander Gladríen alone."

"I promise."

"And if you are ready to visit the sacred circle, promise me you'll wait until I'm awake...so that I might be able to say goodbye."

He remembers. She made the same request when she thought he was leaving for Lameiría without her, before the attack on New Leira. She wants to hug him, to hold on to him, to tell him she'll not go near that circle, ever. But that's unrealistic, all of it. She has her home, and he has his. Their time together cannot last.

Unable to speak, she nods her head.

Ëólas stares at her as if he too has more to say. But he instead swallows his thoughts. "Then I'll see you in a few days." He extends his hand and waits for Adaline.

When she places her palm on his, he presses his lips to the back of her hand, making the synapses in her brain crack and snap and fire. She squeezes her legs shut, ignoring the rush of adrenaline that won't let her fall asleep now. Taking her hand back, she rubs the spot where his lips had been. She opens her mouth to say something, but shuts it and goes into her room, not wanting to watch him walk away.

Alone, Adaline walks past the empty sofas in the sitting room and finds in the bedroom a nightgown hanging from the door of a wardrobe. In less than three minutes, she changes her clothes and uses the water closet—*high up in a freaking tree. How the hell do they manage that?* Pulling back the covers, she crawls into bed, a gloriously soft mattress with sheets and pillows and located indoors.

Finally, her body can stop and just be, even with her mind racing a million miles a second.

Chapter Sixteen

THE WAITING

When Adaline blinks herself awake, she's in the same position as when she lost consciousness: on her side with a pillow tucked between her legs. Despite Ëólas's attention to her lower back, that horse ride left her squirming for at least an hour after he said goodnight.

She doesn't move. She should drag her butt out of bed, put on yesterday's dress, and explore a one-hundred-percent authentic elven city. That's what she does. That's who she is. She can't pass up this opportunity to observe not only a foreign culture but also a completely different species. Only, they don't feel like a different species. Besides, her best experiences abroad always involved visiting her international friends' hometowns, so exploring Ëólas's home without him doesn't seem right. Or fun.

Adaline closes her eyes until someone shuts the door to the sitting room. She jerks her head up. The scent of herbs and baked goods wafts into the bedroom and tempts her to dislodge her stiff joints. After laying the nightgown on the bed, she slips on Lanía's dress, which no longer reaches past Adaline's toes.

Someone hemmed this. I guess that's elven room service? Or Ëólas said something.

She reaches for Ëólas's cloak hanging in the wardrobe, but her hand stops before pulling the silky wrap off the hanger. Wearing one has become automatic. But they're not traveling at the moment, and autumn hasn't quite arrived. The weather's not warm enough to warrant her wearing it. Plus, this cloak isn't hers. She can't keep hiding under it, and she can't take it with her when she goes home. She's better off getting used to not having its protection all the time.

Adaline shuts the wardrobe and leans her forehead against the door. She takes a few deep breaths, expelling all the thoughts and feelings that threaten to drown her, and tiptoes out of her room. She glances around and, not seeing anyone, plops into a chair at the dinette table where she stuffs her face with pastries filled with cheese and fruit. To her delight, she washes her late lunch down with fresh juice that's a blueish-purple color and tastes like mango.

When she's done eating, she stares at the silent room that reminds her of a luxury cabin in the woods. The floor-to-ceiling windows show only foliage, and the accommodations are so lush that she'd rather stay in and read than go for a hike. But she doesn't have any of her books here. Hell, she doesn't have anything that's hers here.

Maybe I should go back to bed.

As Adaline pushes in her chair, someone knocks on her door. She glances at her disheveled bed in the other room, pushes her lips to the side, and cracks the door open. "Yes?"

A tall lady with strawberry-blonde hair pulled up in a high ponytail bows her head. She has the slinky figure of a runway model and the lean arms of a female professional weightlifter. "Good day, my lady. My lord asked me to see to your needs while he's recovering."

Adaline swings the door open. "Is Ëólas okay? Did something happen? Did the spell not cancel correctly?"

"He's fine, my lady, and snoring loudly."

Adaline exhales a puff of relief. "Thank goodness. Um, and you are?"

"Sora, my lady."

"Oh. You know, in a language back home, that means sky."

"It means determination here."

"A good name." Adaline steps aside and gestures for Sora to come in. "What exactly did Ëólas mean by my needs?"

"He didn't specify, my lady. He said only that," she clears her throat, "you'd like me."

"Well, that's just awkward and cryptic. I mean, I aim to like most people. Why would he—Whoa! Are you wearing the guard's chest plate? Are you a city guard? Do they have female guards here? Wait, does Lameiría allow ladies in the army?"

Sora's long face and high cheekbones display only amusement as she too glances down at the leather chest plate with its tree-of-life insignia. "Yes, my lady. We do, and I am a member of the queen's guard."

Whoa. I can't believe I didn't notice sooner. Okay, to be fair, I kinda avoided the guards since arriving in Lameiría, especially after my first encounter. "Why haven't I seen any female guards in New—the Neutral Territory?"

"In New Leira?"

Oh, Ëólas. You're too much. "Yes."

"Because humans don't allow women in their armies. Thus, my lord," Sora pauses and rolls her eyes, "didn't think it wise that we go. At least not yet."

"Oh, that's bullshit. I'll talk to him about that. What else did Ëólas say before he fell asleep?"

"That I'd like you, my lady."

Adaline laughs. "He's such a know-it-all."

"Yes. Yes, he is. But he's also good at reading people, especially those whom he's close to."

Adaline pushes her fingertips against each other while her cheeks turn red. "He's, he's a really good friend."

"Indeed. I was stuck training with him for a century."

"You have? With Merith?"

"Merith trained us both."

"Nice. Oh, training! Can we train today? Fólas started teaching me and—"

"My lord left me your sword."

"Sweet!"

Sora looks about the room puzzled, until her eyes fall on Adaline's empty plate. "You mean your meal?"

On their way to a private garden, Adaline eyes the elven market, still lit with hundreds of lanterns to eliminate the shadows that the sunlight can't reach. Her gaze lingers on the bookbinder. Despite Sora encouraging Adaline to take what she needs, she doesn't allow herself to want a new messenger bag or choose her own dress or even select a pair of trousers like Sora's.

Her new friend volunteers information about the city and elven culture, like how elves don't worry about commerce, that they barter or trade or simply give what another needs. Although Adaline takes a few mental notes, she doesn't ask a million questions for more details. Her natural curiosity is nonexistent—until a petite blonde elf runs up to them.

With large, glossy turquoise eyes, the lady clasps her hands over her chest. "Sora, I heard my lord has returned, but the guards won't let me up to see him. I heard you saw him last. Whatever is wrong?"

Jutting her hip out to the side, Sora crosses her arms under her chest and sighs. "He's fine, Floréna. He just needs rest."

"But why won't they let me up? I've never been denied access to his chambers."

Adaline looks away from the blonde and studies the smithy hammering a sheet of metal into oblivion. She certainly has no reason to tell this young lady why Ëólas is unconscious and when he'll wake up. If Floréna were a servant, she'd know already. She couldn't be a guard either. All the female guards Adaline has noticed today don't wear skimpy dresses with slits up the sides to show off their long legs. That neckline wouldn't allow for training either. A breast might pop out any moment. Maybe Floréna's what Kayla, Adaline's lady's maid, would call a lady of pleasure?

Adaline digs her nails into her palms. *No, no. That's not fair or kind. She could be another childhood friend. A cousin even. Or his...* An elbow jab to her waist nudges Adaline out of her ruminations. "I'm sorry, what Sora?"

"Floréna asked if you're human."

"Oh. Yes, I am." Adaline pushes her cheeks into a smile and prays she's not showing too many teeth.

"I see." Bouncing on her toes, Floréna turns to Sora. "Are you bringing her to the prison? I've been once before, a long time ago when my brother showed me around. I was quite curious about his work back then."

"I'm. No. You've got. It's not like that," Adaline says, not sure why she can't form a coherent sentence.

Sora grips the hilt of her sword and looks at Floréna like a parent about to admonish her child with the hope that passersby won't notice. "The lady is a guest, and friend, of our lord."

"Ëólas?" Floréna draws back and touches her hand to her chest as if she's about to gasp. "From that city."

"The Neutral Territory," Adaline says with a flat voice. *She doesn't call him lord.* "Yes, that's where Ëólas and I met."

"Oh." Floréna eyes Adaline suspiciously. Shaking her head, she turns into all sunshine and rainbows. "Our lord is quite hospitable and charitable. I'm glad you've had the chance to benefit from his magnanimity." Her dreamy tone makes Adaline want to choke her, but before Adaline's forced to fake another pleasantry, Floréna scampers off to frolic with her friends.

"Who is she?" Adaline asks.

"Renor's sister. She's convinced that once she turns one hundred next month, our lord will realize she's the one. She's cute but harmless and happy in her own little world."

"You don't like her?"

Sora takes her time to choose her words carefully. "She is young and takes many liberties that Renor allows."

"Ah. Say no more."

Adaline glances back at Floréna once more, pushes aside the sinking feeling in her gut, and charges ahead, only to slam into an elf hurrying past them. Their shoulders bounce off each other, sending Adaline stumbling sideways and the elf onto his back. "Oh my gosh! I'm so sorry. I wasn't look—"

A hand grabs Adaline's shoulder and shoves her downward until her knees smack into the walkway, and she falls forward onto her hands, her palms stinging from the impact. A steel blade appears at her side, extending past her shoulder and tilting toward her neck. The metal glows gold under the light of the lantern hanging overhead.

Adaline shuts down, not moving a muscle as if the slightest shift could propel her onto a path from which there's no return. She didn't hesitate to challenge Calvden. At least they had a common goal, a common enemy. Here, she has zero idea how to appeal to these people, and the one person who believes in her is unconscious.

"What are you doing?" Sora says to the swordsman.

Adaline doesn't need to look up. The bile in Renor's voice gives him away, adding a hiss to his words. "I'm upholding the law. She harmed one of our citizens, which means her life is forfeit."

As the din of the city dulls, Adaline can feel all eyes focusing on her. Despite the people gathering, no one else steps forward to help, to act as a witness, to argue on her behalf. She doesn't blame them though. She does physically embody everything they fear. At least they're not stoning her. Still, a scream bubbles in her throat, along with the words *fucking racist bigot*, but any burst of anger from her will give Renor justification to act swiftly. She closes her eyes and pictures Ëólas, the way he turns off his emotions and conceals what he's thinking, not giving anything away.

"She hasn't refused arrest, and you cannot execute Lord Ëólas's guest." Sora also knows not to bother arguing about what happened. She won't change Renor's judgment that way.

"Our lord is unavailable, which means I'm still the acting commander general."

While Renor and Sora plan their next moves, Adaline holds her breath and clenches her abs to stop herself from shaking. She didn't hear that voice warn her this time, so either Renor's threats are empty, or Adaline's guardian angel is sitting on the sidelines. The tip of Renor's sword hovers closer to Adaline's pinky, and the candlelight the blade reflects shines on the back of her hand. A bead of sweat trickles down her temple.

Can I do it again?

She closes her eyes and shuts out Renor and Sora arguing. She pushes past the discord of their voices and listens for only the crackle and pop of the candlelight illuminating the alcove beside her. "Please, help me."

Sora steps closer to Adaline, but the small, condensed flame flares into a sphere of fire, shattering its enchanted barrier. As Renor jumps backward half a step, the fireball leaps free of the tea light and falls to the walkway beside Adaline, where it flashes brightly—and just as quickly puffs out into a wisp of smoke that vanishes with the wind.

Huh. Not quite what I expected.

Adaline peeks up at the elves, all of whom blink at the spot where the flame had been. A few whispers break the silence.

With his face wearing a permeant scowl, Renor shakes off his confusion and snaps his attention back to Adaline. He crushes his fingers into her arm and yanks her up, onto her feet. "Fine! Imprisonment then. I'll take her there myself."

"If you insist," Sora says. "But make sure you first stop by the palace and explain to the queen why you're locking up her guest."

"She's not here at the queen's behest."

"Oh, she is now. The queen invited Lady Adaline to dinner tomorrow night."

Renor digs his fingernails into Adaline's bicep and pushes her toward Sora. "I'll go speak with the queen myself."

Moving next to Adaline, Sora grins. "Wise choice. I'll stay with Lady Adaline in the meantime."

Glowering at the two of them, Renor huffs loudly and speed walks toward the palace.

With him gone, Sora exhales, takes her hand off the hilt of her sword, and examines Adaline from head to toe. "Are you injured, my lady?"

After dusting off her hands, Adaline hugs her stomach. "No. I'm okay, thanks. I wish I could say I'm surprised, but I met him last night. I knew then he already hates me."

"Not *you*, my lady." Sora gestures that they keep walking, away from Floréna and everyone else attempting not to stare anymore. "His family originates from

Aerytol, and his parents have yet to recover from their losses. He takes great pride in defending Lameiría, but his judgement is clouded."

Adaline nods. She may understand, but she can only fathom what Renor's seen or heard to make him act the way he did, to make him think his actions were acceptable. "It must be so exhausting having all that hate festering inside him like that. I don't ever want to be like him."

Sora side-eyes Adaline but doesn't comment. Even though she remains vigilant, Sora disappears into her own thoughts for a while, with her stern expression turning gentler.

After they exit the market, training with Sora provides Adaline with a diversion. A few of Sora's friends join them, giving Adaline a chance to watch the ladies spar and observe how their fighting differs from the guys. Listening to Sora's commentary keeps Adaline's mind focused on the here and now, not all the what ifs that kept her awake last night, that will keep her awake tonight. Sora also takes her time testing Adaline's current skill level, praising her commitment to precision and showing ways she can alter Fólas's instruction to make better use of her agility.

Before the sun finishes setting, Sora escorts Adaline back to the palace. Alone in the guest room, Adaline deflates onto the bed and prays she can sleep most of tomorrow away too. Because as wonderful as Sora had been today, the waiting has been eating away at Adaline since the queen first mentioned the sacred circle. Waiting to see the site for herself. Waiting to know if the priestess will allow her to step inside. Waiting to see Cindy and Dax and the Grump again. Waiting for Ëólas to wake up. Waiting to know if he'll tell her to go.

Chapter Seventeen

THE SACRED CIRCLE

Adaline spends the entirety of her second day training with Sora. Thankfully, no one bothers or threatens Adaline. In fact, that Renor never managed to lock her up must have convinced most of the citizens to not pay Adaline any heed. She receives a second break when the queen sends a servant to apologize on her behalf and to reschedule their dinner date for lunch the following day.

When Adaline shuts the door to her room, she bathes, puts on the nightgown, flops onto the bed, and stares at the ceiling, feeling like a hollowed-out version of herself, like half of her has vanished. If she were in New Leira, Seira would have danced her way into Adaline's room and spun circles around the bed until Adaline laughed. Seira would have some perfect way of making Adaline forget all her troubles, and Mercia would have shown up too, spilling whatever news she overheard from her father.

I miss you both. And Seira, I'm so sorry for yelling at you.

Rolling onto her side, Adaline pulls out her phone and hits the power button for the first time since she got lost in the caves. Watching the plastic device flash on and illuminate the elven room with artificial light feels like a betrayal, like she's breaking the laws of nature by using modern technology in this world.

Get a grip, Adaline.

She scrolls through photos of her and Cindy, stopping at them standing in line for a concert at the Kennedy Center. Cindy's shoulder-length light-brown hair and dark eyes gleam as she hugs Adaline to snap their selfie. They've rarely gone a few days without texting. If Cindy had the slightest inkling that her bestie's struggling, she would show up at Adaline's door within minutes—if she could travel between worlds.

Stop focusing on what I can't change.

Adaline closes her camera app and searches her movie library. She has enough power to watch maybe one film, and Judy Garland's *The Harvey Girls* calls to her. But she'd never be able to power her phone on again. She'd never be able to access home again.

She closes all apps and opts for music instead, turning the volume down low and pressing the speaker to her ear so the lyrics replace her thoughts. Remnants of home ease her mind. The music gives her an excuse to feel a myriad of emotions through the lyrics. The last song she consciously hums along to, Maroon 5's "Memories," conjures a collage of scattered images of the ones she's lost, the ones she'll have to leave behind, and the torch she'll carry forever.

When she wakes up late the next morning, her phone is dead. She tries pressing the power button several times, but not even the logo flashes on the screen.

She rests the piece of plastic on her chest, the glass cool against her skin. Despite its uselessness, she tucks her mobile into her pocket and leaves the room to socialize with the queen and meet the king. Outside her door, Sora greets her with a bow, her strawberry-blonde hair once again up in a ponytail.

Halfway down the hallway, a dirty-blond elf turns the corner and hurries toward them. His tan tunic with gold trim highlights his golden eyes, and everything inside her urges her to run to him. But she doesn't have the right. She catches the surge of emotions in a glass jar, screws the lid on tightly, and plasters her face with a subtle and appropriate level of relief.

Ëólas, however, throws his arms around her, pressing one hand firmly against her back so there's no space left between them. With his other hand, he weaves his fingers in her hair and cradles the base of her neck. Forgetting why she held back moments ago, she molds herself to his torso and rests her cheek below his collarbone. One inhale tells her that he bathed, that he's changed up his usual lavender and pine scent for eucalyptus, chamomile, and a touch of lemon. He smells like a cozy evening perfect for snuggling on the sofa and watching a movie marathon.

When they lean back to look at each other over, they both ask, "Are you okay?"

Ëólas flashes a cocky grin. "I'm perfectly fine, thank you. Wide awake and ready for anything."

"And no side effects?"

"None, aside from being famished."

"Well, you have perfect timing. I'm meeting your parents for lunch. You, you are coming, right?"

"Wouldn't miss it." He lets go of her neck and cups her cheek instead as he peers into her eyes. "And you're okay? Nothing remiss happened while I was away?"

He makes it sound like he was on vacation. "Mmm." She places her hand over his and nuzzles her cheek into his palm. "I'm fine."

"Fine?" He stitches his eyebrows together, and his expression hardens. "What happened?"

"Nothing. Everything's fine." The questioning pitch in the last syllable gives her away, but she bites down on her bottom lip and tugs his hand away, threading her fingers between his and tugging him to turn around so they can proceed down the hallway.

He doesn't budge. "Sora, what happened?"

"Renor tried to execute her."

"What!" Ëólas's entire face elongates in shock then contracts in fury, his temples throbbing and his full lips pursing into an unspoken curse. His arm snakes around Adaline's waist and hugs her to him as he scans her body for injury.

"She's exaggerating," Adaline says. "He just wanted to toss me in prison for a few nights. Nothing too serious. Nothing I couldn't handle."

He looks at her incredulously. "Enjoy lunch. I need to go speak with Renor. Sora, don't let her out of your sight."

"Yes, my lord."

"No! Ëólas, you can't." Adaline tugs his sleeve to pull him back.

"He didn't follow my orders. I can't let that go."

"Okay, fine. Yes, of course you need to address that, but you can't make it personal."

"Why ever the bloody hell not?"

Stunned into silence, Adaline can't process what he just said, that he cursed. But as he aims to storm off, her hand latches onto his and pulls him back a second time. "Because. Because you can't force someone to see things, or people, the way you do. If you make this about me, you'll give him more reason to hate me, to hate humans. He'll blame me as the source of his troubles."

Ëólas stares at the floor as he grinds his jaw, and his nostrils flare. He hasn't appeared this mad since she verbally assaulted him on the balcony in New Leira. "Fine. I'll speak with him later about his insubordination."

She reaches up on her tiptoes to kiss his cheek, but he turns his head to say something else, and the corners of their lips brush against each other. A rush of heat consumes her, making her think she's about to self-combust, and her imagination floods her with images of clothing hitting the floor, bedsheets writhing, limbs intertwining, flesh grinding against flesh.

Instead of looking at Ëólas, she pushes past him and run-walks down the hallway. "Come on. We can't leave your parents waiting."

When they enter the same tearoom as the night they arrived, Sora takes a seat in the corner, out of the way. At the same time, another elf rises from his seat. His dirty-blonde hair and diamond-shaped jawline ending in a square chin reveal who Ëólas resembles most. The king's silk robes comprise many layers of navy blue, which match his eyes, and a green overcoat, all with gold trim. Upon his head, he wears a crown similar to the queen's, only his circlet features gold leaves instead of silver. Overall, he appears stern, but the warmth in his eyes gives away his true nature, and Adaline suspects King Aiden to be a secret softy at heart, just like his son.

With a firm nod, the king cups both of Ëólas's cheeks. "There you are. Don't do that again."

"I didn't have much choice in the matter." Ëólas grabs his father's forearms and smirks.

A loud exhale through his nose gives away the king's displeasure, but he doesn't ask for clarification. Instead, he lets go of his son and turns to Adaline. "So, this is the extraordinary young lady."

"I wouldn't go so far as to say that, Your Majesty," Adaline says with a curtsy.

The king chuckles. "I disagree."

Queen Élara walks between her husband and son and takes both of Adaline's hands in hers. "I'm pleased you could join us today, and I'm terribly sorry about yesterday. Several of our generals arrived, and Aiden and I needed to meet with them individually."

"Oh, of course." Adaline glances down at the queen's hands. Their cool temperature slows Adaline's racing heart.

"Speaking of which," the king says, placing his hand on Ëólas's shoulder, "I've instructed our people to gather in the theater tonight so that we may inform them of our plans. The army is set to leave in the morning."

"Thank you, Father."

"With that settled, let us eat." The queen loops her arm around Adaline's and walks her to the dining table on the balcony. After gesturing for her guest to sit next to Ëólas, the queen descends into her chair, next to Aiden and across from Adaline.

A canopy of leaves shields them from the dwindling summer heat, and birds chirp and hop from branch to branch. A gentle breeze rustles the leaves and makes the sunlight dance over them. Meanwhile, servers carry platters of food for the four of them to choose from. Adaline marvels as Ëólas, for the first time, fills his plate with mounds of food, including steaming hot pastries, five apples, seven cookies with different jam fillings, and three loaves of bread. A server brings him two extra plates so he can continue stacking food with one hand while holding a chicken leg in the other as he devours it. Not a speck dirties his face.

He certainly is famished. No longer fearing what the king and queen will think of her, Adaline takes her fill.

The queen watches her son for a while, not in disappointment but rather in relief, and leans back in her seat. Her empty hand seeks Aiden's. When his fingers intertwine with hers and he sips his tea, she finishes the first bite of her roasted potatoes. "Adaline, I'd very much like to hear about this world of yours. If you don't mind."

She swallows a cube of cheese. "Oh, I don't even know where to start. Um."

"Ah, I have this." Ëólas sets down the chicken leg bone, which a server removes immediately. "They have carriages that move without horses. Indoor plumbing that carries hot and cold water in and out of their homes constantly, and metal birds that fly humans high in the sky and make long-distance international travel take only hours."

Aiden looks from Adaline to Ëólas, waiting for them to laugh. "You joke. Don't you?"

When Adaline shakes her head, Élara whispers, "Fascinating."

"We are an innovative lot," Adaline says.

"Indeed." Élara leans forward and selects a stuffed mushroom.

Just when Adaline thinks they can't have any more variety of food brought out, the servers step onto the balcony with entirely different trays, this time with toasted rhubarb, goat cheese spreads with jam and nuts, and a collection of soup bowls.

Ëólas takes a serving of the goat cheese spread, places it next to Adaline's plate, and jiggles his eyebrows. "You'll love this."

"It's so much," she mumbles.

"Yes, but this isn't all for us." Élara nods her thanks to the servers as she passes on this round. "Our people kindly bring us their favorite recipes for us to try, but these trays circulate throughout the entire palace. Anyone may choose what they like."

"Wait." Adaline points at the server carrying the portioned-out soup. "That's the chef?"

"Yes." Élara waves goodbye to the chefs, who proudly carry away their culinary masterpieces. "Now, Adaline, if I may, what can you tell me about your world's connection to magic?"

"Um, well." She absentmindedly strokes the rim of the goat cheese plate with her fingers. "Some religions believe in magic, but I've never seen or heard of a visual display like I've witnessed here."

Aiden drapes one arm around Élara's shoulders. "We elves don't actually practice magic, not like when the world was still young."

As she ponders what to say next, Élara shifts in her seat so that her upper body drifts toward him. "True. Our enchantments are a remnant of magic from long ago. Some elves are more talented than others. But, for the most part, we're able to access only a single element. Have you ever tapped into one?"

Adaline glances at Ëólas, who lowers his loaf long enough to encourage her with a nod to go on. "Yes, Your Majesty. I have."

Élara's eyes gleam. "Which one?"

"A-all four."

"Which four?"

"Wind, earth, water, fire."

"You can speak to the elements, four of them, without using Elvish?"

Adaline nods. "I don't think..." She remembers what Ëólas said when he showed her the marriage vows, and the words come so easily to her. *All that I am, all that I was, all that I'll ever be...* She cuts off her thoughts. "I, I don't think it's the words that matter, Your Majesty, but the intention or the conviction behind them."

Élara's regards Adaline like she's a prize pupil. "Right you are. Still, the elements are more familiar with Elvish, being it's the oldest language."

"And yet no one here has spoken Elvish, or, at least, not around me."

Aiden puts down his teacup and looks at his human guest with remorse. "We are rather protective of our culture."

"Which is completely understandable," Adaline says. "Admirable, even. But the guards I met would sooner kill a human who enters your woods than ask questions." When Ëólas clenches his jaw, Adaline closes her eyes and bites her tongue.

Proceed with caution, Adaline. Don't fuck up a delicate situation.

No one speaks. Debating whether to keep her mouth shut, Adaline lifts her eyes and faces the king and queen. Like two magnets drawn together, they tilt toward their other half. Their relaxed posture eases Adaline's worries and makes her feel as if she were having lunch with her own family.

Instead of displaying a stern look of offense or disapproval, the queen regards Adaline thoughtfully, but when she speaks, gloomy memories temper her tone. "After the war, humans crossed the Forbidden Lands and entered our woods for one reason only. Revenge. Unable to draw us out, they hoped to weed us out. One by one."

Adaline takes her hands off the table and clicks her thumbnails together. "I'm sorry. I—"

"Don't be." The queen waves her hand as if all's forgotten.

But it can't be. Adaline can't let this go, not when she has the queen's undivided attention. Maybe, in time, the queen will come to see things as Ëólas does, but he can't continue speaking for humans. She has to use her voice now, while she has a chance to be heard. "I'm fortunate, Your Majesty. I've never experienced war. I come from a place of privilege where I can do or say pretty much whatever I want."

As the queen sets down her spoon to listen, Adaline sits up straighter and trusts herself to find the right words, words that won't offend or push away, words that invoke empathy and possibility. "But I've traveled extensively and met people with different beliefs and morals and views and laws. I've also lived inside books, studying thousands of years of history. And you're right to be concerned, because I've learned that war and truly evil people always exist in the world. But so do heroes. They rise from the everyday masses. They refuse to accept the status quo and scream for what's fair and just. *They* become a catalyst for change, for good."

Adaline takes a deep breath. When neither Élara nor Aiden object and Ëólas rests his cheek in his hand, opting not to eat another rugelach as he watches her, Adaline continues. "But I've also learned that isolation perpetuates fear and distrust. It becomes all too easy to view other people more as *other* than *people*. So while I deeply empathize with what you and your people have endured, I fear you're hurting yourselves too. Because if the guards can't see an individual for who he or she is, they won't be able to recognize when someone good enters your woods, someone who might help make a difference."

Please don't hate me.

The king and Ëólas exchange a look that Adaline can't quite interpret. As the king's smile broadens, the sides of Ëólas's mouth crease into a frown and he shakes his head. He looks away and resumes eating. The king's eyes dim, and he too becomes more interested in the crumbs on his plate.

The queen, however, nods at Adaline. "I will give great consideration to your words, I promise."

"Thank you, Your Majesty."

After they finish eating, waiting an extra hour or so for Ëólas to clear his plates, the four of them agree to go for a walk. Arm in arm, Aiden and Élara lead the way, talking between themselves. A sweet chuckle from the queen joins the birds' songs above and lifts Adaline's spirits. When Ëólas offers his elbow, Adaline hesitates to accept. But she does, intertwining her arm with his. They follow his parents with Sora not far behind.

The pathway leads downward and away from the palace. As they pass elves coming and going, a few don't look away quickly enough as they stare at the picture of the four of them, easily spotting the one who doesn't belong. Adaline lets go of Ëólas's arm and pretends to smooth out Lanía's dress, which looks and feels as clean as the morning she received it.

"Why didn't you pick out your own clothes?" Ëólas asks.

"I, I didn't have time."

He knows she's lying, but they drop the subject and walk in silence. She listens to leaves swaying against each other, tiny claws scurrying over bark, a wind chime singing in the far-off distance. When daylight peeks through the boughs, she turns her face toward the sun and inhales deeply. She could easily feel comfortable in Gladríen, find peace here, if the forest wanted her. She could explore Lameiría for years, but their walk ends in front of an archway with two life-size marble statues of elven priestesses guarding the entrance. Beyond the archway, six pillars tower inside a grove with branches instead of stalactites reaching downward.

After Ëólas's parents continue into the grove, Adaline halts at the entrance. "What, what are we doing here?" Not knowing this was on today's agenda, she looks at Ëólas, who squares his jaw and rolls his shoulders backward, making him appear taller.

"Keeping my promise. I said I'd help you find a way home, and the priestess agreed to help me do so." He says nothing else and steps aside so that she may go first.

While the world feels like it's spinning a million miles an hour and she's about to topple over the edge, her body carries her forward of its own accord, as if she's no longer in her body but watching these events unfold from above. She screams at her feet to stop, but they don't listen, not until she's standing beside Élara.

The dimensions of the circle appear to be the same as the one in Maryland, both with the six pillars standing nearly eight feet high. In the stone floor, the elves have etched deep loops and curves with sprouting buds and leaves, all of which culminate in the center with an image of the tree of life. Aside from the tree, the rest of the design resembles the one Adaline unearthed in the cave back home. As she suspected, the artwork extends to the pillars. Beneath the symbols etched into the pillars, the protruding shelves hold items that represent the elements: a bowl of water, a lit candle, a pyramid of soil, and smoke billowing upward from burning incense. The two other shelves display a puzzle box and a geode with pale, gray-blue crystals.

Élara and Aiden stroll toward the circle's edge, but Adaline stays put, having regained control of her body. Ëólas keeps his distance too, lingering close behind Adaline, but he remains silent and reticent.

After bowing their heads and whispering something toward the circle, Élara and Aiden face Adaline. Without asking her to come closer, Élara gestures to the pillars. "Do you know why we have more than four?"

Adaline studies the puzzle box and geode. Turning on her academic brain helps her to switch off her emotions. "The puzzle represents the mind. The crystal, I'm not so sure. I'm not a geologist."

"Celestite. We use it to connect with the soul."

"So, mind, soul... What about the body?" Adaline glances at the tree of life, the center of the circle, where she had been standing when her world disappeared. "The person in the center represents the body."

Élara beams. "Ëólas said you're a scholar. Well done." She lets go of Aiden and walks toward Adaline. "I confess I'm curious to see you enter the circle, to see how the elements might react to your presence. I cannot guarantee that reaction will result in you going home. But in order for magic to work properly, you must have clear intentions. What's more, you must know yourself as you are. Indecision or, worse, falsehood of any kind can have disastrous consequences."

Pulling her hands behind her back, Adaline pinches the pad of her hand to smother the migraine pounding her temples.

"Adaline, there's no pressure for you to do this now," Aiden says, almost as an afterthought. But the wrong person spoke up to stop her.

Adaline glances back at Ëólas and searches for Sora too, but she's nowhere visible. Ëólas stands so still, he may as well be one of those statues. He keeps his mouth shut too, offering no encouragement. No goodbye. No nothing. She wants to scream at him, to throw that geode in his face, to rouse some sort of emotion from him—be it remorse or relief. Either way, she'd at least know she means something to him, even if that was mostly a burden. But she knows why neither of them react, why neither of them speak up, because he still believes what he said on the river: She doesn't belong here.

Starting with one small step forward, Adaline approaches the outermost ring of the circle. Cindy and Dax are waiting for her on the other side. Along with her students. Her grumpy mentor and colleagues. The career she's worked the last decade toward. Her condo. Her own clothes. The bed she bought with her own paycheck. Her childhood home.

She closes her eyes, and a magnetic pull urges her to step inside, willing her to move her feet. Burning lemon grass mingled with specks of dirt tickle her nostrils. She hears the water in the bowl ripple and the candle flame flicker, but the sensations from the circle dull. Instead, drips of water echoing deep underground ping in her ears. The air on her cheeks feels cool and damp, and she smells musty, earthy minerals. Voices murmur and fade around her, voices she hasn't heard in weeks.

"Ben, what do you make of..."

"What the fuck happened to..."

"Where do you think she..."

Adaline can see the threshold, the sheer curtain that separates this world from the next. If she takes only a few steps, she can cross through to the other side. Leave this all behind. Never knowing what happens to New Leira. To him. A polar-opposite barrier slams into her torso, a wave of emptiness so intense, so vast, that if she doesn't move, she'll cease to exist.

Opening her eyes, Adaline sees the canopy of leaves overhead and jumps back from the circle before her toes cross the threshold. Her heart pounds so forcefully that she pushes down on her chest to keep it from bursting open. Her ears buzz. The roof of her mouth feels like cotton, and her legs wobble.

"Adaline?" Ëólas asks, his voice barely above a whisper. At some point, he must have moved closer to her because he's right beside her now. "Did something happen?"

She looks at him, at his vacant expression, at his perfected indifference. "No. I, um, I just. Something's off. I don't know." *Why did I jump away? How stupid can I be?*

Ëólas lifts his hand to touch her arm, but he touches only air as she backs away. "It's okay," he says. "There's no rush. You can try again if—"

"Can I go?" Adaline looks at Élara. "I mean, back to my room? I feel, um, drained." *In more ways than one.* "I'm sorry. I don't mean to be rude. I just need a moment to collect myself. To figure out what just happened. Or didn't happen. I mean—"

"Of course, Adaline."

She doesn't wait for any of them. Adaline backtracks out of that grove and follows the path to the palace, ignoring Sora keeping a distant eye on her. As soon as she shuts the door to her room, Adaline collapses onto the bed, buries her face in the pillow, and screams silently. Without comprehension. Without care. Without hope.

At some point, everything in this world became too much, too real, too dire. She's been going at full speed, without pausing to ask herself what she really wants. Because there's no point. What she wants isn't possible.

I don't belong here.

But going home means being alone. Forever. Because no one will believe her. No one will understand what she's seen and experienced and suffered and discovered. No one there will sink into her soul and read her thoughts or know exactly what she needs to hear or not hear. No one there will feel like home, not like this.

When exhaustion and numbness finally overtake her, Adaline plummets to the darkest recesses of her dreams where shadows rise from the ground and encircle her. She's alone, on the ground, the grass cutting her face. A bird caws a death cry overhead, and a male voice shrieks in agony. Her father scoops her up off the ground and runs with her in his arms. Behind him, flames consume their home. The roof collapses, sending an inferno up into the night sky. Sirens blare in the distance as they run down the street of her childhood neighborhood, until Cindy, fully grown, opens her door and begs them to come inside. Before her father steps through the front gate, a woman in the distance screams so loudly that she shatters the world.

Chapter Eighteen

AN OCEAN OF TREES

A gentle but persistent knocking on the door wakes Adaline from her nap. A glance out her window reveals that sunset isn't far away. How many hours do they have left before they have to leave Lameiría? Before she has to leave, one way or another?

Opening the door, Adaline hopes to find Sora. Instead, Ëólas raises his downcast eyes and looks at her like someone with a lot on his mind and no idea how to begin the conversation. She doesn't help him.

"Can we..." Ëólas scratches behind his ear. "Will you join me for a walk?"

I didn't like where the last one ended. "Where to?"

"About." He shrugs his shoulders.

Adaline curls her hands into fists but leaves her room. She doesn't take his arm. *I don't actually have a right to be mad at him, do I?* He's always been honest with her, hasn't he?

Once again, they walk in silence. They exit the back of the main building, pass one of those towers that peeks out of the trees, and meander toward the lone building with its bell-shaped roof perched on the tallest limb. They continue up a staircase spiraling around the trunk. At each new level of elevation, Adaline pauses to admire the city shrinking beneath them. Up here, she can observe the city's rhythm without fearing she's going to create discord. Up here, she doesn't have to mind what she says or does every moment of the day. Up here, she can breathe more easily.

Once they reach the top, the stairs open up to a small platform and the double doors of the lone building. A rocking chair sits to the side, along with triangular shelves holding potted herbs, spices, and fruit. Ëólas holds the door open.

Adaline steps inside but stops abruptly when she sees the four-poster bed in an alcove to the right, framed by floor-to-ceiling windows that reveal the sky blending shades of blue and purple together. "Is this your room?"

Ëólas pokes her between her shoulder blades, urging her to stop blocking the doorway. "My home, yes." When she doesn't move, he walks around her, sits on the bench near the door, and takes off his boots and socks.

She turns away from the bed. "Is it inappropriate for me to be here?"

"No." His answer is so nonchalant that she's embarrassed for suggesting otherwise.

At least no one in Lameiría will accuse me of being a gold digger.

"I want to show you something." Standing up, Ëólas leads the way past his wardrobes and chest of drawers.

Keeping her eyes focused straight ahead, she follows him through his sleeping quarters and into the sitting room—past the fireplace and sofas, the desk, and the dining table—to another set of double-doors. Tree branches divide the glass panes.

They don't deviate much from the theme around here. Not that they should. Ëólas's home invokes comfort and simplicity, and that sofa begs for her to sit on it and curl her legs to the side.

Pausing at the doors, Ëólas offers her his hand. As her palm skates across his, he clasps her fingers and pulls her toward him, keeping his eyes on her the whole time. As she comes nearer, she inhales that lemon and chamomile blend and tells her heart to hush, to quiet down, to stay dormant. Before she can linger next to him, he pushes the doors open and escorts her outside onto a large, oval deck. They walk around a single, long bench with cream-colored cushions and stop at the far side. Adaline rests her free hand on the railing while Ëólas holds the other, his fingers curling between hers. An ocean of treetops stretches out beneath them as far as the eye can see with the sun kissing the horizon.

"Oh," she whispers.

"You like it?"

Adaline nods, unable to take her eyes away from the view. His hand feels warm. Familiar. A perfect fit. She doesn't let her eyes deviate from the sea of autumn leaves. "I've never seen anything like it. It's breathtaking, really."

"Indeed," he says, his husky voice too close to her ear.

She steps away to get some space, to stop him from hearing how fast her heart is beating. He lets her go. He always lets her go.

"This is my favorite spot in all of Lameiría." He points to the left. "You can just barely make out the Neutral Territory. And to the right of us lies the sea."

She squints into the horizon. "I can't see any of that."

"Mmm. Elves can see things much more clearly." But he's not facing the sea; he's looking at Adaline.

She feels see-through. Paper thin. He must know she could have gone home today, or rather that the doorway was close, that she had a chance, but something pushed her back. Élara had warned her to be honest with herself, and she hasn't been. Not for a long time. The closest she's come to being truthful was when she broke up with Derek the night before she hitched a ride with Beccah as they sped off to the cave site.

"What happened?" Éólas asks.

With Derek? Good question. Adaline shrugs.

She closes her eyes, takes a deep breath, and wills the cool air to settle her nerves, but all she smells is him, that damn fresh scent that lures her away from the railing. It's so intoxicating that it's not fair. Elves probably don't even realize what they can do to a woman, how they can mess with her senses and mind and cause confusion.

He steps closer. "Please let me in."

Let him in. Her breath catches. Her muscles tense. The blood in her body travels downward, and her inner thighs pulse. Being here is dangerous. She might slip up, might embarrass them both, might ruin their friendship. *Doesn't he need to go to some big meeting in a theater? Rally the troops?* Instead, he's forcing her into a damn corner at the edge of the world. With her hands shaking, she walks around him and sits down on the bench, pressing her knees together. Her chest burns, and her throat feels dry.

Facing her, he rests both hands on the railing behind him and leans backward. "It's my fault."

Oh god. Please don't give me the whole "I'm sorry if I've given you the wrong impression" speech. She contemplates jumping off the balcony to end her embarrassment as quickly as possible.

But when she looks up, he's the one unable to make eye contact with his chin dropped to his chest, his expression pained. "I've not been honest with you. When...when that elf killed the old man in the cave, you asked me how anyone could be so cruel."

He swallows hard and crosses the divide, taking a seat next to Adaline, but he still doesn't look at her, only at his hands. "Before I met Rioran, I hated humans. I resented them for trapping me in this forest, for breaking the world. Not long after my father assigned me to border patrol, a man entered our woods. He was the first I'd ever seen, and I didn't think. I didn't ask questions. I didn't give him the option to explain himself or ask for help or to just turn around and leave. When I saw him enter my homeland, I killed him. Within seconds. I didn't even realize what I had done until he looked at me, confused and scared. I pushed him off my sword with my boot like he was filth on my shoe, and he collapsed into a heap of bones. He was old, Adaline, a grandfather most likely, and he had blue eyes. Blue as an iris."

Adaline's chest caves inward, her spine curling forward, as her eyes cloud over. How many times had she admonished those elves in the cave, not realizing she had been reminding Ëólas of his own choices, his own mistakes? Has he been working with Magnus to wash his hands clean, to apologize for the past?

Ëólas stares at his palms, his eyes haunted by his failure. "Do you think less of me?" He closes his eyes and waits for her answer.

Looping her arm around his, she leans her head on his shoulder. "No. I know who you are now, and I believe in you. I can't imagine you ever doing that again, and if you did, I'd probably yell and cuss you out...a lot, but I'd also try to understand and help you."

He exhales a long, audible breath and sits up. "You're extraordinary, you know that?"

As he turns to kiss her brow, Adaline hurries off the bench and rubs her arms while angling away from him. She's not extraordinary. She just can't blame him, not entirely, for the way his culture shaped his behavior toward humans. And yet, despite the influence of his culture, he has managed to think for himself and change his beliefs. He's the extraordinary one. He can face the truth.

I just keep avoiding it over and over again. "I'm not special. I'm a coward. Derek knew it, called me out on it."

"What do you mean?"

She could run back to her room and shut the door on this conversation. He'd let her too, giving her all the time she needs until she's ready to stop running.

Stop running. As much as that thought terrifies her, she can sense relief behind it too. Release.

You must know yourself as you are. That's what Élara said. "People keep saying I'm kind, but I'm not. There's...something wrong with me, and Derek's just one example of that. I mean, I've never been good with relationships, always ending them before giving the guy a chance, before giving us a chance." But that's not where the problem started. "Then Dad died, and I lost Nan seventeen months later. And I just...disappeared."

It's too much. She's been carrying too much, burying too much. The treetops start to blur together. The sunset, out of focus, multiplies into three, creating two ghost suns that drift on the sidelines.

"Derek showed up at my office, said he was taking me out for lunch. I tried to push him away too, but he didn't give up on me. Every time I cried on his shoulder, I figured that was it. He's had enough. But he kept popping back up. I don't remember when things changed, but we started dating, and he knew when to nudge me out the door to rejoin the world and when to let me grieve. He listened to all of my research theories, cooked my favorite dishes, and even ground coffee beans every morning for a fresh brew. He was perfect."

Ëólas crinkles his brow but doesn't interrupt.

"But I couldn't love him back. I tried. I kept willing myself to feel something, anything. He'd done so much for me, so I hoped if I acted the part, I'd feel something eventually. But when he started talking about marriage and ring shopping, I couldn't pretend like his joy wasn't strangling me. I strung him along for seven months, giving him hope, playing the part." *Fucking someone I didn't love.* "And then I threw him away. I crushed him. I mean, what's wrong with me that I couldn't love a genuinely great guy who did nothing but love me?"

She glances at Ëólas, all three, blurred versions of him, waiting for him to scowl at her, to call her out for being cruel. He doesn't though, so she continues. "But Derek's only a piece of the puzzle. The truth...is that I'm scared to go home."

With her hands balled into fists, she grits her teeth and spits out, "I'm scared because I'm so fucking angry. I'm angry at my parents for leaving me, and I'm angry at Nan for dying too. I know they didn't choose to go, but I don't care. And I know it's stupid and irrational and selfish, but part of me is angry at Cindy for finding the love of her life and building her own family now. And I feel—"

If only she could gouge her heart out of her chest and throw it away. But Loríen and Élara are right: A blocked heart leads to mistakes, mistakes like Derek, and lies erode a person from the inside out. "I feel left behind. Forgotten. I have no one left, and I'm so damn tired of feeling empty all the time."

"And you!" She spins around and jabs her finger at him. "You were perfectly fine watching me leave, that damn stoic expression of yours. You didn't give a shit about me leaving either. Am I such a burden to you that it's easier if I go?"

Before she can cuss him out, Ëólas strides across the deck, grabs her accusatory finger, and pulls her into his arms. "Fucking asshole," she says into his chest as he rests his chin on the crown of her head. She buries her wet face in his tunic, turning the cream-colored fabric tan, but he doesn't pull away. He doesn't say a thing. He just rubs circles up and down her back, and when she shudders, he holds her more tightly. As she inhales his scent, her breaths slow down and deepen. She relaxes against him and grips the back of his shirt, terrified she'll poof away for good, terrified he'll pull away on his own.

"I'm sorry," he whispers in her ear. "I didn't mean to be unfeeling. I didn't want to interfere with your choice." When she dares to look up at him, he wipes the tears from her cheeks. "And I don't want you to feel alone anymore."

I don't, not entirely.

"Adaline, do you want to stay here?"

She gulps. Staying here wouldn't solve her problem either. Because he's part of the problem. He's become a very dear friend. Someone she can't stand being apart from. But she's not welcome here, and he can't stay in New Leira forever. And he'll be king one day. Granted, that's a long time from now. When she won't exist anymore.

"Maybe," she croaks.

"Well, that's a start." He leans back to see her better but doesn't let go, not yet. "But here's something you need to know for certain right now: Stop blaming yourself for not returning Derek's affections. You can't force that, and you don't owe him your heart. And I'm not convinced he was such a *great guy*. Either he was a simpleton for not recognizing your feelings, or he was a manipulative scoundrel for guilting you into keeping him around. If the latter, I'd very much like to go to your world and break his legs."

A burst of laughter breaks through her sorrow. "That's an awfully violent thing to say."

Ëólas shrugs. "Protecting you has become a bit of a habit now." He presses his forehead against hers. "The truth, Adaline Yates, is that you are remarkable. You're brave, tenacious, wise, and immeasurably kind—no matter what you think. You draw others to you, and *I* am a better person because of you. So don't ever think for one second there's something wrong with you."

Adaline exhales all the tension in her shoulders and back, but now her body aches to fall forward and press against him. "You really have to be more mindful about what you say." When he knits his eyebrows together, she clarifies, "If you become friends with more women, they'll misinterpret what you say. They'll get the wrong idea."

"The wrong idea?"

She attempts to laugh, to shake her nerves loose. She's been in his arms too long, and her thoughts are becoming jumbled. "You know what I mean."

He does that curious head tilt again as he waits for her to elaborate.

She rolls her eyes. "Oh my god, Ёlas. Elves may not find humans attractive, but a lot of women might not know that. God forbid you did ever come to my world. Human women will fall in love with you far too easily, and," she looks down at the tiny gap between their chests, "unrequited love is evil incarnate. It's just not fair to the women."

He playfully scowls at her. "Who ever said elves don't find humans attractive?"

"You did!"

His eyes jump open, and his voice cracks like a teenage boy. "When did I ever say such a thing?"

"The night I met you. At the tavern."

"When you drank tree spirits and almost died?"

"I didn't—whatever." Not sure she wants this conversation to continue, she rests her cheek on his chest. "That night, I asked you if elves and humans ever, *you know*, and your *No* was quite emphatic. I got the point." *Which is fine. Totally fine. It makes sense.*

Ёlas rubs the top of her head with his chin. "I wouldn't listen to most of what I said when we first met. After all, I was small-minded and judgmental back then."

Adaline winces. "Sorry."

"Don't be. You were right. Anyway, just because there's never been such a relationship doesn't mean it's not possible. Who knows what might happen when two people see past their differences and get to know one another."

He's not... He's not implying... He doesn't mean... Oh my god, I'm so confused.

Tightening his arms around her, he leans down and whispers in her ear, "Two such people could make history, don't you think?"

With her face frozen in a catatonic stupor, Adaline robotically nods her head. "Uh-huh."

The corner of Ёlas's mouth twitches in amusement, but he takes a step back and rubs her arms vigorously, shaking her awake. "It's a bit chilly now. You should have worn my cloak."

"Uh-huh."

"Well, now that we've cleared things up—"

We have?

"—what do you want to do now?"

Do now? With you?

"We have a few hours before I have to head down to the theater and address my people. You can come with me, if you wish. Show everyone the strength of our union."

Our union? Her cheeks flush, and the heat building between her thighs makes her wish she had undergarments on. *Does he hear himself? What would he do? How would he react if I—*

"Or we could return to the sacred circle, and you could take some time to think through what you want." He casts his eyes downward.

What I want? She imagines pulling her arms out from under his, imagines resting her palms against his chest. She'd take that final step and press her body against his, rubbing back and forth and pulsing as he grew harder. Oh, how she'd love him to sneak his hand under her skirts, caress her inner thighs, slide his fingers between her—

"Or we could go home for now."

She smiles coyly. "Your home or mine?"

"That would be quite the adventure," Ëólas says wistfully. "I wish I could see your home."

Ëólas. At my home. Not running for our lives. No one to distract us. No war on the horizon. Maybe I could be braver there. "Me too."

As they stare at one another, their breath mingles in the breeze. Then the trees, the sunset, and the balcony fade away.

Chapter Nineteen

AN INVITATION

Four walls solidify around them, shutting out the endless twilight sky. A kitchen island takes the place of Ëólas's bench. Outside the panoramic window, buildings made of glass and steel consume the horizon. On the opposite side, an overstuffed, white sofa and vibrant turquoise accent chair form an L-shape in front of a seventy-five-inch flatscreen TV mounted to the wall.

Ëólas holds onto Adaline as his eyes widen and he scans the entire living room, from the kitchen sink to the dining table near the sliding door, to the bookshelves flanking the TV. "We're not in Lameiría anymore."

Adaline glances at the digital clock reading 1:55 p.m. "Nope."

"Your world?"

"Yep."

"Huh."

Adaline twists about, her eyes landing first on her copy of *Pride and Prejudice* sitting on the coffee table, her mail about to fall off the edge of the kitchen island, and her Converse sneakers chucked by the coat closet. Nothing's been ransacked or searched through, and no officers attached caution tape around her door.

She gawks at Ëólas. "Are you doing this?"

"Me?" Ëólas lets go of her and raises his palms. "How could I be doing this?"

"I don't know. We said we wanted answers, and poof: We're in the Wastelands. And you just said you wanted to see my world, and here we are."

"I don't have that level of magic. That's inconceivable."

"Okay, Vizzini."

"Ha! *The Princess Bride!* I remember that story."

Adaline laughs on the inside but rubs her hands over her face. "This is crazy, Ëólas. How I can be home again just like that, without a sacred circle too? Did you make any wishes the day you met me?"

Putting on his thinking face, Ëólas taps his chin with his fingers pressed together. "Yes, actually. When those people attacked New Leira, I was certain everything Magnus and I had worked for had come to an end. I, I prayed to the fae for help."

Whoa. "And you got me."

He stares at her without flinching, without looking away, without any hint of blush. "I did."

"Huh." *Focus, focus, focus. Jump his bones later. Maybe. Gah!*

"Mmm. What about you? What were you thinking about?"

"Me? Oh, um, nothing. I mean, what? When?"

"What were you thinking? Before we came here."

"Oh! Right. I was thinking about how I have no family left, and I was struggling with being alone."

Ëólas nods but doesn't say anything. Unable to stand his intense gaze right now, she turns away from him, pulls her mobile phone out of her pocket, and plugs it into the kitchen charging cable resting on the island countertop.

"You've been carrying that this whole time?" Ëólas asks.

"Never leave home without it." While she waits for the battery to charge enough for the home screen to turn on, she scans the condo again, and her eyes land on the bowl of apples sitting on the counter. "I don't get it."

"Get what?"

"The apples. They haven't gone bad." She walks over to the fridge and opens the door. "And my salad is still fresh."

Ëólas appears over her shoulder and sticks his hand in the fridge. "We have something like this. We use enchantments to trap the cold inside. How do you do it?"

"Electricity." She walks back to the kitchen island, her body on autopilot because she can't fathom that moments ago she was on top of the world, watching a sunset, and having a potentially life-altering conversation with Ëólas. Who's now in her home. In her world. And might be trapped here for God knows how long. *Holy shit. Focus. Facts first. Heart attack later.*

Meanwhile, Ëólas sticks his head in the fridge to better see the light bulb.

"Flip that switch by the coffee mach—by the knife block. The toggle on the wall. The straight white thingy. Yes, that."

Ëólas flips the switch. When the dining room lights blink on, his eyes grow wider than possible. He pulls out a chair, climbs on top of the seat, and peers into the chandelier sconces. "Is there fire in these?"

"Electricity."

He shakes his head in wonder and walks over to the kitchen faucet. When he lifts the handle, water pours into the basin. "Oh, I like that."

When her phone buzzes on the counter, Adaline leaps at it, her hands shaking as she waits for the date and time to update and her phone to explode with a million missed messages. The numbers blink and reset to 1:58 p.m., Saturday, June 8. "What the fuck!"

"What?" Ëólas repeats, appearing over her shoulder again.

"I've been gone only an hour." She looks at him, expecting him to be just as surprised.

Instead, he lifts his hand to touch the lit-up box she's holding but pulls back and hides his fist behind his back as if he remembered his manners. "That item calculates time? On its own?"

"Yes, and it hasn't changed, not much."

"Meaning, time hasn't progressed here."

"Yep." Adaline looks back at her phone, waiting for it to prove her wrong. "I mean, maybe I damaged it? It's supposed to be waterproof though." Before her brain processes what she's doing, her fingers tap the phone keypad and the speakerphone button. "I'm calling Cindy."

"Cindy? As in the—" Again, Ëólas's eyes widen when he hears the phone ring. For once, he has no idea what to do or say, so he waits beside Adaline while he wiggles his toes against the plush carpet.

She bites her bottom lip to stifle a chuckle. Pulling out a countertop stool, she rests her bottom on the edge of the seat and kicks her elven gown out of the way so she can rest her feet on the stainless-steel bar. From her elbows, her tapered sleeves pool on the granite countertop, fall off the edge, and flow onto her knees. She's back in her own surroundings, but she's still out of place. The honking outside, the neighbors chattering in the hallway, and the filtered air feel less believable than the elf watching the seconds count up on her mobile screen.

The phone rings five times before Cindy's peppy voice answers. "Hey, Chica! How's it going? Are those rocks everything you dreamed of?"

"Cindy?" She can't think of anything else to say, anything that would make sense, anything that could explain why she's struggling not to cry at the sound of her best friend's voice.

"Yeah, what's going on?"

"Um." Adaline pauses and silently exhales to release the emotions swelling inside her. "Nothing. Nothing. I just, I missed you."

"You okay?"

"Yeah." *Shit. I dragged that word out too long.*

"Is the Grump giving you a hard time?"

"No, not yet anyway."

"Ugh. Just tell him where he can stick his tape measure."

Adaline laughs, but someone outside knocks loudly on her door. She drops her phone on the counter while her neighbor cries through her door, "Adaline, you home? It's an emergency. I need your help!"

"Are you home?" Cindy yells.

"Um." *How am I supposed to answer that?*

"What the hell. Why are you home?" Cindy asks.

"Adaline, help!" Mark bangs louder on her door. "I can hear you. Saaaaave me!"

"Do you have any weapons here?" Ëólas navigates around the sofas, the dining table, and the kitchen faster than a cheetah as he searches the condo for something to defend themselves with.

"Who's that?" Cindy asks.

"Adalinnnnnnnnne!" Mark cries.

"Oh my god. Everyone, chill out! Cindy, just a second." Adaline runs over to her door.

"Wait!" Ëólas shouts.

Adaline doesn't. When she swings her door open, Mark squeals with delight and bounces inside her condo, only to stop abruptly when he sees Ëólas lifting a dining room chair in front of himself like a shield.

"Oh! I didn't know you're LARPers." Mark claps his hands and eyes Ëólas up and down. "How adorable. How authentic. Oh my god, Adaline, did you make this dress yourself? The embroidery is fabulous!"

While Ëólas lowers the chair and tucks it back under the table, Mark covers his mouth with his hand and whispers in Adaline's ear, but he speaks so loudly that anyone in the hallway could hear them. "Who's the cute elf?"

"Mark," says Adaline, "what's your emergency?"

"Oh, that! Brandon's cooking for our dinner party tonight, and his recipe calls for red wine, but he's using Holland House. God help me. Please, tell me you have a Merlot or even a Cabernet?" As Adaline retrieves a Merlot from her wine rack, Mark shoots his hands into the air and cheers. "Oh, I love you! You're my hero. Thank you." He kisses her cheek and heads to the door, only to turn back. "Wait, I thought you couldn't make our little soiree? Aren't you supposed to be knee high in dirt?"

Adaline tosses her hands in the air. "Plans changed."

"Oh goodie! Come by tonight. You know how late our events go." Mark waggles his eyebrows. "Bring the cute elf too."

"No!" shouts Cindy over the phone. "Adaline, if you're home, you're coming to dinner tonight. She's mine, Mark. Tonight's the big night."

"Ooooh. Finally!" Mark's upper body sags forward as if he's the one who's been waiting ten years to get engaged. "Thanks again, Adaline. See you later."

"Wait! Mark, I need my spare set of keys."

Mark plops a fist onto his hip. "Oh, poop. Do you know where you lost yours?"

Another world. "I, um, can't say." *Literally.*

After Mark runs down the hall and retrieves her keys, she shuts the door behind him and locks it, making sure she didn't accidentally catch the hem of her dress in the door too. She walks over to her phone, where she can feel Cindy's anger radiating from the speaker, and spends the next ten minutes convincing Cindy that the Grump isn't sabotaging her work.

Even though Cindy relents, she's not convinced. "Fine. I'll ask for details later. Who's the other guy with you?"

Adaline stares at Ëólas, who lifts both of his palms toward the ceiling and offers zero suggestions. "He's, um, a colleague from overseas, and he'll be staying with me for a while. To help with my research."

Ëólas nods in approval.

"Well, bring him tonight too," says Cindy.

"Oh…" *Would he want to?*

Resting his arm on the countertop, Ëólas bends forward and speaks into the phone. "I'd be delighted to join you this evening. Thank you kindly for the invitation."

"Oh, a Brit. Great, I'll tell Dax to update the reservation, and I'll text you the info for La Salsa de Vida. It's kinda fancy. Wear the black lace dress. See you tonight. Also, if Dax finds out you've been LARPing without him, he'll never forgive you. Love you. Bye!"

Finally, the condo is silent again. *I think I have whiplash.*

Ëólas messages his temples. "Is that typical?"

"Depends on the week." Adaline walks over to the sofa, collapses into the plush cushions, and looks up as if answers could fall from the ceiling. In the photos on the bookcase, her dad and grandmother stare expectantly at her.

Ëólas sits down on the accent chair and eyeballs the pen on the coffee table, next to the book. Unable to resist, he picks it up and studies every angle before accidentally clicking the top and jabbing his thumb with the tip.

Adaline squishes her lips to the side as her cheeks balloon. "Are you okay?"

Putting the pen down gently, he rubs his thumb. "It marked me."

"It'll wash off. Ëólas, why are we here? Why now? And why were you able to come with me?"

"Because we have something to learn here." He picks up a coaster, rubs his fingertips over the cork texture, and examines the underside. "The first time you traveled, I learned elves and humans can, in fact, learn to live together. The next time, we discovered Āranol's plan. Maybe when you and I have similar goals, a fae opens a doorway? I don't know. Maybe I'm crazy. But it stands to reason that we have something to learn or discover here. Maybe we're closer to learning how you're connected to magic."

Adaline sits forward, rests her elbows on her knees, and clasps her hands together. "Have you—" *Please don't think I'm crazy.* "Have you ever heard a voice in your head? Someone speaking to you. Someone who's not there."

"Yes. Once."

"Really?"

"Yes, I told you about it. The voice I heard on the wind, the one that told me it's time for change. That voice helped convince me to work with Magnus."

Adaline rests her forehead against her clasped hands. "I've heard a voice. More than once."

Ëólas's mouth falls open. "A fae speaks to you? Regularly?"

"Not regularly. She warns me when I'm in danger."

Forming an O-shape with his mouth, Ëólas squeezes his cheeks as he ruminates. "Fascinating."

"What do you think it means?"

"I haven't a clue."

"Well, that makes two of us. But if you think we might find more answers here, maybe we should go back to the cave site? Granted, that means facing my team and explaining why I ditched them for a few hours. But if we leave now, we can be there in an hour, if we can beat traffic on—Oh, fuck me. My car's in the shop and won't be ready until tomorrow." Adaline pushes her fist into her forehead while a notification makes her phone buzz on the counter. Hopefully, that's Cindy texting her with the restaurant info, but she's going to have to text the Grump something. And soon.

"Can we walk?"

Adaline laughs. "The cave is like 60 miles away."

"You're telling me that, instead of walking for two days, your *car* can get us there in an hour?"

"Yep. If there's no traffic."

"Traffic?"

"Too many cars on the road."

"By the fae." Ёólas slumps back in the chair and droops his arms over the sides.

Slapping her thighs, Adaline sits up. "Alright, here's the plan. We need to get you clothes. And shoes. And I'm not missing Cindy's engagement party this time. So, I'll suck it up and message the Grump, and we'll head back to the cave site tomorrow afternoon. Sound like a plan?"

"Wonderful."

After telling Ёólas to make himself at home and enjoy examining everything, she drags her feet back to the kitchen island. Chewing the inside of her cheek, she texts Ben while wincing the entire time: *I'm sorry to have run off like that. Cindy's mom has been hospitalized, and I panicked.*

She waits for Ben to reply, for his grumpy self to emerge full force with a series of curses, for him to scream about her lack of professionalism, for him to reiterate how much he didn't want to join her on this excavation. At the same time, she also prays to the universe that she didn't just jinx Cindy's mom. She'll never forgive herself if something does happen to Doña Mariana.

Three dots bounce on her screen, making her stomach twist into knots, until Ben's reply dings: *I've got things handled here. Stay safe.*

She rereads his message ten times, waiting for him to follow up with a tirade, but he never does. That's it: seven words. He doesn't even call her out for leaving her backpack or luggage behind. Adaline leans her head on the counter, pressing her forehead against the cool, granite surface like an ice pack. The fact that Ben believes her lie, because he knows how much she's lost already, makes her want to vomit. But facing Ben can wait until tomorrow.

With Ben settled and Ёólas flushing the toilet for the fifth time, Adaline tiptoes past the sofa and accent chair, ducks into her bedroom, and shuts the door. Her dresser cluttered with three stacks of books, her ladder shelf with the miniature statues she's collected from her travels abroad, and the sewing basket with the purple scarf she hasn't finished crocheting all sit undisturbed, unchanged, unfazed.

She slips off Lanía's dress, folds the fabric carefully, and rests it on her dresser. Then she opens her underwear drawer. On the right, she's stacked a pile of colorful, comfy, cotton undies and nude bras. On the left, a black lace pushup bra with a matching thong draws her attention. Her eyes dart back and forth between her options. After rolling her eyes, she takes a pair from the right.

When she opens her closet, she pushes aside her sundresses one at a time. June is too hot for jeans, but Ëólas has never seen her legs. Well, except for when he massaged her calves and she hiked up her dress during the never-ending horse ride. She grabs a sundress, the longest one she owns. The black fabric with miniature sunflowers hugs her chest but falls loosely to her knees. Last, she secures her hair on both sides with a barrette, lifting her waves away from her shoulders. She feels oddly exposed after all the layers she's been wearing this past month.

Glancing around her room once more, she heads to the door and reaches for the knob, only to stop. She backs up a few steps and drops onto her mattress. Falling backward, she spreads her arms out on her plum-colored duvet.

I'm home. I'm actually home. But do I want to stay? What if Ëólas and I are somehow bound together?

Bound together. The vows echo in the recess of her mind like a song on replay that she's been humming without realizing it. She laughs at herself.

He's still a prince. And I'm just me. Who can talk to the elements. Sort of. When my life is in danger. Which seems to be a regular occurrence when I'm there. But maybe that just proves that I can make a difference. And if I can, even in the smallest way, how can I stay here?

Adaline sits up and hangs her head. She's not going to be able to think about much else while Ëólas is here. Neither of them knows how long he might be stuck in this world. What's worse, even though she lost only an hour or two while in his world, they can't expect the same outcome when they return. Or *if* he returns. If anything, an hour here could be a month there, meaning Āranol and the Morgai could have already attacked Magnus and the city.

"Fuck." Wallowing here won't help. Guessing and panicking won't help either. Right now, Ëólas needs her help. And clothes.

Ducking into the back of her closet, Adaline grabs a T-shirt and walks into the living room where Ëólas scowls at the pages he's flipping through of *Pride and Prejudice*. With a shake of his head, he puts the book down, and when his eyes fall on Adaline, his muscles lock in place so that he cannot move or look away.

"It's, um, hot this time of year." Tucking a rogue curl behind her ear, she hands him the faded shirt with The Beatles crossing Abbey Road and stares over his shoulder so she can more easily ignore him frowning at the cotton blend. "You should take everything off from the waist up. Use the guest room, the door to the left of the bookshelves. I know the shirt isn't much, but it was my father's."

Gently, Ëólas folds the shirt over his arm as if he were carrying a dinner jacket. "I'm honored. Thank you."

When he shuts the door to the guest room, Adaline grabs a wristlet from her desk drawer and tosses into the zippered pouch her spare keys, her mobile phone, and the new credit card she hadn't activated until just now. *No license, but hopefully that won't be an issue.* From the hall closet, she retrieves a golden-yellow cardigan to cover her shoulders and Derek's forgotten flip-flops. *Poor Ëólas.*

Within a few minutes, he exits the guest room, his new wardrobe a fun mix of casual college student meets forest ranger. Ignoring her amusement, he points to his ears. "What about these?"

She tosses her wristlet from hand to hand. "They're not super pointy. People will just think you were born that way."

"I was."

"Ah, yes. I just mean..."

"I know what you mean," he laughs.

"Ha. Ha. Okay. But seriously, if anyone does mention your ears, it just means they're an asshole."

Chapter Twenty

THREE CORNERS

Despite the fact that some unknown fae has spirited Ëólas away to another world, one stuffed to the brim with humans, he walks down Bethesda Row as if he were back in the Neutral Territory with his eyes taking in every shop window display, every person dashing past them, and every source of honk and holler and giggle. When an airplane flies overhead, he stops in the middle of the sidewalk and watches the white dotted trail fade away. Adaline holds his hand to pull him back down to reality, and they continue onward. But he isn't the only one easily distracted right now.

If I do go back, I'd still be Magnus's ward. And even if I can convince him to let me stay in New Leira when he leaves, Ëólas visits only a few months a year. I'd hardly see him.

For their first stop, Ëólas ditched the flip-flops for suede ankle boots. Every now and again, he bounces a few steps forward and rocks back and forth on his heels. "How do they make the squishy interior that hugs my feet?"

Adaline shrugs. "I have no idea."

"Can I keep these? Add a few enchantments, and they'll last forever."

"They're yours to do with as you please."

"Fantastic."

Next, Adaline leads Ëólas through the clothes racks and selects different materials, styles, and sizes for him to try on, but the mound in her arms quickly multiplies until she can no longer see straight ahead. Thankfully, a sales lady comes to their aid, a curvy twenty-something with luscious, shimmering, thick hair that flows down her back. If her silk blouse were to burst open, the catapulted buttons would blind someone. Told to sit in the corner just outside the try-on room, Adaline mindlessly refolds the clothing that didn't fit or feel right to Ëólas.

I can't imagine what New Leira is like without him there.

When Adaline peeks into the fitting room, the sales lady slides her hands down Ëólas's arms, her fingertips lingering over his biceps. The light-blue cotton and linen blend fits him perfectly, allowing him room to move but also falling against his lean body so that Adaline can make out the silhouette of his muscles and a concealed pendent that dangles above his abs.

The sales lady tells Ëólas to turn around so she can examine his shoulders, and her eyes ogle his ass in a pair of skinny jeans, the cuffs folded once over his boots. "This is perfect. Do the jeans fit right in the waist?"

As he turns about, he lifts his shirt to look at the waist, revealing a row of sculpted abs that no man, no living creature, in any world should ever have the right to show off. Then again, he does spend his days at the training grounds and walking miles and climbing trees.

I guess he earned those. She hugs the pile of clothes she folded to her chest. After she plucks off a loose thread and tosses it to the ground, her eyes jump back to Ëólas's stomach.

The sales lady examines his waist and licks her lips. "Are they too tight?"

As she dips her fingers into his waistband, Adaline drops the clothes, letting them spill around her feet. She leaps into the fitting room, sprints to Ëólas's stall, and skids to a stop in between him and the saleslady who jumped backward to avoid Adaline knocking her over.

Taking a step back to push Ëólas into his stall, Adaline spreads her arms to block the doorway. "He's fine. I've got things from here. Thanks so much for your help."

With a forced grin, the sales lady leaves, glancing back at Ëólas until she's gone. Spinning around, Adaline shoves him further inside the stall, her hands lingering on his chest. "Do you always let women stick their hands down your pants?"

He lifts his palms, and his face goes blank. "Is that not normal?"

"No!"

"Oh."

"Button up your shirt two more times, too. Only models show off their pecks."

No matter how hard she tries, she can't erase the scowl on her face and soften her tone. At least Ëólas does as Adaline says while she sorts the clothing they're buying. If he'll be here a month, he'll need at least a week's worth of everything. She slams two more shirts onto the purchase pile.

He can learn how to do the laundry too.

They exit the store with Ëólas carrying six large shopping bags. The further they get from that sales lady, the more Adaline's able to slow her pace.

He's never once indicated that he might be physically interested in me. Sure, he's sweet and attentive and supportive. Aside from one random, roundabout comment about making history, which could apply to anyone, he's never ogled me. He's never suggested that he might...that we might...

Ëólas stops abruptly in front of a dessert shop. "You're mad at me."

Exhaling loudly, Adaline faces him. "No, I'm not. I just have a lot on my mind. I'm sorry." *He's a prince. Maybe he's used to having ladies fawn all over him.*

"I thought ruminating was my job?" When Adaline cracks a smile, Ëólas nudges her with his elbow. "If you need someone to talk to, I'm a pretty decent listener."

"Thanks. I'll keep that in mind. Let's head back to drop off your stuff, and I need to change for tonight. Remind me to make sure you try cheesecake after dinner."

"Deal. May I ask something though?"

"Sure."

Putting down half the bags, Ëólas reaches into his pocket and pulls out a crumpled piece of paper. "What are these numbers?"

Adaline glares at the digits. "How you can contact her. She wants to be your next lover."

With his nostrils widening and his brows dipping downward, Ëólas walks over to a trashcan and throws out the paper.

"Not interested in making history, huh?" The words burst out of her mouth before she can slam her hands across her mouth and shut herself up. Spinning away from him, she picks up his bags and stares at the cakes in the display window. In the glass, she watches Ëólas walk up behind her, his breath on her neck.

With his eyes never leaving her reflection, his hand slides down her wrist, and his fingers brush the inside of her palm as he takes the bags from her. "What have you been pondering so intensely, Adaline? Where's your mind been all day? All week? Let me know when you're ready, and we'll talk."

Ëólas clings to the metro's overhead bar as the train jostles them downtown. People sporting NHL Washington Capitals' T-shirts and faces painted red and white fill the train, pushing Adaline and Ëólas further into a corner. A group of drunk college kids squeezes around them, hollering, cheering, and making plans for their next party. Their torn jeans and oversized shirts clash with Adaline's black-lace dress, attached nude lining, and deep V-neck. One of the college guys sidles up closer to Adaline, and his side-eye lingers on her décolletage. She turns in toward Ëólas, her flared hem mingling with his legs, as he puzzles over the stained ceiling.

"Let's win this cup!" a passenger hollers. The entire train roars in response.

Using her handbag to cover her cleavage, Adaline waits for Ëólas to make eye contact with her again. "You're taking this rather well."

His eyes fall on a homeless man who boards the train, pushing his shopping cart of possessions ahead of him to make way. People clear space for him, or rather run away. He lays down across two seats where he falls asleep.

Ëólas forces himself to turn away. "I don't know what to say."

The train car slows down and stops in the middle of a tunnel. Everyone moans, and the Caps fans cuss loudly. The lights on the train flicker a few times before going off, and the emergency lights cast an orange hue on everyone. Even though most people keep their noses tilted toward their phones, Ëólas's eyes dart about the train in every direction.

Adaline places her hand on his chest, over his heart, willing him to relax. "I've got you. No elf hunters here, promise."

When he looks down, their eyes lock. He places his hand over hers and breathes slowly. The white lights flicker on again, and the train lurches forward. The sudden momentum shifts the crowd, and Adaline stumbles forward, her body shoved against his. Cheers erupt around them.

Do you fancy me? Can you stop being so damn honorable for once?

As the train speeds ahead, Ëólas uses his one free arm to hug Adaline close to him, to shield her from the next mass of people shoving their way into the train car and pushing her and Ëólas further into the corner, her shoulders hitting the car wall. As he massages her back, his thumb fiddles with her concealed zipper. Beneath her curls, his featherlight touch skates over her bare back until he begins massaging a knot she didn't realize had formed at the base of her neck. She closes her eyes so he won't see them roll back in her head. When she glances up at him, he's fixated on the ticker tape displaying the metro stop names.

Damn it. I can't keep going on like this. Get your shit together, Adaline, and be bold, even if I might have a heart attack in the process. Tonight, I'm getting answers.

As the train jolts to a stop, the passengers rock backward, but Ëólas holds her in place until the train conductor announces their arrival. Outside the metro, Adaline takes Ëólas's hand and leads him to the restaurant, her cheeks flushed and her heart racing but her nerves steeled.

Before they go inside, she swings in front of him, leaving little space between them. "Are you ready for this?"

"Yes." He clears his throat. "I'm from a country called England. I work at the University of Reading in the Anthropology Department, and I'm thirty years old."

"Well done."

"Thank you. I'm a good student."

"Professor."

"Right."

"Okay, let's go. And don't leave me alone. Otherwise, Cindy will try to grill me about what happened with work, but tonight's her night. I don't want to do anything that will take away from that."

"Understood." He bows his head, demonstrating he'll be on his best behavior.

When they enter La Salsa de Vida, the tropical yet spicy tune "La Gozadera" immediately tempts Adaline to swing her hips and shimmy her arms to the rhythm. The dance floor, not yet cleared of tables, promises late-night entertainment, and the upstairs seating has a prime mezzanine view of the live band that's begun their sound check.

A group of Dax and Cindy's friends wait by the podium. Adaline spies Dax first, punching a friend in the arm while fidgeting with the lump in his side pocket. Seeing Adaline, Dax excuses himself from his LARPer buddies and navigates through the crowd to greet her and Ëólas. The dopey grin on his face makes his bulbous cheeks shine. Adaline throws her arms around his neck and kisses his cheek. With her arm hooked around Dax's, she introduces him to Ëólas, who automatically bypasses Dax's outstretched hand to shake his forearm.

Dax tilts his head, then grins wider and clasps Ëólas's forearm in return. "Thank you for derailing Adaline's work plans so that she can be here tonight."

Ëólas laughs. "I'm glad it worked out. She's spoken of you and Cindy so many times over the last month that I'm glad to finally meet you both."

"She has, huh? I don't know if I should be worried." As Dax chuckles, his gaze locks on Ëólas's eyes. "Nice contacts."

With Dax and Ëólas making small talk, Adaline scans the gathering group. When Mikkel walks through the door, she screams, throws her arms in the air, and jumps at her old college roommate, who hugs her fiercely, lifting her feet off the floor. Neither of them let go right away.

When her heels touch the ground, she grabs his arms and squeezes. "What are you doing here? How long are you in town? Why didn't I know you were going to be here?"

"It's good to see you too, my dear," Mikkel says in his thick Haitian-Miami-Maryland accent. "I'm in town for three days before I fly down to Florida to see my grandmother. After that, I'm off to New York, London, and

Prague for meetings before returning to Nairobi. And last, Cindy told me not to tell you. She didn't want you to feel worse about not being able to come tonight. And yet here you are. What happened?"

"You wouldn't believe me if I told you. It's all good though." Adaline gestures with her thumb at Ëólas, who's popped up behind her. "This is my colleague, Ëólas. He's helping me with my research while he's in town. Ëólas, this is one of my best friends from college, Mikkel."

"A pleasure to meet you," Ëólas says. "You must be a friend of Cindy's too?"

"And Dax. I met them through Adaline, and we've been close ever since. You're from Britain? England or Wales? I can't quite place the accent."

Ëólas casually tosses his hand away. "Somewhere in between. You can't find it on a map."

Adaline pats Ëólas's arm. *Well done.* "Mikkel and I spent most of our nights playing board games and watching reruns of *Gargoyles*. But about two years after we graduated, he moved overseas for work, so I get to see him maybe once a year now." The corners of her mouth dip downward. Mikkel's another friend who's moved on in life. She needs to do the same, to keep looking forward instead of backward.

As they wait to be seated, Mikkel draws Ëólas into a conversation about Mikkel's work and how he assists with mass population migration due to climate change evaporating drinkable water. Finally, Ëólas is the one asking a million questions. Even here, in another world, his confidence and easy manner help him to slip seamlessly into new company. The more she watches him debate politics with Mikkel and Dax, Adaline's sense of pride grows larger. Her two worlds have collided, and Ëólas has taken everything in stride, even meeting the closest people she has to family.

Now this is a perfect moment.

Sensing another person approaching from behind, Adaline steps aside to make room among their growing group. An arm snakes around her waist, an arm not belonging to Ëólas. She turns around, not yet comprehending what's happening, and gasps as Derek plants a kiss on her lips. As his ChapStick rubs off on her, all of her hopes for tonight implode inside her stomach.

"Derek, what? Why?" Placing her hands on his chest, she steps backward so an arm's length separates them. With her hand covering her mouth, she glances at Ëólas and pleads with her eyes that he not interfere. He gnashes his teeth but turns back to Mikkel, even though Ëólas keeps Derek within view the entire time.

Derek's gray eyes sparkle as he takes in her dress. "Dax texted me with the updated reservation info."

Fuck! I never told them we broke up.

"I was so relieved when he said I could be here," Derek says. "I know things got a little heated yesterday, but I thought about everything you said, and I hope we can talk." Taking her hand, he leads her to the opposite side of the waiting area.

Not once does he notice Adaline's mouth hanging open or her eyes glazed over. Her feet automatically follow him while she keeps waiting to wake up, to realize she's having another nightmare. But somehow, Derek manages to trap her in a corner of the restaurant.

Away from their friends, Derek looks her up and down. His long, parted bangs frame his steel-gray eyes, and his matching dark gray polo accentuates his stare, making his gaze sharper and harder to avoid. "Wow. You look stunning."

"Derek, I'm sorry Dax—"

"No, I'm sorry." He takes a deep breath before he speaks. "I want you to know I heard everything you said about us moving too fast and that you don't feel the same way. And it's okay. I get it. You need more time. You've been through so much the last two years, and I got overexcited and tried to skip ahead. It makes total sense you got scared. We don't have to talk about marriage, not until you're ready. I'm okay waiting, because you're worth waiting for."

Taking both of her hands in his, he gazes at her with the same devotion as Pygmalion did with Galatea, as if Derek knows with absolute devotion that Venus will grant his wish and Adaline will fulfill his desires. He leans in to kiss her again, but Adaline dodges to the left and spins away from him. His smile falters for half a second.

"Derek, I didn't—"

"Hey guys! Table's ready!" Dax shouts over the din.

Holding her hand, Derek pecks her cheek and guides them through the crowd to follow their friends and the hostess. Adaline stumbles behind him, unsure what to say or do to end this without causing a scene, without clueing Cindy into what's going on, and without derailing Cindy's once-in-a-lifetime moment because of Adaline's drama.

But, but I already ended it. Why do I have to go through this again?

Ëólas doesn't move until Adaline walks past him, his glare fixated on Derek's fingers tugging her wrist. Silently, Ëólas follows Adaline's lead. As they walk up the winding metal staircase to the second-floor balcony, she slips her hand out of Derek's. He moves backward to let her take a seat, and she drops into the last chair to the right, thinking Ëólas is right behind her. But Derek jumps into the chair next to her, forcing Ëólas to sit at the end of the table.

This is not a sign from the universe. No way. If I was meant to be with Derek, he would have traveled with me to the other world, somehow. This is just shitty timing, nothing more.

Derek drops one arm around the back of Adaline's chair, so she rests her arms on the table and leans as far forward as possible. Nibbling the inside of her bottom lip, she tilts her head sideways and looks at Ëólas, her brows sagging. He rests his chin on his steepled hands and lifts his eyebrows as if he's watching a game of chess and waiting to see who will make the next move.

Facing Adaline, Dax remains standing near the center of the table. He must expect Cindy any moment now.

Crap. Okay, I'll drag Derek outside after dinner. No, wait. We might still have time to get this over with now. "Derek, I need to speak with you out—"

"Heeeey!" Cindy chimes, waving at all of her friends.

Dax beams at his soon-to-be fiancée in the magenta dress Adaline helped Cindy pick out. He kisses her tenderly and pulls out her chair but waits as Cindy walks around the table to greet each of their twelve friends. When she reaches the end, Adaline jumps out of her seat and grabs Cindy in a bear hug. She smells like cherry blossoms, and the strength of their embrace encapsulates a lifetime of sleepovers concluding with cookie-dough ice cream, the mutual loss of a parent, and an unspoken vow to drop everything when needed and be there for each other.

Cindy's the last link to Adaline's past, a past she's almost ready to relinquish. She hugs her dearest friend more tightly.

Cindy squeezes Adaline just as fiercely, and they rock side to side. Her life is about to change too. But before letting go, she whispers in Adaline's ear, "Are you sure you're okay?"

"Yeah, I'm just so damn happy I could be here after all."

When Adaline drops her arms, Cindy knits her brows together and scrutinizes her friend's face until her focus jumps to Adaline's hair. "Whoa, it's so crazy long." Pulling a section of Adaline's hair away from her shoulder, Cindy runs her fingers down the length until it drops to the middle of Adaline's thigh.

"Magical extensions. Apparently, I needed a change." *Oh, Seira. I miss you too.*

"Uh-huh."

"You don't like it?"

"It's freaking gorgeous, like mermaid hair. I'm just surprised you didn't tell me."

"Sorry. We do have a lot of catching up to do, but it can wait until tomorrow. Go sit down, and tell Dax to stop taking his damn time."

"I know, right?" Cindy winks her fake lashes and pinches Adaline's elbow.

"But before you do, I'd like to introduce you to someone." Without warning, Adaline's cheeks burn. "This is Ëólas."

She steps to the side, giving Ëólas space to stand up and enabling her to block Derek, who's chattering away with the person next to him. As Cindy extends her arm to shake Ëólas's hand, he clasps her fingers and kisses the back of her hand. Cindy side-eyes Adaline and grins.

Ëólas nods his head hello. "A pleasure to finally meet you, Cindy. I've heard much about you and your family, particularly your younger sisters. I'm delighted I can share in tonight's festivities. Thank you kindly for the invitation."

"Aww." A blush creeps up Cindy's cheeks. "You're so welcome. I can't wait to get to know you."

When Cindy walks behind him, she locks eyes with Adaline and mouths *Oh my god!* while fanning her face. She continues around the table until she takes her seat next to Dax, who orders appetizers for everyone, including Cindy and

Adaline's favorite bacon-wrapped dates. Adaline looks over the menu with Ëólas, their shoulders not quite touching, and suggests what he might like to try.

"What are you in the mood for?" she asks.

"How about the quintessential American meal?"

She points to the burger section. "It's bread with meat in the middle."

"Another sandwich?"

Adaline chuckles, recalling the confusion on his face when she wedged slices of meat in between bread in New Leira. "Yes, but it's juicy and tasty. I warn you though, the portion sizes are crazy."

"Perfect. I'm feeling famished again."

Adaline shakes her head but doesn't comment. She returns to her own menu but can't ignore the intense wave of energy radiating at her from the middle of the table. Peeking over the leather-bound menu, she catches Cindy flicking her eyes back and forth from Derek to Ëólas and pursing her lips as she analyzes Adaline's body leaning away from her boyfriend. Adaline pushes her brows toward the ceiling in all innocence and sits up straight in her seat. Only, when she leans against Derek's arm, her shoulders automatically curl inward.

Damn it. Cindy saw that.

As Derek brushes his thumb over Adaline's shoulder, he turns to Ëólas. "I'm sorry. Do I know you?"

"Um, no," Adaline cuts in. "This is Ëólas, my new colleague." She gulps and forces her next words to sound neutral. "Ëólas, this is Derek."

After the guys wave briefly at each other, Adaline blocks her view of everyone and everything with her menu and reads the same words over and over again. When the server asks if she'd like to order a drink, she blinks a few times before defaulting to, "Sangria. Just bring the whole pitcher. A few actually."

The clanging of metal against glass makes everyone at the table turn to Dax, who stands up and clears his throat. Adaline pulls her phone out of her purse and starts recording. Within two seconds, Ëólas appears over her shoulder. He squints at the digital screen, and a whispered "Whoa" escapes his lips. She stifles a laugh.

After Dax thanks everyone for coming downtown to help them celebrate, he retells the story about the first time he met Cindy at an outdoor showing of *Forrest*

Gump, about how nervous he was asking her to prom, and about how they lost each other for a few years.

"We took some time to figure out who we wanted to grow into, and we did pretty good. But the moment I saw her again, I knew I didn't want to grow into anyone that didn't include her, because Cindy has always been my perfect match." Dax gets down on one knee and pulls out of his pocket a plastic toy can, something from a kid's play kitchen, with a picture of dancing peas and carrots. As Cindy laughs and tears trickle down her cheeks, Dax pops the lid off and tilts the can until a ring tumbles onto his palm.

Cindy shoves her hand in his face, which makes everyone laugh, including Ëólas.

Dax takes her hand and kisses it. "Can I ask first?"

"Oh, fine." She dances in her seat but doesn't withdraw her hand.

"Lucinda Maria Seguar, would you do me the honor of becoming my wife?"

"YES!" Cindy squeals, forgetting about the ring, throwing her arms around Dax's thick neck, and peppering his cheeks with kisses.

When Dax does finally slide the ring onto her finger, their table and four more around them clap and cheer. Cindy and Dax wave thanks to everyone, and Cindy kisses him three more times. As he takes his seat again, she tilts her ring in the light to watch it sparkle like a kaleidoscope, even as the servers arrive with the appetizers and take everyone's dinner orders.

Ëólas leans closer to Adaline. "If you hadn't told me about the meaning of the ring, I'd have no idea what's going on."

"I'm glad we covered that topic then." *While we were running for our lives. My god, the Wastelands feel like another lifetime. If not for Ëólas being here, I'd think I'd gone mad.*

She pushes all thoughts about the other world away. Tonight is a celebration, a reprieve. She blows Cindy a kiss, and in return, Cindy holds up her hand to Adaline and bounces in her seat. Adaline laughs to herself. She's never been like Cindy, not when it comes to romance. Adaline has never longed to go ring shopping. She never imagined the colors of her bridesmaid dresses or the theme she'd want. She never flipped through bridal magazines, drooled over a wedding gown, or pre-planned the menu. The pomp and circumstance never appealed to her—except for the music selection. Okay, and the dessert menu. Her wedding would require creamy New York-style cheesecake. Now Adaline's drooling.

She sneaks a peek at Ëólas chatting with Mikkel and presses her palm against her heart. She doesn't need a wedding. She doesn't even need a groom. If Ëólas is open to having her for the next twenty years, that's enough. Having him is enough.

Chapter Twenty-One

SANGRIA

After the servers place the appetizers and pitchers on the table, Adaline lurches forward, pours herself a glass to the rim, and sucks down the tangy sweet beverage until only one-third remains. She also arches her back so her shoulders don't touch her chair or Derek. Finally, he takes his arm back to pour himself a glass, and Adaline's spine curves into the cushioned chair.

I can get through this night.

Mikkel, in all his diplomatic glory, takes over the conversation at her end of the table for a bit. Bobbing her head and sipping her sangria, Adaline doesn't interject until Mikkel haphazardly mentions that he's meeting up with Maggie tomorrow.

Adaline nearly spits her drink back into her glass. "Wait, wait, wait. You're seeing Maggie again? *The* Maggie? The girl who got away last year?"

"She didn't get away. We live worlds apart." Mikkel waves Adaline off, but the goofy grin on his face gives him away. "And she's finishing her PhD research. You know how time consuming that can be."

Adaline scrunches her nose. "But have you been in touch this whole time?"

"I might have seen her two months ago at a convention in Geneva."

"Mikkel!"

"I'm trying to give her space and not distract her."

"Oh, no!" Adaline slams her glass down on the table, drawing Cindy's radar. "You already are distracting her. You think you're doing the right thing by keeping your mouth shut, but what you're really doing is driving her insane, making her spend every waking moment scrutinizing every interaction and conversation she's ever had with you because she's second-guessing if she's been imagining the chemistry between you the whole time."

Mikkel waves his hand dismissively. "No, she's not."

"Hell yes," Cindy says. "You're messing with her head. Tell Maggie how you feel. You can't keep this casual for another two years."

"*Two* years!" Adaline screeches.

"She knows," Mikkel says. "We text every day, and we've been talking about meeting up in Turkey in three months."

"That's not enough, Mikkel." Cindy wags her finger in his direction. "You have to be upfront with her. That's the only way you'll know if you two can make this work."

"Do words speak louder than actions here?" Ëólas asks, his head still volleying back and forth.

Mikkel points at Ëólas. "What he said. Actions speak louder than words."

"Not always!" Adaline scowls at Mikkel, making him shrink in his seat. "Sometimes we need to hear the words said out loud, to drown out the voice in our heads that tells us we're not good enough."

Ëólas scoffs and looks at Adaline incredulously. "How could Maggie ever think she's not good enough for Mikkel?"

"Because he's an intimidating guy who works with presidents and world leaders and has the power to make an actual difference in the world for thousands of people. And with her being so far behind him, how can she ever hope to be equal to him, to be worthy of him?"

"Achievements alone don't make someone my equal," Mikkel says.

Ëólas points at Mikkel. "What he said."

"Well, I guarantee she doesn't know that." Adaline finishes the last of her drink while wishing she could crawl into a hole. Then again, with her luck, it'd be a rabbit hole, and she'd be lost in Wonderland again.

Ëólas and Mikkel stare at each other, waiting for the other to provide a new defense, but both of them seem hesitant to argue the point further and lock their mouths shut. Standing up, Cindy announces in an overly cheery voice that she needs the bathroom and gestures for Adaline to join her, but Adaline shakes her head profusely and stares at the bottom of her glass, which is now empty. With a loud huff, Cindy sits back down, darts her eyes to Ëólas once more, and sips her sangria while flashing Adaline a wicked smile.

Thankfully, multiple conversations resume around them. Ëólas sits quietly at the head of the table while Adaline can't stop tapping her foot. Neither of them attempt to enter any conversations, not even with each other.

Without rhyme or reason, Derek cranes his neck around Adaline to better see Ëólas. "So, um, how long are you going to be in town?"

"I'm not certain. Depends on what Adaline and I discover over the next few days." Drumming his fingers on the table, Ëólas reaches for an empanada from the tapas sampler platter and takes a large bite. "Mmm, that's nice."

"Cool, cool, cool." Derek bobs his head a few times while he decides what to say next. Sitting sideways in his seat, he looks at Adaline like she's holding the Nobel Peace Prize, not half a pupusa. "You're lucky, you know, to have Adaline's insight. She's brilliant."

Don't roll my eyes. Don't roll my eyes. Don't roll my eyes.

Ëólas puts on his indifference mask, the one he wears when the council members bicker with each other and he has to listen with patience and respect until he can present his ideas and shut them up. "I'm well aware, thank you. We've been working closely together for a while now, and I've come to trust her unequivocally, mostly because she's so formidable. We've had our fair share of arguments, but I always found her to be correct in the end. I learned my lesson. I'll never be so daft as to ignore her words again." Without taking his eyes off Derek, Ëólas plucks a pineapple chunk out of his drink and gnashes it between his teeth.

Leaning forward, Adaline severs the tension in half as she reaches for the pitcher and pours herself another drink, using her fork to direct extra alcohol-soaked fruit into her glass.

With a half laugh, Derek scratches the back of his head. "Yeah. She has a lot of passion for her work."

"She certainly is passionate." Ëólas sucks a cherry off its stem.

Oh my god. What's he doing? Cherries can't be fucking universal in their meaning, right? I might kill him. I might actually kill him if he makes my friends think I've been cheating on Derek.

Placing a hand on Adaline's knee, Derek gazes lovingly at Adaline while she slurps the bottom of her second glass. "I know you love sangria, honey, but have some appetizers." He puts together a plate for her, a selection of empanadas, dates, and her favorite chicken tamale. Unfolding her napkin, he drapes it over her lap and returns his hand to her knee.

When Adaline catches Ëólas gripping the butter knife, she shakes her head ever so slowly and doesn't breathe again until he puts it down.

"So, Ëólas—Hey, isn't that Hercules's sidekick? Iolaus?" Derek asks.

"Different spelling." Adaline shoves two bacon-wrapped dates in her mouth at the same time and nearly chokes.

"Oh, okay. And you'll be here for a few days. Cool. I'll probably see you on campus then. I teach history, primarily U.S. history. I hope you're enjoying your trip on this side of the pond. Where are you staying?"

"With me." Adaline pushes the food aside, jabs each and every fruit with her fork, and eats them all.

Looking at her like a lost puppy, Derek rubs his thumb over her knee and begs, "Why?"

"Why not?" She brushes Derek's hand off her. When she pours herself a third drink, she ignores Cindy's intense stare.

"Oh," Derek says, his tone curt. Inclining his body close to hers, he whispers in her ear, "You, you don't know him well enough. I can stay too."

Who the hell does he think he is! Clenching her jaw, Adaline says as quietly as possible, "We should talk now. Outside."

Derek crosses his arms over his chest. A spark flares in the back of his eyes, an ember that falters and dies out faster than Adaline can register. He grips her knee again, only this time he digs his fingers into her skin, leaving his mark in the shape of little half-moons. "I can't, in good consciousness, leave you alone with him. You only just met the guy. He could be a psycho in disguise, him and his ridiculous ears."

A waterfall of dark purplish red flows from the pitcher onto Derek's chest. Adaline doesn't recall actually moving her arm or picking up the pitcher because everything becomes too much of a blur as Derek shifts from arguing to screaming. He jumps up, knocking over his chair, and hurls profanities into every corner of the restaurant, releasing a torrent of rage she's never seen from him before. The ice cubes and fruit tumble down his shirt and disappear under the table. Their friends leap to their feet too, but no one says anything while they try to piece together what just happened. At some point, Ëólas must have stood up too because he's positioned himself in front of Adaline.

The pitcher rolls at her feet.

"What the hell was that for?" With a groan of disgust, Derek plucks an apple slice out of his shirt pocket and throws it on the floor. "And who the hell do you think you are?" Derek gets up in Ëólas's face and raises a pointed finger that Ëólas grabs and twists behind Derek's back.

Adaline pulls on Ëólas's bicep. "Don't break his arm! You'll get arrested." Pushing the pitcher away with her foot, she turns to Derek. "I'm so sorry. I don't know what came over me, but you need to leave."

"What? Why? I've done nothing but be there for y—"

"You still don't hear me. I meant everything I said to you yesterday, and you still took this opportunity to push me into an uncomfortable situation, hoping I'd just go along with you again. I'm done. It's over. What about that isn't clear enough?"

"But I love—"

"You need to go, man. I'll walk you out." Mikkel puts his arm on Derek's deflated shoulders and escorts him downstairs while servers speak with Dax to make sure everyone's okay and clean up the mess. Stepping up to the railing, Ëólas watches Derek leave the building. Cindy, dodging the puddle and chunks of mango slices, makes her way to Adaline and holds her hand to help it stop shaking.

She leans her head on Cindy's shoulder. "I'm so sorry I ruined your night."

"Oh, stop. It'll take a hell of a lot more than this to bring me down right now." Cindy gives Adaline a big hug. "Plus, that's the most alive I've seen you in months. Best engagement gift ever."

"Drowning Derek? I thought you liked him?"

"Meh. It's hard for me to like someone who's wrong for you."

I really needed that.

After they hold each other a bit longer, Cindy returns to her seat, and at the same time, the trays with their meals arrive.

But Adaline walks next to Ëólas and rests her hands on the railing. "That was embarrassing."

Ëólas slides his hand next to hers, their pinkies touching. "I knew you'd handle it, sooner or later." With an I-told-you-so smirk, he points to his ears. "Besides, he proved he's an asshole."

"Oh my god." Adaline rolls her eyes but chuckles along with him.

The rest of the night, the dinner table boasts several lively conversations, tasty dishes that Adaline keeps telling Ëólas to try, and two glorious slices of cheesecake: one with a chocolate ganache topping and another with a fresh fruit spread. She passes Ëólas a fork. "I wasn't sure which might be too sweet for you."

"Nothing about this looks like cheese, aside from the wedge-like shape." He holds the fork up between them. "Why do I have a miniature meat server?"

Cracking up, Adaline digs the four prongs into the fruit slice. As the creamy texture mingles with bursts of strawberry on her tongue, she closes her eyes and moans softly. *Every world should have cheesecake.*

"That good?" Ëólas asks, his eyes lingering on her lips.

"Oh yeah. Your turn. Try the bite of chocolate first."

She pulls a chocolate square off the cake and hands it to him. As it melts in his mouth, his eyebrows shoot upward. He tries the cheesecake itself, and an unbridled smile stretches across his face. "I see what you mean."

If only they could have more moments like this, sweet snippets carved out of the chaos. If she had to do it all over again—the panic of never seeing home again, the helplessness of being attacked, the terror of thinking she's about to die at a stranger's hands—she would. She has zero regrets about her adventure, because the wonder, the magic, the people, the mission, they all make her braver.

I'm going back with him. Even if he doesn't want me, I have to go back.

In their corner of the restaurant, Adaline and Ëólas alternate between the two slices, their forks dancing around each other and their upper bodies drifting closer, until Cindy plops in the seat next to Adaline.

Relinquishing the last bite, she takes Cindy's hand and tilts it back and forth to better see the cushion-cut diamond. "He did good."

"He did, didn't he?" She hugs her hand to her heart and gleams. "Time to hit the dance floor, Chica. Ëólas, you want to join us, or are you going to hide up here with the men?"

At Dax's suggestion, Ëólas opts to hang out with the boys. They line up along the balcony while the ladies head downstairs. The restaurant turns up the speakers, and Adaline and Cindy merge with the music. Adaline occasionally steals a peek at Ëólas and his animated conversation with her friends. Knowing he's okay, she gives in to the music, swinging with Cindy and taking the lead. Every time her hips and arms sway to the beat, she casts off the worst bits of the last month.

"Why didn't you tell me about Derek?" Cindy swings under Adaline's arm, then grabs both of her hands as they break step back and forth, the hems of their dresses swishing away from their thighs.

"I ended things only yesterday." *Sort of.* "I didn't have time to fill you in."

"About the blond model you brought to dinner?"

Adaline scoffs even though her face grows warmer, but that's just because of the music and Adaline rock stepping to the fast-paced beat. "He's a colleague."

"Who you're in love with."

"Whaaaaat?" Adaline spins around Cindy's back. Holding her friend's waist and hand, they switch into a swing step. "It's not like that. I mean, maybe. We haven't worked this out yet."

"But you're jumping his bones tonight."

"What?" Adaline, pretending to look like the epitome of innocence, twists Cindy away and back again.

"Please, you're wearing your pushup bra, the one you *hid* from Derek."

Spinning away from her friend, Adaline abandons the dance floor and heads over to the bar. She needs something stronger. "I need a Paloma."

Cindy follows. "Hey, what's going on?"

Adaline waves her hand to get the attention of a bartender. Left waiting, she turns to Cindy and word vomits on her best friend, whom Adaline's been aching to speak with for weeks. "It's just really complicated. He lives overseas, you know? I'd have to move really far away. With ridiculously limited internet. And he comes from a prestigious family, one that most likely would freak out if he actually brought me home. And so many people look up to him. And he's so considerate, sometimes too much so. And sometimes he pisses me off to no end, but most of the time being with him is the easiest thing in the world. But I don't actually know if he's interested in me. And even if he is, I'm not sure if he'd be up for something long term. And he's not into the whole marriage idea. I don't even think I'm his type." *Not with a human.* "He's just so—"

"Go."

"What?"

Cindy waves the bartender away and grabs Adaline's hands. "Move. Do whatever you need to do, but don't let him get away."

"But."

"No buts. Look," Cindy says, counting off on her hand. "One, you love traveling, so move overseas. Two, tell his family to fuck off if you have to. Dax's mom ruined our relationship the first time, and my cowardice nearly cost me everything. Don't be a wimp. Three, I don't care how impressive Ëólas is; you're fucking amazing. Don't roll your eyes at me. And four, I've never, ever seen you in love before. Not once. So don't you damn let this go, or I'll be spending my wedding fund on buying your ass a plane ticket so you can wake up every day in that beautiful man's arms."

You don't know what you're saying, just how far away I'll be, that I won't even be at your wedding or meet your babies or watch you become the abuela. But...

Adaline throws her arms around Cindy's neck and holds on for dear life, knowing this could very well be the last time. For years now, Adaline's life has revolved around preserving the past. Letting go isn't easy. It's not without tears and heartache. But she's ready now, ready to jump off that cliff and enjoy the exhilarating free fall that awaits. Even though she doesn't know how she'll land, that's okay. She'll figure it out.

I love you, Cindy. "No matter how far I go, you'll always be my sister."

"Damn right." Cindy holds Adaline close, then playfully punches her shoulder. "Why don't you guys come over for dinner tomorrow night so Dax and I can get to know him more? I'll set up Settlers of Catan. But no more sangria."

I wish you could get to know him more. Hopefully, that pang will lessen with time.

CHAPTER TWENTY-TWO

A LIST

They return to Adaline's condo past midnight. She props her back against the front door while Ëólas takes off his shoes. He glances at her three-inch heels, at her flexed calves, at the lace hem of her dress that extends two inches beyond the nude liner. When he stands in front of her, they're almost the same height now, chest to chest, nose to nose.

The intensity of his gaze makes her more conscious of the sangria sloshing around in her stomach. Neither of them breaks eye contact. The tension between them gathers, condenses, and rolls together, building between them like steam trapped in a boiling pot of water. The lid has to go.

What do I say? Do you want me as your lover? I want to be your next lover? The word *next* lodges in her throat. *Be brave.*

Ëólas shoves his hands in his pockets, as if he's subconsciously letting her know that he has zero intention of touching her again. "If we find answers at the sacred circle tomorrow, you know you don't have to come back with me."

A lump forms in her throat, threatening to strangle her from the inside out. *Did he overhear my conversation with Cindy? Is he pushing me away like I did Derek when he got too attached?*

Adaline lowers her eyes and bunches her face into a knot. The pot's boiling, alright. She clenches her fist, then shoves his chest as hard as she can, forcing him to take several steps backward to give her space. "You're such an asshole. How can you say something like that!"

He doesn't bother to take his hands out of his pockets, to defend himself, to fight back. Instead, he looks at the floor, at the distance between them. "You have friends here. A life. You don't have to give that up."

"Don't you think I know that? But you honestly think I can slip back into this life without ever knowing what will happen to you and Magnus and New Leira? You think I'm okay with never seeing Seira or Sallie again? Or the guys who've become like my brothers? Did it ever once occur to you that maybe I'd prefer to be a part of history rather than dig it up? Damn it, Ëólas. I know what I want, and you and your infallible gallantry aren't going to stop me."

His eyes snap to hers. "What do you want then?"

His arms twitch at his sides, and his body tilts a hair forward, but he doesn't move, doesn't risk pissing her off further. His eyes lock with hers, and the heat behind them gives her hope. She latches onto that single spark, uses it like a tether to pull them both together. The closer they are, the harder it is to breathe, to think, to find the right words. Slowly, she traces circles around the top button of his shirt, the one she told him to close up. He swallows hard.

"What do you want?" he repeats, but his voice is thicker, heavier, hoarser.

She spreads her legs, slips one knee between his thighs, and shifts her hips to rub against him, just once but enough to test if she can break through his chivalry, if she can find more proof to give her the courage to be honest with him, to say the words throbbing in the back of her mouth.

He frees one arm, wraps it around her, and holds her closer. When she pulls one side of her cheek up into a smirk, his hand drops to the small of her back, and he crushes her between him and the door, the backward momentum giving them an excuse to grind against the other. With her hand still on his chest, she grabs his shirt, her nails scratching his skin through the thin fabric. The pressure between her legs builds, and her cheeks flush. As he slides his thigh between her legs again, her thong rubs her in all the right places. Her breath hitches. He lowers his cheek beside hers, the corners of their mouths touching, and whispers his question for a third time.

Apparently, actions aren't enough for him either right now.

"I want you," she rasps, pulling him closer, burying her face in his neck, inhaling his scent. *I want you more than anything else, in this world or any other.*

With both hands, he grabs her rear, digging his fingers into her round bottom, and presses his entire length against her, revealing that he can barely fit inside his jeans anymore. "Thank the fae."

His lips brush across hers and knock down the last of the wall they both built the day they met. They linger in the middle of that first connection for a long second, savoring the hard-won reward, the undeniable evidence of their aligned desires. Slowly, their lips dance and mingle and cascade against each other as they yield and merge again, neither wasting time to pause, neither creating a window for this to end. As she parts her lips, desperate for more, to continue down this path she hardly allowed herself to imagine, he deepens the kiss, crushing his mouth against hers and pushing his tongue inside her, demanding as much from her as she's longed for from him. Their breath mingles, and their lips sync into a unified rhythm that equally takes and gives and makes all of her troubles and doubt fade out of existence. When his hand grabs her knee and pulls her leg around his hip, he grinds against her again, and she rolls her hips to feel him fully against her.

She's unraveling quickly, and she doesn't care. She finds his belt buckle and tugs it loose. But his other hand releases her bum and captures her fingers. Letting go of her lips, he leans his forehead against hers. They both breathe heavily, needing a moment to find their voices.

After kissing her passionately but quickly one more time, he leans back to take in her flushed cheeks. His eyes follow the path of her V-neckline and linger on her cleavage where her mounds press together. She wriggles beneath him, squeezing her knee wrapped around his hip, teasing him to keep going.

Instead, he exhales slowly and locks eyes with her again. "What else do you want?"

Adaline wiggles her imprisoned fingers. "Isn't that obvious?"

His grin widens, and his golden eyes darken. "We'll get there. But what else?"

"I don't know what you mean. My list of demands?" *You, inside me, right now.*

"Yes. I need clarity. Before we take this further."

"Oh." Adaline shimmies her hips from side to side, making him groan but drop her leg. She grumbles. *Fine. What do I want?* "A job."

"What sort?"

"I'm not sure yet, but something that allows me to help."

"A position on the council?"

Adaline crinkles her nose. She's seen enough of the way they bicker among themselves. "I hate politics. But I want to stay in New Leira. When Magnus leaves, I don't want to go with him." *I want to stay with you.* Watching Ëólas leave will kill her. She'll spend every night waiting for his return, his touch.

As if reading her mind, he trails the back of his hand along her side, his featherlight touch causing her to shiver and her head to grow foggy. He nuzzles her nose with his and peers into her eyes, coaxing her to tell him more. "What else?"

"At least—" She bites her bottom lip to stop the tears from forming. Her next demand seems too big, too much of a risk. She doesn't want to cry, not now, not when they're negotiating. "At least twenty years with you." She can't look at him, can't face his reaction, so she closes her eyelids to trap the tears behind that thin wall. They still escape, and her voice cracks as she says, "And promise you won't forget me."

Damn it, damn it, damn it. No matter how much her logic brain yells at her to stop behaving this way, her tears fall freely and make her chin itch. She clamps her mouth shut and swallows the cry that wants to follow. Only when his hands cup her cheeks does she open her eyes.

Beyond the blur, his nose and mouth pinch together, as if he feels every ounce of her pain. He wipes away her tears with his thumbs. "I could never in a million lifetimes forget you." He skates one arm behind her back and hugs her tightly. "I am beyond relieved to know you consider New Leira home." He nips at her lips again, pulling her away from the edge of despair. "What about Lameiría? Might that be a home to you as well?"

She looks at him through her damp lashes, still not daring to hope he'll keep her with him. "I, I'd like to help bring about change there too, but you think your parents will let me visit again? I mean, what will your people think about us?"

"Oh, Adaline." Lifting her chin, he presses his lips against hers, his touch tender and sweet, a balm for the cracks threatening to break her apart. "Thank you for being so honest. It's my turn now. If you're certain you want to return with me, I need you to understand I'm going to ask you to marry me."

Her tears solidify on her cheeks, and her heart stops beating long enough for her to make sure she heard him correctly. *He doesn't know what he's saying. He can't mean that.*

How can everything around them be moving at a glacial pace and yet time also seems to be speeding up? She can't move a muscle, can't speak, because if she does, she'll shatter reality or find herself lost in an alternate universe where he's disappeared.

He takes her shaking hand and places her palm over his heart. "Is it really so impossible for you to entertain the idea that my feelings might equal your own? I am utterly and completely in love with you."

An automatic reply tumbles out of her mouth. "No. No, you're not."

He doesn't realize what he's saying. He doesn't see how he's hurting her, torturing her, dangling in front of her the idea of a future neither of them can have.

With a faint laugh, he flashes a disbelieving half smile. "I think I know my own heart."

"No, you don't." She sounds like a broken record unable to skip past the crack. "I, I don't have as much time as you, and you're going to be a king, and I'm just me, and—"

Securing her within his embrace, he speaks slowly so that each of his words can penetrate her remaining defenses. "I have been in love with you for quite some time now. Don't you see how I cannot tolerate being away from you any longer? That I keep losing my resolve to give you space, to not touch you, to wait for you to decide what you want?"

She can't look away from him, his eyes, his nose, his lips that she aches to taste again. He glides his lips across hers and trails kisses along her jawline and downward. She needs her logic brain, but his breath on her neck overrides her better judgment. Forget everyone else. Him—she can't hurt him. "But I'm human. I'll get old." She shudders, remembering that lady in Feídra né Morna who gagged at the way humans age.

"The scales will balance." His breath lingers on her neck, and he sucks that tender spot that electrifies her, searing her core.

Her hips rock toward his. "But I'll be whittling your life down to practically nothing," she whispers.

"Can you bear the thought of us not being together?" He rubs the tip of his nose against hers. "Doesn't the very idea feel like fate's squeezing your soul into oblivion?" When she nods, his lips move closer to hers, the space between them shrinking with every microsecond. "It's the same for me. I'd rather have a shorter life in which I can spend every moment of every day loving you, than be cursed with a longer life that's barren."

That's how I feel. Staying here without you would leave me empty.

"Adaline, I promise I'll never forget what you'll be leaving behind, what you'll be giving up to stay with me. I'll make sure you have everything you want and need from this day forward. My only requests are that you continue to be yourself, the woman I fell in love with. Pursue your career in my world. Research whatever delights you. Ask a billion questions. Follow your passions. But please," his voice strains, "keep me with you. Even if you must travel between worlds again, take me too. Because you're my one, mé ellador. I want to go where you go."

"Oh my god. You, you really love me as much as I love you."

"Infinitely," he says. "I'll even convince Magnus to name the city New Leira as a wedding gift."

As she laughs and cries in his arms, he kisses and tells her again he loves her, giving her the words she needs to hear aloud to fracture the last of her disbelief, and a new vision fills every crevice of her heart, one of her standing by his side and helping both of their peoples. *Their* people, united. The vision, so bright and certain, swells inside her chest, making her body ache, but she doesn't struggle to contain the waves of happiness flooding her because this bliss belongs to the both of them—just like the seemingly small moments in between the difficult times, when it's just the two of them and she can love him fiercely.

Wherever he goes, I'll go too. As long as I can stay in his arms.

And in his arms is where she wants to be, right now, in bed.

Adaline slides her hands up his chest, around his shoulders, and grips his neck. Threading her fingers through his dirty-blond hair, she pulls him down to her and melts her body against him. With his kiss becoming more frantic, more demanding, she moans and takes his tongue into her mouth while her body vibrates from his hands wandering, seeking, and understanding every curve of her body. She parts her legs, anticipating his fingers making their way to her most sensitive spot, and reaches for his belt buckle, unfastening the clasp and pulling the leather strap inch by inch until it falls to the ground. He releases a guttural growl that rumbles in the back of his throat and makes her more ravenous, delirious even, to find out how else she can make him show how much he craves her too. Tracing the side of her breast, his hand encircles one. Even through the fabric, she feels the heat of his hand squeezing and exploring and delighting in her, and she moans her need for more.

"I can't resist that sound," he groans in her ear.

"We should move this to the bedroom."

"Agreed." He kisses the inside of her neck and sucks the soft flesh until she dissolves under him. "But we need to discuss a few more things."

"Oh god. What now? This is the longest foreplay ever."

Too many layers separate them. She unsnaps his jeans and drags the zipper down, giving him space to breathe, to grow, to find her. She slides her hand along his length, along the concrete evidence that he wants her too, making him shudder and struggle to gather his thoughts.

"You're accustomed to waiting a year before marriage." His breathy words make her neck quiver. "If you wish to wait that long, we can enjoy most everything, but for the final act."

"What? No, get inside me now."

"Mmm. One way or another, absolutely." His hand dips under her dress and between her thighs. Stroking her skin, he teases, drives her mad, making her hum for him. Hooking his fingers around the bottom of her panties, he tugs, pulling the elastic away half an inch. "Remember what I said about magic? It's not so much the words that matter."

"It's the intention. Yes."

"Well, it's impossible for me to be with you, fully, without that being my intention. And I don't want to rush you into mar—"

"I already told you what I want." She can't recall how long she's subconsciously known he's the one, but it's been a long time now, before they traveled to the Wastelands, before that guard abducted her, before he gave her that sword. Regardless, the feeling's been settling into her bones, weaving their fates together thread by thread, until her entire being craves his presence all the time. "I've been hearing the vows inside my head since the day you showed them to me."

"You too?" His simple confession sets her entrance on fire.

"Yes, and I'm ready, mé ellador. Are you?"

"Am I?" With his finger rubbing along her underside, he nuzzles his forehead against hers. "I see I've been too quiet, given you too much space, my love. I'll rectify that going forward, but I need you to know I have never loved anyone as much as I love you, and I never will."

With her chest so full it aches, Adaline extracts herself from his grasp. She could cry with relief, with gratitude that her life took this most unexpected turn, but she'd rather show him the extent of her love another way. Taking two steps back, she unzips her dress. The sleeves brush down her shoulders. The neckline tips forward, first exposing the soft curves of her décolletage and the black lace bra cupping her mounds. Ëólas's eyes follow the fabric as the dress caresses her belly, skates past the tiny V of her thong, and flutters to the floor, the garment gathering around her heels.

His cock rises as he ogles the entirety of her, his gaze tracing her lingerie. "Those are coming back with us. Do you have more?"

She chuckles and slips her heels off, never giving up eye contact with him. "Yes. A few. In different colors."

"I love colors. All sorts of colors. We should go shopping again."

Her cheeks pull up in a naughty grin. "How about you take these off and show me what you want now?"

"By the fae."

As she hugs his neck, he grabs her bare bottom and lifts her up. She winds her legs around his waist and kisses the length of his jawline, the hollow of his neck, and he carries her over the threshold into her bedroom. When her feet touch the carpet and her thighs bump the bed, he stares at the center of her bra, his frustration visible when he can't find a latch or ribbon to undo. She takes his hands, guides them behind her back, and helps him find the hooks.

"That makes no sense." But he shuts up and inhales deeply as her bra falls away. "Better than I imagined."

He imagined me too. Hee hee.

He floats the backs of his hands alongside her breasts and over her nipples, his eyes dilating as her nubs rise in response. Taking both generous mounds in his hands, he plays with one bud, circling it with his thumb before pinching it. She yelps and nods for him to keep going. He flicks the tip of his tongue over the other, and the cool air that clings to her bud makes her shiver with need. Flashing her a ravenous smile, he sucks on her peak, pulling her further into his mouth, and swirls his tongue around her nub. The pressure and connection consume her. She grabs a fist full of his hair and claws his upper back, telling him to suck harder.

When he stands up, his fingertips still titillating her sensitive flesh, she unbuttons his shirt, forcing herself to do each one slowly, to torment him as much as he has her. But each new reveal of his chest, of his abs, of his V directing her eyes to his hard-on makes her squirm and clench internally. She pushes the blue cotton off his sculpted shoulders, down his arms, and reaches for his jeans. To help, he grabs his pendant, pulls the long chain over his head, and tosses it onto the floor. Kneeling down, she looks at him through her lashes, tugs his pants to his ankles, and pulls them off. The fact that he's still wearing his linen shorts from back home makes her arch an eyebrow.

He shrugs and unties the lace around his waist, letting them fall to the ground. "As much as I'm enjoying the view of you down there, we can save that for another time, if you're so inclined."

"Oh, I'm inclined alright."

She takes his hand, lets him pull her up to standing, and slips off her last miniature garment so that nothing separates them now. No misunderstandings.

No assumptions. No clothing. She walks into his open arms and savors the instant connection of their bodies pressed against each other, a perfect fit. Being with him like this, naked and cherished, allowing him to see every part of her, inside and out, feels natural and beautiful and worth celebrating.

Of course she could never love anyone else. She's always been waiting for him. "When do we say the vows?"

"You'll know what to do, but, essentially, before you let me in."

Done with foreplay, she sits on the bed and positions herself in the center. She takes in his lean body, all the dips and outlines and delicious bits she'll get to know intimately as the years roll by. As he climbs over her, he slides between her legs and folds his arms around her. Crushed between the bed and his weight, she's never felt more secure.

He takes her mouth first. His tongue reaches deep inside her, and she matches his need with her own. She could kiss him for hours, for days, for years. She'll never get enough of his body against her own, never get tired of his hands setting her skin on fire, never get enough of his lips blessing her all over. She rolls her hips against him, rubbing herself along his length, urging him to enter. As she writhes, he growls, sliding his hand between her thighs. She spreads her legs wider and locks her heels behind his knees. When he slips his fingers between her folds and encircles her button, she whimpers and cries out and bucks beneath him.

Oh god, yes. That's it. Now.

Grabbing her hip, he presses his tip to her entrance. Her core aches to pull him inside, both the one between her legs and the one nestled within her soul. Curling her toes, she pushes down on his lower back, willing them to fuse together. When their lips lock again, she pours all of herself into that kiss, every version of herself from the beginning to the end, along with all the hopes and dreams she's ever entertained and all the despair and heartache she's suffered.

When both grow insatiable, their moans and whimpers lapping her heart, Ёlas stretches her open, filling her entrance. Without a word spoken aloud, he uses his last kiss to carve his vows into her soul, and she does the same, even with the slight changes they both instinctively make, changes that define them and the relationship they've been nurturing.

Mé ellador, all that I am, all that I was, all that I'll ever be, I share equally with you, for all of time.

The words continue to echo inside her head like a drum beat steadily speeding up. When Ëólas thrusts inside, she kicks her heels into his buttocks, shoving him in deeper, and surrenders to destiny's demands, as payment for fate stepping in and delivering her perfect match.

I'm his, and he's mine. He's really mine.

Pressing his chest closer to hers, he rolls his hips into her over and over again. She clenches around him, her hips undulating in unison, and a warm, golden light envelops their bodies. With every thrust, energy bubbles and builds inside her core, threatening to tear her apart. It's not just the impending orgasm but also the forging of an unbreakable bond as they rock their separate journeys closer and closer into alignment. And when their futures collide together, the waves of ecstasy pulsing throughout her body tell her she'll never be alone again. He'll always be a part of her, and she'll always be a part of him.

Forever.

Chapter Twenty-Three

THE BOND

When Adaline wakes up the next morning, her lower body is deliciously sore. Every languid movement stimulates a different tender muscle that reminds her of last night's euphoria. Once wasn't enough for either of them, and her inner thighs throb more than after that horse ride. With a satiated sigh, Adaline rolls over, and Ëólas lifts his arm to make room for her. She snuggles up against his chest, kissing his cheek, and trails her hand over his abs, tracing the outline of each muscle. With a sigh, she leans up on her elbow to peek at the clock reading 11:00 a.m. behind his head. The shop will have her car ready in two hours. They have time.

As she snuggles in tight, he kisses the top of her head. "Good morning, mé ellador."

She tilts her chin up to see him better, to stare into those golden eyes that no longer conceal his emotions, that look at her with adoration. "I love that word. My one."

"Mmm. It's more than that. Mé ellador means my one, my love, and my spouse. For us, it's impossible for those three to be separate."

"When you say *for us*, you mean me too, right?"

"Always." With the arm holding her, he walks his fingertips up and down her arm.

"Good, just checking."

Draping a leg over him, Adaline shimmies on top and places her hands on either side of his shoulders to prop herself up, without disturbing his long hair tucked neatly behind his head. His pleased and comfortable expression makes her never want to leave this bed. His fingers, however, find their way to her breasts brushing up against his chest, but he lets go long enough to push her hair away from her face while she rolls forward and kisses him good morning.

For a long while, they enjoy sweet kisses, taking turns nipping the other and exchanging goofy, cheerful grins. Wanting more, she sits up, giving him better access to play with her breasts. In the daylight filtering through her parted curtains, she watches the different emotions that run across his face. Like her, he displays mostly a mix of content playfulness. He even pushes his hips off the bed, making her breasts bounce, and flexes his pelvic muscles so his cock taps her rump hello twice. Adaline laughs out loud.

Dragging his hands to her hips, he holds her in place but lets her fingers dance over his abs. "May I ask you something, without you laughing at me?"

"I promise that if I do laugh, it's only because I think you're adorable."

He grumbles. "I suppose that will suffice."

"Your question?"

He oscillates his head from side to side. "Do you think... What are the chances that you're, mmm, already with child?"

Her hands stop moving. "None." *He wants kids so soon? God help me. I can't keep up.*

"Really?" He sits up on his elbows, and confusion washes over him. "But every time I turn around, another woman's having a child."

Now Adaline throws her head back and laughs. "It's not that simple, my love. Besides, I'm on birth control."

"You can control that?"

"Yes. It's called an IUD. My doctor put it inside me. It's a piece of metal in my uterus that—"

"Inside you!" Ëólas fully sits up and examines her belly, his fingers touching the birthmark beneath her left breast and the scar along her backside, the one defect on her olive skin. "Did it hurt? Does it hurt?"

"No, and that scar isn't from getting the IUD. It's from a bicycle accident. I fell against a broken wire fence. Needed lots of stitches for that one."

His fingertips move to the birthmark. "And this one? It's like a star kissed you."

"Mmm. I wish I had a more magical story, but that's what's left of my hemangioma."

"Your what?"

"It's just something that babies can be born with, extra skin cells, I think. It fades over time though. My grandmother has one too. Had one."

He kisses her lips, silently reminding her she's not alone. "It runs in the family?"

"I don't think so, but I loved that she had one. It made me feel special, more connected to her."

"Maybe we'll be lucky, and our child will have one too."

"Are you rushing babies on us?"

"No, not at all." Ëólas grabs her bottom and pulls her hips against his. "Despite my reactions, I'm happy to wait, if you are."

"Yes. But I do want them. Eventually."

"Good." He puckers his upper lip and rocks his head from side to side. "I do, at the very least, need one heir."

"Wifely duties already?"

"Not for a long while, I hope. I'd like time to savor you."

"I want to be savored."

"Good. We're in agreement then."

With a nod, she pushes his shoulders down. Lacing her fingers through his, she presses against his palms and angles her hips so that she's directly on top of him. As much as she relishes the sensation of his fullness beneath her, all she wants right now is to bottle this moment, to keep it safe, so she can clearly remember this first peaceful morning, absent of danger, when they're truly themselves, together.

She can hardly recall the second-guessing and self-doubt that once plagued her. Logically, she knows she suffered silently for weeks. But in their place, she feels only the connection she shares with him, the half of his soul residing inside her. Whenever she thinks about him, a new warmth radiates within her chest, like an eternal internal embrace.

Wiggling her fingers between his, her palms grow warmer. The sensation increases until a spark of light illuminates between their palms.

The flash nearly blinds her, and she lets go, yanking her hand backward. "What was that?"

Ëólas sits up and pulls her close again. "That, my love, was the bond."

"The bond? Our bond?"

"Yes, see." He holds his hand up again and waits for Adaline to place her palm against his. "Now, think about how much you love me."

Well, that's easy. The instant she does, a soft, bluish-white light illuminates between their hands, the tether binding their souls. The energy pulsating between them is not only intense and powerful but also effortless and comforting. "It's beautiful."

"Yes, it is. To be honest, I wasn't entirely certain it would work the same way between us, but there it is. Even more evidence that you're my perfect match."

Adaline throws her arms around his neck, wraps her legs around his torso, and holds onto him as she silently thanks the universe that they can be together like this.

The first elf-human couple. Wow.

But her smile slowly fades. Even though they may know this relationship was always meant to be, not everyone will view their union in the same light. Some of their friends might even reject the idea. "What's everyone going to think?"

"I don't particularly care." He leans back, kisses her nose, and smooths her messy locks behind her ears. "I'll make certain you're treated like the princess you are."

"Um, what now?"

"You're my wife, so naturally... You do realize it works that way, right?"

"Yes, but no. I mean, I don't know anything about being a princess." The way she says it, *princess* sounds like a dirty word.

She shudders, topples off Ëólas, and buries her head in her pillow to hide her mortification. The pressure in her temples builds. Her hands become clammy, and her heart rate speeds up. She's not a princess. She's done nothing to deserve the title, and she still knows so little about Ëólas's people and Lameiría as a whole.

"My love." He rubs her back, massaging her spine and bottom. "I don't expect you to be anything other than your wonderful, charming if not abrupt self. For anything else, I'll be beside you the entire time."

"But what will the people of Lameiría think?" she asks, the pillow muffling her voice. "What about your parents? Will they be okay with this?"

"Ha! My mother recognized my feelings for you the first moment she saw us. Well, more specifically when I ordered Renor to unhand you. I'm not the type to threaten my own guards."

Swiveling around, Adaline latches onto his wrist. "She knew? And she's okay with it?"

"Why else would they have invited you to lunch?"

"But, but they took me to the circle! I almost disappeared right then."

"Yes, but you chose not to. Granted, I almost yanked you out myself, despite my word that I'd help you home."

"Ëólas! I thought you didn't care." She swats her pillow and sits up on her knees. "You broke my heart."

His shoulders suddenly curl inward as if she punched him. "I'm so sorry, my love. But when you didn't leave, that was the first time I had hope that you felt the same way about me. Before that, I thought my love unrequited."

"Are you fucking kidding me? Every night, I kept dreading the moment I'd have to give you up. I kept—"

A sledgehammer hits her heart, and she doubles over on the bed, gasping. The fear of losing a soul mate, the agony of watching the person she loves most turn away from her, the shame of *the one* thinking the worst of her—the feelings aren't new, but their remnants still hurt. Except, the pain she's feeling isn't hers. It belongs to him.

"Breathe," he whispers, lying beside her, caressing her cheek. "The bond is still new, and our emotions heightened. I'm sorry you're feeling my pain."

"You, you were hurting just as much as me. Maybe more, I think."

"No, your denial shielded you a bit, but I'm so sorry I hurt you."

"Me too."

He pulls her into his arms and kisses her shoulder, her neck, her earlobe. "I love your sweet little ears," he murmurs.

Laughter helps the agony of the past recede, but now that he's broached the topic of what he'd been thinking and feeling all along, she needs to know more. "Can I ask you, when did you realize? About me?"

"Consciously or subconsciously?"

"Both."

"Subconsciously, the day I met you."

"Same."

"Consciously, hmm. I think, maybe, when you told the story of *The Princess Bride*. You were describing Westley saying goodbye to Buttercup, and the sorrow on your face, the agony in your voice, well, I wanted so desperately to hold you."

"I was thinking about you, leaving New Leira."

He parts his lips to speak, but instead chooses to kiss away her heartache. "Oh, and one more thing we need to clear up."

"What's that?" Her hands return to his abs.

"You are my type. Feisty and bold and compassionate and wise."

"Thanks? I mean, yay. But that's kinda random. Why would you think that needed to be cleared—Oh!" She whacks his chest. "You heard my conversation with Cindy! But how? You were up on the balcony."

"Ah yes. Well," he winks, "I do have larger ears."

"Ëólas!"

Before she can smack him again, he maneuvers himself on top of her, using his knees to nudge her legs apart. The more she admonishes him, the more he makes up for his secrets with sweet kisses and roaming hands until she's panting beneath him, begging for more, and riding the waves of ecstasy.

Adaline pours the pancake batter onto the griddle, and the medallions sizzle. With Ëólas in the shower, she turns up her music selection and dances from the sink where she places the empty measuring cup, to the refrigerator where she pulls out the orange juice, to the stovetop where she cracks five eggs in the hot frying pan. Showered and dressed herself, she pauses cooking to pull her hair back into a low ponytail and returns to dance-cooking. Her booty shakes to Taylor Swift, and she rock steps to Imagine Dragons.

The bathroom door creaks open, and Ëólas steps out. Scrambling the eggs, she glances over her shoulder and drools at the sight of his naked torso. No matter how many times they made love in the last ten hours, she's not used to having instant access to his sexy self. She licks her lips and eyes his sweatpants that hang low and show off the V. That beautiful, glorious V that she wants to lick and—

The smell of burning bacon pulls her back to the stove. She flips each one as well as the pancakes. Last, she shreds sharp cheddar cheese into the eggs. As Ëólas takes a seat at the kitchen island, which also houses her oven and stove, he slips his necklace back on, tempting her to ignore the pancakes and ogle his pecks.

How can male nipples be such a turn on too? "Did you enjoy your shower?"

"Marvelous. The water felt a bit off though."

"Ah, the chlorine. And who knows what else."

"Why?"

"To kill microorganisms that can make people sick."

"Huh. Humans sure have learned a lot."

"In some areas, yes, we have."

"Including how to make scandalous dresses that make me envision sliding my hands up your skirt."

She glances down at her A-line sundress, this one a marble blue. "Is that a bad thing?"

"Absolutely not."

"Good." She sticks her tongue out at him. "Then we don't have to argue about my right to wear what I want."

She plates his breakfast and passes him a large serving, assuming he's still ravenous, hopefully from all the sex and not lingering side effects from that strength-borrowing spell. She places in front of him the butter and syrup, scoots onto the seat next to him, and demonstrates what to do with the condiments.

He points at the golden-yellow pancakes. "They weren't made in a pan, and they don't look like cake."

Adaline chuckles, but she's too hungry to tease him. "Go figure. Eat up."

He waits for her to take the first bite. The moment the sweet goodness hits her belly, her insides fill with happiness and satisfaction, even if they are having breakfast at noon.

"Dessert for breakfast," he comments, but he devours everything.

After they eat, Ëólas collects the plates and puts them in the kitchen sink. Turning around, he leans his backside against the counter, crossing his arms over his smooth chest. Between his nipples and long hair dangles that necklace. Adaline's not sure which to look at more.

Why's he wearing a necklace? I mean, of course guys can wear a necklace, but what's the pendant? Her gut twists and turns, pushing her around the island to stand in front of him.

"So, what should we do for the next hour?" he asks. "I'm perfectly happy carrying you back to bed, but I'm also curious to see more of this world. What do you propose, my love?"

She's not sure she heard him, except for the love part. "What's with the necklace?"

"This?" Looking down, he uncrosses his arms and holds the pendant between his thumb and finger. "It's the crest of my family. All the royal families have one. Lameiría's symbol, obviously, is the tree of life. I'll have one made for you as soon as we return home."

"What's it made of? Onyx?" Something about the black stone feels oddly familiar. Unease makes her take a tentative step forward.

"No, something far rarer: Aerylite. It's said to be a gift from the fae."

Aerylite? Like Aerytol? She can't place why that word sounds familiar, like something she heard from a story long ago. She can't recall the memory, but the shape of the pendant, the delicate chain, the size of the outer circle, the style of design, it's so familiar. Similar.

"Adaline, what's wrong?"

An image of Nan shutting a jewelry box flashes in her mind. "My, my grandmother had a necklace like that, only hers was silver, and it wasn't a tree in the middle. It was more like clouds or grass with a few stars or maybe flowers."

Now Ëólas looks both confused and ill, and the gravity of his words makes his voice deeper. "Where did your grandmother get such a pendant?"

"I don't know. She just always had it." Adaline saw it only a few times throughout the years, but whenever she did, Nan would drop it into a box and lock it away in her desk drawer. Adaline tried asking about the pretty piece of jewelry, but her grandmother's face would turn dark, distant, and cold.

Ëólas's pensive expression adds to her growing uneasiness. "The pendant you're describing belongs to the elves, specifically the Aerytolíans."

So many thoughts, so many ideas, so many possibilities string together, overwhelming Adaline's senses and making the room spin: Her father's work with the sacred circle. Her grandmother keeping that pendant hidden, like she was ashamed of it. The soldier asking if she's from another world.

Her legs unsteady, Adaline retreats to the living room and sinks onto the accent chair. "Oh my god, Ëólas. What if my family played a part in the betrayal?"

No, no, no. Not now. Don't tell me our happy moment is already over. Don't tell me this is why we had to come back here, to find out this.

Taking a few deep breaths, Ëólas runs his hands through his hair. The kitchen feels eons away, with him mentally disappearing into his ruminations. He probably doesn't even register she's still in the room.

She hugs her arms around her waist and rocks back and forth. There's that feeling again, of always being alone, always feeling slightly on the outside of everything. Is it because her family did something horrible that they've had to pay for through the generations? And how can Ëólas love her if—*No. That's not an issue.*

"Maybe the fae sent me to the Neutral Territory as a form of recompense?" She looks at him, praying he'll say something, anything, so at least she'll know where he stands on this.

Ëólas finally sees her again, hunched over in the oversized chair, mentally pleading for him to respond. He walks over, kneels down so they're eye to eye, and rests his hand on her knee, reestablishing their connection. "Whatever we discover, I love you. I believe in you. The fae didn't just send you to my world; they sent you to me. And that's not a coincidence. That's fate."

Placing her hand on his, she looks at their intertwined fingers. Their lives have become interwoven. Inseparable. "Whatever we discover, I'm going to do everything I can to help bring our people together."

"I know." He doesn't look at her with fear or judgment, only admiration and adoration. As proof, he kisses the back of her hand, and their connected palms kindle a glow that pulsates between them, keeping them in sync.

"Forget the cave," she says. "Maybe the answers we need are actually in Nan's house. I think it's time for me to go home."

CHAPTER TWENTY-FOUR

THE TRUNK

After picking up Adaline's car from the shop and texting her colleagues that another emergency's delayed her further, she and Ëólas set off immediately, before Adaline can spend the next few hours throwing up over a toilet while thinking about what secrets her family might have kept from her. Aside from his hesitation at trapping himself inside a car with a seatbelt and the initial whiplash of Adaline flying onto the highway, he thoroughly loves the speed of automobiles and every so often sticks his hand out the window to feel the wind rushing by.

Huh. I might have a daredevil on my hands.

For the thirty-five-minute drive, Adaline gives Ëólas a crash-course on music genres. Soon enough, he's a natural at using her smartphone to stream various stations and search for specific artists. The wonder never leaves his face as they both dance in their seats and steal glances at each other, making Adaline wish they had more time to just be.

The drive itself is too short. When they pass the stone wall that leads to Nan's paver driveway, her nausea returns. The car rolls to a smooth stop in front of the three-story mansion, and the afternoon sun hides behind the sandstone exterior and mansard roof. On both sides of the front door and the arched window above it, double pillars stand at attention.

Ëólas's eyes widen. "This is a lot bigger than your condo."

"Yeah, but it's not a freaking palace in a tree."

"Does anyone live here now?"

"No. Nan left the house to me, but I haven't been back since the funeral. Cindy's mom, Doña Mariana, lives across the street, and she's been looking after things for me."

After finding the spare key under the garden rock, she lets them into the grand foyer. *I really wish I hadn't left my messenger bag in New Leira.*

The coffered ceilings and white marble flooring lead to a curved staircase with iron panels that divides the second floor into two separate living areas. Everything's spotless, as usual, but instead of baked cookies and a warm hug, silence greets her. Without Adaline having to utter a word or a sigh, Ëólas takes her hand.

Rather than drowning in a deluge of emotions, she points to the archway to the right. "Through there, we have the kitchen, dining room, and Nan's sunroom. To the left, that's the living room, which connects to the library and dad's office."

"Got it. Where do we start?"

Adaline glances upstairs and at the hallway that leads to Nan's room. Pursing her lips, she drops her eyes. "The library."

When they enter the two-story library, Ëólas whistles. "Now that's a lot of books."

"Yeah. Dad was a collector, that's for sure."

In the center of the room, an oak desk and empty chair face floor-to-ceiling arched windows and the evergreens that separate their backyard from the neighbor's. All other walls feature built-in bookshelves with a sliding ladder. Two leather chairs frame the large fireplace, above which Adaline's father mounted his American revolution saber and the black leather scabbard beneath it.

Ëólas walks over to the fireplace and admires the long, sleek blade, particularly the solid steel hilt and the spiral pattern carved into the hardwood grip. "I thought you don't do swords in this world?"

"Not so much anymore. That's a historically accurate replica."

"The blade's so thin."

"It was designed for those fighting on horseback."

"Hmm."

"What?"

Squinting, Ëólas points at the top portion of the scabbard. "There's dried blood on this."

Adaline walks over and scrutinizes the same spot. "I don't see anything. Huh."

They glance at each other, then spend the next two hours looking through her father's desk, papers, and filing cabinets, skimming documents about his own anthropological studies. Despite Ëólas's frustration with English's "blatant disregard for spelling phonetically," they also look through the library shelves, checking if her father's books might hint at something. Not finding a crumb, Adaline sits down and stares at her feet, thumping madly on the carpet, while Ëólas keeps searching.

I have to go into Nan's room. With a humph, she gets up. "I'm, I'm going upstairs."

He returns a book to the shelf and climbs down the built-in ladder. "Do you want me to come with you?"

"Not yet. I need some space for this. But I'll call when I need you."

"Okay." He kisses her three times before she goes.

The last time she walked down that corridor, she knew she'd find Nan in bed, already gone. This time, she has no idea what awaits in that room. With her hands shaking, she turns the knob and pushes the door open. The stillness of the room screams at her. Nan's sweater hangs around the back of her desk chair. The book on her nightstand has the bookmark wedged two-thirds into the story, and her hairbrush sits on the vanity beneath the picture window that overlooks the backyard.

Adaline picks up the brush and stares at the gray strands of hair caught in between the bristles. Holding it to her chest, she scans the room, trying to decide where to look first. She tries the desk drawers. They're not locked this time, but she can't find the box containing the necklace. She does, however, find a blank birthday card with a Post-it note attached: *Adaline's 29th.* After returning the card to its resting place, she silently shuts the drawer.

Where would Nan have put that necklace? Where would she have hidden her secrets?

She hears Nan's advice in her head, advice she gave a million times over the years: *Whenever you need answers, look to your own feet.*

She pats the hairbrush bristles on her palm and stares at the huge classic trunk suitcase at the foot of Nan's bed. Setting down the brush, she peels back the blanket covering the trunk, careful not to snag the linen on the clamps, slats, and straps.

For as long as Adaline can remember, this trunk has sat in front of this bed. Only once did she ask what was inside, and Nan had said, "The past and the future." When Adaline asked if she could look inside, Nan wrapped her arm around Adaline's small shoulders and ushered them out of the room. All she said then was "Soon." That promise stopped Adaline from thinking to ask again, even though that was twenty years ago.

Adaline undoes the buckles and lifts the lock. As the trunk creaks open, scents of cedar, roses, and lemon waft through the air. On the top tray rests an eight-by-ten black-and-white photo of Nan and her son a few years before Adaline had been born. Edwin stands behind his mother, resting his hands on the back of her chair and smiling beneath a bushy mustache Adaline never had to bear witness to. Nan's glossy eyes stare beyond the camera. In her late forties, maybe, she had parted her long dark hair down the middle, and she wears the same knowing smile that used to lean over Adaline as Nan tucked her in bed and kissed her goodnight.

They look so young.

With a sigh, Adaline runs her fingers over their faces, over their hands. She closes her eyes and takes several slow breaths before resting the picture on Nan's bed.

I'm taking that back to New Leira with me.

Next, Adaline finds a long, cylindrical canister made of aged leather and a small, decorative wooden box resting on top of tissue paper. Retrieving the canister first, she pulls off the top and withdraws a rolled-up piece of canvas roughly thirty-inches long. As she unfurls the first inch, her breath hitches.

How could Nan store an oil painting in such conditions? What was she thinking!

Dreading the sound of paint cracking, she slowly peels back another inch. The paint thus far looks pristine.

Curiosity overruling better judgment, she unrolls another inch and another until the entire painting is in full view. Adaline gasps at the sight of the colonial family portrait. The gentleman's waistcoat, the lady's gown and headdress, and the style of painting itself appear to be from the seventeen hundreds. Everything about the painting screams it belongs in a museum. And yet, despite the man's long hair and woman's bonnet, their faces unmistakably belonged to Nan and Edwin.

Adaline spreads the painting out on the floor, weighing down the corners with Nan's brush, purse, and book, and backs up until she bumps into the wardrobe. The implications continue stabbing at her skull as she glances back and forth between the eight-by-ten and the painting.

"Éólas," she whispers.

A few moments later, his feet walk past the painting, and his frame blocks the photos, freeing her from staring at those faces.

"What's wrong?" he asks, placing his hands on her arms.

She points at the pictures. "That photo of my dad and Nan is thirty, maybe forty, years old. That painting looks like it's three hundred years old."

Not leaving her side, he studies the painting. "Are they your ancestors?"

"I suppose. I mean, the condition of the painting suggests it's a forgery. It should have deteriorated in that canister. But the clothing. The mannerisms. The style of painting. It's all so authentic. That's Nan's smile, one hundred percent. I don't understand."

They both stare at the painting for some time.

"What else is in the trunk?" he asks.

Adaline sinks onto her knees and crawls over to the trunk, bumping her knees against the wood slats. She pulls out the small box engraved with constellations and the moon high in the sky. Inside rests a stack of cards, the top few of which are Nan's and Edwin's licenses and social security cards. Adaline shuffles through the various forms of identification. As the years recede into the past and the social security numbers change, the photos of her father and Nan remain the same. Sometimes her dad used his full name, Edwin, and sometimes he stuck with Eddie. Only once did he switch to Edward. Nan never deviated from Arraya Yates.

"They never aged." Adaline places the stack of cards aside. "How can humans not age?" She looks at Ëólas, who's turned into a Grecian stone statue while he ruminates. "Please think out loud!"

He blinks awake. "I'm, I'm sorry. Habit." Hesitantly he asks, "Why are there no photos of your grandfather or your mother?"

"I, I don't know. I mean, my grandfather died before my father was born, and the movers lost my mom's photos after we lost her and moved in with my grandmother."

"Convenient," Ëólas mutters. "What was your mother's name?"

"Aurellia. She was from Portugal."

"Does she still have family there?"

"I don't know."

"You never asked? About your mother's family?"

She shrugs. "It's hard to miss something I can't remember."

Ëólas sits back and smacks his head against his knees. "You say that every time I ask you about your mother."

"No, I don't."

"Yes, you do."

"I, I don't like this conversation." Adaline pinches the pad of flesh between her thumb and finger. The sharp, sudden pain helps dissipate the pressure building around her temples.

"What are you doing?"

"Pressure point. It helps migraines go away."

Ëólas scoots forward and takes her hands in his. "What about your grandfather? What was his name?"

"Nan's husband? Erol."

Ëólas's eyebrows shoot up so quickly that she expects them to pop off his face. "What?" she asks.

Squeezing her hands, he exhales slowly. "Erol was the last king of Aerytol."

Adaline lets go of Ëólas and clamps down on that pressure point again. "The king? But you always mention the queen."

"Yes, because she's the one who descended from Aeríoléna and Tólen, the first queen and king of the elves."

Adaline looks back at her grandmother's portraits and shakes her head. *What are we missing? Why are there so many similarities, and yet nothing lines up perfectly?* Just with most research, these answers are leading to more questions.

"Well, my grandmother was clearly human. You think she might have—"

"Married an elf? I've been pondering the same. That, and the possibility that, well, Adaline, are you certain Nan is your grandmother by blood?"

Falling back on her bottom, Adaline lays down, throwing her hands out at her sides as she stares at the ceiling. There's that spinning, nauseous feeling again in the pit of her stomach. They need answers. That's why they came here, and they're so close.

But now, she's not so sure she wants to know the truth. "Seriously? First, you think I might be partially elven, and now you're saying I might be adopted. I feel a major identity crisis coming on, one that will require a lot of therapy."

"I'm only proposing theories, and you asked me to think out loud." Ëólas lies on top of her, propping himself up on his elbows and yet crushing and securing her with his weight.

She runs her hands up and down his back. With his presence and touch grounding her, she forces her fears aside and thinks aloud too. "Yes, I'm certain Nan's my biological grandmother. I look a lot like her, and we have the same birthmark. What about Erol? Could he have survived and come here?"

"No. When my grandfather fought to defend Aerytol, he found Erol's head and oversaw the burial. They were childhood friends."

"Oh god." Adaline grabs her neck.

Ëólas nods and rests his head on her chest. "When Lameiría learned of the attack, my father ordered our people to assist. Alderton responded the same, and that began our first war with them. Humans forgot over time, but my grandfather hasn't. Nor the people of Aerytol who sought refuge in Lameiría. Elashor's not particularly thrilled with my efforts in New Leira."

"Elashor?"

"My mother's father."

Adaline strokes his head and holds him tight. "Do you regret it?"

He looks up at her, his gaze returning from a long-ago memory shrouded in sorrow. "Never. My efforts brought you."

They lay in silence a bit longer, her stroking his head. Him, thinking between her breasts.

Leaning on his forearms, Ëólas removes his weight from her and peers into her eyes. "Adaline, your access to magic, that's an Aerytolían trait. Your family's not aging and the sacred circle being here—is it possible Nan changed her name?"

Adaline laughs so hard that the carpet scratches her shoulders. "My grandmother wasn't a queen. Maybe she was once queen of the PTA and her charities, but she wasn't queen of some ancient, magical kingdom. I just can't believe that's possible, even with all the evidence piling up. I mean, why wouldn't she tell me that? You think she could have mentioned it during the last twenty years: 'Oh, dear, after you're done with homework, I need to tell you about the time I used to rule a kingdom in another world. Oh, and by the way, I had plastic surgery, and I'm actually an elf.' I mean, that's ridiculous."

"You're mocking the way I speak now?" He pretends to bite her collarbone.

"I'm not. I told you she had an accent like yours. Don't look at me like that. It's just a coincidence." *Granted, one of many right now.*

"Where's the pendant?"

Adaline points to the trunk, not sure if it's actually in there, but she lifts her head to watch him dig through the top tray. After he opens a small velvet box, he pulls out the pendant that matches his in size and style, only Nan's necklace is silver and features the night sky.

He gulps. "Adaline, it's made of Aerylite."

"Yours is black."

"I have raw Aerylite. This is purified, which again is something only the Aerytolíans knew. My love, you must be descended from them in some way." While Adaline sinks further into the ground, Ëólas's voice grows louder with awe and excitement. "Maybe, maybe when the queen cast that spell, she didn't perish into the earth. Maybe she came here. And changed her name to Nan. Maybe even her appearance."

"Nan's not her name." Adaline says this as if everyone should know that. "Nan is a British nickname for grandma."

"By the fae, Adaline!" Ëólas kneels down beside her.

"Oh god. Don't say it."

"Was her name Arraya?"

"For fuck's sake!" Adaline covers her face with her hands and prays the room will stop spinning. "I think I'm going to throw up."

"Adaline, don't you realize what this means? You're Aerytolían. You're the rightful queen of New Leira, of Aerytol." As Adaline groans into her palms, Ëólas clicks his tongue. "I sense my enthusiasm is not your own."

"Sorry to disappoint you and everyone else who's going to have outlandish expectations of me now. I'm not a queen, Ëólas. I'm an assistant professor of cultural anthropology."

"Well, you were destined to become queen regardless. You married me after all." When Adaline looks up at him quizzically, he chuckles. "I'm referring to Lameiría, my love. I'll be king one day, which means you'll be queen." He sits back and clicks his tongue ten more times. "Hmm. If I married the Queen of Aerytol, that means I can't—never mind. We'll have to figure out how that will work."

"Please don't call me a queen, and please stop talking about politics. I hate politics." She sits up, only to curl her knees under her torso and extend her arms far in front, sinking into child's pose to stretch her back. Burying her face in the carpet, she takes deep breaths.

This can't be happening. There has to be another explanation, one that doesn't mean I'm partially an elf and a freakin' queen. "Can't we just have a normal honeymoon?"

"What's a honeymoon?"

Yoga isn't helping. Adaline drags her hands across the carpet and sits up. "After you get married, you take a vacation, and you travel somewhere exotic and get lots of fruity drinks with little umbrellas in them, and you have lots of sex—"

"Well, I like this idea."

Ëólas scoots forward until their knees touch. Leaning forward, he kisses her softly and nibbles her neck, and the tingling sensation makes her laugh inadvertently. As he switches to sitting down with his legs crossed, he pulls her sideways onto his lap, wraps one arm around her waist, and grips the underside of her knee with this other hand to hold on to her securely. Draping her arms around his neck, she kisses him again, borrowing his joy. But the moment their lips part, the merriment of their playfulness fades. She strokes his cheek with her thumb, and part of her wishes she'd never mentioned the pendant.

The corners of Ëólas's mouth dip downward. "Why are you so distraught, my love? You are a miracle. When the people learn we've found the Queen of Aerytol's rightful heir, they'll—"

"Be horribly disappointed I'm human. Or half human. Or a quarter elf. What does that even mean?"

"Where's that relentless optimism?"

"It died the moment I learned my whole life has been a lie. That my family lied to me. That my family left me alone to figure this out by myself." When Ëólas cocks an eyebrow, Adaline bites her lip. "Okay, not alone. Not now. But you know what I mean."

"I do, but thank you nonetheless. Anyway, they must have had a reason."

"Says every person ever who tries to justify lying."

"I'm not saying I agree with their methods, my love, but I imagine that reason is similar to why my family swore to keep Seira's abilities hidden."

"What do you mean?" A shadow of an idea crosses her face. She's not sure she can bring herself to vocalize the sudden thought, but the more the words echo inside her head, the more she knows she's right. She worries her bottom lip and stares at Ëólas as she asks him to tell her the truth about Seira. "She's Aerytolían, isn't she?"

Ëólas nods.

Seira and me, we're related. She's family. I still have family! That's why she latched on to me the moment I arrived. Did she suspect then too? Did she know all along?

Small moments flash into Adaline's mind, moments that she thought peculiar but couldn't bring herself to examine more closely, like the first time she met Seira and she said, *Adaline! You made me wait such a long time.* Or the way Seira cared for Adaline, making her clothing and brushing her hair, crawling into her bed to ward off nightmares, or yelling at those who weren't nice to her. The last time they saw each other, Seira called Adaline out for not being herself, for being lesser. And from day one, Seira called her neir nía, a term of endearment that literally means little sister but that elves use among close female friends and kin.

"Oh my god, Ëólas. She really is my tíer nía."

"Yes, she is."

Despite all the shock she's dealt with today, Adaline peppers Ëólas with thank you kisses, making him laugh, but stops abruptly. "Wait, why isn't she queen?"

A cloud drags a large shadow over the house, blotting out the summer sun and allowing the shadows in Nan's room to emerge.

The tension in Ëólas's shoulders becomes more noticeable as he holds Adaline. "When Seira found her way to Lameiría, she was still a child. She didn't speak for a few decades. Elashor looked after her, keeping Seira's natural abilities far away from the capital. But her magic has always been, well, unstable. I don't know what happened to her before she found us, but she's remained detached, never answering direct questions, except for one."

"Which was?"

"When I began working with Magnus, she told him the truth. I was horrified, but I realized that could only mean Magnus really is honorable. Both he and I wanted to reinstate her as queen, but she refused. Magnus asked why, and she said, 'Because I'm not the rightful heir.'"

Adaline snuggles against Ëólas's chest, tucking her head beneath his chin as she imagines Seira in Lameiría, waiting for her neir nía, for her own family, to return. *How alone did she feel, waiting for me? I've been thinking only about myself, but this is so much bigger.*

"My love?" Ëólas's gentle voice pulls her back to him. "This also means something else, something about us."

"Please, tell me it's something good."

He brushes his lips against her forehead. "Most certainly. If you have elven blood in you, that's all the more reason to believe you and I will have a long, long life together."

Adaline sits up straight and looks him in the eyes. *Not twenty. Not fifty. But hundreds of years. With Ëólas. With the family we'll make together.* "You really think so?"

"I do."

Could we really be so lucky? She lays her head on his shoulder, and they sit together quietly while he massages her back and helps her mind unwind.

"Why wouldn't they tell me?" she whispers.

He brushes her hair off her shoulders, but his dark expression reveals his worries. "The only reason I can fathom is that they were trying to protect you."

"From what? There's no threat here."

"Maybe. But maybe they were trying to delay your return."

"Because Aerytol is no longer safe." Adaline continues down this train of thought, connecting each dreadful piece at a time that threatens her hopes and dreams. "Because our enemies don't approve of elf-human relations. That's why people have been attacking New Leira. That's why that guard abducted me, not only because they're terrified of a union like ours but also because his boss must know about my family."

The abomination. That's what the guard called me. Because I'm a half-breed.

Ëólas's entire countenance changes as all color drains from his face. Even his golden eyes look muddied. His chest shrinks inward, and his shoulders droop. "When we go back, I want you to stay in Lameiría. Magnus and I will handle this war, and you—"

"Absolutely not! This war isn't only about me. It's about stupid racist bullshit. It's the manifestation of prejudice and fear mongering and intolerance, and I won't put up with that kind of crap. I won't let these assholes destroy our home again."

Leaning back, he regards her for a few moments, tucking her hair behind her ear. "You sound like a queen, minus the cussing."

"I'm sure queens cuss too. But I'm serious, Ëólas. This war is bigger than me."

"But I fear you'll be at the center of it."

"And Seira! And you! You married me. That makes both of us a target. I mean, look at what happened to my grandfather."

Adaline grabs her neck again. *Elashor found his head.*

Oh god. No. She's put Ëólas in even greater danger. *No, no, no. Not him.*

Adaline scrambles off Ëólas's lap to get away from him, not that she can break this off now. But if they don't tell anyone they're married, if they pretend not to like each other, if she stays away from him while they're in New Leira—If only she could rewind time and spare him.

This isn't fair to him. He didn't know what he was getting himself into. She backs away from him.

Ëólas jumps up and runs after her, grabbing her wrist and not letting go, not to hurt her, not to scare her, not to trap her, but because he looks petrified she'll disappear forever. He pulls her into his arms, pressing his chest to her back, and buries his face in her neck. "I asked you to keep me with you."

"But, but I'm putting you in danger, and I can't lose you too. I won't." How many hundreds of years did her grandmother have to survive without her Erol? How could Nan go on? How could she breathe day in and day out with only half of her heart?

She clings to Ëólas. "There has to be more. Something more to help us."

Through their connection, Adaline senses the war raging inside Ëólas as he forces himself to lower his arms to her hips, giving her the chance to step away. *He's just as terrified of losing me.* She takes his hands, lacing her fingers through his, and pulls his arms around her waist. She leans against his chest, and he inhales the scent of her herbal shampoo.

"We can't make decisions based on fear," she says.

"Very wise, my love."

"Thank you." She turns around, kisses him once, and leads him back to Nan's trunk. "To think, she kept all of this under my nose, and I never once thought to sneak into her room and take a peek."

"I imagine crossing the Queen of Aerytol would have been terrifying."

"Honestly, no. I never felt anything but safe with Nan. Maybe that's why I never suspected."

Kneeling in front of the trunk, they pull out the remaining items on the top tray, including a stack of documents with details for offshore accounts and property in different locations around the world—stuff that would help Nan and Dad relocate every forty or so years.

With Ëólas's help, she lifts and sets aside the shelved tray, and a layer of tissue paper conceals the remaining items. Adaline pulls back the tissue, revealing a white lace gown. Even in the bedroom's limited, indirect sunlight, the embroidery and iridescent gemstones illuminate the inside of the trunk. Beside the gown rests a sheathed dagger, a pair of white flat shoes that look as if they were made yesterday, and a forehead circlet. Pearls and amethyst decorate the delicate silver band befitting a queen.

Ëólas retrieves the dagger. "Aerytolían designs." He shows her the floral, airy knots that she recognizes from the cave floor. He sets the blade aside, and Adaline rifles through the papers.

If I have access to magic, surely Nan would have left me with an instruction manual, right? "Anything else in there?"

"That's about all. Well, and a rock." Ëólas lifts a smooth gray stone out of the trunk.

"Seriously, a rock? That's it?"

"A vibrating rock?" He rolls it onto his palm to show her better.

The moment Adaline sees it, she snatches it out of his hand. "I know what this is."

Amazed, relieved, and terrified, she holds the stone in her hands and closes her eyes. It pulses against her palms, and a memory flashes into her mind, a memory she hasn't thought of since she was seven years old. She's lying in a hospital bed. The machines beep, and the lights are too bright, unnatural. Her backside throbs from where that broken wire fence tore her open.

Nan's weathered hands rest on Adaline's forearm, and her face, softened with age, looks careworn, like she's been holding a vigil for centuries. Her voice, however, remains kind and encouraging. "What happens when we drop a rock into the water?"

"It makes rings," Adaline says with an accent matching Nan's.

"Yes, and the rings grow bigger. So big that they eventually touch everything below the surface and even the grass at the water's edge. You'll know when you're ready to face those rings. In the meantime, I'll safeguard this stone."

When Adaline opens her palm, the memory fades, and she's back in Nan's bedroom with Ëólas watching her intensely.

"What is it?" Ëólas asks.

She looks at the stone and shakes her head, unable to conceal the awe in her voice. "It's my memories, and I know how to get them back. I have to enter the sacred circle."

Chapter Twenty-Five

THE VISIT

"Are you packing this too?" Ëólas holds the pendant, oscillating back and forth, out to Adaline.

She's already packed Nan's portrait, dress, and other elvish belongings into a duffle bag. "Nan didn't let me touch it. Maybe that's because she didn't want this for me."

"She didn't let you touch it because you would have known you're not entirely human."

"What do you mean?"

"When Aerytolíans touch Aerylite, they have a unique reaction."

"How so?"

"I'm not entirely sure, only that it's obvious."

"Huh." Looking at the pendant like she's allergic to it, she holds her duffle open for him to drop the necklace inside. She zips the bag shut, and they proceed downstairs to add these bags to the trunk of her car, which already holds the boxes Ëólas helped her pack up from her condo.

She only just came home, and they're leaving so soon. She walks into the kitchen, looks at Nan's favorite tea mug still sitting on the drying rack, and switches off the light. As they make their way to the front door, Adaline runs back to the kitchen and packs up the mug too. She picks up her bag again when someone knocks on the front door. With a single glance between them, Ëólas walks backward until he disappears behind the archway into the living room.

Adaline opens the door just as the streetlights outside blink on. Standing on her doorstep are two women, Cindy's mom and abuela.

"Adaline!" Doña Mariana lunges forward and hugs Adaline hello.

"Tanto tiempo sin vernos." Abuela pats Adaline's cheek and smiles so much that all her dimples smile too.

"Lo siento." Adaline returns both of their hugs in a daze.

Why do I feel ambushed by Cindy's family?

She didn't expect to see Doña Mariana again, that round face that constantly reminds people how fiercely she loves her kids, which includes Adaline, being that Doña Mariana's been her surrogate mother these past twenty years.

Adaline shuts the door as they step inside Nan's house. "Te he extrañado tanto."

"We've missed you too." Doña Mariana rubs Adaline's arm. "But I know you needed space. Now that you're here though, I need to speak with you."

With a mischievous grin, Doña Mariana and Abuela take off for the living room, most likely to look for the guy Adaline arrived with. Tossing her hands in the air, Adaline follows after both women. The spacious light-gray room, with its white trim and cathedral ceiling, doesn't give Ëólas anywhere to hide, unless he ducks down behind Nan's extra-long dark gray sofas or silently slips through the library door again. Apparently, he chose to do none of those.

Spotting him in the corner, Doña Mariana goes to shake his hand. "Ah, there you are. Nice to meet you. I promised Arraya I'd keep an eye on Adaline, so I had to come over and see you for myself."

"The pleasure is all mine." Ëólas takes a seat across from them and beside Adaline. An oblong coffee table is his only defense. "I've heard much about you and your daughters."

"I wish I could say the same about you." Doña Mariana twists her hair up behind her head and holds it in place with a clip, her signature move when she's ready to get down to business. "But you've appeared out of nowhere, or rather," she gestures at Ëólas's ears, "from another world."

Adaline nearly falls off the sofa. *What!*

"Adaline, dear, no need to panic," Doña Mariana says. "Mother and I came by to find out if this person is someone you trust and if we can help fill in any missing gaps for you in terms of your family's history."

Unsure whether to hide or scream or ask questions, Adaline blinks at both women who have been inside this home more times than she can count, who attended every birthday and holiday, who babysat Adaline whenever needed, who took her to get her ears pierced. They've known all this time and never said a single word to her. Just like Nan and Dad.

Sensing her rising anger, Ëólas holds her hand, which makes Abuela hum happily.

"I met Arraya the day I was born," Abuela says with her gravelly voice. "She and my mother were best friends and, before that, my grandmother's best friend and, before that..." She waves her hand back and forth as if time were a fly she could swat.

"You knew. You knew this whole time." Adaline looks from one woman to the other. "How come no one told me? How come Nan and Dad didn't tell me that I'm, what, a quarter elf?"

"Half, honey," says Doña Mariana.

Ëólas intertwines his fingers with Adaline's, and both Seguar women beam.

"You found the one after all." Doña Mariana nods at their hands.

"But how do you know this?" Adaline asks.

"Arraya came to our world in the 1500s, pregnant with your father. After she gave birth to Edwin, they traveled south until they met my ancestor, Juan, in 1540 when he joined Francisco Vasquez de Coronado's march into the Rio Grande. Long story short, our families have been looking out for each other ever since."

"And my mother?" Adaline covers her mouth, afraid to ask, "Was she really from Portugal?"

"No, sweetheart," Abuela says, shaking her head. "She's from your world, from a kingdom called Alderton."

"Holy shit!" Adaline drops back against the sofa cushion and looks at Ëólas. "Well, what do you know? I was legitimately Magnus's ward, only on my mother's side."

They both half laugh and turn back to Doña Mariana for more answers, but her mother stands up and heads into the kitchen.

"Come, I'll make tea," Abuela says. For being seventy-five, she's still spritely, thanks to looking after her grandkids.

Everyone follows Abuela into the gourmet kitchen, but Adaline takes over making their drinks while Ëólas rests his back against the fridge and the Seguar women sit at the huge granite kitchen island in the center of the room. As Adaline turns on the tap and fills the electric kettle, she stares out the picture window. The swing bench she used to sit on with Nan creaks in the breeze. With no one here to take the floral cushion inside before a rainstorm, the fabric has dulled and turned gray.

Adaline turns the tap off and sets the kettle on the base, switching on the power. "If Dad grew up here, how did he meet my mother?"

Getting up, Doña Mariana opens the white cabinets and retrieves a few different boxes of tea, including Nan's favorite, chamomile. She pulls out two rooibos teas for her and Abuela. "After so much time here, your father decided to try to find a way home. Arraya tried over the centuries, but most of her magic left her when she came here. She said that doubt, fear, regret, and anger weakened her abilities. And, well, after what happened to her home and her husband, Arraya was never quite the same."

Ëólas, crossing his arms over his chest, hangs his head. Adaline sidles up to him and places her arm around his waist. He drapes his arm around her too, and she relaxes against his side.

Of course she wasn't the same after losing her soul mate. "Did my father have magic?"

"A bit. He wasn't very skilled. Growing up here, he never really connected to magic. Anyway, your father and grandmother moved around the world, never staying too long in any one location. But when that hiker discovered Arraya's cave and the local authorities roped it off, Eddie moved back to Maryland while Arraya stayed in England. He began working at American University so he could stay close to the circle while keeping other people away."

Oh my god. Dad wasn't researching the site. He was protecting it. Adaline pulls four mugs out of the corner cupboard and fumbles not to drop them. "Wait, wait, wait. The cave belonged to Nan?"

"Yes." Abuela nods. "She said it came with her from Aerytol. She cast a massive spell to preserve destiny and protect your father, and the whole dang circle came with her." She laughs as if she's retelling an old family joke.

"Whoa."

After Ëólas takes three mugs out of her arms and puts them down in front of Abuela, Adaline slams her mug down on the counter. "But why didn't they tell me?"

"I don't have all the details." With the steam rising from the boiling water, Doña Mariana walks around Adaline standing still from shock and grabs the kettle. "Your father, he struggled to speak about your mother. But in your grandmother's trunk, you'll find a stone with—"

"I have it." Adaline pulls it out of her pocket. "She took my memories, didn't she?"

"Not without your permission," says Abuela. "But if you've got that, you'll know what to do."

Doña Mariana pours the boiling water into all the mugs, and everyone steeps their tea bags in silence. The oversized kitchen feels cold.

Dad must have eventually found his way home, where he met my mother. Did he bring all three of us back here? Or just me? Leaving her tea to cool, Adaline turns the stone over in her hands as if doing so could conjure her mother's ghost. "Is, is my mother dead?"

Casting her eyes downward, Doña Mariana blows away the steam wafting in her face. "I'm sorry, Adaline, but I don't know. Whatever happened to her, happened in your world."

My world? This is my world. "Why didn't Nan tell me before she died?"

Placing her hand over Adaline's, Abuela waits to answer until Adaline looks at her. "Because your father hoped that if you married someone from this world, you'd have a normal life here and never have to go back, never be in danger again."

Go back. Again. Meaning I was born there? And I was in danger then too?

Grinding his teeth, Ëólas abruptly turns away from them and sets his mug in the sink with so much force that the ceramic cracks and breaks. The pieces clatter against the stainless-steel basin. Placing both hands on the counter, he hunches his shoulders.

Adaline hugs him from behind, resting her chin on his back. "He was wrong."

"No, he wasn't."

"Don't you dare tell me we'd both be better off having never met. I'll never forgive you for think—"

"That's not what I meant." Ëólas spins around, making Adaline back up. He reaches out and cups her cheek. "We just need more details so we can make certain history doesn't repeat itself."

"Agreed." She leans into him. "That's what the stone is for."

Ëólas nods but withholds his thoughts, for now.

Facing Doña Mariana and Abuela, Adaline asks, "Does Cindy know?"

"No. She's your friend. That's between you two."

Yeah, okay. 'Cause that will be an easy, fun conversation.

After convincing Abuela and Doña Mariana that they don't need dinner, they say their goodbyes, and Adaline locks the door behind them. While Ëólas cleans up the mess in the kitchen, including the broken mug, Adaline rests her keys on the foyer table and meanders into the sunroom where Nan spent most of her days in autumn and winter. Nan said this room helped her to focus. Maybe being around nature will help Adaline do the same. She gingerly sits on Nan's wicker sofa and lays her feet on the matching coffee table. The potted and hanging plants Abuela's been nurturing make Adaline feel like she's in a greenhouse.

Is that why you loved this room most of all, Nan?

She tilts her head onto the cushion behind her and counts to ten each time she breathes in and out. She doesn't feel special, magical. She doesn't feel like an elf. She doesn't feel like a princess, let alone a queen. She feels disconnected. From her past. From herself. From the people who raised her. From the people she thought she knew.

Doubt, fear, regret, and anger weaken our abilities. That's what Doña Mariana said. If that's the case, maybe the opposite is true too.

Adaline sits up. Can she think of a time when she felt determined, hopeful, and loved. Yes, when she wanted to show Ëólas this world. "Oh my god." Adaline leaps off the sofa and turns to find Ëólas walking into the sunroom with her duffle draped over his shoulder.

"Are you ready to head back to the condo, or do you want to stay the night here?"

"Ëólas, holy shit. I just realized something. I, I think we might have a classic Dorothy situation going on here."

"I have no idea what that means."

"Yeah, we need to schedule a movie marathon. The point is—I can't believe I'm about to say this. I think I'm the one who's been making us travel." She squishes her mouth into her nose.

"You mean you abducted me?"

"No. I—Oh my god, I did. I'm so sorry." She covers her face with her hands. "That's so embarrassing, but yes. I didn't mean to. I don't know how or why exactly but—"

Ëólas peels her hands away from her face and looks at her lovingly. "After our findings in the trunk, I began to suspect the same. Do you think you can get us home?"

"Maybe. It's all about the intention, right?"

"Mmm-hmm."

"The problem is that I think I travel subconsciously. And truth be told, I'm not in a hurry to go back to Lameiría. I'm, I'm scared to face everyone and deal with those who won't support us."

"My love." Ëólas brushes his lips against Adaline's, and that tingling sensation travels directly to her abdomen. When he kisses her deeper and his tongue slides into her mouth, Adaline grabs onto him and pulls his thigh between her legs. His hands knead her hips until they travel under the hem of her dress, and he slips one hand inside her underwear. "You've mentioned more than once that I think too much. Maybe you do too. Intention. Desire. Same difference."

Kissing her neck, Ëólas works his finger back and forth, massaging circles around her clit and turning Adaline's brain to mush. She wants all of him now, and she'd prefer a bed rather than Nan's wicker furniture. She has no room in her heart for any other feelings than desire.

Ëólas pulls the strap of her dress down and kisses her shoulder, making Adaline picture only his bed, the one she dared not look at before, the one in the treehouse floating atop a sea of leaves. She obediently lifts her arms, and he pulls her dress over her head. Tossing her clothing onto the sofa, he cups her breast, working his thumb around the nipple. As she moans, the stone tiles fade into hardwood planks, and the glass walls and Nan's plants disappear.

In front of the same sunset they left not even two days ago, Ëólas drops the duffle behind him, his eyes glowing with awe as he admires his wife. That look on his face makes her work faster to yank off his polo, which she kicks aside. Grabbing his belt buckle, she pulls him toward the double doors, toward their bed.

CHAPTER TWENTY-SIX

A NEW ROLE

When Adaline wakes up from her sex-induced nap, the other side of the bed is empty and cold. She rolls over and picks up the handwritten note Ëólas left on his pillow. Leaning toward the fire crackling in the hearth, she reads,

My love, should you find this before I return, know I won't be gone long. I just need to handle a bit of business, and then I will rush back to you.

Given that Āranol may reach New Leira as early as six days from now, Adaline intends to soak up as much happiness as she can. She admires Ëólas's fancy calligraphy and inhales the crisp scent of parchment. Returning the note to his pillow, she pushes her elbows behind her and sits up. The four-poster bed with its ivy carvings, the natural wood furniture, and the white linens makes this home a cozy retreat. If only she knew where to find the toilet.

Maybe I can just pop back into my condo, freshen up, and pop back here?

She closes her eyes and imagines the beautiful sound of a flushing toilet. When she peeks one eye open, she's still in Ëólas's bed. "Huh. I guess it doesn't work that way. I wonder what the rules and limitations are."

Adaline swings her feet onto the floor, and instead of being cold and stiff, the boards are toasty under her toes. She opens Ëólas's wardrobe, which looks like it belongs in Narnia, and puts on one of his tunics, a navy blue one. She loves that color on him, how it makes his eyes stand out even more. The intimacy of wearing his clothes makes her giddy and glad she left her sundress back home.

What's Abuela going to think when she finds my dress in the sunroom?

"I demand you tell me why troops are arriving," a female voice calls from outside, "and why I wasn't permitted into your chambers earlier." The owner of the voice flings the door open, and Floréna storms inside, wearing a summery orange-cream dress that hangs off her shoulders and a girdle that highlights her hour-glass figure before dipping between and outlining her long legs. She takes one look at Adaline pawing Ëólas's wardrobe and halts mid-march. Her sweet face twists in horror.

Well, this is embarrassing. Of course Renor's sister has to be the first person Adaline meets upon her return to Gladríen.

"Good evening, Floréna." She tucks her hair behind her ear and clasps her arms in front of herself, making sure the tunic covers her private bits. "Ëólas isn't back yet, but—"

Before Adaline can finish, Floréna lunges at her and smacks her across the face. "You vile cockroach."

Cupping her throbbing cheek, Adaline tumbles into the wardrobe. "What the—"

Floréna, grabbing a fistful of Adaline's hair, drags her out of the wardrobe and toward the door. "I've heard tales of the audacity of humans, but to see it with my own eyes. We've treated you as a guest, and you thought you could—"

"This isn't what you think."

As Adaline tries to pry Floréna's fingers loose, she grabs Adaline's arm and twists it behind her back, forcing Adaline to fall face first onto the floor. Floréna kneels on Adaline's back and screams for the guards.

What do I do? How do I get out of this? "Sora!" Adaline shouts. He wouldn't have left her undefended.

"Sora? You think she'll help you once she learns you attempted to defile our lord's bed? You populate this world like vermin and carry diseases. Our lord would never have a creature like you for a lover."

"He married me."

Floréna's gagging turns into dry heaving, but she lets up enough that Adaline's able to tear her arm free and roll away, making Floréna topple sideways.

Scurrying to her feet, Adaline widens her stance and lifts her arms, ready for another assault as she faces Floréna. "I don't want to fight you. You're making a horrible mis—"

The blonde shifts her weight onto her back foot, telling Adaline to dodge left, which she does, and Floréna flies past Adaline. Catching her balance, Floréna spins around and pulls her hand back for another slap, but Adaline kicks Floréna's legs out from under her. Three guards rush in at the right moment to watch Floréna fall onto her ass.

"She attacked me!" Floréna says, her bottom lip quivering, her finger pointing at the only human in the room. "Take her away."

Damn it. No, these are my people too. Even if they don't know it yet. Kindness. Nan always said to aim for kindness.

Lifting both of her palms in surrender, Adaline calmly faces the guards. "There's been a misunderstanding. Ëólas will clear this up."

The guards look from each other to Adaline and gulp. "My lady, would you please come outside and wait for our lord's return?"

"What do you mean wait? You saw her hurt me." Standing up, Floréna pushes her blonde hair behind her bare shoulder.

"Y-yes, Lady Floréna, but both the queen and Lord Ëólas instructed us to protect Lady Adaline."

"Well," Floréna huffs, "that won't be the case soon enough."

Adaline follows the guards' request and goes outside. The lanterns dangling from the underside of Ëólas's porch twinkle against the moonlight. Without waiting for any further instructions, she sits in the rocking chair by the front door and crosses her legs, trying not to think about how badly she needs to pee. One guard runs off to report Adaline's transgression to Ëólas while Floréna stands poised and triumphant at the top of the stairs. The guards look away from Adaline's bare legs, their faces flush with embarrassment.

"Where's Sora?" Adaline asks.

"The queen sent for her," says guard one. "She'll be back shortly, my lady."

As much as Adaline envisions the satisfaction of punching Floréna in the face, Miss Fake Sunshine will never consider Adaline's words as truth. So, she waits. She doesn't know whom she feels worse for, Floréna when she realizes she's assaulted her future queen or Ëólas when he sees how his people have treated his wife. For his sake, Adaline rocks back and forth to remain calm. She whiles away the minutes, studying the herbs on the shelves beside her and counting the ants as they parade past her toes. Rocking backward, she admires the full moon and the billions of stars overhead, and when the wind blows, it's like she's flying in space. Not even the Air and Space Museum's planetarium can compare to the vastness surrounding her.

How can a place so lovely contain so much hate?

When Ëólas bounds up the stairs, he looks calm and collected, but he's crushed his thumbs inside his fists. He and Adaline lock eyes, and she mouths *I'm okay.* Walking past the guards and Floréna without acknowledging her, he offers Adaline his hand. With her palm in his, she stands up.

He places his thumb under her chin and turns her face to the side. "She struck you."

"She was defending your honor."

While Ëólas clenches his jaw, Adaline takes hold of his fist, unfurls his fingers, and laces their hands together.

Floréna's triumph melts into a pool of muddled confusion. Her voice is smaller too. "Ëólas, I found her rummaging through your things. Taking your clothes. Wearing none of her own. She—"

"You are not a child anymore, Floréna. You ought not be entering my quarters at all." Ëólas's tone is heavy with simmering rage. "You know the penalty for harming a member of the royal family is death." He issues that statement so calmly that Adaline shivers. He slides his arm around her and pulls her close.

Floréna balks. "Surely you jest." She fixates her eyes on Ëólas's hand at Adaline's waist.

Without another word to Floréna, he turns to Adaline. "What do you propose, mé ellador?"

Hearing Ëólas use that term of endearment on someone else, Floréna can't look at either of them as her rosy cheeks turn green.

Adaline taps the top button of his sapphire vest, the color accented with a calm dark-blue-gray silk tunic. "I'm not a fan of these extreme sentences. It was a misunderstanding, and it's not like we've made a formal announcement yet. Go home, Floréna, but we need to work on your views about humans."

Ëólas's frustration rumbles in his throat. "Understand, Floréna, I'm being lenient with you only because Adaline wishes it so. You owe her your life. Go home, and keep this incident to yourself. That applies to you as well," Ëólas says to the guards. "The queen is planning an announcement later tonight, and I will not tolerate anyone else knowing about your disgraceful behavior toward your lady. Now leave us, all of you."

The guards bow at their lord and Adaline and scurry off, but Floréna can't seem to move. Ëólas moves to say something harsh when Adaline tugs him back. Walking over to Floréna, Adaline sighs. She suffered from the hopelessness of unrequited love for weeks. How could Floréna have survived it for decades?

"Everything's going to be okay, Floréna. I hope, given some time, we might even be friends. In the meantime, go home." She gently touches Floréna's elbow and guides her to the stairs. "And as we work toward helping the world open up again, you'll have safer opportunities to travel, which will also make it easier for you to find someone who can barely breathe without you beside them."

When Floréna goes downstairs, her eyes a mixture of sorrow and confusion, Ëólas strides over to Adaline. In one move, he scoops her up, placing one arm around her back and the other under her knees, and carries her to the front door.

He nuzzles her cheek with his nose. "You're kind."

"The world needs more kindness."

"The world needs more of you."

Another breeze tickles Adaline's exposed bottom. "Put me down," she says without actually fighting to get free.

"Are you truly alright?" He carries her over the threshold and toward their bed. "How can I ever apologize enough? How can I help you feel better?"

"Find me a toilet! I really have to pee."

After using the facilities located downstairs, because apparently their treehouse has a second and main floor with another entrance beneath the deck, Adaline flops onto the sofa opposite the fireplace, tucking Ëólas's shirt around her bum. The mantel holds a few wood-carved animals, a deer and bird that Ëólas made himself.

Beside the crackling fireplace hangs a new dress with rich azure tulle and chiffon, a narrow bodice with a sweetheart neckline, off-shoulder sleeves, and a midnight-blue ribbon around the waist. It's quite the Cinderella-esque dress in terms of color but is much more form fitting. She laughs at the irony though, especially given no one here has ever heard of that fairytale, and she's happier to wear this one, rather than Nan's packed away in the duffle bag taunting her from beside the fireplace. If she wore Nan's dress, she might as well request a group of elves to build her a billboard announcing her lineage, given everyone in Lameiría will recognize the Aerytolían style with its open back and iridescent color.

Adaline sighs. How a fireplace within a tree doesn't catch fire no longer distracts her from the thoughts she kept trying to beat back since she returned to Gladríen.

Even though we're only announcing our union tonight, how long can we keep my lineage a secret?

From the stairs hidden in an alcove to the right, Ëólas comes upstairs and mentions something about speeches and a celebration. She doesn't really hear him, even when he kneels in front of her. She stares past the dress. She can't stay in Ëólas's tunic all day, not if she's going to walk down to the sacred circle later tonight. To unlock those memories. Memories that can't be good if her grandmother sealed them away. Then again, maybe she still has time if the announcements are first. Are they? She should have listened to him.

"My love?" he asks. The guilt chiseled on Ëólas's face regarding Floréna draws Adaline back to him.

"Where were you?" She keeps her voice soft, but he hangs his head. "That wasn't an accusation, mé ellador. You can't be with me every minute of every day. Besides, I think I handled myself alright, no?"

"You were brilliant." He kisses her knee.

"Did you take care of what you needed to?"

"Yes."

Drifting in from the open deck doors, a breeze ruffles the hem of her new dress, bringing with it a citrusy scent and a sizzling sound that reminds Adaline of a fajita platter. "Dinner?"

"It can wait." He reaches into his pocket and pulls out a small purple cloth pouch that he places on her palm. "For you."

Unsure why he's giving her something when she already received the one thing she wanted most, she glances at him skeptically but tugs the two tiny strings. The cloth falls open, revealing a silver band with six amethyst gemstones shaped like petals, all surrounding a central diamond. "You, you made me a ring?"

Ëólas takes the band from her hand and slides it onto her left ring finger. "I apologize for not giving this to you first, but I did say I planned to ask you to marry me *after* we returned here."

She stares at her hand, dumfounded, and tilts the timeless flower back and forth in the fire's light, casting her own kaleidoscope of orange, red, and yellow on the walls and ceiling. She never considered wearing such a bauble, never understood Cindy's yearning for one. But Ëólas got this ring just for her. He remembered her traditions and made sure she didn't miss out. And now she has a constant reminder of their love, a visual symbol she can take with her always, and one that sits so prettily on her hand too, even if she can't see it properly anymore because of her blurred vision. "When? How?"

"I asked the jeweler to make it before I canceled that spell."

Her heartbeat slows to a crawl. *He had this made, before he took me to the circle and I almost disappeared on him?*

The enormity of his love, of the insecurity and hope that he too carried, of his willingness to stand back and let her choose her own path, crashes over her like a tidal wave that holds her down until her chest might burst, only she doesn't fight to escape. She holds onto the pressure, taking it in little by little, until the feelings settle deep within her so she'll never forget what they both endured to reach this point.

Within the glow of the fire, she slides off the sofa, into his arms, and looks at those liquid-gold eyes. "I love it. I'll treasure it forever. Thank you so much."

"I'm elated you love it so." He rubs his thumb over the gems and kisses her, the flutter of his lips making hers tingle. "My love, I know you're nervous about tonight, but I'm never going to let anyone or anything come between us. Whatever comes our way, we'll face it together. Because we're a team, now and always."

"I wouldn't have it any other way."

As Ëólas escorts Adaline toward the queen's garden, Adaline uses one hand to hold tight to the crook of his arm and the other to lift the azure layers so she won't trip. Occasionally, she feels the stone in her pocket tap her thigh as they walk.

"Okay, let me see if I got this straight. We're meeting with your parents while we wait for your grandparents to arrive, the same grandparents who don't approve of New Leira." When Ëólas nods, she continues, "After, we'll go to the theater to address your people."

Ëólas, wearing his signature navy-blue and green layers, arches an eyebrow.

"Our people," Adaline corrects, even though that still sounds foreign to her. "There, we'll announce your plans for the war and our union, and while everyone's dancing the night away as a celebratory send-off, we'll sneak over to the sacred circle to unlock my memories. Right?"

The circlet on his head doesn't budge even as he nods. "Correct."

"Whew. It's going to be a long night."

Before they take two steps into the garden bordered with rose bushes, Élara rises from her bench and walks over to them. The moonlight makes her raven hair shimmer and her pale green gown glow.

She takes Adaline's free hand in her own, and when Élara speaks, her voice hums as softly as a choir. "Aiden will join us shortly. At present, he is instructing the guards to report to us about the humans in our prison. I believe we have only four, but we will review each of their situations and—with your input—discuss new options. We hope you will consider our efforts to reevaluate our laws as proof that we eagerly welcome you into this family, Adaline. If you should feel so inclined someday, please consider calling us Mother and Father.”

Words fail Adaline. She glances at Ëólas, who seems to radiate from the inside out with his silent jubilation. When she faces Élara, the queen waits patiently for Adaline’s response.

How can this lady be so intimidating as a queen and so endearing to family? Adaline sucks in a sharp breath. *Oh my god. She’s like Nan.* She takes Élara’s hands, but the queen pulls Adaline into a gentle yet firm hug.

When they separate, Élara smiles fondly at her new daughter and leads her to a table set with tea and biscuits. “A snack before the festivities?”

“I never turn down a cup of tea,” Adaline says. *Or coffee. I so do miss coffee.*

Opposite his mother, Ëólas sits next to Adaline and fills their three cups, content to lean back and let the ladies bond.

“Now, Adaline, when you and Ëólas return home after securing the Neutral Territory, we’ll host a week-long festival to celebrate your union.” Élara drops a sugar cube into her cup. “Please, let me know what traditions you want included, and invite as many friends as you like. I’m not excluding your family and friends. This wedding celebration will also serve as a testament to our people and yours that our laws are changing.”

Adaline pinches her arm under the table to make sure she’s not dreaming. “That’s, that’s amazing. Thank you.”

“Will Elashor attend?” Ëólas passes Adaline a biscuit that she refuses with a head shake, still full from dinner.

“He doesn’t have a choice in the matter,” Élara says. “Not even my father would dare question destiny’s design.”

Adaline squeezes Ëólas’s hand. “Your support means so much to me. To us.”

“Truly,” Ëólas says.

As his father walks into the garden, Ëólas stands up. In a hurry to mimic her husband, Adaline pushes her chair out to rise too, but Ëólas’s hand on her shoulder tells her she doesn’t need to.

Reaching the table, Aiden kisses Élara's cheek, pats Ëólas's shoulder in a congratulatory sort of way, and kisses the back of Adaline's hand. Before letting go, he pauses and examines her ring. "Very pretty and a sweet tradition. It suits you, my dear."

"Thank you." Taking her hand back, Adaline smiles at the ring again. "I need to get one for Ëólas though."

"Matching?" Ëólas grimaces.

"Ha, no. Most guys wear a rather simple band but thicker, maybe with a design etched into the metal."

"Oh, that's alright then. I like that idea." He winks at her.

With the four of them sitting around the table, Ëólas's parents share stories about his youth, about what a curious, vivacious child he had been.

"He used to disappear for weeks on us," Élara says, taking another sip of tea. "We'd find him at the furthest reach of Lameiría. One time, when he was barely twenty, he climbed the tallest tree and refused to come down for a year. We had to send him materials so he could build his personal quarters up there."

Wait, what? "Is that our home?"

"Yes, my love." To punctuate his next words, Ëólas taps his hand on the table. "But don't believe the exaggeration. Merith made certain I came down for training."

"A mother's allowed to boast, and I have only one to boast of. Permit me to indulge, my son." Putting down her teacup, Élara leans forward, and her golden eyes sparkle with curiosity. "Adaline, do you have a large family?"

"Mother." Ëólas's warning tone makes Élara sit back as he finds Adaline's hand under the table.

"What? Am I not allowed to ask? Have I offended you?" Élara asks, concern evident on her face.

"It's fine," Adaline says. "My family back home is gone. My father, Edwin, passed away two years ago, but he was a scholar like me."

"Illness?" Élara asks, her voice quieter.

"Car accident."

Ëólas chokes on his tea. "That contraption you drove me in?"

"I'm a good driver!"

"At four times the speed of a horse, yet you couldn't ride a horse?"

"I went to driving school for cars, not horses."

"What's a car?" Aiden asks, trying to follow the conversation.

Ëólas proceeds to explain how an automobile works, at least the bits he could observe. The effortless conversation between the four of them catches Adaline off guard. The cadence of their laughter, the banter given and reciprocated, and the absence of insecurity remind her of many late-night conversations with her own family. Even though those evenings inevitably ended with Dad rushing off to resume his studies or Nan stepping away to read a book or Adaline driving back to her condo, those small, regular get-togethers had been her safety net. No matter what happened at work or in her personal life, she could seek shelter from life just by going home. No one prepared her for the sudden loss of that shelter, not that anyone could have. But still, through Ëólas, she's been given that gift a second time, and she won't take this family for granted.

No matter what happens with Aerytol, we'll protect this family too.

At the mention of in-door plumbing, Ëólas and Aiden lose themselves in conversation. Élara, shaking her head at them, asks Adaline more personal questions about her childhood, her interests, and, inevitably, her mother.

"My mother passed when I was very young." When Élara expresses her deepest sympathies, Adaline shrugs. "It's okay, really. It's hard to miss something I don't..."

This time, Adaline hears herself, hears the automatic reply that doesn't sound like her, that sounds like Nan. Ëólas pauses his conversation, glances at Adaline, and attempts to distract his mother by asking about her plans for the wedding celebration that will fill Lameiría with song and dance and sleepless merriment. Adaline tries to focus on Élara's words, but the stone starts vibrating in her pocket, so much so that even her teacup becomes a blur.

Although Élara's lips continue moving, they slow down as time stretches away from Adaline. The dripping of water echoes in her ears. The crackle of fire. The roar of wind. The tumble of a rockslide. The feeling of being pulled inward matches how she felt when she approached Gladríen's sacred circle.

The stone, it's calling to me. Or maybe I'm calling to it.

Her attention snaps back to the present only when everyone stops talking and stands up. Her teacup is empty, although she doesn't recall finishing it.

Ëólas extends his hand to her, helping her out of her seat. "My grandparents have arrived." He leads Adaline, still in a daze, toward the garden entrance, behind his parents. "Are you alright?"

"I'm fine." Adaline reaches up and smooths out the wrinkles on his brow.

He snatches her hand and kisses her palm, making her forget about the stone, at least for a little bit. As they approach Elashor and his wife, Élara and Aiden step to the side so Ëólas may present his bride.

Elashor, the source of this family's golden eyes, keeps his hands clasped together in front of his stomach as if forming a shield while he studies everything in the garden, except for Adaline. His silver hair has dark highlights that make her wonder if he once had dirty-blond hair too.

So, this is the former king who used to be childhood friends with my grandfather. Who buried my family.

His wife, who looks only slightly older than Élara and has the same raven hair, watches Adaline's every movement, from her toes to her fingertips. Her gaze grows darker as Ëólas slides his arm behind Adaline's back. For two individuals nearly a thousand years old, they both look younger than Nan before she passed. Though they have few wrinkles, their faces seem thinner, paler, almost transparent so that Adaline can see the faint-blue veins beneath their skin.

Ëólas and Adaline halt in front of them both. "Elashor and Neira, this is my wife, Adaline." Ëólas presses his hand against the small of Adaline's back, reassuring her of his constant presence.

When Elashor finally looks at Adaline, he narrows his eyes and tightens his jaw. His chest heaves ever so slightly, as if someone punctured his heart with a needle and he's slowly losing all this breath. He says nothing to acknowledge her.

Regardless, Adaline curtsies. Élara and Aiden move to stand beside Adaline and Ëólas, and in that moment, Adaline decides to love them both.

"Where is she from?" Neira says, her tone sharp, her gaze unyielding.

"She's King Magnus's ward," Ëólas replies, keeping his promise that Adaline's origins are her own to reveal.

The lie tastes like mercury in her mouth. *Lying to family can't be right.*

Elashor steps forward. Adaline digs her feet into the grass so not to flinch or step backward. The earth helps her legs feel as steady as a mountain while Ëólas keeps his hand against her back, and Élara steps forward, preventing her father from looming any further over Adaline.

She follows his eyes as he studies her long curly hair, her cheekbones, the tip of her chin, her small nose and heart-shaped face—all features she shared with her grandmother. He glowers at her olive skin, green eyes, and of course her round ears that she inherited from her mother.

"Can't be," Lord Elashor mumbles.

He recognizes me? Somewhat.

"Welcome, child." Neira's tone is as cold and flat as the slate path she treads upon to join her husband, who's already walked past their group.

Together, Elashor and Neira pass through the garden, leaving the rest of the family behind, and make their way toward the theater where Adaline now has to face most of Lameiría.

No problem. Easy peasy.

Élara squeezes Adaline's shoulder encouragingly before excusing herself and Aiden. They catch up to her parents, waiting at the opposite garden exit, so Élara and Aiden can lead the way.

Ëólas's eyes have grown cold and his jaw rigid. She places her hand over his chest, and the bond between them sparks and jump-starts his heartbeat. Color returns to his cheeks. As he presses his forehead against hers, his breathing resumes a normal rhythm. Knowing he wants to apologize, she places her finger on his mouth long enough to silence him.

"What about your other grandparents?" *Maybe they're nicer.*

"Trapped in a faraway kingdom. My father traveled here on his own when he was very young. When the war happened and the borders shut down, well, my father hasn't seen his parents since." He kisses her forehead, trying to smooth out the wrinkles now on her brow, and offers his arm, which she accepts. They exit the garden together.

Adaline frowns at Elashor and Neira's backs. Nan would never have allowed anyone to judge her like that, and Adaline can't help but wonder if she just let Nan down.

Chapter Twenty-Seven

THE STONE

Arm in arm, Ëólas and Adaline stroll through the city, past musicians strumming strings and piping flutes in alcoves, past dancing circles overtaking balconies, and past merchants displaying the skills of their trades before an eager audience. The entire forest is alive with songs and laughter as elves race back and forth on the walkways, ladies with ribbons flowing from their hair and blokes discussing whom they should woo next. The chefs constantly cook new food, and even though Adaline's never seen a pig in the forest, something smells so much like bacon that she's soon drooling and following that scent. People pass out patties, pastries, and pies and share recipes while teaching others how to make the delectable treats over camp stoves and firepits. It's like Adaline's back in D.C., attending a free arts festival with live music and cooking lessons and an introduction to different crafts.

She and Ëólas stop to watch a group of painters. While Ëólas watches someone paint a seascape, Adaline's eyes keep drifting back to a wooden crate turned sideways. Over the slats, the artist has finished painting a meadow and has moved onto dabbing fluffy white puffs of sheep. Adaline aches to pick up the brushes, but someone demonstrating bookbinding draws her attention away. Behind them, another group of elves roll wine barrels up to a makeshift bar. As more people pour into this concentrated portion of the forest, the more laughter and wine they pass around.

When an elven lady offers Ëólas a goblet, he gives the offering to someone else.

Adaline's mouth salivates at the thought of more tree spirits. Granted, getting drunk tonight would be a bad, bad idea. "Do you refuse the wine because of me?"

"No." Ëólas nods hello to the people they pass. "We have official obligations in a short while. Also, I'd rather not test if our wine will kill you."

"You're joking."

"I'm not." So he doesn't have to shout over the strings and pipes, he speaks into her ear. "And I've seen firsthand how much a sip affects you."

"That wasn't a sip. I guzzled the whole cup that night."

"You what?" Ëólas releases a torrent of laughter. "I should have suspected then."

Huh. We had a clue hidden in plain sight the whole time.

They continue their stroll, but Adaline watches Ëólas continue chuckling to himself. She could watch him for hours, that unbridled merriment, the way his youthful joy encourages everyone around him to relax and savor the present moment too. Everyone around them smiles brighter when they see him delighted. A few people gravitate toward them, drawn in by his light, and wish him well before reluctantly returning to their own revelries. They love their prince. Their trust in him is evident on all their faces.

Again, Ëólas whispers in her ear, "If you keep looking at me like that, I'll have to sneak off with you somewhere, and we're already pressing our luck with time."

"What do you mean?" She tries to sound innocent, as if she hasn't been thinking the same thing. Taking a large step sideways, she widens the gap between them. She's not ready to face what his people will think once they realize whom their beloved lord married.

"There you are!" Renor runs to them and halts in front of Ëólas. "Her Majesty awaits you at the theater."

Renor doesn't bother to look at Adaline. She may as well not be there, but Ëólas gives him a laser death stare that forces Renor to acknowledge her existence. He nods once and looks away.

Is this what it's going to be like, Ëólas ordering people to show me some common decency?

She steps forward, interrupting Ëólas's line of sight. "Lord Renor, a pleasure to see you again. You must be quite exceptional in your role to assume so much in Ëólas's stead. I hope when Ëólas is back, you'll have a chance to relax. I've heard so much about how the elves indulge their passions throughout the ages. What are you studying at the moment?"

Please have a hobby or something we can talk about. Does he even know I saved his sister's life? And stole the person she loves. Oh man, this family's going to hate me forever.

Renor glances left and right, debating his exit strategy. Reluctantly, he regards her, purses his lips, and speaks as though every word requires his life force. "My top priority is upholding the wishes of my queen and king, and they have requested that you hasten your stroll toward the stage."

Renor does an about-face and walks off, leaving Ëólas and Adaline to follow behind.

Adaline nibbles her thumbnail as she watches Renor's back. "I don't think he's going to come around."

"Pay him no heed," Ëólas says. "He's uncertain what Floréna did to be bound to their family's home. And he's still mad at me for giving him mugnite duty."

"What's mugnite?"

"The sludge at the bottom of the toilets."

"Huh?"

"The muck that devours waste. It's dormant except for when we give it something to feed on."

Adaline coughs and gags. *Oh my god. Way to terrorize children who already fear falling in the potty. I'll never look at another toilet here the same way again.* "Why would you give him such a horrific job?"

"He disobeyed my orders."

"I disobeyed your orders in New Leira. Multiple times."

"You did?" He pretends to sound shocked at this revelation. "I suppose my subconscious love saved you." He shrugs. "Then again, Magnus was technically responsible for you, so my hands were tied."

"Dang. Remind me to never work for you. To be fair, it also doesn't help that Renor probably thought you two would be brothers someday."

"Why would he think that?"

"Seriously? You have no clue?" *That Floréna's in love with you?*

"Clue about what?"

"Oh, dear." Adaline loops her arm around Ëólas's and shakes her head as they walk deeper into the forest.

They pass through a tight, circular grove of trees and walk downhill along one of many stone paths that lead to a center stage, its smooth golden-brown planks rising maybe half an inch off the packed dirt floor covered in magenta leaves. The amphitheater must hold several thousand elves when full, not to mention if they fill the staircases that wind around the tree trunks. The platforms up top look like reserved box seats.

When Adaline and Ëólas reach center stage, Élara touches the back of Aiden's arm, a simple gesture that hints at her excitement. She hurries forward and, clasping Adaline's hands, transfers her natural ease to her daughter. "We will celebrate this night for eons because tonight marks the beginning of a new path for us all with the first ever human and elf union. Even though some will struggle with the idea, we four will guide them through any confusion and uncertainty."

At the mention of *first ever*, Ëólas drifts closer to Adaline. "We will, indeed."

I guess no one celebrated my parents' marriage, at least not as a historical moment. They must have hidden the truth, like they hid me. Because they knew this world would view me as nothing more than an abomination? "Thank you for being so kind and welcoming."

Élara air kisses Adaline's cheek, releases her hands, and asks Aiden to accept a wooden box that a nearby guard's holding.

After taking the square, ash-gray wooden chest, Aiden congratulates both Ëólas and Adaline. He chooses few words to express his sentiments, but his eyes, as prominent and enchanting as rare woodland bluebells, reveal his delight at seeing his son happy. Turning to Adaline, he lifts the box's hinged lid. "Every parent prays their child is fortunate enough to find their destined partner. You have fulfilled ours. This, my dear, is for you."

Inside, Adaline finds a silver circlet, matching Ëólas's, with the same miniature sapphires and emeralds imbedded in the leaves. She seizes Ëólas's hand, latching onto him instead of reaching into the box to pick up the delicate band. *I've never been into jewelry, so why do I want to wear that so badly?* "I, I don't know what to say. It's lovely. Thank you."

"I'm glad you like it," Élara says. "It was mine long ago."

Whoa.

"We wanted to show you this now so you'll be prepared when Élara gives this to you after her announcement." Aiden waits for Adaline's nod to close the lid and passes the box back to the guard. After he too air kisses her cheek, he joins Élara to greet a handful of people slowly making their way to the bottom of the theater.

While facing and waving to his people, Ëólas dips his head closer to Adaline. "I thought you'd prefer a warning."

"Oh my god, yes."

"But you look happy."

His face and his body posture display only confidence and ease, but, internally, Adaline can sense him battling the same range of emotions churning inside her.

She threads her arm around his. "I am. I really am."

Ëólas studies her a moment longer, making certain she's being honest, and shifts his attention to scanning the new arrivals gathering at the amphitheater's entrances, his brain most likely calculating who will volunteer to join him. Similarly, Adaline studies the faces of the generals and guards, trying to familiarize herself with people who might soon be their allies in New Leira. A tall, strawberry-blonde bounds down the stone path, her high ponytail swinging behind her. When Adaline waves hello, Sora stops halfway, places her hand over her chest, and bows her head.

The gesture makes Adaline ask Ëólas, "Um, did something happen?"

"The queen released Sora from palace duties and reassigned her to you."

"To me? Meaning Sora's coming back with us?" When Ëólas nods, Adaline bounces on her toes. "That's so freaking fantastic! Wait, is Sora okay with that?"

"Why do you think she and I were fast friends? She has a thirst for adventure too. She's thrilled."

"Oh, that's wonderful."

"Agreed, but we're needed now." Ëólas jerks his head in his father's direction.

Taking center stage, Aiden explains where people will sit and the logistics of the evening, pointing to the front row where Élara's parents and the council members will be seated only a stone's throw away. While Aiden explains the order of tonight's announcements, Adaline looks at the thousands of seats encircling her and can't fight back the growing feeling that the audience will be waiting for her to falter.

Just like her classmates did during her dance recital. "They want me to mess up," she told Nan years ago. Hiding backstage, Adaline sat on a deflated moon balloon, despite her solo being next. When she missed her turn, another classmate danced past her and claimed center stage. Her father left his seat in the audience to find his daughter, and Nan gave them space to talk alone.

Rotating his flat cap in his hand, Edwin crouched down to her level. "I've watched this routine twenty times, Adaline. You've never missed a step. Why are you back here?"

"They hate me." Adaline traced the ridged tracking of her pink skirt. "They want me to mess up so I won't be the teacher's pet anymore."

Sitting next to Adaline, Edwin bumped her shoulder with his own. "You want to go home? Sell your tutus and slippers?"

"No!" She tapped the edges of her slippers' platforms together. "I want to dance."

"Then dance and screw them! Gah, don't tell your grandmother I said that."

Adaline giggled, and her father tickled her side, making her continue laughing until the current song reached its crescendo.

"The truth, kiddo, is that there will always be those who don't want us to be ourselves. If you start hiding now, that's what you'll be used to. Always hiding. Always being half yourself." His voice sounded further away the longer he stared into the shadows. But before Adaline could ask if he was okay, he scrubbed his face, slapped his thigh with his hat, and stood up, offering Adaline a hand to get off the balloon. "Life already has enough dark moments, kiddo. I'd rather you dance through life."

Back then, he had been right. When she switched to private lessons, dancing and playing music were the only times she felt at ease being herself. But how could he offer her that advice when he actively participated in keeping half of her hidden? Did he regret that choice? But the consequences of being herself have turned deadly. And her life isn't the only one at stake now.

Élara interrupts Adaline's ruminations by quietly sharing that her first speech will remind everyone of the Neutral Territory's mission, that elves and humans can and should coexist in peace, and that mission honors the land upon which it's built.

My grandmother's homeland. The same land I'm supposed to protect. As queen.

Adaline exhales slowly, hoping she can mask her emotions from Ëólas's stare. In her pocket, she turns the stone over in her hand and focuses on its smooth, cool texture.

Elashor and Neira enter the grove, and the crowd at the top parts to allow them through. At the bottom of the pit, Adaline feels like an insect in their eyes. Already their gazes are trying to unravel her secrets. The stone grows warmer, hotter, in her hand. They glance at her pocket, as if they can see through her, that she's only half as good as them, only half a person. She's not protecting herself; she's protecting a lie.

"Create your own circle," whispers that same voice. A voice just beyond reach, just beyond the edge of this world. A voice Adaline vaguely recalls like a lost dream.

Crap. Please tell me I'm not in eminent danger.

Keeping her voice low, Élara takes center stage. "I will declare that when we lost our high queen, Lameiría lost its path too. Elves are not meant to hold on to grief, fear, and anger. And the queen's greatest hope has not been lost. Ëólas, Adaline, you two should join me here, and I will announce that destiny has chosen you two as proof, that your efforts in the Neutral Territory led you to find the one. Ëólas, that's when you should formally introduce Adaline to our people."

Ëólas offers Adaline his hand. She latches on, borrowing his calmness, his fortitude. Her stomach, however, keeps doing somersaults. She presses her lips closed to stop herself from throwing up.

"She's ill." Lady Neira's loud, flat voice makes all eyes turn on Adaline.

She thinks the rodent has brought them disease.

"Are you alright?" Ëólas asks.

"I'm fine." Adaline squeezes his hand harder as his grandparents approach them.

It's just a stage. Like so many I've been on before. This is just another performance.

The stone vibrates against her thigh, and she hears the waves of a lake slapping a shore. Looking about, she expects a river to burst through the grove and wash them all away, but she can't find any sources of water around them.

Not letting go of Adaline, Ëólas turns to his mother and says in a hushed tone, "I'll list the benefits of the world changing but that we'll have to overcome those who abhor the idea of elves and humans coexisting. After, I'll go into detail about what Adaline and I discovered and that an attack on the Neutral Territory is an attack on Lameiría."

Stepping onto the stage, Lord Elashor twists his noble face in disgust. "You plan to summon our troops to defend your little project?"

Adaline glances at Ëólas, at his steeled gaze, but through their bond she knows he's anything but calm on the inside. The wind howls, rattling the leaves circling them. But everyone's clothes and hair appear undisturbed. She waits for him to speak louder, to fight to be heard over the roar of the wind, but he keeps his volume just the same, as if he doesn't hear the wind at all.

"The Neutral Territory is more than just a neighboring city. It represents the future of all kingdoms, especially that of Lameiría." Ëólas steps closer to Adaline and holds her hand over his heart. The warmth of their bond tingles from her hand, through her arm, and into her own chest.

"And Alderton thinks the same? They have agreed to fight *with us* this time?" Elashor asks.

"I have not yet had the chance to speak directly with Magnus, but I know where he stands on this matter."

Elashor balks. "Your assumptions and efforts will yield only the same results."

"Father." Élara steps forward, placing herself between Elashor and Ëólas. "We are unified in this matter. If you aim to cast doubt among our people, you should return home. I will permit nothing more than determination and support."

Ëólas kisses Adaline's brow. The stone vibrates again, and the fire within the lanterns strung around the grove and market stalls crackle and pop. As their glow burns brighter, the scent of smoke and charcoal permeates the night air. Wondering if anyone else senses the change in the lanterns, Adaline glances at Sora and the other people debating whether to take their seats at the bottom of the theater, but they're preoccupied with staring blankly ahead as though their queen and former king are not quarreling.

With a sneer, Elashor throws his hands about. "You expect me to remain silent while you invite war upon our people?"

"I expect you to trust your queen." Élara's fierceness is a thing of awe.

Elashor and Neira nod, but the gesture is perfunctory at best. They turn to leave.

No, no, no. Ëólas's family can't split apart.

"Wait! Please," Adaline says. "We all understand your fear. I can't imagine living with that for so long. It's a part of you now, and I'm sorry for that. I truly am. But we're family now, and I just hope—"

"Hope?" Elashor repeats, his voice hollow. "You have no concept of what we lost. The high queen and king were magnificent. They were kind and gentle and welcomed the lost into their home." He gnashes his teeth and spits, "They invited evil disguised as progress into their home, and their efforts resulted in their heads severed from their bodies. They were executed, child."

Adaline grips her throat. *Nan, what do I do?*

A gentle breeze stirs the leaves, causing them to dance around the hem of her dress. The soil deep beneath them turns over and makes way for the tree roots stretching their limbs. The flowers and bushes stand taller and stretch their petals.

Adaline pulls back her shoulders and lifts her chin. "My family didn't raise me to be a coward. They raised me to..." *To what? Dance through life despite the pain?*

Study history to avoid repeating the past? Always choose kindness whenever possible? Oh. They did prepare me for this.

Finding her voice, Adaline evokes her grandmother's poise and confidence. "My family raised me to seek the truth and trust in myself."

She takes the stone out of her pocket. When Ëólas sees it, he nods he's with her. He's always with her.

"Caution is not cowardice," Elashor hisses.

"That's enough." Élara claps her hands together with a boom to silence everyone. "Our focus ought to be on encouraging our people's support, not dredging up the past."

"I'm sorry, Élara, but that's not true." Letting go of Ëólas, Adaline walks over to her and Aiden. "The past holds the truth, and with our family fracturing, I think you need the truth just as much as I do."

"What truth?" Élara glances at the stone in Adaline's hand. "I don't understand."

"It contains my memories. My grandmother, I think, put them in here."

"Your memories?" Aiden asks. "Memories of what?"

"We're not sure yet." Cutting everyone off before they can ask more questions, Ëólas places his hand on Adaline's back, ready to guide her out of the theater. "We need to go to the sacred circle. Now. The speeches will have to wait."

"No, it's okay. I'll just cast a circle here." She ignores Neira's gasp.

"You need us to gather the elements?" Ëólas asks.

"They're already here." Adaline waves her hand around the stage. "Since I've had this stone, the elements keep calling to me, and I heard the voice too. Élara, Aiden, you might want to back up. Mé ellador, when the time comes, would you please take the place of the soul pillar?"

Ëólas smiles proudly.

"You can't just create your own sacred circle!" Neira clutches her necklace as if to ward off evil. "Only a priestess has that right, and humans can't do magic."

"I don't think that's true. Regardless, my grandmother wasn't human." Adaline doesn't bother to address everyone's confusion while she moves to the center of the stage, and Ëólas gets everyone to move farther back.

Closing her eyes, Adaline clutches the stone close to her heart and listens to everything except for Neira's protests and the generals' murmurs. The smell of charcoal and the sound of crackling fire invokes memories of roasting marshmallows that simultaneously crisp and liquify, Nan applying copious amounts of Neosporin after Adaline's first attempt at flipping pancakes, Cindy and Adaline lighting candles for their spa sleepover, and the fire in Ëólas's hearth flickering to life when they made love this evening.

A lantern near the stage shatters. Several people gasp, but Adaline tunes them out as the ball of light rolls downhill, leaving only a scorch mark behind, and stops a few feet shy of Adaline to her left. The flames billow in the wind but do not set the stage on fire.

The wind carries memories within its bursts, a laughter that reminds Adaline when she and Cindy flew a kite that tore free from their hands and soared into the sun, her dad screaming in horror when a carnival ride launched them into the sky and flipped them upside down, and music from when she convinced Ëólas to dance the night Lori was born.

The wind swirls together, forming a docile tornado behind her.

The smell of moist soil transports Adaline back to her grandmother's garden, where they'd plant and prune flowers, spread mulch, and create compost while Adaline told Nan about her day at school. The scent of minerals takes her back to the cave where the bluecaps answered her song and to the Rialto in New Leira where the citizens came together to plant twelve vameires for the memorial.

Two of Lameiría's tree roots burst out of the ground, slither onto the stage to Adaline's right, and twist together.

When Adaline hears the water splashing along the riverbanks, she remembers floating on her back, her father's arms beneath her, and his voice insisting he won't let her sink. She remembers Nan rowing them out to the center of the lake and reading sonnets while Adaline daydreamed. She remembers floating downstream with Ëólas while the river carried them and their stories to safety.

In front of her, a spring erupts from the ground, splashing and sputtering upward through the stage's wooden planks.

For mind, Adaline calls upon family game nights with Nan and Dad huddled around the living room coffee table and all the colorful crystals that lined Lady Loríen's shop.

A mound of dirt rises like a large anthill until a geode emerges, which Élara quickly places on the stage, leaving room for only one more element.

Looking at Éólas, Adaline places her hand over her heart to feel the bond between them, and he takes his place as the sixth pillar, standing off to the side in front of her.

One by one the elements illuminate, creating a ring of light around her. She keeps her body perfectly still in the center. With the elements all contained, silence befalls Lameiría. No one dares to speak. The spring starts to overflow, filling the stage with a shallow pool of water no higher than Adaline's ankles.

She raises her hand, takes a deep breath, and releases the stone.

Everyone hears the kerplunk, its echo hanging in the air.

As the first ring appears, a wall of mist three times Adaline's height rises from the pool, displaying an image of wooden beams and a white stucco wall inside a cottage. Two nightstands painted lavender flank a single bed covered with a quilt. The ring of water slowly expands, and beings like water sprites rise from the pool. Their bodies, made of living water, solidify into people and voices from the past.

Chapter Twenty-Eight

A BEDTIME STORY

"**P**lease, Papa. Tell me a story." With her parents behind her, Adaline crawls into a small, simple bed. At four years old, her American accent is nonexistent. Instead, she speaks like everyone else in the Neutral Territory.

Her mother places a candle, the only source of light in the room, on the nightstand. After tucking the periwinkle quilt up to Adaline's chin, Aurellia hands Adaline a rag doll with black yarn for hair and green button eyes.

Laying down beside her daughter, she brushes her light-brown hair away from her eyes. "I'd like a story too, but let's make it a short one tonight. Your father has a long journey ahead of him tomorrow."

Adaline rolls toward her mother, whose wool skirt acts as a second blanket, and snuggles into the crook of her arm. "Poppa's going to snoop in King Rioran's court again?"

"It's not snooping." Crossing his arms over his chest, Edwin leans his shoulder against the doorframe and sticks his tongue out at Adaline. His tan tunic bunches against the woodgrain, revealing a small hole at the seam, and a short dark-brown beard covers half his face, making him look like a teddy bear. "It's research. Now, hush up if you want a story."

As Adaline pretends to button her lips, Edwin kneels beside her bed and rests his arms on the quilt. His hands, washed clean from a day's work of herding sheep, reveal scratches scabbed over but few wrinkles. "Once upon a time, in a land not so far away, there lived a wise queen and a kind king. They looked after all of Aerytol and shared their wisdom with the world."

Aurellia pokes Edwin's forearm. "I thought we agreed on a short story, Eddie."

Adaline giggles. Edwin shrugs. With a loud exhale, Aurellia combs Adaline's hair with her fingers, and Edwin continues, "The queen and king realized that elves and humans weren't getting along so well. And—"

"Why?" Adaline asks.

"Patience, please. Let me tell the story." He boops Adaline's nose. "They weren't getting along so well because all they saw were their differences. The humans lacked patience, and the elves lacked imagination. To help bring the people together, the queen and king invited elves and humans alike to live in Aerytol. At first, the people did come together, and they built a magnificent city that merged human ingenuity and elven sustainability. Within a few hundred years, the human population had grown much faster than the elves, so much so that they outnumbered elves four to one."

Adaline attempts to whistle her amazement. "That's fast! Where did all the babies come from?"

"Heh. Um." Edwin scratches his head and scrunches his nose.

When his mouth emits no other sounds, Aurellia snuggles her daughter. "Ask me that again in a few years."

With an exhale, Edwin takes Adaline's hand and tugs gently so that she looks at him. "Anyway, here's the important part, Adaline, something I want you to always remember: Not all humans are bad, and not all elves are good. In fact, both of them can be rather stupid."

He pauses for a moment, as if he's debating whether to go on, and the corners of his mouth turn downward. "One night, a bunch of boys drank too much. They got rowdy and boastful and started fighting. Sadly, one of the boys died—an elf whose father was captain of the queen's guard. The other boys panicked and tried to conceal the incident, but the captain discovered the truth. Although the queen punished the guilty individuals, the boy's father blamed all of mankind. The queen tried to help him release his pain, his rage, but he couldn't."

"I don't blame him for that." Aurellia kisses the crown of Adaline's head. "I'd rip the world in half if anything happened to you or your father."

"Did the captain die of a broken heart?" Adaline asks.

Casting his dark brown eyes downward, Edwin nods. "In a way, yes. He tried to convince the queen that Aerytol would be better off if she banished all humans from the capital. The queen refused, and he grew resentful. His son's death had introduced a crack, like in a pane of glass. He used rumors to push on that crack, causing fractures of hate and distrust to spread between the elves and humans. He wanted the humans to prove time and again that they were the troublemakers. He needed to make the queen worry, but then she and the king learned they were expecting their first child, a baby boy."

Aurellia places her hand on Edwin's, and Adaline watches the long look that passes between her parents.

"Go on," says Aurellia.

Edwin looks at Adaline and ruffles the hair on her head. "Sometimes, when an Aerytolían conceives a child, a fae visits them in their dreams and reveals a glimpse of their purpose, their destiny, how best they can help the world with their unique gifts. The queen's purpose was to unite elves and humans. Before her parents entered the Immortal Realms, they told her that whenever she left this world, she would safeguard a beacon of hope."

Despite her eyelids growing heavier, Adaline forces them open again. "What did the fae reveal about the baby boy?"

Edwin looks at his wife as though he needs nothing more in life than her. "That the prince of Aerytol was destined to fall in love with and marry a human."

Adaline snuggles closer to her mother.

"The queen and king were elated to know their unification efforts would bear fruit," Edwin says. "And she confided in the captain about her dream, hoping he'd finally realize he needed to release his anger."

"I wish he did," Adaline says, her voice little more than a murmur.

Edwin hangs his head. "Me too, my darling. Instead, he became enraged. He could not tolerate the idea of an elf-human union, so he convinced the humans the queen planned to enslave them and cut their numbers in half to protect her unborn child. Out of fear, the humans rioted and stormed the castle."

"But that was a lie!" Squeezing her hand into a fist, Adaline sits up in bed and hits her comforter. Her mother coaxes her back down, pulls her into a hug, and strokes her arm. "Poppa, I don't like this part of the story."

"I know. But the only way to fight those lies is to preserve and share the truth. Everyone, including your mother's people, believe humans killed the Aerytolíans. But they didn't. They don't know that amidst the chaos, the captain confronted the queen. He accused her of losing her way, that the fae would never condone human blood mingling with elves, let alone with the Aerytolían bloodline. So, he renounced his oath to defend her."

Edwin stops. "Maybe that's enough for tonight." He kisses Adaline's forehead and stands up.

"That's why the captain killed grandpa?" Adaline asks.

Edwin stops in the doorway and lets out a long, quiet sigh. "Yes, sweetheart."

Adaline crawls out from under her covers, lifts her arms, and waits for her father to scoop her up. Aurellia doesn't protest. She sits back and watches her two loved ones, her shoulders sagging and her eyebrows wilting.

Holding onto his daughter, Edwin nuzzles her forehead with his cheek. "My sweet girl. I should have told you about Dorothy instead."

"Please, Poppa, how did Grandmother and you survive?"

Edwin sits down on the edge of her bed, shifts Adaline onto his lap, and clasps her bare feet, keeping them warm. "When the captain cornered my mother, she used every ounce of her magic to cast a spell that would protect destiny's design."

"And that's what sent you and Grandmother to another world?"

"Yes, sweetheart. That's where I grew up, in another world inhabited only by humans." When Adaline tugs her father's round ears, Edwin does the same to her. "I'm getting to that. Get back in bed. When Aerytolíans are young, the fae bless us with a gift, one that will help us to better manage the responsibilities placed upon our shoulders."

"We sure do get a lot of help," Adaline says. "What makes us so special?"

"Special." Edwin laughs to himself. "I never really thought about it that way. We're just different, and that is a story for another night."

When Adaline pouts, Edwin swats her bottom, nudging her back under the covers and into her mother's arms. "Anyway, when I turned five, I received my gift, which allows me to help my family blend in. My mother and I could stay in one place a lot longer because I could slowly make us appear older." As Edwin explains this, wrinkles form all over his face, and his hair turns gray, but in the blink of an eye, he's young again.

"Poppa, do you like that other world?"

"Very much so. It has its flaws, its tragedies, just like home. But humans are rather remarkable, and I admire their endless curiosity. After a few hundred years though, I grew restless. I studied every culture, every religion, every philosophy I could access, hoping to discover a source of magic that would allow my mother and I to return home."

"Why can't Grandmother come home?"

"Our magic isn't infinite, Adaline. Traveling between worlds is exhausting. When you run from here to the center of the village, how long must you rest afterward? Now, imagine running around the entire planet a few times over. It's a miracle she survived at all. To cast a spell that broke open the barrier between worlds cost her greatly. She succeeded only because the fae permitted her to do so."

"How do you know that?"

Edwin just winks. Adaline scoffs and pulls the blanket over her head as if she's given up and intends to go to sleep. When her father eases himself off the bed, a little voice escapes from under the covers. "When did you meet Momma?"

Throwing back his head, Edwin stares up at the ceiling, grabs a fistful of his short yet thick brown hair, and laughs to himself. "Enough already, young lady."

"Oh, you don't want her to know?" Aurellia teases.

The bed sheets rattle with giggles.

"Whose side are you on, my love? Short version, Adaline: I went back to my mother's circle, the one she brought from Aerytol, and I applied my research methods by combining mystical traditions throughout the world. Destiny must have decided it was time I came home because the spell finally worked. Poof! I returned home, well, to the Forbidden Lands. I didn't have enough magic left to change my appearance, so, within moments, I was fleeing from Lameiría's border patrol. They're terrifying, you know. Anyway, I kept running until I reached Alderton where I met your mother. End of story. Off to bed."

"But why did Uncle Jamie punch you in the eye?"

Pinching the bridge of his nose, Edwin closes his eyes and grimaces at the memory.

"Because you don't tell a woman you just laid eyes on that you're going to marry her. It's rather creepy," Aurellia whispers in Adaline's ear. "Uncle Jamie was protecting me."

"Uncle Jamie is rather fierce," Adaline says.

"That's one word for him." Giving up on escaping this night, Edwin lays down next to his daughter.

As she closes her eyes, her breathing grows slower and heavier, and the water sprites resurrecting the past fade, dissolving the image of Adaline snuggling down between her parents.

Still, she asks one last question, her voice echoing throughout Gladríen's theater. "Do you miss Grandmother?"

"Every day," Edwin whispers. "She desperately hoped to meet you."

Another ring spreads in the water, and the image shifts to a different room in the same cottage with a wide fireplace burning several logs. Above the fire, a large soup pot hangs from the hearth's bracket. A ten-foot-long wood table appears in front of the fire, several feet away and covered with flour, metal canisters, and a loaf of bread rising under a tea towel. Adaline, at maybe five years old, sits on the floor in front of the hearth, her long wool skirt tucked under her knees.

Her mother, carrying carrots in her apron, drops them on the table and starts chopping them, taking her time while humming. A flare of orange flames makes her turn around. "Adaline, do put the fire back in the firebox." With a large knife,

Aurellia pushes aside the carrots cut into medallions, grabs a goose hanging above the mantle, and plucks feathers. "I don't want the house to burn down."

"The fire won't burn the house, Momma. It's only dancing." Standing up, Adaline brings the flames flickering on her palm closer to her mother, who backs up and shields herself with a damp cloth.

"The fire doesn't go beyond the hearth. No exceptions."

With a sigh, Adaline plops down in front of the fireplace and extends her palms toward the logs burning and crackling. "Off you go. You heard her." The flames hop into the larger fire.

"Why don't you help me with dinner? While you chop these potatoes, you can tell me all about the stories the fire tells you."

Grabbing a purple potato, Adaline dips a washcloth into the water bucket on the floor and scrubs the dirt off the tough, wrinkled skin. "The fire doesn't tell stories, Momma. That's the wind."

"And what good stories have you heard of late?" Edwin, coming inside, shuts the door, kicks off his boots, and greets Aurellia first, giving her a kiss and a naughty smile that confuses Adaline and makes Aurellia smirk.

After he kisses his daughter's forehead, he sits in the wooden chair beside her and watches his two women cook. A few moments later, Aurellia throws a potato at him, which he catches with one hand. He washes his hands in the basin by the window and takes over chopping duty while his wife does ten other things in the kitchen.

Edwin leans around the table to see Adaline scrubbing away. "So, who have you been spying on this time?"

"I'm not spying! It's not my fault the winds like to gossip. If you don't like it, I won't tell you what the princes are up to."

Both her mother and father stop their work and gather around her.

When her father playfully pinches Adaline's cheek, she jumps up. "They keep talking about creating a place where elves and humans can mingle freely!" Adaline squeals, leaps into her father's arms, and gives him a big hug. "Poppa, we won't have to hide anymore."

She looks at them both, waiting for them to ask questions, but they keep their reactions hidden behind vague smiles. They don't say or ask anything more and resume making dinner, leaving Adaline to grab another potato and scrub it so hard that the skin rips.

After fast forwarding through dinner and painting lessons with her mother, Adaline quickly runs off to bed. When her parents say goodnight and leave her door open a crack, she counts to one hundred, slips out from under the covers as quietly as a mouse, and wiggles her shoulders out the door. On her hands and knees, she slinks across the floor and lies down, peering around her father's desk so she can see her parents chatting. With their backs to her, she exhales soundlessly.

Sitting on the arm of the accent chair, Aurellia wraps her arm around Edwin's shoulders and rests her cheek on top of his head. "Is it time to introduce her to Queen Élara?"

Edwin hugs her waist. "Not yet. Elashor worries me. He's bitter and blind. Élara has her own reservations too, but the boy... Still, the moment they all realize Adaline has magic, they'll look to her. We should let her be a child a little longer. She'll be queen for the rest of her life."

"Why can't you be king? Why place all the expectations on her?"

"My love, I'm not a king. I'm a professor of anthropology and a shepherd. Besides, you've seen the way the elements respond to her. They've never listened to me like that."

"Well, Adaline's information means you don't have to sneak into Lameiría anytime soon."

"It's not really sneaking when I just walk in."

Aurellia's laughter dances around the room, making the fire glow brighter. As she massages the back of Edwin's neck, she becomes quieter, more thoughtful. "You really think they'll accept me? They hate humans so much, Edwin. They blame us for everything."

"They'll come around, especially when they find out what really happened." Edwin turns his head sideways and peers up at his wife. Taking her hand, he kisses her palm and skates his beard back and forth, making her squirm, laugh, and pull her hand free. "Do you think you can one day accept them?"

"I'm afraid of them," she whispers.

Against the candlelight, Edwin's ears elongate, and his beard disappears.

"Not of you." She kisses his cheeks and lips several times before resting her forehead against his. "Never you."

As one ring fades and another grows wider, the golden glow of candlelight turns as bright green as a meadow on a sunny afternoon.

"Ugh! He hasn't made up his mind yet?" Alone, Adaline tosses seeds onto the ground. The chickens descend and cluck madly around her. The wind howls beside her, brushing her curls across her face. She peels her hair away from her mouth and whispers into the wind, "Please, tell him it's time for change."

The wind loops around her, flipping her hair over her face and playing with the hem of her dress. When it drifts away, the side yard stills.

Adaline follows the current until it vanishes. "We have to work together. To fix what's broken."

Leaving the chicken coop, she meanders toward the pasture where her father, a speck on the horizon, tends to the sheep. She lays down in the grass and hums in tune with the birds chirping and the sheep baaing. When the sun touches the horizon, someone stroking Adaline's back wakes her up.

"What are you doing out here?" Aurellia squats at her daughter's side. "I thought you were with your cousins. Isn't Nora supposed to be teaching you how to make a four-panel dress?"

Adaline, sitting up, wipes the sleep from her eyes. "I, um, wanted to come home."

"Are you alright?" Aurellia scoops Adaline up into her arms and carries her back into their cottage.

When they sit on the sofa, Adaline drapes herself against her mother's chest and inhales her scent, which smells sweet like currants and warm bread. "I don't like

Allex. Auntie made treats for everyone, but he wouldn't share. Even after Baby Sofie started crying, he still wouldn't."

"Where was Auntie?"

"Milking the cows or feeding the ducks. I don't know."

"And what did you do?"

Adaline buries her face in her mother's neck. "I asked a bird to shit on his head."

Her mother's chest spasms a few times, and her shoulders shake. As Adaline sits up on her mother's lap, Aurellia bites her lip and forces the corners of her mouth downward. Her eyes sparkle, and the tip of her nose is bright red, making Adaline giggle too.

After bopping Adaline's tushy, Aurellia shakes the amusement off her own face. "It's not funny. And I don't want you using that vulgar word." She watches Adaline bob her chin in agreement while poking her finger through a hole in her mother's apron. When Adaline's done fidgeting, Aurellia lifts her daughter's chin and looks at her thoughtfully. "The challenge, sweet girl, is that you can't force someone to see things the way you do."

"I tried negotiating. I really did. And he didn't care. He wouldn't listen to any of us, not even Nora, and he wasn't being fair."

"No, he wasn't. And Allex can be mule-like. But what happened after the bird came to your defense?"

Adaline looks away. "He started crying and shaking his head, and the sh—um, I mean, poop got on the treats."

"How could one bird's poop do that much damage?" Aurellia asks in awe.

"More than one bird might have heard me."

"Oh, Adaline! Did your cousins see you talking to the birds?"

"I don't think so. They were too busy trying to calm Baby Sofie."

"So instead of comforting your baby cousin, who absolutely adores you, you were busy organizing an aerial assault on a seven-year-old child that resulted in no one getting what they wanted?"

Adaline bursts into tears. "I'm a terrible person!"

She tries to run away, but Aurellia hugs Adaline and rocks back and forth until her daughter's sobs reduce to a whimper.

"You're not a terrible person, Adaline. You just have to keep working on your negotiation skills. I can only imagine how difficult this must be for you, having to hide what you can do. But it's only for a little while longer."

"But why must Poppa and I hide if Ëólas and Magnus are going to create a safe place for us?"

"Because the princes are still young. What's more, we don't yet know who will support us and who might not be so happy to learn about our family. And we must protect our family. Always."

"You don't think that captain is still alive, do you, Momma?"

Her mother takes a long while to ponder this. "Your father hasn't heard mention of him in Alderton or Lameiría, so perhaps he is gone. But the damage he created... Adaline, when you listen to the wind, have you ever heard the name—never mind."

"Who, Momma?"

Her mother whispers in Adaline's ear, "Morgán."

Adaline shakes her head. "Was that the captain?"

"Yes, but don't go asking about him, my sweet girl. We don't want to risk his attention, and you never know what one might hear riding on the wind."

"I only listen, Momma."

Her mother kisses her forehead and each of her cheeks. When she tickles Adaline under the arms, her daughter falls over, laughing like the rag doll forgotten by her mother's painting drying in the corner. After Aurellia pulls Adaline up into a hug again, they sit close together, neither in a hurry to start dinner.

"I'll find a way to make it up to Allex," Adaline says, her head rising and falling with her mother's breaths.

"I know you will, because you are inherently kind. Never forget that, Adaline, because the world will always need more kindness."

Chapter Twenty-Nine

THE VOICE

Another ring of water expands across the pool. The image of the cottage drips apart like rain and falls into the water at Adaline's feet. Immediately, another wall of mist emerges, raising the image of a brown barn with a weathered roof and double doors left open wide.

"Grab that will you?" Edwin points to the shears, which Adaline picks up and passes to her father. Sitting on a stool, he pats a sheep's back and murmurs in its ear to be still, be calm.

Adaline watches him shave the sheep, and the rest of the flock waits patiently in a long line. "Where's Momma?"

"At the neighbor's. Mrs. Forent's husband has been ill for a few days now, and the rest of the family is starting to show symptoms. Taking care of a sick husband and eight sick children is too much for any one person to handle."

The wool falls in clumps onto the floor, silent tufts of what once was and what can be. Adaline collects them into baskets. "Will Momma get sick and die?"

Her father pauses but quickly continues his work. Another long strip of wool falls around his boots. "No, I don't believe so. She has half my soul after all."

"Was it painful, giving that away?"

"No, not at all. Well, not for me."

Adaline looks up quizzically as her father's cheeks turn red.

"Never mind. You can ask your mother for specifics when you're older." He continues his work, making certain not to stab the sheep with the tip of the shears.

Meandering over to the doors, Adaline stands outside the barn and plays with the tip of her long braid draped over her shoulder. As she searches the horizon for her mother, thick, black clouds roll across the evening sky, plunging the land into premature darkness. The wind picks up, and tufts of wool roll further into the barn.

Adaline turns to help her father when she hears a woman's voice in the wind. "They've found you," she whispers.

Adaline spins around, her heart racing, and searches the horizon again, only this time not for her mother. The horses start neighing and galloping back and forth across the meadows. The chickens squawk and scream as their feed bucket falls over. The sheep abandon their line and start running into each other.

"Shit!" Edwin yells. "Adaline, I need your help."

She doesn't move. She doesn't look away from the horizon. Still, she sees nothing. She exhales and turns to her father, but that voice pulls her back again. "They've found you, Adaline." Her voice is hardly louder than a whisper, but her tone is urgent. "Run!" she screams in a hushed voice.

Adaline sprints into the barn and grabs her father's hand. He looks down, confused, but she keeps tugging him to the back of the barn. "The wind says they've found us. We need to run."

She expects her father to pick her up, to tell her everything is okay, that the wind is just gossiping and playing tricks. Instead, Edwin races up the ladder and onto the hay loft and jumps down with a sword Adaline's never seen before. He straps the sheath to his belt with practiced movements. When he does scoop up Adaline, they don't run into the cottage. Edwin sprints out of the barn and whistles for a horse. One comes galloping their way, but before her father can get on, shadows emerge across the horizon. One by one they pop up, increasing from three to five to ten. Adaline clings to her father, digging her fingers into his shoulders. Despite her protests, he puts her on the horse, alone.

"Poppa?"

"Go to the Forbidden Lands. Make your way to Lameiría. You know the way."

"But—"

"Border patrol won't harm a child. Get to the woods, and they'll take you directly to Queen Élara. Don't tell her who you are, not yet, but if you must show her your magic, she'll keep you safe. I'll come find you there. If anyone gives you trouble, ask the trees for help. They won't tolerate anyone hurting you. You need to go now, sweetheart. Tell Benley to ride fast and hard, and do not stop for anything. You understand me?"

"Poppa! Don't make me go alone."

The shadows form into riders on horseback, all of them galloping toward them.

"Fuck!" Edwin says. "Listen, Adaline: Fear, regret, guilt—negative emotions like those weaken our magic. Focus on how much Momma and I love you, how this family will never stop fighting for each other, and you will be able to do wonders. Now go."

He slaps the horse's rump, and Benley takes off at full gallop. Adaline looks back at her father as he draws his sword.

Clutching the reins, she leans forward into the wind. "Please, wind, tell momma to stay away."

A gust races off toward Mrs. Forent's home. Adaline looks back a few more times. As her home disappears behind a hill, she sees her father fighting the invaders, but a few others gallop after her. She sinks down lower, hugging the horse's neck and whispers into his ear words of encouragement. Benley gallops faster.

Adaline's certain everything will be okay, until the wind returns, carrying with it her mother's erratic, frantic screams. Her face turns pale. She closes her eyes, but she can't shut out her mother's cries.

"We fight for our family," she whispers. "Like how Grandmother protected Poppa."

Adaline summons up every image she can of her mother kissing her cheek, cuddling next to her as she drifts off to sleep, wiping her face clean, splashing her during bath time, combing her hair, and smelling like currants and bread. She tugs the reins sideways, and Benley changes direction. "We can do this. Head for Mrs. Forent's. We have to help Momma."

The wind rushes a twang-like sound into Adaline's ear, but before she can look back to understand if that means danger, an arrow thwaps sideways into Benley's shoulder. A second arrow follows immediately behind, thudding into Benley's thigh. The horse rises up, throws Adaline off his back, and collapses away from her.

Adaline scrambles back toward the horse, but he flails his legs to keep her away, to make her flee. She sprints as fast as she can, begging the earth to strengthen her legs. If she can make it to the ruins, maybe border patrol could intervene. She doesn't have to make it all the way to the forest. If she tells them who she is, they'll help her mother too. But three horsemen quickly surround her, their hooves stopping, pushing her back.

The first one sneers at her. His muted gray eyes make him look like the undead as he circles his horse around her. "Is it human?"

"It looks human," says the one with red hair. Sniffing in the air, he wrinkles his nose and gags. "She smells human too."

The riders laugh as pee trickles down Adaline's leg. They make her feel small, insignificant, a mistake. Her parents would never let them treat her this way. She clenches her hands into fists. Her nostrils flare, and her whole body radiates. She channels her strength into the earth, which starts trembling. The horses back up and try to gallop away, to free themselves from their reins. No matter how much the riders tell their steeds to steady themselves, the horses become more agitated. Adaline whispers into the wind, which hisses in the horses' faces and up their noses. They rear up, throw off their riders, and gallop away, trampling the third rider who screams once then doesn't move. The other two, sprawled on the ground, look at Adaline like she's the monster.

She runs in the opposite direction, back toward Poppa.

"Grab that thing," shouts Red as they get to their feet.

Their legs are so much longer than Adaline's. Gray Eyes grabs her hair, which Momma braided earlier this morning when they talked about the fall festival and which songs Adaline wanted to perform for the village. He yanks her so hard that she feels like her scalp detached from her head. With a scream, she falls onto her bottom, but he doesn't let go. He pulls her braid again, forcing her to stand.

Red, stalking over to her, slides his sword out of the scabbard, the sharp steel blade reflecting the only light peeking through the clouds. The wind whips up and bangs the blade against Red's chest, making him stagger backward.

"Put that away," says Gray Eyes, now holding her wrists. "Ãranol will want her alive."

"No, he won't. He'll be delighted the last of the Aerytolíans are gone. We'll have finished his father's work for him."

Red raises his sword, but Adaline kicks Gray Eye's shin. He lets go long enough to smack her across the face and kicks her legs, causing her to fall onto her knees. A few black birds flying overhead screech and get Adaline's attention. When she asks them for help, the birds dive at Gray Eyes. He lets go to shield himself, but the birds flap their wings and dig their feet into his cheeks as they scratch and peck out one of his eyes.

Adaline jumps up, but Red grabs her arm and twists her back to him. "Let me go!" She punches his chest, and her little fist bounces off his breastplate. "I'm just a child."

He grabs her throat, and when he squeezes, all sounds turn hollow and echo-like.

"You," Red's spit flings onto her face, "are nothing more than an abomination." He squeezes harder, and the world and his hatred fade into darkness.

When Adaline opens her eyes again, she's draped over someone's shoulders, someone who's running. Her arms hang limp down the runner's backside. Rain pelts her head, dripping down her cheeks and off the tip of her nose.

"I've got you, sweetheart." Edwin runs away from Red lying on the ground with one leg bent at an unnatural angle.

Skidding to a halt, Edwin looks right, left, then right again. His chest caves inward, and his shoulders droop. He slides Adaline off his shoulder and into his arms, keeping her face against his coat. She pushes off to turn around, but he drops his sword and pulls her tight against him, pressing her face against his side. From the corner of her eye, she sees more riders galloping toward them.

Her father gets on his knees so he's at her height and cups her face, his hands like blinders as he makes her look at him and only him. Rain drips down his eyebrows and cheeks, but he forces a smile, for her. His eyes are as wet as the puddles collecting around them. The horses, pounding the earth as they race toward them, sound like thunder.

"Adaline, you have been the best part of our lives, filling our days with immense love and endless amounts of silliness. I am so proud of you, sweetheart. Proud and amazed. You are a gift. A miracle. And no one can ever change that fact. I am so grateful I got to be your father."

The horses are so loud now, almost right on top of them. Edwin pulls Adaline into an embrace, one she can't turn away from, and she hugs him back. She wants to kick and scream and launch herself at the threat that's almost upon them. Is that what her grandmother did?

"Look to your grandmother," says that woman's voice riding the wind.

Adaline peeks up and peers over her father's shoulder. As the riders dismount and run at them, Edwin buries Adaline's face in his neck, covering her eyes.

"Look with your heart," the woman whispers.

Adaline's instincts tell her to claw and scrape her way to safety, but her father holds her still.

He takes a deep breath and exhales slowly. "I love you."

"Let go," the voice breathes in Adaline's ear.

The horses neigh their own battle cry. Thunder booms overhead, and a sword hisses upon exiting a scabbard.

Adaline releases her fists and inhales the scent of wet wool and soaked grass. She remembers her father chasing her around the chickens, telling her bedtimes stories until the wee hours of the morning, teaching her how to shear the sheep so she doesn't pinch her fingers too, and smiling ear to ear when she showed him how water can bend itself out of a bucket.

She doesn't know her grandmother's spell. She doesn't know the words. But she taps deep inside her core and prays to save her father, to save their future.

The world begins to sound muted. The horses and their neighs, the valley suppressed under the heft of rain, and the puddles at their knees fade away. Her father begins fading away too, becoming less than a ghost, but she holds on tight to him, to those memories. A moment later, she and Edwin are kneeling in front of a fireplace. They're so close to the roaring flames that they almost materialized on the hearth. Edwin yanks his daughter away from the blaze and collapses on his bottom, holding Adaline in his lap, their wet clothes soaking into the area rug.

Inside the large room, a bookcase reaches the ceiling. A world globe on a desk shows a map Adaline doesn't recognize, and a box flashes pictures and sounds of people arguing and laughing at the same time. Behind a plush red sofa, a woman with long brown hair and wearing trousers walks into the room. The moment she sees Edwin and Adaline soaking wet and muddy, she drops her mug. The ceramic shatters into pieces, and tea splashes the hardwood floor. The woman runs over to them and slides onto her knees. As she touches Edwin's shoulder, the grief that washes over her face is palpable.

Edwin leans his head on the woman's shoulder, not yet letting go of his daughter. "Adaline, this is your grandmother."

Another ring fades, and the water sprites replay the next memory, every detail of which Adaline now recalls with agonizing accuracy.

With tear-stained cheeks and puffy eyes, a seven-year-old Adaline wakes up in bed. Only, the blanket covering her is not the floral comforter her grandmother bought her last week in London. Instead, she wakes up in her own bed in the cottage in Alderton. The bed squeaks when she swings her feet onto the floor and stands up. The dresser drawers are empty, with their clothes and belongings tossed and broken on the ground. She steps over a shattered vase and picks up the torn-off head of her rag doll, which she cradles in her arm. The floorboards creak beneath her bare feet as she walks into the main room. The cushions of her parents' favorite chair are ripped open, and her mother's pots and herbs lay about the floor, upside down and cracked.

"Hello, there," says a voice from inside her parents' room. An elf with light-brown hair and chartreuse eyes emerges in the doorframe. He looks Adaline up and down with a sad expression, like he's seen too many people suffer and pities the little girl in front of him. "I've heard tales of the ghost child who haunts this home every night. But you don't seem like a ghost to me."

Adaline hugs her doll's head to her chest.

"My name is Ãranol. What's yours?"

Adaline plays with the black yarn comprising her doll's hair.

"You know, our families are old friends." Ãranol leans against the door frame and clasps his hands in front of himself. In place of a breastplate or a sword at his side, he wears a silk tunic, vest, and cloak in shades of turquoise and gold. His light-brown hair reminds Adaline of springtime when she and her mother would plant bulbs. "I know a lot about you too. Hmm. I bet you even have Aeríoléna's kiss, right?"

Adaline touches the left side of her ribs as if to protect the birthmark she, her father, and her grandmother share.

Ãranol snaps his eyes to the spot below her heart, making a mental note of the telltale mark's location, and he smiles like he's already won the game. "I thought so. See? Our families have known each other for centuries. We're practically family."

Mumbling into her doll's face, Adaline asks, "Where's Momma?"

He moves sideways, not close to Adaline but a few steps around the perimeter of the room. Adaline moves in the opposite direction, her steps matching his, keeping the distance the same.

"Would you like to see your mother? I'd be happy to bring you to her." He takes one step forward, and Adaline takes one step back. He pauses and squats down so they're similar in height. His cloak, folding around him, covers her father's chess pieces strewn about the floor, the chess pieces he carved himself. "Here's the dilemma you and I face, little one. Every night, you come back looking for your mother, and every night one of my soldiers tries to, hmm, *bring you* to her. But you disappear. How much longer are we going to have this little dance?"

Adaline glances at the front door.

"She cries for you every day. She misses you terribly. Won't you let me take you to her? I have a pretty brown horse outside whom I'm sure you'll adore. He even has a funny name: Beardless."

Adaline looks at the door again.

Āranol extends his hand. He doesn't move, doesn't rush forward. He stays perfectly still while he lets Adaline think. She looks at her mother's broken easel, the paints her father bought splattered on the floor. She nuzzles her doll, and the yarn absorbs her tears.

"You want to see your mother, and my father would like to meet you. Seems to me we can help each other." With his chartreuse eyes never wavering, Āranol keeps his voice musical and gentle.

Adaline inches forward. He smiles the way her father did when Adaline asked the soil to arrange itself in shapes and make pictures. She slides her small hand into Āranol's. Slowly, he stands up. "That's better. Let's go meet Beardless, shall we?"

As they walk toward the door, Adaline's toes squish into her mother's red paint, leaving a trail of tiny smeared toe prints behind her. Beardless waits for them a few feet outside her home. She looks for Benley, but he's nowhere to be found.

"Beardless loves children. Would you like to feed him?" Āranol reaches into his saddlebag and pulls out a carrot that he hands Adaline.

The sheep wander the valley. The grass smells crisp and fresh. Despite the damage inside, she keeps waiting for her mother to call her name and ask her to make the soup broth boil faster.

Adaline offers the carrot to Beardless. A handsome horse, he swishes his tail while he eats. His brown coat is darker than Benley's, but they both have a white diamond patch on their noses. Āranol walks behind Adaline and hands her another carrot, which Beardless greedily munches on.

"Can we go see Momma now?"

"Of course." Āranol's chin hovers just above Adaline's shoulder, the pointy tip of his ear brushing the side of her hair. "Let me help you up, and we'll be on our way. You can see her tonight."

Adaline reaches up to grab the saddle. Āranol places one hand on her waist, and a searing concentration of pressure pierces her lower back. After her initial sharp inhale, pain blooms across her back and seeps into her abdomen. Her heart slows down, and the world turns black and white.

Taking a step backward, Āranol lets Adaline crumple to the ground. From his saddlebag, he pulls out a rag and uses the cloth to wipe her blood off his dagger. With her bright eyes staring up at him, he kneels down beside her and sighs. "I'm sorry. None of this is your fault. Your father never should have conceived you."

With the last ring growing larger, the mist displays a sterile, white room. Adaline's eyelids are too heavy to open, and her limbs feel stiff. Her backside hums with a numbed throbbing sensation, and a steady, unnatural beep near her ear refuses to let her go back to sleep.

"She should awaken in a few hours," says a male voice, and a door clicks shut.

"We'll leave for the States once she wakes up," a woman says quietly. "The last thing we need are the authorities sniffing around."

Does that voice belong to the woman Adaline heard in the wind? No, they're not the same. This voice belongs to her grandmother. Nan. She told Adaline to call her Nan.

Someone else in the room paces back and forth, their heels clacking on the hard floor. When Adaline peeks her eyes open, her father, not noticing her, pulls at his hair. "I need to figure out how to get back. I'll kill every last one of them."

Adaline shuts her eyes.

"You'll get killed, you mean," Nan says.

"Not with my gift. I'll change my appearance again and sneak into their ranks. I just need Adaline to stay here, to stop traveling in her sleep, to forget how she can even do that."

"She needs time to learn how to master her gift. Right now, she's traveling instinctively. You think you're going to convince her to let you go after she's lost her mother? We need to be patient, Edwin. When she's older, we can go back."

"I don't want her to go back!" Edwin thumps his forehead against the wall. "Let her stay here. Let her live here."

"You want her to share our fate, watching everyone she loves grow old and die and having to start over again elsewhere? And without your gift, how will she appear to age over time? Technology is getting more advanced. Hiding won't be so easy."

"Perhaps that won't be the case for her. If she stays here, she could marry a human. Maybe she'll become more like them. Let the elven half of her die."

"You don't mean that."

"Don't I?"

Adaline's never heard her father so angry. She tries to raise her hand and reach for him, to show him she's okay, but her arm is too heavy, and something's tied to her arm.

"She's Aerytolían, Edwin. She has a destiny. You saw it yourself, didn't you?"

"I don't care anymore. If we remove what we can of her memories, this world will become her home. I'll figure out how to get back to Aurellia on my own. I did once before. I'll do it again. We'll leave Adaline out of it."

"Edwin, you can't—"

"That world doesn't want us anymore, Mother. Do you know what I heard your *dear friend* saying? Even Elashor believes wholeheartedly that humans are a plague. That world is broken, and I won't sacrifice my daughter to save it."

"You're grieving."

"I'm furious. I have no idea what happened to my wife. I don't know if she's hurt or worse, and while I'm trapped here, those bastards keep trying to murder our child. They almost did this time. Your world is not mine, Mother. This is my home. We'll make it Adaline's too."

"Poppa." Adaline's throat burns.

"I'm here, sweet girl." Rushing to her side, Edwin places his large hand over hers, lending her his warmth.

"I can try, Poppa. I want to go home."

"No, sweetheart. It's not safe. Please, stop looking for your mother. I'll handle that."

"Is Momma okay?"

"Of course she is." Edwin places his hand over his heart. "I'd know if she weren't. She's alive, and I need you to trust me that I'll find her."

She tries to talk more, but words hurt. When her father leaves to get her water, she turns to Nan sitting in the chair by her bed. "How do I find Momma?"

Nan's wavy dark-brown hair falls off her shoulders, behind her back, as she lifts her chin high, and the gleam in her eye makes her heart-shaped face glow with confidence. "My dearest, someday you will help your homeland in ways you can't yet fathom. But first, you have to grow up. Your mother will manage. Destiny chose her for Edwin, so I'm certain she's exceptional in her own right."

Adaline angles her head so she can see her grandmother more clearly. "How do you know that?"

"Because." Wearing a pencil skirt, Arraya crosses her long legs and sits back as she drifts into her memories. "Destiny helps us to find only the most exceptional individuals to be our partners. They must deserve the benefits they gain when we share our soul with them."

"Like what?" The more Adaline talks, the more her voice sounds like a frog, but she needs to know what advantages her mother might have.

"Oh, it varies. At the very least, they gain longer lifespans, a stronger connection to the elements over time, and the promise of eternal rest in the Immortal Realms." Arraya smooths her skirt even though her appearance is flawless. "Your grandfather developed quite an affinity for earth. He loved visiting the crops around the palace, making the plants grow beyond their typical size. He once brought me a giant peach the size of a dog."

Giant fruit can't help her mother. Closing her eyes, Adaline's tears fall without a sound.

"My dear girl, everything will be okay." Removing the distance between them, Arraya stands beside the bed and strokes Adaline's cheek. Her gentle touch and firm voice make ignoring her unimaginable. "I know you want to see your mother now, but we can't help her if we lose you." Nan places a stone in Adaline's palm. "Your father needs you here, and we have to be patient. We have to be wise."

Adaline encloses the stone in her fist.

With a kind, encouraging voice, Nan asks, "What happens when we drop a stone into the water?"

"It makes rings."

"Yes, and the rings grow bigger. So big that they eventually touch everything below the surface and even the grass at the water's edge. You'll know when you're ready to face those rings. In the meantime, I'll safeguard this stone. Let me help you now so you can help your mother when you're ready."

As Nan teaches Adaline what words to say in Elvish, the stone pulses, vibrates, and extracts the pain, the terror, the grief. Adaline's tears cease to flow. Her face relaxes, and she lets her eyelids close. But she holds onto her guilt. She can't forgive herself for not being enough, for not being able to save her mother now. That guilt burrows into the furthest recesses of her mind and builds itself a nest so it can haunt her in her dreams, even as Nan promises, "It's only for a little while, my dear, and this will ease your burden too. It's hard to miss something you don't remember."

The last thing Adaline hears before drifting off to sleep is Nan whispering, "I have faith in you, Adaline. You have always been my greatest hope."

Chapter Thirty

A Decision

The last image rains into the pool. The light emanating from the pillars fades. The miniature tornado turns into a breeze that drifts away, and the water from the spring recedes into the ground, taking with it the water sprites and leaving behind a ring of mud.

Picking up the stone, Adaline stares at the damp, smooth gray surface. It's empty now, nothing more than a hollow shell, because she remembers the entirety of her childhood in Alderton, the village in Meadowbrook where her mother's family lived, and the trek she and her father took to the old palace ruins when Adaline turned five.

Above all else, she remembers her mother.

Remembers her sun-kissed olive skin and mossy green eyes. Remembers how she would hum as she hung up the wash. Remembers how her eyes would shine as she held her pallet, mixed colors, and dabbed paint on a canvas in quick, carefree motions. Remembers that her favorite dessert was strawberry cake with white icing. Remembers that she used to dance when making the bed and cooking breakfast. Remembers her smile—her smile that could turn tears into giggles and rainy days into adventures and bad moments into snuggle fests.

We were happy.

She hears Ëólas's feet cross the stage, and his boots stop just before her. She exhales and lets the stone roll out of her hand. When it hits the stage, it shatters into dust. "I need to find out what happened to my mother."

He places his hands on her arms. "I'll help you."

Clenching her fists, she digs her heels into the stage. "We have to stop them. We can't let Āranol and Morgán destroy Aerytol, not again. I want to protect my home."

She lifts her chin, and Ëólas nods. Even in the dead of night, his golden eyes give her hope.

Yet everything between them is still so new. They confessed their feelings, enjoyed euphoric intimacy, and got married only twenty-four hours ago. Now he's caught in all this drama. He had no idea what he was marrying into, no idea what destiny would ask of him. But looking at him now, at the determination and empathy on his face, that ever-present connection between them tells her that he has no regrets, and if the situation were reversed, she'd fight the entire universe to keep him safe too. Hell, she might have to.

Nan's voice pops into her head. *Destiny chooses extraordinary people for our partners.*

Well, he certainly is that.

Besides, he chose this path before Adaline entered the picture, from his first conversation with Magnus. His choices, his efforts, his goals meant he and Āranol would fight regardless. Maybe that's why destiny chose Ëólas, because her path would inevitably converge with his, no matter how long it took her to return here.

But what about Morgán? What happened to him? And what do I bring to the picture? How can I help Ëólas in this war?

Maybe, just maybe, the two of them working together can make the difference. Maybe that's the price they're both willing to pay. But they can't change the world alone.

"I will help, my lady," says an unfamiliar voice.

Scanning the theater to find who spoke, Adaline gasps. Every elf in Gladríen, maybe more, has filled the amphitheater. The seats, the aisles, the tree limbs hanging overhead—all of it overflows with people who couldn't resist the display of magic. Tears stain many of their cheeks. Others cling to their loved ones with their faces twisted in a mixture of agony and regret. Sora stands tall with her hand resting on her hilt, just like Merith does when standing behind Ëólas. Others yet can't bear to lift their eyes and face her, including Elashor and Neira. Renor has sunk onto his knees.

Adaline steps closer to Ëólas, who places his hand on her back and looks at her reassuringly.

The elf who spoke up steps forward, crosses his arm over his armor, and bows deeply. "My soldiers and I will fight beside you."

Ëólas nods his approval, but Adaline instinctively shakes her head. "I don't want anyone risking their lives."

Yes, she's ready to fight. But wars mean lives lost. She can't fathom ordering troops into battle, never being able to know, to remember, the names of every person lost along the way. And how can she jeopardize Lameiría in the process, siphoning off their own protection and making them a target?

With Aiden beside her, Élara walks up to Adaline. She turns in a slow circle, making certain all her people are watching, and does the unimaginable. She kneels in front of Adaline and bows her head. Aiden follows her lead, followed by Sora and the general who spoke up. Like a rippling wave, every person in Gladríen rises, only to kneel and lower their eyes. Not one of them looks scared. If anything, they look determined.

Adaline takes in the entirety of the theater while her mind struggles to process what's happening. But when Ëólas moves to kneel beside his mother, she grabs his hand and pulls him back. Their fingers intertwine, locking their palms together.

"Your father was right," Élara says, her voice echoing as she rises. "Lameiría will support you. I speak on behalf of every elf here when I say we would give anything to see Aerytol restored, my queen."

Before Adaline can think of how to respond or what to do, another general joins the first and mimics the same signs of allegiance. "My troops and I would be honored to defend the rightful queen of Aerytol."

"As would we," says yet a third, followed by three more.

Even Renor steps forward, which leaves Adaline speechless and not sure how she should feel about allowing the person who nearly beheaded her to join this fight. Then again, maybe they have something in common after all—the desire to go home. Adaline nods at Renor, and his eyes turn glossy.

It's happening, Poppa. We've reached the beginning. She wipes away a tear. "Thank you, all of you. I'll take all the help I can get."

As the generals bow again, she turns to Ëólas, who looks at her as though he already sees the queen her parents knew she'd become. His confidence helps her to push aside her doubts, at least for now. Nothing can go wrong with him on her side. They're a team, and they're both responsible for defending Aerytol and all its people who dared to hope again.

Ëólas smiles at Adaline. His brows are soft and his eyes full of pride. "I'll be by your side the entire time."

She throws her arms around his waist and hugs him. Feeling scared is nearly impossible when she's in his arms. "Destiny must be on our side. I can do anything with you, mé ellador."

When she utters those last two words, silence befalls the amphitheater. The sniffles, the awed whispers, and rustling of clothing and armor halts. Even the lanterns silence their burning as everyone leans forward, making sure they heard her use those two words when referring to their lord.

Oops. As Adaline's cheeks redden and Ëólas kisses her forehead, everyone in the amphitheater erupts in cheers, jumping to their feet, applauding, shouting their elation.

Ëólas tilts his lips toward her ear. "That's one way to announce our union."

"Heh. Yeah."

Side by side, they both wave to the crowd while Élara and Aiden kiss their son and daughter-in-law's cheeks and formally welcome her into the family in front of thousands of witnesses. After a guard passes Aiden the wooden box, he lifts the lid, and Élara places the circlet on Adaline's head. Her first tiara.

If only her parents could have seen this day.

Elashor and Neira, however, are nowhere to be found.

As the celebration rages throughout Lameiría, Adaline and Ëólas meet with various generals and organize their departure. Each one affirms their loyalty, their whole beings glowing with joy at meeting and speaking with Arraya's heir. Adaline smiles and nods and contributes where she can, but troop placement is Ëólas's expertise. He never leaves her side as more people come up to congratulate them. Previous residents of Aerytol, many of whom were children when the city fell, mention Adaline's resemblance to Queen Arraya, and Adaline assures them they'll always be welcome in Aerytol should they wish to go home.

After a few hours of dancing, toasts, speeches, and declarations of support, Adaline excuses herself to use the privy. Ëólas begins to escort her back toward their home, but another general catches his attention. She tells Ëólas to do what's needed, and reluctantly he agrees. With Sora close behind, Adaline excuses herself and leaves. When she walks past the privy without stopping, Sora doesn't ask questions, which Adaline appreciates because she has no more words tonight.

She makes her way through the silent city, the din of music and revelry growing ever distant. When she reaches the stairs leading to their treehouse, Adaline hoists her skirts and walks as quickly as she can. At the top, Sora stops while Adaline runs inside, slams the door behind her, and leans back, huffing and puffing. She kicks her shoes off into the corner, places the circlet on the vanity, and crawls onto their bed, her Cinderella-like dress serving as the only blanket she needs. The moment the pillow cushions her head, Adaline lets go of the smiles, the reassurance, the confidence that Lameiría needed to see tonight.

She allows herself to feel everything, to relive when that dagger pierced her back, when the Morgai destroyed her childhood, and when Adaline left her mother behind. Her chest heaves up and down as she clutches another pillow close to her chest. She screams into the down feathers. Screams until her throat turns raw. Screams until her body can't produce another sound.

When the door creaks open, Adaline silences herself. She lays as still as possible but doesn't turn around. She hears boots dumped in the corner near her shoes, and the bed sags as Ëólas curls up behind her. He threads his arm beneath her own and presses his body against the curve of hers as he holds her. Adaline releases a long, slow exhale, but she holds back from crumbling again.

Ëólas brushes her hair off her cheeks and snuggles closer still. "You don't have to pretend with me. I'll be here the whole time."

Adaline twists around and holds onto him as she sobs. When she's released everything she's been pushing down for decades, she drifts off to sleep with Ëólas beside her, holding her just as tightly as when he first came to bed. Before her consciousness fades, she prays Āranol won't haunt her dreams anymore.

When Adaline wakes up, she hears the faint hum of music and celebration in the distance, even with the sunrise announcing their upcoming departure. But Ëólas doesn't stir. He lies beside her, forehead to forehead. She watches him sleep, admiring that wide jawline and square chin, his slender nose, and long black lashes. The morning rays peeking into their room highlight the gold in his dirty-blond hair. She contemplates brushing a few rogue strands off his forehead and behind his ear, but she'd rather keep admiring him.

How could anyone out there think he and I aren't meant to be?

He's so much a part of her. Adaline presses her finger gently against his lip, which Ëólas kisses, his eyes still closed.

"You're awake," she says.

He smiles. When he opens his golden eyes, sunlight washes over her, warming her inside and out. He glides the back of his hand along her arm, then under the covers and over her waist, kneading her flesh and pulling her up against him. She entwines her bare leg around his, and the pressure of his member poking her mound helps her to vaguely recall him helping her out of her dress earlier this morning. She kisses him softly, and he twitches between her legs.

But he pulls his lower half away, and Adaline frowns. She wants to keep feeling his reactions to her.

"How are you?" he asks.

"Better. Really, I am. I just had a twenty-year backlog of suppressed emotions I needed to release. Thanks for staying with me."

"Always." When he kisses her, his lips linger over hers so that she can cherish the taste.

She's still amazed how a single kiss can rush downward, make her mindlessly wrap her leg around his waist, and pull him back to her. She's proud of herself when he grows harder and pokes her again. Ëólas's hand trails down her waist, over her thigh, and grabs her rump as he grinds into her. She pulls her leg up higher, opening herself more to him, which he no longer resists.

With her skin flushed and her core throbbing, she pushes his shoulder until he's on his back, and she climbs on top of him. They come together so naturally, so easily. The delicious need for more outweighs the soreness that vanishes the more she rocks back and forth on him, her hands pressing against his abs. His touch on her breasts, the way he oscillates between being gentle and greedy, makes her simultaneously quiver and rock faster.

Gripping her hips, they combine their efforts, and he thrusts deeper inside her. She calls his name as she gives in to the connection that continues to grow between them, to this wholeness that fills her to the brim. She can't bear the thought of anyone tearing them apart, of anyone hunting Ëólas the way they hunted her family. The seed of her determination settles inside her center, its roots burrowing deeper until she's about to burst at the seams, and her resolution blooms inside her.

She will never let anyone take this away from them.

When she collapses on his chest, he strokes her back with the tips of his fingers. She snuggles against his chest and circles his nipple with her middle finger. Round and round she goes until Ëólas kisses her head, and she looks up at him. Like a rabbit, Ëólas twitches his nose at her, and she giggles, relieved he has a silly side too.

"I needed this. Thank you," she says.

"Anytime you need this, I'm happy to oblige." His golden eyes are darker now, a satisfied sunset after a long day. "Are you certain you're okay though? That was a lot of information last night."

"It's a lot to process. Your people sound happy though." Music and laughter linger in the air around them. She listens more closely, the way she used to as a child when she wanted to hear news from Alderton or Lameiría. Cheers for Aerytol's return drift into Adaline's ear. She turns her head, pressing the side of her face against his chest, cutting off half her hearing.

"Our people." He massages her scalp, creating a rhythmic motion that forces her to close her eyes, and he hums an old elven tune about a lad who fell in love with a star.

Hugging her arms close to his torso, she inhales lavender, glad to have that familiar scent back. "I love your smell," she mumbles, almost ready to drift off to sleep again. "It's so comforting."

"Mmm. That's why I add lavender to my baths, to help me shed the day's political frustrations. I'm glad you like it too." After massaging her scalp, Ëólas moves to her shoulders. Her muscles yield under the pressure of his hands kneading her back and forth.

Heaven. "I think I've always loved you."

His hands stop, and his palms collapse on her. "I'm sorry."

Adaline looks up at him and opens her mouth to speak, but she's not sure what to say, how to make that sad face go away, let alone what changed his mood.

"I was not kind to you when you first arrived. I didn't trust you. I didn't trust..." He glances up at the ceiling while mentally admonishing himself but puts on his brave face and looks at her again. "The first moment I saw you, I thought you were the most beautiful being I'd ever laid eyes on, even with your peculiar clothing. And then..." His eyes gloss over.

Adaline sits up, letting the bedsheet fall down around her hips. "You don't have to apologize. I get it. You have so many people you're responsible for, and you took on this huge gamble with the Neutral Territory all on your own. Of course you'd be cautious of me."

"I was judgmental and small-minded." He brushes his knuckles along her cheek.

"But you're not now. Besides, I was confused too."

"How so?"

"I couldn't understand why I needed your approval. I always noticed when you were absent, always tried to guess what you were thinking, and I was so damn jealous when I saw you laughing with your friends. I wanted so desperately to earn your trust. No, your attention."

Ëólas sits up and kisses her. She folds her legs around him, and they taste each other for a while, just enjoying the closeness between them. No more walls. No more misunderstandings. No more guessing games. No more suppressed feelings.

He leans his forehead against hers. "I was so confused when I asked Delós and Jósep what you'd been asking them. I thought for certain you'd give away ulterior motives. And yet they'd share only your constant curiosity and kindness. Jósep adored you, you know? You were the first human he trusted." Ëólas wipes Adaline's cheeks dry.

"He was one of my first friends here," she whispers.

"I know."

"We have to stop Ãranol and find out what became of Morgán."

"We will. And when I face Ãranol, I'll shove a dagger in his backside and make sure he never takes another breath again." Gripping her back, Ëólas traces the scar she thought she got from a bicycle accident.

Adaline kisses each of his cheeks and the tip of his nose. Now's not the time to think about Ãranol, about the past. Too many memories want to resurface at once, and it's overwhelming, making her brain physically hurt trying to sort it all. She wishes Lameiría had its own therapist so she can properly process all the memories bombarding her senses. Not to mention the guilt. How will she ever reconcile choosing to forget her mother?

How am I going to find out what happened to her? "Ëólas, what, what if my mother's in Hell City, in Feídra né Morna? We were so close. Can we go back?"

"I thought about that a lot last night, and I understand the desire. I want to find her too, truly. But please don't take us back there, not yet. When we first arrived in Lameiría, I assigned several scouts to cross into the Wastelands, take birds with them, and report back their observations of Ãranol and the Morgai. But last night, I sent more. They're to head directly to Feídra né Morna to inquire about your mother. And before you protest, they volunteered. Lameiría is elated you've come back to us."

Adaline rubs her forehead. "I, I don't know how to be a queen, Ëólas. You've had your whole life to prepare for this role, and you've earned it. Me? I got the gig just because of who my grandmother was." She lowers her voice to a whisper. "I'm terrified of letting everyone down, especially you."

"My love, you could never disappoint me. Besides," he bumps her forehead with his own, "you have a tendency to step forward and assert yourself when you're provoked enough, which is another trait of yours I admire."

"Meaning?"

"Meaning when Āranol or anyone else dares to threaten the people of Aerytol, I know you won't walk away. It's not in your nature. In the meantime, I will help you tackle those insecurities of yours one at a time."

"Oh, really. And how do you plan to do that?"

Ëólas spins Adaline around so that they swap places, with him on top and pinning her to the bed. "By worshiping you myself."

I mean, if you insist.

One smoldering look from him reignites her desire. He kisses along her jawline and her neck while using those hands of his to massage her breasts and his thumb to play with her nipples. She runs her hands up and down his muscular back and grips his hips to pull him down so she can feel the full weight of him keeping her safe. Nothing could sneak between the bed and him.

He closes his mouth over hers, and their tongues search for each other, dance around each other. He slides back inside her, and they both moan. He thrusts once, and Adaline arches her back, ready for the barrage, ready for wave after wave of ecstasy to give her a reprieve, ready to clench him and make him beg for more too.

Only Ëólas suddenly collapses on her and buries his face in the pillow, next to her cheek. He balls his hands into fists and groans angrily.

Um, what just happened?

She arches her hips once more, and the rod inside her confirms he's still hard. He's also proven their first night together that he can keep going, so... "My love?"

Ëólas lifts his face and turns to the door. "We'll be there shortly." His voice is no louder than if he were speaking only to Adaline. When he looks at her, the pain on his face melts her heart.

Oh right, super elf hearing. Oh god. Please tell me no one died. "What happened?"

"The queen requests our presence," he says in a flat tone. "Sora's waiting outside."

Adaline groans and drops her legs. But when Ëólas begins to get off her, she crosses her ankles around his back and locks him in place. "Sora, give us a few more moments! This queen needs to collect herself and get ready."

Ëólas arches both eyebrows. "Now you accept your role?"

"Oh, just hurry up! We have five minutes. Let's make them count."

CHAPTER THIRTY-ONE

THE EARTH

When Ëólas climbs off Adaline, they use the basin and cloths on the vanity to wash up. From the doorway, Sora passes him a bundle of clothing with dark-blue and gold layers, which he hands to Adaline. "From my mother." Within seconds, he throws on black trousers and a forest-green vest over a lighter tunic.

As he's buckling his belt, Adaline unfolds the individual pieces, including a royal-blue ladies' tailcoat with black trousers and riding boots. "Oh, I love her. Now *this* is travel worthy. Why don't you go ahead, and I'll be along shortly."

"No."

His short, abrupt response causes her to pause pulling on her own panties that she brought from back home. With one leg in the hole, she lifts her eyes to understand what's running through his head. "Huh?"

"I am not leaving without you." He sits on the bed and begins unfastening her coat's twenty buttons.

Without another word, she continues getting dressed, using her own bra as well and opting for the black full-coverage version for comfort, but she keeps glancing at him. Despite his stoic indifference, his eyes contain the shadows of darker thoughts.

He's afraid to leave me, even with Sora outside.

She pulls on the tight-fitting trousers that feel like a comfortable pair of opaque leggings, but thicker, and fastens the buttons at her hips.

He's worried. But about what? That I'm in danger? Well, shit. That tracks. If Āranol has spies in New Leira, he could have them in Gladrien too, and the cat's out of the bag now. It's only a matter of time before the Morgai find me again. Fuck.

Trying not to panic about how overprotective Ëólas might be in New Leira, Adaline puts on a silky gold undershirt that falls an inch below her hips, and Ëólas holds open the tailcoat as she slips her arms into the long sleeves that flare at her wrists. Together, they fasten each tiny, close-knit button along her torso. While the upper portion fits snuggly, the coat tail falls like a dress that stops short a few inches above her ankles and leaves her trousers exposed so that she can move freely and ride a horse with ease. Last, she quickly combs her hair, pinning back the sides with barrettes, and Ëólas slings her duffel onto his back.

Stepping outside, they wish Sora a good morning and hurry to the palace. When they enter the queen's tearoom, Élara rises from her seat, informs them Aiden's already left for the front to make certain the troops are ready, and hands Ëólas a tiny piece of curled paper.

As he reads it, Élara explains aloud, "Merith sent word. Animosity is rising in the Neutral Territory. Without specifics about the war, the divide between the people has escalated."

Ëólas massages the center of his forehead, just above the bridge of his nose. "We're set to leave, but we're still six days away. I can rush troops ahead, but—"

"We might have another option," Adaline says. "I, I might be able to travel us there faster."

"Do you think you can control your gift like that?" He faces her but withholds his excitement. "You're still traveling instinctually, no?"

"Well, yes. But I'm worried about our friends, and we can't keep leaving them to prep for Āranol's arrival on their own. So, I'm hoping that my dominant instinct right now is to help our friends."

He looks at her, searching for any sign of reluctance or fear, so Adaline tucks those away into the far recesses of her mind. Of course she's excited to see her friends again, to return to the Rialto bridge, to have breakfast with Seira and Mercia, to check in on baby Lori, and to help Magnus as much as possible. Now's not the time for her to panic about their friends' reactions to their union, or Magnus's reaction to her lineage, or the council's freak out that technically they have no say in New Leira anymore, or, worst of all, that everyone there immediately defers to her as queen when they have hundreds of lives at stake. No, she doesn't have to worry about that at all. Surely, that will sort itself out while they're working together to stop Āranol and the Morgai.

I mean, what could go wrong? I should have at least four days before Lameiría's army reaches the city and spills the beans. Plenty of time to acclimate to this new, um, old identity.

Adaline smiles confidently or, at least, tries to, but her facial expression only makes him study her more intensely.

Coming to Adaline's rescue, Sora steps forward. "I think Queen Adaline ought to try. I'll inform the troops and lead them to Aerytol myself the moment you're gone."

"Agreed," says Élara. "I have every confidence in my queen."

Adaline gulps and refrains from asking the ladies to hold their horses with the honorifics. Again, Ëólas carefully studies her, so she nods her head vigorously. Perhaps too vigorously.

"Uh-huh." He eyes the patio through the glass doors. "Alright. Let's just take this outside. Mother, Sora, would you please excuse us?"

"Of course." Élara kisses them both on the forehead and clasps Adaline's hands. "I look forward to the day when we all come together again in Aerytol. Now, pop off and settle this matter, Your Majesty."

Cool, cool. No pressure. After promising to do her best, she stares at Ëólas's offered hand. "Um, shouldn't we send for Aiden?"

"No, Father and I said what we needed to last night."

Taking his hand, Adaline follows him to the doors, only to turn back for a moment. "Sora, travel safely, and see you soon. Élara, thank you. For everything." *Especially for giving me the love of my life.* "I hope I'll see you and Aiden soon."

"Aiden and I are always here if you need us."

The two ladies disappear from view as Ëólas leads her outside. The sun, not yet risen above the trees, peeks sunlight upward, through limbs and boughs and between leaves, making Adaline almost feel like the world's turned upside down.

A wind chime hanging from a branch near the doorway jingles quietly in the breeze. And on the lower-level walkways beneath them, footsteps come and go along with the occasional conversation.

Off to the side from the tearoom doors, Adaline steps into Ëólas's arms, closes her eyes, and clicks her heels together three times. Nothing.

Okay, time to be serious.

She squints hard, holds her breath, and conjures images of her favorite covered bridge, Delós's mandolins on display at his stall, the candles lining the shelves of Sallie's shop, and the patio on which she and Seira sipped tea the first day they met. Still nothing.

"Everything okay?" Ëólas asks.

"I'm not sure. I'm thinking only about New Leira, but maybe I'm thinking of too many places."

"Mmm. Last time we traveled, I guarantee you had only one thought."

Yeah, your bed. "Exactly."

"What do you love most about New Leira?"

She tilts her head up and looks into his eyes. "It's where I met you."

"Ah, well." Even though the corners of his mouth tug upward, his cheeks turn red. He glances at the doors as if to make certain no one's nearby. But, with elf super hearing, his mother and Sora might have heard Adaline's answer.

Wait, what? Hold on. Adaline scans her memories of all the people she's observed in New Leira. Not once did she see a couple kiss in public. *Huh.*

She shakes her head. "It's okay. I've got this."

Instead of closing her eyes, Adaline focuses on the tree behind Ëólas. She clears her mind until the grooves in the trunk blur together, and she envisions her chambers—the squat vanity, the lush area rugs with grapevine designs, and the loveseat beneath the window.

The more she visualizes the details, the harder she tries to latch onto what's not in front of her. But she remembers what the voice had said, about letting go. And Adaline does. She stops trying to force her chambers to appear. She stops thinking and instead looks with her heart, to Kayla not thinking Adaline less of a lady when she didn't know how to clean her teeth with linen, to Mercia teaching

Adaline how to stitch and insisting that Adaline would make a great queen, to Seira brushing Adaline's hair and surprising her with several new dresses that actually fit her body.

When she lets go and trusts herself, trusts her gift, trusts where she wants to go next, traveling into her chambers becomes as easy as taking one more step to cross the threshold from one room into another—an ordinary action that she does multiple times throughout the day *without* thinking about it. This time, she just has to take that last step with her soul and know, without any inkling of self-doubt, that she will. Adaline exhales to discard all uncertainty, and the canopy of trees, the outdoor table and chairs, and the palace itself transition into Adaline's private chambers in New Leira.

"Ha!" Ëólas scoops her up and swings her around so quickly her feet fly off the floor. "My love, you're brilliant!" Setting her down, he kisses her cheek and runs for the door.

"Wait!" A tad dazed from the transition, Adaline tugs his arm and pulls him away from the half-open door. "We haven't actually discussed what we're going to tell everyone. About us, I mean."

Ëólas jerks his head backward. "The truth, no?"

"Oh."

At the sight of Adaline's face turning pale, Ëólas shuts the door slowly. He walks past her, sits down on the bed, and remains quiet and pensive as he carefully selects his next words. "You have concerns about telling everyone about us. I, I don't understand. Please, help me."

Adaline walks back and forth, giving her mind a chance to catch up with her racing heart. "Are you sure Magnus and everyone else will be okay with this? I mean, Thoren kept trying to push me to consider Magnus, and Merith basically told me to not even think about you."

"He did what?"

"Yeah. No one's going to see this coming," she says, gesturing back and forth between the two of them. "And how's the council going to react? We need to make sure this city comes together right now. What if our union freaks everyone out, and the divide gets worse? Like, the elves think you're too sympathetic to the humans because you chose me, or the humans accuse me of siding with the elves for marrying you?"

While clenching his teeth, Ёolas digs his fists into his thighs. "How long do you propose we keep our union a secret, Adaline? Until Sora and the others arrive? Are four whole days enough?"

"Maybe." When he looks like she stabbed him in the heart, she wedges herself between his legs and places her hands on his shoulders. "I didn't mean it that way. It's not about the length of time. I just don't want to deal with everyone all at once. I'd rather make sure our closest friends are on board with this first."

Ёolas leans back on his palms and exhales a loud puff of air. "Alright. We'll start with Magnus first and seek his advice on the best way to inform everyone. Is that better?"

She bends forward and kisses him tenderly. "Yes. Thank you."

"I'll have a private word with Merith later."

"If you must."

"I must." He slides his hands along her hips, beneath her coattails. "We'll need to tell them about you too, about your grandmother."

"I know. But, again, let's first speak to Magnus privately. And Seira. I want to make sure I don't draw attention to her."

"Deal."

They seal their plan with a kiss that lingers and continues, their tongues seeking each other as their bodies become further entwined.

When their lips part, Adaline pushes his hands off her bottom and pulls him off the bed. "Tonight. No matter what awaits us outside that door, tonight will be about us. Okay?"

"Absolutely." He gives her a naughty smirk and backs her up against the door. His lips trail down her neck, and as she moans, he whispers, "I'm going to make sure you scream tonight."

His words make her reconsider their primary objective right now, but he reaches around her and pulls the second door open beside them. When he gestures for Adaline to go ahead, she does, with a sigh. First, they rush to the king's study where the guards inform them that Magnus and the council are out assessing the city. While Adaline constantly looks about for Seira, they hurry out of the castle and down the hill into New Leira, following the guards' directions as they relay where last they saw Magnus's party.

Adaline pauses in front of Sallie's shop. The kids and their grandmother scurry about to help customers because even though they're still mourning their father, they can't afford to close the shop. She cranes her neck, hoping to catch a glimpse of Sallie, but she's nowhere visible.

Ëólas touches Adaline's back. "You can check in on her after we find Magnus."

"Yeah, you're right." She looks back over her shoulder one more time, without luck.

Walking away from them feels like walking away from home. She always thought Sallie's family reminded her of Cindy's, but they also reminded her of Uncle Jamie and all the cousins she left behind in Meadowbrook, if they still live there. Luckily, she'll have plenty of time to find out.

As she and Ëólas walk briskly through the streets, crossing bridges and looping around the city, the people hurry from shop to shop or continue their own work at their stalls. More than a few tense faces relax when they see Ëólas and Adaline passing by. But the usual din now includes the sounds of hushed conversations punctuated with hammering, as if someone's building something so large that Adaline can hear their construction from almost anywhere.

After a few more twists and turns, they find Magnus and Jorrel, the elf who still reminds Adaline of a panda, walking down Front Street while playing mediator between the two council members who always argue about resources.

Huh. I still have no idea what Jorrel does.

"That's enough. We need to—" Having spotted Adaline and Ëólas, Magnus's exhausted frown flips into a grin that stretches further across his face as they approach him. "Well, about damn time."

The entire council and the guards behind them turn to greet Ëólas, bowing their heads. With a wave of Magnus's hand, the council members move aside, giving their lords space to speak first. Merith, however, allows the tension compressing his biceps into steel beams to fall away for most likely the first time in over a week. Adaline can only fathom how worried he must have been, to be captain of Ëólas's guard and to have lost his prince. Thoren widens his stance and scowls as if he caught his children sneaking off in the middle of the night to engage in underage drinking. At least Hamon and Fólas don't hold back their delight. Hamon's eyebrows shoot upward as he takes in Adaline's elven coat and trousers, but he nods in approval, and Fólas looks like the party just arrived and is ready to order a round of drinks.

There they are! All of my guys. If she didn't have so many eyes on her, she'd hug each of them in turn.

Magnus walks up to Ëólas and Adaline first, with Merith and Jorrel not far behind. "Thank the fae!" Clasping Ëólas's forearm, he shakes firmly and uses his other hand to pat Ëólas's shoulder. "You better have a damn good story for us, and I hope you have more information regarding what's happening so we can plan more effectively."

"Quite the story indeed, but it's best we return to the castle," Ëólas says.

The brotherly ease between them makes Adaline beam. When Magnus turns to her, her instincts take over, and she gives him a hearty hug, which he returns in earnest. She doesn't know how yet, but she's going to find a way to thank him properly for being brave enough to come up with the idea for New Leira. She owes him most of all. If not for Magnus, she might still be trapped in a half-life and worlds away from her ellador.

Gripping both of her arms, he gives her a once-over to make sure she's visibly okay. He chuckles when he takes in her clothing. "Now we both have ventured into Lameiría and come back to tell our tales."

"Very true. It's so good to see you again, Magnus. All of you." Adaline looks at each of her friends in turn and lets the relief and joy on their faces strengthen her for the conversations yet to come. She also spots her first personal guards, Moren and Tumin, and waves hello to them, making them blush.

Aww.

When Magnus lets go of Adaline's arms, he turns to Ëólas. "Thank you for keeping her safe."

Before Ëólas can respond, Jorrel jumps forward and bows deeply, his straight black hair falling forward. "My lord, I am ready to inform you of everything that has transpired during your absence and the decisions I made in your stead."

Oh, so that's what Jorrel does. He's like Ëólas's secretary or envoy.

While Ëólas gently lets down Jorrel that his report will have to wait, Hamon sidles over and mumbles in her ear, "What the hell happened?"

Merith scowls, and Hamon steps aside.

Staring at both Ëólas and Adaline, Merith scolds them with a tone and gaze so serious that Hamon wipes the smile off his own face. "You had us worried. You cannot disappear in such a manner again. Either of you," Merith says, staring at Adaline like a teacher reprimanding a mischievous student.

Casting her eyes downward, Adaline debates apologizing. *I mean, I did abduct his lord.*

Ëólas places his hand on the small of Adaline's back and turns to leave. "I don't think we need to worry about that again, Merith. But we have much to discuss and should head back to the castle now. Magnus, we should convene first."

Ëólas keeps her beside him, despite the barrage of questions from the council members and their efforts to place themselves between the two of them so they can speak quietly with him. But one, loud declaration from Ëólas that, "Now is not the time," makes the elven council fall quiet.

After Magnus orders his own council members to be patient, the three of them lead the group back to the castle. Magnus and Ëólas chat in hushed voices while Adaline stays close to Ëólas's other side. Even though she can't hear their words, the sound of their voices together reminds her of when she used to hear pieces of their conversations in the wind, how she wondered what they looked like, and how much she wanted to meet them both. At last, the three of them are together now, and they will be for a long while yet.

As Adaline hums to herself, she overhears Magnus mention ground spikes and catapults. *Okay, not quite like the reunion I'd hoped for, but it's a start.*

Along the way back to the castle, Adaline spies not only the Rialto in the distance but also Sallie running up Front Street, her skirts hiked up in her hands. Seeing Adaline, Sallie stops abruptly, and her torso sags forward with relief. She steps off to the side to avoid blocking the king and his entourage long before they'd reach her. Meekly, she dares to wave at Adaline, who breaks away from the royal procession to sprint ahead.

Ëólas calls after Adaline, but when she glances over her shoulder, he's busy gesturing for Moren and Tumin to stay close to her. When he looks at her again, the vibrancy of his eyes tells her that he's happy to see her among friends. With Magnus whispering in Ëólas's ear, Adaline turns back to Sallie, and they embrace each other fiercely.

"I was terrified you had been hurt, or worse." Sallie's voice cracks. "We've had too many losses already, and the children keep asking for you."

"I've missed them too. And you. I'm fine though, really, and everything's going to be okay. I promise."

Over Sallie's shoulder, Loríen approaches them, carrying in her arms baby Lori. Even without Adaline being present to push people together, her friends remained friends after all. Sallie keeps her arm looped through Adaline's as she leans forward to peek at the sleeping baby girl.

A perfect start to a new beginning. Adaline leans her head on Sallie's shoulder.

The wind picks up, lapping waves against the water's edge and hinting that autumn lies just around the bend. The city should be planning for the harvest festival, at least those from Alderton should. Even back home in Maryland, she's always loved the smell of candied apples, spiced hot cider, and leaves tumbling about her backyard. All of that stayed true, both here and at Nan's.

Perhaps I didn't lead two different lives after all. But how did I forget to listen to the wind?

As Sallie leans forward to cradle baby Lori into her own arms, Adaline whispers hello into the wind. Her old friend caresses her cheek. The gentle touch feels familiar somehow, like that between sisters.

"Adaline," that ethereal voice whispers.

Goosebumps rise up on Adaline's arms. Only a few days ago, the idea of a tree or a cave or a river helping her seemed too farfetched to consider. But Adaline will never doubt that voice.

As Lori curls inward, seeking her mother's milk in her sleep, Adaline backs away from their group, trying to distance them from whatever harm approaches. She turns to find Ëólas, and from the corner of her eye, a man wearing a worn leather cap, pulled down low on his brow, steps into her path. With his light-brown eyes, threadbare linen shirt, and muddy boots, he looks like any other worker on the human side of the city. But at his waist, a narrow piece of metal reflects a glint of sunlight. He lifts his chin, and his face, flawless and ageless, contorts into a snarl as he extracts the rest of his dagger from its sheath.

What surprises Adaline most isn't his audacity or desperation to attack her in public, or even how Ëólas's face can shift muscle by muscle, replacing his calm amusement with sheer terror, as he breaks into the slowest sprint ever rendered. No, what surprises Adaline most is the calmness that overcomes her.

As the dagger inches toward her torso, an image of her father taking her Trick-or-Treating pops into her head—a random, inconsequential moment. She wore her newest tutu with a classic pair of Chucks, and her father pulled out of storage an early American colonist costume complete with a tricorne hat, which Adaline now realizes might not have been replicas. For a split second, she laughs to herself, until the memory vanishes.

Pulling his arm backward, her attacker steps toward her and screams out each syllable of the word *abomination*. He sucks in a deep breath, filling his lungs, and grips his hilt more firmly. Without hesitation or remorse, he looks her in the eyes.

But above his scream, Adaline hears more clearly Nan, leaning over her flowerbeds, dragging the trowel through the soil, and telling Adaline that the rosebuds love listening to her school adventures as much as Nan does.

The flash of that memory feels more concrete than the dagger slicing the wind in half and inching its way toward Adaline's torso. Ëólas, frozen in time, has one foot kicked up behind him, and he's raised one arm in front as if to pull himself forward faster. Merith's confusion at his lord's reaction begins to melt into widening alarm. The two guards sent to watch over her are still too far away, even as their hands move for the hilts of their swords, and Magnus hasn't turned his head enough yet to comprehend the source of Ëólas's reaction.

Within the beats of time slowed down, Adaline recalls her mother's buoyant laugh, the kind of happiness that should have birthed faeries as it bobbed up and down throughout the cottage, and the sound of her father turning another page to continue reading to her late into the night.

Beneath her right breast, the tip of the dagger punctures a hole in the coat Élara gifted Adaline that morning, the one Ëólas helped button up himself because he refused to leave her side. His fear of losing her was palpable back then. Now it's suffocating. Yet here she is, face to face with someone all too eager to end her life with a dagger aimed between her ribs and ready to slash her liver. Fólas's self-defense lessons echo in her head, that the larger the wound, the more likely the victim will die.

All of Adaline's thoughts focus on her husband, on the person whom destiny deemed to be her match, the person whom she vowed to protect just this morning because she can't let history repeat itself and force them apart.

As the blade's tip slips a millimeter into her flesh and a bead of blood soaks into her gold tunic, Adaline grounds herself into the earth. Without understanding how and why, without overthinking the feasibility of what she wants to do, without reverting to her academic brain, she thinks back to the moment she cast that circle in Lameiría, the way the roots burst through the ground, the way the earth element seemed to come alive and hear her internal call.

Now, she visualizes the tether connecting her to the ground and grabs onto it. In fact, the luminescent bond between her and the earth isn't all that different from the one between her and Ëólas.

The attacker broadens his smile as her wound widens another millimeter. Refusing to give into her panic, she glares at him and tightens her jaw. She jerks her arm skyward, tugging the earth with her. Hearing her internal plea, the soil beneath the cobblestones punches upward too, and several flying bricks hit the attacker's hand and gut, causing the dagger and his glee to fall to the ground. As he caves inward from the initial impact, another brick punches him in the face, smashing his jaw and nose to the side. Sallie and nearby merchants scream and jump back, but Adaline thrusts her hands forward so that the soil propels the bricks in the same direction, away from the bystanders. Unfortunately, that also causes Moren and Tumin to dodge projectile bricks while they struggle to finish unsheathing their swords. A few cobblestones fall into the river, lost for all time.

While Magnus and everyone around him gasps, staggers backward, and shields their eyes from debris raining down, Ëólas rushes closer, his eyes locked onto her wound. As he pivots so that he can slide in front of her, Adaline focuses on the ground and pulls her hands apart. The earth responds, ripping the street open just enough to create a two-foot-deep hole behind her assailant.

Spitting blood, the man sneers at her. Before he can stand erect again, Adaline yanks her arms backward as if she were pulling a tablecloth. The exposed earth beneath his feet whips toward her, knocking him backward, and he falls ass-first into the pit behind him. The earth piles on top, trapping him so only his toes, hat, eyes, and nose remain visible above the otherwise mostly flat ground, aside from the broken stones piled up beside him.

That's enough.

The earth settles down.

Chapter Thirty-Two

THE TRUTH

A moment later, Ëólas skids to a stop in front of her, blocking her view of the man buried alive and the frantic citizens. Pressing his hand firmly against her side, he shouts for Loríen. "I need your assistance now."

"Ëólas, look what I did." *Holy cow! How the hell did I pull that off? Can I even do that again? And how—*

The world tips sideways as Adaline falls into Ëólas's arms, her head spinning as nausea punches her gut. She slouches against him, trusting he'll keep her standing. When she can sense his panic rising, she finds her footing and forces herself to stand up even though she could use a quick nap. Ah, this is what her father meant, that their magic isn't infinite. "Sorry about that. Nothing to worry about."

Ëólas holds onto her arm, not yet willing to let go, even when Adaline mouths to him, *That was the magic, not the wound.*

Sallie tears her apron away from her waist and hands the linen to Loríen, who rips the fabric into strips and wraps them around Adaline's ribs. Ëólas uses the rest of Sallie's apron to wipe blood off his hand, but a streak of red remains that he can't stop staring at.

Loríen ties off the bandages, making Adaline wince. "I need to get the lady to the castle so I can see if she needs stitches and make sure she doesn't get an infection."

"The wound isn't deep." Pressing her hand to her ribs, Adaline thanks Loríen but insists, "Really, I'm fin—"

"Get more guards to distance Adaline from the crowd," Ëólas shouts to Fólas, who dashes off and begins organizing his subordinates. Hamon, being co-captain of the city guard, doesn't wait for Magnus to tell him to do the same.

Adaline taps Ëólas's shoulder. "Hello. I'm okay."

Nodding mechanically, he moves his hand to her back. Only when Merith places himself in front of Adaline does Ëólas breathe more easily. With his sword ready, Merith stares down the crowd, daring anyone to try something again. Moren and Tumin position themselves on either side of Merith, forming a living shield.

Likewise, Magnus orders guards to secure the greater area. Even though Sallie's trying to find a gap that will allow her to return to her shop, the rest of the city's people don't shy away from gathering closer, clogging the streets and bridges as they try to see for themselves what happened and ask everyone nearby to relay their version of events. More and more people stare at Adaline in awe. The council members, whispering to each other, never look away from her either. But now, Magnus and Ëólas aren't allowing anyone to leave until the guards question everyone present.

We'll be here all day.

After making certain she's not bleeding through the bandages, Ëólas looks toward the castle. "We need to get you out of here."

"No, Ëólas we can't yet. We need to explain what's going on." She pulls her elbow away from him and turns to Magnus, making his way to them.

Magnus eyes her bandages, props his hands on his hips, and observes the prisoner trapped in the ground. "Now that's something. Adaline, how are you?"

"Bleeding," Ëólas says. "We need to clear a path through the crowd."

"He barely scratched me. And we need to speak with Magnus, now." Granted, she can't fathom how they can step away from this situation and plan a course of action, not with so many eyes on her. Worse, the human council member, Lord Otto, whose daughter tripped Adaline during the ball, keeps staring at her like a newfound treasure to exploit.

We seriously need new council members.

Despite her protests, neither Ëólas nor Magnus hear her. Waving his hands left and right, Magnus directs guards to force the people to move backward, either onto the bridges already packed or against the shops lining Front Street. People bump into each other and fall over as they stare and whisper and point at Adaline.

The crowd grows rowdier, and Ëólas's neck muscles tense with adrenaline. His pupils dilate, and his breath becomes heavier as he scans the crowd for potential threats. Hesitantly, he turns to Loríen. "I'll get her to the castle while you fetch your supplies. Let's try your methods first."

Loríen bows her head in apology. "My methods don't work on adult humans."

"Ëólas, stop!" Grabbing his cheeks, Adaline turns his head and forces him to face her as she speaks calmly. "Hey, look at me. See me." She locks onto those golden orbs, coaxing him to see past the darkness of what almost happened. "We need to address the people. We can't leave them like this. They're scared and confused."

She sweeps her hand at the crowd, and the citizens flinch backward and duck as if expecting her to hurl bricks at them. Even Sallie takes a step back.

When he finally blinks, Adaline cups his cheeks more gently and tilts her face closer to his, shutting out his view of everyone else. "I need you to trust me. Can you do that? Please."

Even though he can't yet shed the worry twisting his face, he holds her hands. "Always."

"Thank you."

With her thumb, she rubs his cheek twice and forces herself to drop her arms, to let him go, but he holds on to her until Magnus eyes their entwined fingers and arches an eyebrow. Even though they quickly step apart, Magnus glances back and forth between the two of them. Ëólas meets Magnus's gaze and smirks, not in a boastful way but more in admittance that Magnus's suspicions have been right all along, and Magnus's eyebrows shoot upward. He sucks in his cheeks to stop himself from chuckling and walks back to the council members to stop their bickering.

Oh, I guess Magnus does know?

Before Magnus can silence them, Lord Otto pushes to the front of his group and loudly comments above the city's din, "How does the lady have access to magic?"

Magnus halts mid-step, and the crowd hushes, waiting for an answer.

Adaline takes a step forward, but Ëólas pulls her back. His eyes fall to her ribs, which now show a drop of blood bleeding through the bandage. He opens his mouth to object, but Adaline's unyielding gaze convinces him to have faith. He drops his arms to his sides, letting her know he'll follow her lead and watch her back as she faces the council.

"I need to speak." She glances at Magnus, who nods his approval. Pulling her shoulders back, she lifts her chin, cups her hands in front of her torso the way Nan did when giving speeches, and speaks with a loud, clear voice. "Everything you think you know about Aerytol's fall is wrong."

Magnus tilts his head back in surprise, and Fólas and Hamon exchange confused looks. Murmurs hiss throughout the streets, but everyone quiets down quickly to let her continue.

"There are people in this world who abhor what we're doing here. They hate our ideals now as they did five hundred years ago. They don't see this city and its purpose the way we do. Or the ways in which we're similar. Or the friendships we've built." After glancing at Sallie and Loríen standing together, Adaline turns in a circle to take in everyone who's crowded down Front Street, down the side streets, at the riverbank on the other side, and along the bridges. "They don't believe in the future we're creating, and they are willing to do whatever it takes to stop elf-human relations because fear and hate have consumed them."

Adaline pauses to press her hand to her wound and apply pressure. Each time she inhales, her flesh burns. Ëólas moves to inspect her bandages, but she shakes her head no. Thankfully, he halts and clamps his mouth shut.

Get to the point, Adaline. "The army marching this way wants nothing more than to destroy everyone in this city, humans and elves alike. These are the same people who lied about what happened the day Aerytol fell. The same people who convinced Aerytol's human population that Queen Arraya intended to enslave them to protect her unborn child. The same group," she takes a deep breath, "of elves who tried to kill their queen—"

Gasps and shouts of disbelief cut her off. At Fólas and Hamon's direction, the guards lining the streets demand that everyone quiet down.

Within the lull, Adaline finishes. "Those elves sought to ruin Aerytol because they refused to accept destiny's proclamation that Arraya's son would marry a human."

The crowd erupts again, with protests gaining in volume from across the river on the elven side of the city. Even Magnus falls back a step and looks to Ëólas for confirmation. Solemnly, Ëólas lowers his eyes, and Magnus clamps his hand over his mouth.

Adaline lifts her hands and pats the air downward, asking for the crowd to hush, to give her a chance to explain. "Please, you need to hear this. Morgán betrayed his queen, and his followers tried to destroy her message. But they failed. And they'll fail again, because—"

"Not elves, my lord," an elven council member begs, looking at Ëólas. "There must be a mistake. Elves couldn't. We wouldn't. We can't."

Ëólas silences the speaker with a single glare and looks to Adaline, indicating everyone else should do the same. The determination on his face encourages her to keep going, to make them face the truth. Taking a deep breath to steel her nerves, Adaline walks over to the prisoner, stoops down, and rips off his hat, revealing his leaf-shaped ears.

As everyone cries out in shock and disbelief, she shouts so everyone can hear her. "All of us have a bit of darkness inside us. No one is exempt from that possibility."

Adaline gestures for Ëólas to come near, for them to work together to convince everyone of the truth. He stands beside her and calls for silence, which Magnus reinforces. Soon enough, the only sound throughout the city is the water rushing downstream.

With the city watching him, Ëólas angles himself so that he faces the riverfront but also keeps Magnus in view. "When we chose to leave Lameiría and partake in this venture, we did so because each of us here believes not all humans are bad. Now, we need to accept the fact that not all elves are good."

As Ëólas repeats her father's words, she swallows her emotions and doesn't give people a chance to react. "Lord Ëólas and I have returned from the Wastelands, where we discovered Morgán's followers."

"The Morgai," Ëólas continues, "now led by an elf named Ãranol, built a city along the sea, where they've been tormenting humans for centuries. We cannot overlook the crimes the Morgai have committed, and we can no longer think ourselves better than our neighbors."

Turning to Magnus, Ëólas places his hand over his heart, bows his head apologetically, and extends his hand as he walks up to Alderton's king. "Lies and deceit turned our people against each other. I am here to make amends, my friend. Lameiría stands with Alderton. Our army is ready to defend the Neutral Territory and all its citizens. With Queen Élara's blessing, reinforcements will begin arriving within four days."

As Magnus digests everything, he stares at Ëólas's hand. Not bothering to look back at his council, he squares his shoulders, grabs Ëólas's forearm, and shakes firmly. "And we are honored to fight beside Lameiría, to safeguard all of Aerytol."

A cacophony of applause and hurried conversations mixed with cheerful tones and concerned objections surrounds them. But Adaline focuses primarily on Magnus and Ëólas and the commitment evident on both their faces. As long as Lameiría's prince and Alderton's king stick together, they'll be able to convince New Leira's citizens to stick around and help defend this city. With the people informed and the peace treaty intact, they should return to the castle to review their strategies for dealing with Ãranol and the Morgai. Okay, and Adaline could use some ointment or something on her wound.

She pulls her hand away from the bandage, and a quarter-sized red dot covers her palm. *Shit. If Ëólas sees this, he'll freak out.* As Ëólas turns to her, she quickly covers her ribs again, but Hamon clicks his tongue in disapproval.

Before he can call to his king, Lady Síena speaks up first, and her question grabs everyone's attention. "This has all been quite the revelation, Lord Ëólas, and of course we follow your lead. But please, how does the lady possess magic? Who is she?"

Once again, all eyes shift to Adaline.

Oh, right. That.

Still playing the role of her protector, Magnus shifts his feet hip-width apart, grabs his belt, and puffs out his chest like he usually does in preparation of a speech. This time, he's probably formulating an elaborate backstory or deflection, but Ëólas mouths *wait* to Magnus and doesn't do anything to distract or silence his council. Instead, he waits for Adaline to choose how to handle this. If she casts her eyes down or shows signs of distress, he'll take charge of the situation and end this now. But the conversation, the speculation, won't end. Not ever. If she wants these people to trust her, she has only one option.

Nan, give me strength. "My mother, Aurellia, was a painter and shepherdess from Alderton, where I was born and raised until I turned seven. My father, Edwin, grew up far away from here." She takes a deep breath. "And he was an elf."

Lady Síena narrows her eyes. "Are you implying—"

"I'm not implying anything. I'm stating. Arraya was my grandmother."

First, a blank expression floods Magnus's face. Then he recedes so deeply inside his thoughts that Adaline can't begin to guess what he's thinking. Likewise, the citizens on both sides of the river don't make a sound, and their unexpected silence leaves Adaline more vulnerable than ever. Thoren's gob-smacked expression would have had her laughing hysterically for hours, if not for the gravity of the situation and her stomach twisting in knots that he'll never trust her again. At least Merith, with those observant silver eyes, looks at her the same way he did the night he discovered her singing and dancing in the elven tavern, as if he recognized a kindred spirit.

If time allowed, she'd speak to each of her friends now and explain why she unintentionally withheld this information from them, but the severity of Lady Síena's expression promises that this conversation is far from over.

"How is that possible?" Lady Síena asks.

"Arraya's last spell, inlūmras né leira, sent her and my father to another world where Morgán couldn't hunt them. My father managed to come back for a time. That's how I lived in Alderton, until we fled from the Morgai." Adaline clenches her fists and grimaces at the earthbound prisoner.

Burying the elf alive would be so easy, even if she did so for only two weeks and six days, just before he'd suffocate to death. The earth rumbles beneath her prisoner, but Ëólas reaches for and tugs Adaline's hand, pulling her away from the edge of her own darkness.

With him beside her again, she focuses on finishing her story. "My family didn't want me to come back here until we knew it was safe. And because of Magnus, Ëólas, and all of you, Aerytol is once again a beacon of hope between our two people. You've rekindled my grandmother's dream. You're fulfilling her greatest hope by unifying our people."

The crowd's buoyant whispers reinforce her faith in them and their commitment to see Aerytol thrive. While the council members murmur among themselves, Ëólas places his hand on Adaline's waist. She steps closer to him, eager to sidle her body against his, to feel his warmth, to have that tactile connection again, but all he does is peel her hand away from her ribs and check her wound again.

She pushes his hand away and frowns. Her voice falls flat as she says, "Shouldn't you join the council?"

"No. They don't have much say in what happens next."

"Which is?"

When he looks up, she expects him to continue acting like she's about to pass out on the street any moment, that she's a delicate wallflower who needs her husband to carry her back to the castle. Instead, he takes her hand in his and stares at her with the same unyielding admiration she's shown him whenever he's taken charge and cared for his people's needs. And in that instant, she feels like his equal.

I wish I could kiss him right now.

"Adaline, the only thing that matters next is having Loríen look at that wound. At least it's stopped bleeding, but still. Can we please wrap this up now?"

Intertwining her fingers with his, she steps closer to him and breathes in that lavender scent. *Perfect timing.* "Okay."

As they face the council, Magnus remains silent but again stares at their entwined hands. This time, they don't let go, and Magnus chuckles to himself as if he's confirmed his own thoughts.

"Princess Adaline," Lord Otto says, his voice sticky sweet as he scratches his palm, "we are honored Alderton could lend its resources, finances, and protection to help rebuild the Aerytolían legacy. We have much to discuss, but we mustn't force you to strain yourself further. My king, as the princess's guardian and dear friend, perhaps it's advisable that you escort her back to her chambers?" Rubbing his palms together, he grins at his innuendo. "You've taken such a personal interest in safekeeping the lady thus far. I'm sure you'll continue to give her your undivided attention and support while we continue to evaluate what's in the best interest of the Neutral Territory."

Ew. Gross. Does he not see me standing right here? Holding someone else's hand?

The three of them stare at Lord Otto as if he's speaking a foreign language no one's ever heard of before.

"You blind fool," Magnus says. "The lady's already made her choice."

Lord Otto puzzles over Adaline holding Ëólas's hand. "Ah. Well, we have plenty of time to discuss our options."

Are you fucking kidding me? My marriage isn't a political option. "Okay, that's enough."

"Agreed." Ëólas turns his back to Lord Otto, whose face grows redder by the moment. "Fólas, ah, there you are. I need you to work with Hamon to safeguard the city. And dig up our new guest. I want him unharmed, for now. Adaline and I have questions for him. Magnus, I trust you can handle the rest. Merith, stay with me while I escort my *wife,*" he says loud enough for all to hear, "back to the castle and see to her wound."

Magnus claps Ëólas on the arm and beams at Adaline. "Wonderful. Exactly as I hoped." He kisses Adaline's cheek and whispers in her ear, "As I said, all hope is not lost."

Before he can pull away, she grabs his hand and holds fast. "For you too."

When he shakes his head and steps away, Adaline decides how she's going to repay her friend, her king, her protector. Despite everything else going on right now, she'll have to go back to Meadowbrook, back to her roots and her childhood cottage, not only to lay the past to rest but also to discover whatever happened to Uncle Jamie's family and find out if her cousin Nora is the same woman Magnus fell in love with all those years ago.

Somehow, I've got to help Magnus find happiness too.

With Magnus at the helm for now, Ëólas and Adaline take their leave, with Merith in front and Tumin and Moren following closely behind.

Before they take five steps though, Lord Otto calls them back, his tone no longer oozing with fake adoration. "Lord Ëólas, would you please clarify for the people if the lady is claiming her birthright? Or is Lameiría claiming it for her?"

Grinding his jaw to suppress a scowl, Ëólas glances over his shoulder. "Why are you addressing that question to me?"

As Lord Otto opens his mouth, Adaline lifts her hand to cut him off and makes no attempt to conceal her lack of patience with this matter. "Lord Otto, that's not what matters right now. We need to focus on protecting our people, understanding our enemies, and shoring up our offensive and defensive tactics."

"Which we will continue to prioritize in the coming days." Magnus's steadfast gaze reassures her that their goals are still aligned.

"Thank you, Magnus." *On so many levels.*

Surrounded by guards, Adaline and Ëólas walk toward the castle on the hill, with Loríen having gone to retrieve her supplies. Along the way, citizens pause their daily doings to bow and watch Adaline's small procession, proving that news travels quickly. She smiles and waves, blocking out the pain throbbing at her side. But with each step, the enormity of everything she has revealed hits her in the stomach like a bowling ball thrown backward. There's no turning back now. No pretending like she's an orphan wandering the streets and eager to make friends. And no avoiding the political repercussions that lie ahead.

What keeps her steady, aside from the love beside her, is knowing she's been headed down this path since birth. She may have forgotten that for a while, but she's back now. And she's far from being on her own.

Despite the people staring at them, Adaline looks at Ëólas and doesn't bother to conceal the depth of her love and faith in their aligned path. They've already overcome the seemingly impossible by escaping a soul sucker, convincing rebels to trust their enemy, sharing the truth with all of Lameiría, and, Adaline hopes, uniting the people of this city. Yet their teamwork has only just begun. "The next several days will be interesting, that's for sure."

"No matter what, we're going to safeguard New Leira. And you." Ëólas kisses the back of her hand. "You have my word."

"I know," she says. "Because together, you and I can do extraordinary things."

EPILOGUE

Adaline rolls onto her back, taking the comforter with her, and drapes an arm over her eyes to block out the sunlight. Her mind races to recall her last conversation with Ëólas, after Loríen finished her enchantments and excused herself from Ëólas's chambers. Well, their chambers. Which must be at least thrice the size of Adaline's old room on the other side of the castle. In addition to the spacious bedroom complete with multiple wardrobes, a long sofa in front of a grand fireplace, and area rugs in shades of blue, green, and gold, his quarters also include a sitting room and private kitchen.

Basically, he has a condo inside a castle. Not that he gave her a tour while pulling off her coat, ushering her into bed, and posting Merith's handpicked guards outside and inside the sitting room. He even stationed guards beside the balcony windows, as if a dragon might show up any moment.

Oh, that sweet, worried husband of mine. Husband. That word still sounds unbelievable too. As does queen.

Still, they've got bigger concerns at the moment. What she needs to do is drag her ass out of this insanely comfortable bed, find Ëólas, and join whatever meeting he's started. First, she shifts her hip and waits for her wound to prickle. But her ribs feel only numb.

"Huh," she says aloud.

In response, a small finger taps her nose three times, making Adaline turn her head to the side. When she blinks her eyes open, a set of periwinkle orbs stares back at her.

"Miss me?" Seira chimes, lying beside Adaline. Her blonde locks drape over her shoulder like a summer blanket.

Adaline exhales, and her heart feels compressed inside her chest. *My cousin. My family.* "So much." With all the pieces falling into place, Adaline curls onto her side and tucks her hands under her pillow. *Ëólas can wait a few more moments. He'll understand.* "I'm sorry for arguing with you before I left."

"That's alright. I'm elated you're you again. Did you have to get stabbed though?"

"Wasn't my first choice. And it wasn't deep. More like a bad scratch."

"That needed four stitches." Seira, lying above the covers, fluffs Ëólas's pillow and snuggles up closer.

After Adaline sticks her tongue out at Seira, they smile the way best friends do when they share an unspoken moment of understanding.

"Did you know all along?" Adaline asks.

"Know what, Neir Nía?"

"That we're family. That I'll be queen. That Ëólas and I—all of it."

"All of it," Seira repeats with a curious tilt of her head, leaving Adaline guessing if Seira's simply repeating Adaline's words or confessing.

Alright, let's try something more concrete. "How are we related?"

"Our grandmothers were sisters."

Holy shit. A straight-up answer. And Nan's sister, huh. "Asería? She escaped into Lameiría?"

"No, to Kershran."

The kingdom to the east. So, Asería hid among humans too, but without dad's gift. How did she manage? And how did Seira find her way to Lameiría, alone?

Seira's gaze drifts beyond Adaline, and the color in her eyes dulls. Sensing Seira's not yet ready to share her story, Adaline shuts her mouth. As much as she's dying for details, she doesn't want to open old wounds. Then again, she might have to push Seira to reveal what she knows if she has information that could end the on-coming war.

Shit. I should go find Ëólas.

Adaline stretches under the covers, her foot knocking two crystals onto the floor. Sitting up on her elbows, she counts the fourteen other crystals Loríen placed around the bed. "Overkill."

"No, it's not, Neir Nía."

"Ugh. Spare me another lecture, please."

Tumbling out of bed and wearing only her gold tunic and trousers, Adaline heads over to a large wardrobe. She can't parade around the castle with bloodstains on her abdomen. "I need to find Ëólas. Let me just change into one of his—"

"You could just wear your own clothing." Seira points to the wardrobe on the opposite side of the bedroom.

"Oh. I never heard anyone come in." *I'm surprised I can still sleep so soundly. Maybe that's a bad thing.*

"That's because I moved all your belongings myself, right after you left my chambers, yelling at me."

"What? Why?"

"I said I'd do something drastic, and you and Ëólas were taking the longer route. Seriously, I'm surprised you didn't jump into his bed the day you met. Why did you drag that out so long?"

Adaline's mouth hangs open as she contemplates a million different responses, most of which begin with cusses.

"Oh, don't look at me like that, Neir Nía. At least you two didn't wait the whole year. That would have doomed us all." Seira flops backward onto the bed and props her head up on her hand. "A full heart strengthens our magic."

Without starting an argument, Adaline crosses the length of the room and opens the other wardrobe, beside which rests her duffle bag. On the bottom shelf, she finds her messenger bag, Timberland boots, and the clothing she wore the day she arrived. As beautiful as the gowns hanging above are, she's not in the mood for pageantry right now. She grabs her tank top and flannel, putting on both while noting that she hasn't felt a twinge of pain since waking up. Her flannel warms her bare shoulders and makes her feel more like herself. Even as a child in Alderton, she preferred trousers when riding Benley and helping her father in the meadow.

In front of the standalone floor-length mirror, she begins tying the flannel into a knot at her waist. Pausing, she drops the red and black cloth, lifts her tank, and unwraps her bandages. Not a single mark remains. Not even a scar.

Damn. If only I'd had Lorien's crystals after I met Āranol.

With a shake of her head, she sits down at the foot of the bed and pulls on the riding boots Élara gave her. "Are you coming with me?" *I need to find Mercia too, after I check in with Ëólas.*

Seira exhales loudly and then stands at attention. "I don't know how much help I'll be, but, yes, my queen. Lead the way."

Outside, Moren and Tumin confirm that Adaline's been asleep most of the day, but Adaline thinks that has more to do with the amount of magic she used than the wound she received. She'll have to test that theory later. With six guards in tow, Adaline and Seira go to the king's study. Granted, people might be calling it now the queen's study, but nothing's been decided yet, and who knows how this situation will pan out.

Politics is usually one big cluster fuck.

"Seira, let me know if anything is too much," Adaline says as they approach the doors to the study. "I'm sorry to pull you into this, but—"

The doors burst open, and Ëólas rushes out of the room, causing everyone to jump backward to give him and Adaline space. *Of course he heard me coming.*

His brows are still slanted with worry. "You shouldn't be out of bed. You need rest to make sure you heal properly."

She steps back from him before he can loop his arm through hers and haul her off to bed. "I'm all healed."

"Waiting for your wound to stop bleeding doesn't constitute being healed. Rest is the only way to make sure—"

"Ëólas, the wound is gone. Look." She lifts her shirt and shows him her stomach. "Not even a scar."

Afraid to touch her, he rubs the tip of his finger over the spot that had been bleeding not too long ago. "You healed faster than elves."

"Elf-human hybrid bonus?"

"Maybe. Or maybe the wound sealed itself, but you could still have internal injuries." He pushes his hair away from his face and ponders the possibilities. "You should still go rest and—"

Adaline jabs his shoulder with her finger. "Hey, I said I'm fine. Good as new. I need you to believe me when I say I'm okay."

"I'd be more apt to believe you are okay if you say that only when you actually meant it."

"Ooh. Touché. Fine, I'll be perfectly honest with you from now on. Deal?"

Ëólas exhales. "Deal." He tucks her into his embrace and smiles when she nuzzles her head against his collarbone. "I can't stand the thought of you being hurt again. I need you to keep learning self-defense, please."

"I will. I plan on making sure I can keep you safe too, you know. I can't bear the thought of you being hurt either." As she pulls back, she rises on her toes to kiss him. But noticing the guards all turning away with red cheeks causes her to deflate and lower her heels to the floor.

Keeping my lips to myself isn't going to be easy. Adaline frowns.

With a smirk, Ëólas kisses her brow. The tingle of his lips still makes her heart flutter and her worries melt away, at least for the moment.

"Come on." He ushers her and Seira into the study where her friends have gathered, the original five guys who knew about her arrival from another world.

Facing them makes her both want to squeal with glee and run out of the room. She clutches Ëólas's elbow and searches their faces for signs of disapproval. Merith, Hamon, and Fólas look at Adaline as if their little sister's all grown up. Ignoring his colleagues, Thoren maintains a straight face from the other side of the room, but he can't hide the twinkle in his eye that gives her hope.

Magnus, lounging on the sofa opposite the bookshelves, slaps his thighs and gets to his feet. He meanders over to Adaline, positions himself in front of her, and looks like he's about to lecture her. Then, with a sweep of his arm, he bows. "Your Majesty, Alderton humbly acknowledges the rightful queen of Aerytol."

Adaline blinks at him, waiting for the punchline. "You've got to be kidding me. It can't be that simple."

"Of course it is." Magnus clasps his hands behind his back and puffs out his chest as he flashes that dashing smile. "As your guardian, it was my job to care for your land and property until you came of age and married. Seeing as how you've met both requirements now, I ought to return what is rightfully yours. I'm only fulfilling my oath." Then he leans in and whispers behind his hand, "My council would be daft to deny you your title and start a war with every elven kingdom."

Magnus winks at Adaline, which makes her shake her head in disbelief.

Then, to boggle her mind further, Merith approaches, crosses his fist over his heart, and drops onto one knee. His long, silver hair falls beside his cheeks. "My lady, I give you my solemn vow to uphold your orders and fight for Aerytol."

When Fólas kneels beside Merith and lowers his head too, Adaline looks at Ëólas, unsure what they expect her to say or do next. Nothing feels right, neither words nor actions. Should she commend them? Or thank them? Or accept their oaths? Looking amused, Ëólas shrugs his shoulders, indicating she can do or say whatever she wants.

"Please, get up," she squeaks. When they do, she leaps forward and hooks one arm around each of their necks. "I missed you guys. All of you. Thank you for keeping the city safe while we were gone."

Merith and Fólas return her hug, both of them pressing one hand against her back. Then, with a suppressed laugh, they shake their heads and step back, allowing Hamon to saunter over.

"I told you she's not going to be a fan of decorum." Hamon playfully socks her shoulder, which results in Thoren punching Hamon's arm for real. "Ouch. I'm just saying."

"You're right," Adaline chuckles, giving Hamon a brotherly hug too. Then she clasps Thoren's forearm, remembering how far they've come since their first meeting and his inclination to run her through. *God, I hated him. But I think he might be a big softy too.*

"Good to have you home," Thoren mumbles, his nose turning red as he sniffles and looks away.

"It's good to be home. I, I don't know what more to say, except to you, Magnus." She grasps his large hands and squeezes firmly. "No matter what, we have to keep working together. Alderton's my home too, and I won't tolerate discord between our two kingdoms."

"Agreed." Magnus kisses the back of her hand. "I look forward to your coronation, Your Majesty."

My coronation. I can't even.

When she feels like she's about to throw up, Magnus says, "Don't worry, Adaline. Coronations take a long while to plan, and I won't be leaving right away. At the very least, we have a war to stop."

Ëólas secures his palm at the small of her back, right where his hand belongs. "Ãranol won't stand a chance with Alderton and Lameiría working together."

"Good." Adaline moves closer to Ëólas so they're hip to hip. She also keeps one eye on Seira, who's wandered over to the window and disappeared into the background. *I hope this conversation won't upset her.* "Speaking of Ãranol, have we agreed on a course of action?"

A few strands of Seira's platinum blonde hair blow in the breeze. Otherwise, she remains still. But Ëólas's expression darkens.

Reaching into his pocket, he takes out a tiny piece of paper that he shows Adaline. "Remember I sent scouts into the Wastelands after we first arrived in Lameiría?"

"Yeah." Adaline puzzles over the miniature handwriting. "They haven't found anything. I don't get it. They've had, like what, five days. How can Ãranol's army be unaccounted for? Doesn't he have about a thousand Morgai with him?"

Ëólas and Magnus exchange a look that makes the hairs on the back of her neck stand up.

But Thoren's the one to speak up first. "It means he's changed tactics, my lady. He could strike at any moment."

"We suspect," Merith hastily adds. "He might have also encountered obstacles that have delayed him."

Like Mr. Toad. Oh god, please let them be delayed.

"Regardless, I doubt he's retreated, even if he knows you've returned." Ëólas's hand radiates warmth into Adaline's back, keeping her grounded. "I informed everyone about what's transpired at Feídra né Morna—and about your recovered memories. They agree he wouldn't so easily give up."

Fólas grinds his teeth as he seethes, "That sick, twisted excuse for an elf doesn't deserve a quick death."

"Good. We can all have a go at torturing him," Hamon says.

"I appreciate the sentiment, but you're telling me that after everything Ëólas and I went through in the Wastelands, we've lost the advantage?" Adaline's gut twists and turns. *This can't be good news. They're right—Ãranol wouldn't give up. He didn't give up hunting me even after I first escaped him.*

Magnus's voice pulls Adaline away from her ruminations. "Regardless, a portion of my army will arrive in the Neutral Territory in the next two days. Between my troops and Ëólas's, the city, er, um, New Leira, will be well guarded."

Adaline's cheek puffs into a half smile. "Thank you, Magnus."

"It's a good name," he says.

Ëólas briefly tickles her lower back and grins, having fulfilled his wedding promise. Adaline rises onto her toes, tugs his arm downward, and quickly plants a kiss on his cheek. Leaving him to turn scarlet in front of Magnus and the others, she walks over to the window next to Seira.

As much as Adaline wants to hold on to the joy of today's reunion, the task before them grows heavier as she watches the city off in the distance, the shadows growing longer as the sun sets behind the castle. Specks of people dash in and out of buildings and go about their business with no clue what the future will bring. They're just trying to build a home for themselves, for their families. And because of that, their lives are in just as much danger as Adaline's.

The ruins of the old palace prove what can happen when those in power underestimate evil. The fallen columns, the collapsed left wing, the broken balconies—she remembers all of it from her last visit to the ruins, to her grandmother's first home. Nan underestimated Morgán once before, and his treachery resulted in tragedy for all of Aerytol.

God, I hope he's dead. But even so, Āranol must have something else up his sleeve. He's still coming, I'm certain of that. And we're going to have to be ready. For anything.

Adaline turns about to face her friends, her family. The title they want to give her doesn't matter, not really, because no matter what challenges Āranol throws at her, her resolve to protect this city and find her mother won't waver.

"We can't wait for them to strike." Adaline looks to Ëólas, who has been her north star from day one, even when she didn't realize it. "When both Alderton's and Lameiría's forces arrive, we should deploy a portion to meet Āranol head on. Either we'll meet up with the Morgai far away from New Leira, which hopefully will keep the city safe, or we'll continue on until we take Feídra né Morna."

I hope that's a solid plan. "Of course, I'm welcome to all suggestions, and if you think—"

"I agree." Taking her hands, Ëólas joins her in front of the window, his thumb pushing against the ring he gifted her. He has his work cut out for him too in the coming days, giving her space to come into her own while he continues to be the leader everyone's come to trust. "We have a lot of logistics to sort through, but we'll figure it out."

With their friends vocalizing their agreement, Adaline closes the distance between her and Ëólas, lifting his hands close to her heart. But the movement of Seira nodding her head makes Adaline turn around and press her back to Ëólas's chest. He rubs her arms while Seira's lack of enthusiasm permeates the room and corrodes everyone's confidence.

Not turning away from the window, Seira says in a cold, detached voice, "He's becoming desperate, now that he knows you're back."

Everyone watches Seira, their faces falling as their carefully laid plans begin to crumble. But none of the guys dare to speak up, to ask for clarity, to risk Seira accidentally unleashing whatever magic she too must possess.

That's why everyone's been so cautious with her. But negative emotions weaken our magic.

Adaline steps forward. As Ëólas's hands fall away from her arms, she angles herself so she can study Seira's placid expression. "You mean Āranol?"

Shaking her head, Seira stares at a speck on the windowsill as if she's gazing into a crystal ball. "No, his path's undetermined."

What the hell does that mean? If Seira's not referring to him, then—Oh god. He can't still be alive. "Do, do you mean Morgán?"

Sinking downward onto the floor, Seira shrivels to half her size. She pulls her legs to her chest, tucks her chin into her knees, and rocks back and forth. Her arms tremble. Her breathing becomes erratic, and her pupils shrink, turning her eyes dark purple. Stories passed through the generations wouldn't create this type of reaction. No, only firsthand trauma could do this.

Oh, Seira. What did Morgán do to you? "What do you know, Seira? Please, help me so I can—"

"I don't know!" Leaning against the wall, Seira presses her palms to her eyes and cries out. "It's all so muddled. There are far too many possibilities. I never know if I'm speaking up too early or too late, and either could send you down the wrong path. The last time I was too late—" Seira's face turns ghostly white. Rolling onto her side, she clutches her stomach as if she's about to throw up. Then she grabs her hair, pulling at her scalp to rip her thoughts out of her head. "Make it go away," she cries. "I don't want to see. Don't make me see it again."

Whether Seira's referring to the past or present, Adaline doesn't know. And she doesn't care. She won't torture her cousin for details. Kneeling next to Seira, Adaline strokes the back of her head. "Breathe, Tíer Nía. Breathe. I'm here, and I'm not leaving you alone. We're together now, and we have friends helping us."

Adaline glances at Ëólas and the others, all of whom look equally pained to see Seira suffering but also determined to end this, to end Morgán. "We're going to stop him. I promise." *Whatever he did to you, I'll kill him myself.*

When Seira settles down, Magnus passes her a goblet of wine, which Seira sits up to accept, but the smell or sight of the crimson liquid makes her wince. She sets the goblet aside on the stone floor and rests her head on Adaline's shoulder. Together they take their time, breathing in and out until Seira's tears stop falling.

Not wishing to rush her cousin, Adaline leans against the wall and motions for the guys to have a seat on the sofas, which they refuse while their queen is on the cold, hard floor. *They're the best, really. We're fortunate to have such friends.*

Adaline wiggles her shoulder, making Seira sit up and look at her. "You don't have to worry so much, Tíer Nía. Even with your help, all we can do is address one problem at a time and have faith in each other that we'll figure this out. Okay?"

Instead of responding with words, Seira touches Adaline's ribs, the spot that used to be bleeding. "But he's on the cusp," she whispers. "A decision hangs before him, one that could make the world come undone."

Adaline and Ëólas look at each other, neither knowing how to respond. How are they supposed to safeguard Aerytol if Seira just foretold the end of the world? *Well, fuck.*

ALSO BY ERIN P.T. CANNING

Adaline and Ëólas's story has just begun!

Join them as they rally their peoples to stop Āranol's plans and work together to unlock Adaline's gifts in book three, ***Fire and Fortitude***, available now.

If you enjoyed reading this, please consider leaving a review. Nothing more helps authors to keep going and encourages other readers to take a chance on a book than your reviews. Thank you again.

All of my books blend fantasy, adventure, and romance as my characters explore other cultures, make unexpected friends, and discover their hidden strengths as they fight for what they desire most.

For regular updates, bonus chapters, free book recommendations, and more, you can subscribe to my newsletter by visiting my author website.

ELVISH LANGUAGE GUIDE

As a lifelong lover of fantasy, I created pronunciation rules for my book. Here's how these Elvish words and names sound, followed by a pronunciation guide.

Aiden (eye-den)
Ãranol (ah-ruh-nol)
Ëólas (ee-oh-lus)
Élara (ee-lara)
Elashor (el-uh-shore)
Feídra né Morna (fay-druh knee more-nuh)
Fólas (foe-lus)
Gladríen (glad-ree-en)
inlūmras né leira (in-loom-russ knee lear-uh)
Jósep (joe-sep)
Lameiría (la-mear-ee-uh)
Loríen (lore-ee-en)
mé ellador (mee el-luh-door)
Morgán (more-gain)
neir nía (near knee-ah)
Neira (near-uh)
Renor (reh-nor)
Seira (sear-uh)
tíer nía (tea-er knee-ah)
vameires (vuh-mear-ehs)

Vowels

A

schwa = a (as in uh)

short = ã (as in ah / apple)

long = á or eí (rarely ay)

E

short = e (eh)

long = é *

* é becomes ë or í when pronounced separately in front of another vowel

I

short = i*

long = ai

* i becomes y when used as and to blend two words into one

O

short = o

long = ó (as in oh)

schwa = õ (as in aw / ball)

U

short = ū (as in oo / ooze)

long = ú

Diphthongs

eir = as in ear or weird

ae = as in air

au = as in ouch / house

oi = oy as in toy

ACKNOWLEDGMENTS

I am blessed with the most amazing husband, who cooked and cleaned and handled bedtimes and made me coffee when I was up until two in the morning, making sure I'd hit my deadline for this book. Thank you a million times over for supporting my author career and believing in me. David, I love you forever.

My beta readers! Thank you, Michelle, Nadia, and Rita, for your honest feedback and constant encouragement. You three helped me to keep going during the holiday season and its inherent extra layers of chaos. Your hysterical and enthusiastic comments left me smiling for hours, and your questions and concerns helped make this book even stronger.

LeAnn, thank you for your flexibility with my crazy long word count and helping this book to shine as brightly as possible. Editors like you are a treasure.

To my cover designer, Tatiana, who redesigned this entire series into a collective work of art, thank you for creating such a stunning visual for my universe and my genre. Your work is breathtaking.

Danielle, I also have to thank you for helping out with my podcast so that I had more time to finish this book and give it the attention it deserves. You're a lifesaver.

As fortunate as I am to have such an amazing team, **the hours I spend in front of the computer take on a whole new level of meaning because of you, my readers.** You are the key to every author's success. Thank you for investing in Adaline, her friends, and the world we've discovered through her, and thank you for spreading the word to help others discover Aerytol too. Most of all, thank you for your constant encouragement with your reviews and interactions on social media. Seeing you post and talk about my books, getting messages from you as you're reading the chapters, is one of the greatest gifts I've ever received. You keep me going, and for that I'm forever grateful.

About the Author

Erin P.T. Canning has worked for twenty years as an editor, encouraging other writers' individual voices and teaching them how to hone their writing skills. She always planned to write a book. While she focused on her family, she stopped writing for six years. But something deep inside was missing. Depression, anxiety, and anger forced her to search for herself, both for her sake and her family's.

Despite fearing her skills had atrophied, Erin started writing again. For as long as she can remember, her imagination has been her safe place—a never-ending adventure where she can travel to far-off lands, find people who believe in her potential, and be the hero. By giving herself permission to be imperfect, she finished writing her own shitty first draft in 2022. *Ruins and Redemption* celebrates Erin making her own dreams come true.

Now, she spends her days helping writers become the authors they're meant to be and her evenings writing a blend of fantasy, adventure, and romance as her characters explore other cultures, forge unlikely friendships, and discover their hidden strengths as they fight for what's right and what they desire most.

She earned her BA in Literature from The American University and MA in Writing from Johns Hopkins University, and she lives with her husband and their two boys in Maryland.

You can find Erin on Facebook and Instagram (@erinptcanningauthor). You can also catch up with her regularly by going to her website, www.erinptcanningauthor.com.

www.ingramcontent.com/pod-product-compliance
Lightning Source LLC
Chambersburg PA
CBHW032116310726
48972CB00001B/247